My dad used to say everyone has a hunger.
I never knew what he meant until now.

FERAL

Sierra Prynne

Book One in *The Garden of Beastly Delights* series

To my parents, who read every draft,
and to Lori, who saved my life.

CHAPTER 1

"What do you want to do with your life?" Why did *every* college application ask some version of this question? It was such a vague, subjective invasion of privacy—if you even had an answer ready to begin with, which I certainly did not. Did they *want* us to lie?

I sat in the little hallway between the kitchen in Tommy's Pizzeria and the service counter, on a chair wedged between a whining refrigerator and a stack of wholesale cans of tomatoes taller than I was. My hiding place from Tommy, where I could fill out college applications in peace while waiting for delivery calls. It was an old game between us; if I kept out of sight, I won and he'd leave me to it. If he spotted me and there wasn't a delivery order, he'd make me mop the dining room where customers routinely dropped entire slices of pizza face down on the linoleum floor.

"How long you still working, Nat?"

Tommy was a...*rotund*...man. I should have heard him coming long before he appeared beside me.

"Thirty-seven minutes," I said, glancing at the clock on the wall. Thirty-seven minutes before I needed to drive across town to my Tuesday/Thursday night babysitting job.

"I hate to do it to you, kid, but spill on aisle three."

I turned slightly so I could see past him into the dining room, where a toddler had marinated the floor with orange soda. I grabbed the mop.

I found the mopping part of the job almost meditative. Sweep, dip, wring. A welcome distraction from…other things. After next week, after finals had come and gone and I'd intentionally purged the trauma of calculus from my brain, I'd be a high school senior. And after that, I didn't know. The future loomed large and empty before me. I had always thought I'd have some semblance of an idea about what I wanted to do with my life by now. But how could I know that when I didn't even know who I wanted to be yet? You actually have to experience life to know that. I spent all my time working or studying, hoping a school might take pity on me and offer me a scholarship so I didn't have to bankrupt my mom—or bankrupt future me with loans—to afford college.

"What's up, *Dummer*and?"

I felt a shoulder hit mine from behind, barely softer than a punch, before I registered their presence around me. The always-together trio of rich brats everyone at school called Glam Radio because that was the name of their vanity influencer brand. One platinum blonde, one golden blonde, one strawberry. My shoulders rose against my neck instinctively as I watched the three of them take the booth in the corner we reserved for parties of eight or more. Even ruder, considering they were basically like carbon copies of one another and had so few individual thoughts they barely qualified as one whole person.

"Can we, like, get a menu, or what?" asked Kayla, the leader.

"What a dive," murmured her flunky, Juliet.

"You actually order at the counter," I said, motioning behind me, "but you know that already."

"I don't want to do that," Kayla said. I felt her eyes on the back of my neck as I sped up my cleaning, managing to smear the last of the soda farther across the floor. "Hey, Dummerand."

I forced myself not to react to the mispronunciation of my last name.

"I'll give you a big tip if you order for us and bring it over here."

"We know you and your mom need the money," said her other lackey, Joanna.

Their snickers felt like little needle pricks down my back, but I should have been used to it by now. If laughter could actually leave scars, I would have been disfigured long ago.

"Babe, don't waste the cash. I'll get it," a deeper fourth voice said.

I turned, already knowing who it belonged to. Kayla's boyfriend, Paul, a transfer student from Norway so tall he had to duck under most normal doorways when entering rooms. The repetitive movement, paired with almost always having to look down to talk to people, had twisted his pink lips into a permanent, stoic pout. His long, dark blond eyelashes naturally curved away from his powder blue eyes.

"She is totally staring at him," Joanna whispered.

I jerked my gaze away, moving aside as Paul carried a large pizza to their booth. Notes of warm dough, honey, and sandalwood flooded my nose. He dropped into the seat beside Kayla and wrapped his lean arm with the fine blond hairs around her neck. He pulled her in for a kiss. When I realized I was staring again, I turned away.

I hated myself for liking him, just as much as they found it amusing. But honestly, it wasn't *him* I wanted. Not really. Beyond the dollish good looks, he was as full of himself as the rest of them. A hot piece of hotter air. I just…

I wanted someone to wrap their arm around me and pull me close, envelop me in warmth and comfort and desire. To breathe in someone else's scent and let it awaken me from my nose to my toes. I wanted to be wanted at least once. And not just by anyone. By someone who I wanted…and who was *proud* to be with me.

But I wasn't delusional. The pizzeria's front room was mostly windows, and the harsh fluorescent lights reflected everything happening back in on us. I caught sight of my own reflection and winced. My dark, wavy hair was tucked under a baseball cap and looked slightly matted where I had leaned against the refrigerator in the back room. And compared to Glam Radio and their visiting Scandinavian demigod, my short height and curvy figure made me look like a hobbit. Paul the giant was just as likely to step on me as actually see me.

Knowing he was just a placeholder for what I wanted didn't make it any easier not to look at him. I finished mopping and pushed the bucket back to my hiding place behind the tomatoes, their giggles of derision amplified in the small space. Tommy was there waiting for me, eyeing me softly. This place was the size of a matchbox, and he'd heard everything. His pity somehow soured my mood worse than Glam Radio's ridicule had.

"Order's up, on the east side," Tommy said. He waved a full warming bag at me, perfuming the stale storage room air with parmesan and garlic. "You can head out early. Just drop this on your way."

"Really?"

Tommy smirked. "Must be your birthday."

I was out the door, legs cartoon pinwheeling beneath me, before I shoved my Penn State application prep pamphlet into my backpack. He didn't know it, but it *was* my birthday. My seventeenth. Any seventeen-year-old *should* spend her birthday swimming in gifts and adoration from family and friends…and I could once babysitting was over. I'd celebrate with a low-key meal of Indian takeaway with my mom and friend Scarlett when I got home. We'd watch movies and order expensive pastries from the twenty-four-hour bakery down the street. And then, I'd slink back up to my room to keep studying, playfully guilt-tripping my mother for *dooming* me to a spring birthday, which fell on the week before finals every year. Poking fun at her was a time-honored tradition.

Even with the warming bag insulation, the pizza scorched my hands. I flung open the passenger side of my beat-up, old yellow car and slid the boxes onto the floor as quickly as I could. I dropped into the driver's seat and plunged the key into the ignition when something caught my attention out of the corner of my eye. A black Lincoln Town Car limousine with tinted windows pulled into the parking lot, as out of place as a panther and just as graceful. It idled for a long moment, purring, before the sound died, and the driver's door opened.

A strange sort of déjà vu feathered my senses. I had met the man who emerged from the car before—I was almost sure of it. My stomach twinged with distrust. He was older, in his late fifties, maybe, with blue serious eyes that made him seem like a ghost in the darkness. His face was a Roman bust forged from cold flesh and just as placid with indifference. Even with the obvious effort he had put into taming his short crop of black hair, it looked mussed and almost furry in the dark. He wore an impeccably tailored suit of deepest blue, and his tie had an unusual geometric pattern that seemed familiar and yet so *decidedly foreign*.

Gah, *where* did I know him from?

He stood for a long moment, observing the pizzeria as if he'd never seen one before, wincing at the drizzle that was beginning to fall like it was offending him. I couldn't smell him, but I could tell from here *eau de parfum of impatience* clung to him like a cloud.

My phone pinged in my hand with directions, and I glanced away. When I looked up again, he was gone. I twisted the key in the ignition, flooding the parking lot with light. Delicately pressing on the gas, I pulled slowly past the town car, past the pizzeria windows, and spotted him talking with Tommy—more bending over him—with a displeased, urgent expression on his face. His attention flitted briefly in my direction before he suddenly fixed his gaze on me through the window. There was no warmth there. Whoever he was, some part of me whispered it was better not to know. I slammed my foot on the gas and tore out of the lot, leaving my déjà vu behind me.

CHAPTER 2

"He sounds like a creep," said Scarlett, leaning over me to grab more chana masala.

"Nat was being pretty creepy herself, staring at his '*furry black hair*,' his '*steely eyes*'?" My mom nudged me at the table. "Must've been cute."

"No," I replied too quickly. "Blue eyes. I said he had blue eyes."

"Check out that blush."

Cute, no. *Sinister*, maybe. He was too old for me, anyway.

"Maybe for you," I murmured. "He was like fifty."

"See, he's a creep," declared Scarlett. "Hitting on a teenager."

"We never even spoke."

"Definitely stay away from him, Nat," Mom said. "I don't want to worry about you more than I already do. And please don't turn out like me. I married older—*twice*—and look how that turned out."

She waved her hand around at our small apartment, making light of herself and keeping the insecurities I knew plagued her at bay. I gave a gentle frown. Our two-bedroom wasn't a palace, but it was so inviting in its own way. Cozy. We rented it from a school friend of my dad's. The wood floors may have creaked with even the slightest pressure, but my mom lovingly oiled them every six months until they shone. And the lemon oil perfumed the air every time you walked in, like it was haunted by citrus. The windows were ancient single-pane things, but she'd followed a DIY tutorial to put in Swedish winter windows on top of them, to keep the place warmer in the cold New England snows. Her art—the paintings she did after working as a bookkeeper for local dentist offices all day—cluttered the walls, transforming the whole thing into a gallery.

Then there was *my* art, tucked away in the bookshelves and in drawers. My *book nooks*. Delicate little three-dimensional miniature scenes which I had painstakingly cut from assorted materials and painted by hand. My favorite—a street scene of a magical alley festooned with fairy lights that actually twinkled, and dragons curled on windowsills instead of cats, and cobblestones where I had added tiny flecks of mirror to cause the illusion of a puddle reflecting the lane back at itself—sat in a place of honor on an end table by the front door where all who entered could see it.

We might not have had a lot of money, but this place was lovely. It was home.

And of course, there was my best—and let's be honest, only—friend, Scarlett, who always seemed to be here, filling the apartment with enough energy for three families. She'd just discovered that if she shaved part of the side of her head and braided the rest of her golden blonde hair, she looked like the type of Norse goddess to which people built altars. I watched her take another selfie and post it in between mouthfuls of curry. She did everything with an effortless grace I'd never understand. And where the kids at school seemed to resent that I was happy to be friends with anyone, they seemed to admire that she fit in at the periphery of any group.

I glanced down at my scrawny knees and knobby elbows where bruises patterned my skin like leopard spots. Pizza delivered, I had arrived on time for my babysitting gig to discover some species of malevolent creature had switched the two kids I normally watched with sugar-crazed acrobats who took turns leaping from the stairs into my panic-stricken arms.

"You okay, kiddo?" My mom nudged me again.

"Yeah, of course, just tired," I lied.

"Becky," said Scarlett as my mom's eyebrow rose playfully on her forehead. "Ms. Damarand. You gotta make us coffee."

"Oh, I do, do I?"

"Yes," said Scarlett, shaking my mom's arm. "We've got movies and cake still. If she falls asleep during either, I *will* cut her hair."

Scarlett had wanted to give me a French bob for months, since she'd seen *Amelie* for the first time and decided I was a dead ringer for Audrey Tautou, which was only true in a bizzaro world where Audrey had an incurable olive tan and a much sharper nose.

My mom laughed and got up to make coffee. "Good luck with that."

"Yeah, I would murder you."

"You are such a chicken," Scar tutted. "It's just hair. You're seventeen. Shave it all off except for a rat tail—who cares? It'll grow back."

"I like my hair like it is," I fibbed.

"No, you like what you know works. How do you know other things aren't better? You could be a fox and not even know, hiding everything under baseball caps and old tee shirts your dad bought on trips you weren't even alive to go on. Try being brave for a change."

My back bristled, the way it always did when Scarlett was hurtful…and right. The hiding—me hiding myself—had started when puberty hit, when I'd looked down to see two large, uninvited guests on my changing body. At first, I'd been excited…and then not so much when boys and men—and even girls and women—had started to pay more attention to them than they did to me. Invasive, sometimes handsy attention. As much as I loved Scarlett, it was the one insecurity I knew she wouldn't understand.

"I'm brave," I murmured, embarrassed by the weak sound of my own voice. Scarlett gave my arm a dismissive pat.

"Come on, Scar," my mom said. "Do you remember how hard it was to convince her to get her ears pierced?"

"I don't like pain. Who does? You can't hold that against me forever."

"You cried so loud they made us leave the store," said Scarlett, smiling at my discomfort. "You kept shouting, 'You broke my ears!' It was so cute. Then you punched that security guy in the nards and became my hero." Scarlett scooted her chair around the table a little and hugged my arm sincerely, melting my resistance. It was impossible to stay mad at her. "I miss that little ballbuster. Don't be a chicken."

At least until she said things like that. I shrugged out of her grasp, and the seat, and brought my plate back to the counter to serve myself more spicy paneer jalfrezi.

"I'm not a chicken."

"It's okay to be scared sometimes, Nat," said my mom. The coffee maker burped and bubbled in response.

"Yeah, about real things, like finals and stuff," added Scarlett. "Not about whether you'll look good with different hair—which you will."

"That's easy for you to say," I fired back, returning to my seat. "You're not scared of anything."

"That's because I don't live in the future," said Scar, stealing a hot pepper off my plate and popping it into her mouth without a second thought. "I'm destined to live a big life. The only people who get to have those are the ones who make every moment count. They *declare* who they are and who they want to be with every action they take. *That's* bravery."

"Figure out who you are, and do it on purpose," said my mom, rejoining us with cups of steaming coffee, cream, and sugar. "That's the Dolly Parton way."

"Yes," said Scarlett. "Ask yourself *what would Dolly do* and you'll never go wrong."

God, I *hated* when Scarlett was right, and she was always right when it came to these sorts of life things. She'd barely lived longer than I had—and couldn't even pass World Geography without cram sessions using mnemonics I made up for her—but she still seemed to have so many things figured out.

If I were honest with myself, I'd said no to cutting my hair just because it was easy. An easy no that kept things exactly as they were. An easy no that didn't require me to put myself out there or get hurt.

I sighed. "Fine, you can cut my hair..."

"Are you serious?" squealed Scarlett. She clapped. "Shaved sides, too?"

"No!" my mom and I said at the same time. We glanced at each other and chuckled.

"Baby steps," I added as the phone in my pocket suddenly pinged. I pulled it out to turn it off when a notification caught my eye. "Huh..."

"What?"

I glanced at my mom's happy face. What I was about to say would hurt her, I just knew it.

"Archer Mahon just friended me."

"Who's Archer Mahon?" asked Scarlett.

Mom paused with the coffee cup halfway to her mouth. She plopped it back on the table and leaned over to see.

"Hello?" Scarlett tried again. "Who's Archer?"

I eyed my mom, waiting for some reaction. She bit her lip. A small line appeared, running along the bridge of her nose between her eyes—never a good sign.

"My ex's son," Mom offered.

"Natalie has a stepbrother?" Scarlett said, wrinkling her nose.

"No. Kinda...but I've never met him."

Ping! My mom took hold of the phone and my hand. I could feel the tension in her still-gentle grip.

"It's Cassian now," she said, worry creeping into her voice.

My heart twinged for her; they were from a time in her life—our life—that she'd tried so hard to forget. I took the phone back. Sure enough, there were two new friend requests on my profile.

"Who's Cassian?" asked Scarlett, eyes darting between us.

"My other ex-stepbrother," I said, watching my mom get up to return the cream to the fridge, lost in thought.

"Whoa, okay, why don't I know you have stepbrothers?"

"Because I don't, hence the *ex*-part." I got up and went to my mom, hugging her from the side. "You okay, Mom?"

She didn't answer—didn't have the chance to. A sudden knock drew our collective attention to the front door. I glanced once more at my mom. She seemed to be frozen, processing by the counter.

"I'll get it," I said.

I tiptoed over and peeked through the peephole.

"Who is it?" whispered Scarlett.

"I dunno. I can't see anything." This was partially true. *Some*thing was outside, looming large enough to block the viewing hole.

As I opened the door, dread crawled up my spine like a spider. Standing outside, silhouetted in the yellow glow from the streetlight, was the strangely familiar older man from the pizzeria.

CHAPTER 3

"Bruce?" My mother seemed to hiss the name of the man standing on our front landing. Her eyes narrowed to slits.

He removed his Oxford shoes before stepping inside.

"Hello, Rebecca," Bruce said, almost bowing at my mother. His English accent was smooth and unharried. "It's good to see you looking so well."

My mom glanced away, her body language tight and unreadable until she slammed the coffee pot back into the machine like she was crushing a bug.

"I know this is an odd hour to be calling," he added in the stilted silence, stepping farther inside, all but saying that even though it was an intrusion, he had no intention of leaving. He studied Scarlett briefly before turning back to me. His blue eyes were red up close. Irritated. "You must be Natalie."

He offered his hand to shake. It floated between us for several seconds as I glanced between him and my mother. As my eyes met his again, that déjà vu struck once more, this time like a mallet. Resentment burbled up from somewhere deep inside me, and he lowered his hand as I tucked mine into my hoodie.

"That's me," I said.

"You've certainly grown up," he said. I blinked, putting actual effort into trying to remember him. He motioned respectfully to the round, four-person dining table with the stains and nicks on it as if it were an antique instead of something we'd found abandoned by the side of the street. "May I?"

"Do we have a choice?" my mother asked, her voice almost sounding natural. "Coffee or tea?"

"Coffee's fine, thank you, Rebecca."

Scarlett searched my face for information as he swept past and selected a seat at the table.

"Who is he?" she mouthed.

"The guy from the pizzeria," I mouthed back.

He had something in his hand—a dark gray leather attaché so thin it looked like a skipping stone, from which he removed an even thinner leather folder embossed with a green seal. A seven-pointed star with a Latin phrase underneath.

"Beautiful, isn't it?" I must have been staring.

I nodded, motioning to the Latin. "Ne te qu?"

"Ne te quæsiveris extra," he said, his eyes shining. "Your mother knows what it means."

My mom eyed him dryly before turning to me, smiling the tempered, indignant smile I knew meant she *did* know, but was leery of giving him the satisfaction. She was exhausting her social politeness quota.

"It's Emerson," my mom said, taking the seat across from the man at the table. She motioned to the last open seat for me. "It means, 'Man is his own star.' A poetic phrase rich people misuse to claim poor people are poor because they don't work hard enough."

"Self-determination," countered the man, almost smirking, "The exact opposite reason I'm here to see you tonight. Fate has such a delightfully piquant sense of irony."

"I'm very self-reliant, thank you," said my mother before he'd even finished. He eyed her baldly and plunged on.

"Actually, I'm here to see you, Lady Natalie," he said, placing the leather folder on the table in front of me. His fingers lingered at its edge, like it was a sacred, delicate thing in need of protection. "I'm afraid I come bearing sad tidings. Your stepfather, Lord William Mahon, the Most Honorable Eighth Marquess of Ayr, is dead."

William. *Will.* I hadn't heard that name in nearly five years. It was off-limits in our house.

My Mom and William had met at a resort in the Caribbean, back when she worked for a law firm that compensated for a lack of Christmas bonuses with an all-inclusive work vacation instead. I was nine then, old enough to remember how tired she was when she'd left that December morning and how *alive* she had looked when she came home ten days later, smiling infectiously, wearing a flower in her hair and a locket around her neck that hadn't been there before. She looked truly happy for the first time in who knew how long.

I had listened to her carry on hour-long phone conversations for weeks through the thin wall between our bedrooms. Then, on Valentine's Day, her secret someone, *Lord William Mahon,* had arrived at the door like a vision in a navy sweater, with silver-streaked brown hair and a twinkle in his robin's egg-colored eyes. In his arms, rare blush orchids for my mom and a teddy bear dressed like a princess for me. I still had the toy, hidden on a shelf in my bedroom.

Mom and Will had married not long after, in a frenzy of hushed arrangements and long, threatening phone calls from his estate in the United Kingdom, warding him off marrying some *poor American commoner*.

"Especially one who's been *married before* and *has a child!* For heaven's sake, William…" I'd once overheard a man tell Will.

I'd once overheard *Bruce* tell Will.

Although Mom suffered the worst of it, I never forgot how those cutting words hurt me, too. That old nursery rhyme about sticks and stones had never married into the British aristocracy.

Like something out of a fairytale, we'd moved out of the apartment into a beautiful mansion in upstate New York, on its own acreage, with its own lake. Will had taught me to swim, as well as tricks for how to remember long, rambling numbers, like important dates and formulas, for school tests. Tricks I still used to pull mostly A's in my high school classes now.

I heard a chair scrape indecorously across the wood floor and turned my head just in time to see my mother disappear toward her bedroom, her eyes full of tears.

"Mom?" If she had exhausted her social politeness quota, anger had replaced mine. "Well done, Bruce. You go around telling everyone the love of their life is dead like that?"

Scarlett eyed me with sudden desperate empathy as my words sunk in. She was up like a shot, running after my mom.

I rose to join her.

Bruce took firm hold of my hand, his piercing eyes unblinking.

"Let go of me," I said. He didn't; I tried to pull away, but his grip only tightened.

"Tough decisions are coming, Lady Natalie," he said.

"Why do you keep calling me that?"

"Your stepfather was a busy man, a secretive man. A man for whom 'the impossible' was merely a matter of perspective. He had his dalliances, his weaknesses like anyone. But he rarely made mistakes. As his second hand, I respected his judgment in almost all things… although once again, he's made a decision in death that I find difficult to understand. One he's not here to explain. One he's left me to ponder at great length. Yet here I am, in Pennsylvania, trying to respect it."

His gaze moved across my face, studying me, searching for something. I bristled under his stare.

"You *destroyed* his marriage to my mom," I accused. "You're a monster."

"You are correct," he said, his tone a mixture of indifference toward my mom and begrudging admiration toward me for standing up for her. "Their marriage never should have happened. It was spontaneous and selfish. An aberration of behavior that hurt many people, whether you believe me or not. He abandoned his wife and sons to come play house with you and your mother. He put other *pressing* matters on hold, too—"

He cut himself off and looked away suddenly.

"Those two years cost him more than you know, dear child," he said, starting again. "And if I might speak honestly—"

Loathing roiled in me. "Seems like you're already being pretty damned honest—"

"I see nothing here now, save the tears of a pretty widow, that would have bewitched him so completely into making the choice that has brought me here tonight."

Again, his insult struck like stinging tentacles. I yanked my hand out of his grasp.

"My mom is bawling her eyes out in the other room," I said. "I cried when you people forced Will to leave us. But I suppose those weren't actual tears, either. We were putting on a show for no one."

Bruce tapped the table, thinking.

"I apologize for the offense," he said. "As cruel as it is of me, it *is* a relief to see your mother so heartbroken. I didn't know she actually cared. I thought—"

"You thought she married him for his money," I said flatly. "So, she could flounce around in a pretty dress and call herself a Marquess."

"A Marchioness," he corrected.

"Whatever. Same difference."

He winced. "Not quite. We will need to work on that."

"Don't bother," I said. "I'm sorry about Will and what his sons went through, but it sounds like we're not your responsibility anymore. You've delivered the bad news. Now, you can go back to England with your snooty tail between your legs and leave us to the rest of our *common lives*."

I inched toward the hallway and heard the screech of his chair as he rose behind me.

"Forgive me," he said, his voice breaking. I turned back. "I don't want us to start off on the wrong foot."

I blinked at him, incredulous. "Start off…?"

"Your stepfather negotiated a most unusual arrangement for you. Lord Mahon…" A pang of pain seemed to ripple over him. He tried again. "*William* didn't leave his estate to his sons. Lady Natalie…he left everything to you. From this moment forth, until your renunciation or death, *you* are the Most Honorable Ninth Marchioness of Ayr. And I am at your service."

CHAPTER 4

Lord William Mahon had slipped in and out of our lives like a pretty dream.

"Wake up, little bird. We have a surprise for you."

My mom had woken me at the crack of dawn one rainy May morning a few days after my tenth birthday with a small pack of my clothing ready to go.

Will had been standing by the front door, looking every bit the handsome British gentleman. He took my mother's suitcase and my bag and flashed me a reassuring smile as we navigated the rickety wooden steps of our apartment to the alley below. Even though I couldn't—and still didn't—care very much about cars, I could still remember the smell of the plush beige leather in the backseat of Will's Audi and the brand-new blanket he had carefully tucked around me. Seats adjusted, belts fastened, he drove us north. I fell into the deep, dreamless backseat sleep that only kids know and woke hours later alone in the car. Heavy rain streamed down the windows, blurring the world beyond into impressionist art. I opened the door onto a dewy meadow of soft white and yellow wildflowers, stretching from the edge of a mercury-gray lake to a driveway curling up a slight hill to a literal red brick castle.

"Nat! Over here." I ran as fast as my little legs could carry me to the porch where my mother stood. "What do you think?"

"It's a castle."

"It's home, my dear girl," Will said, joining us from inside. He placed a hand on my back and patted playfully. "Do you approve?"

All I could do was nod.

The rest of our ramshackle collection of heirlooms and small tokens arrived several days later, hauled inside by two confused moving men who ogled the scratched, upcycled dining table, looking for proof that it was actually priceless as they *gingerly placed* it on the black-and-white marble tiles of the kitchen. Everything we owned fit in a single room. Spread out among the twenty-eight rooms of the castle, the bits and baubles of our ordinary life looked like kitschy affectations. Will had reassured my mom that they would fill the halls of the house with joy and comfort. True to his word, Sotheby's decorated the entire house for us within the week.

To tell you the truth, I remembered it like a summer camp I got to visit on weekends. I was sent off to an insanely expensive boarding school almost immediately. Will *insisted.* I thought he was trying to get rid of me—and maybe he was. But every weekend, without fail, he and my mom would arrive to pick me up and bring me home. He'd give me the type of warm fatherly hug I hadn't had since my dad had died and ask me about my week. He'd fix me my favorite breakfast on Saturday and teach me to play chess on a board he had built himself.

It was during these chess lessons that I'd gotten to know him as more than the overcompensating father figure we both wanted him to be. We'd discussed my plans for the future.

"Are you quite *sure* you want to be an accountant?" he asked.

I squirmed. I had no idea how to tell a rich man that I'd spent every Sunday of my life before he appeared at the breakfast table with my mom, poring over supermarket coupons and creating budget menus for the week based on what we could afford.

"Well, no one *wants* to be an accountant," I said.

He laughed. "Exactly! You're ten. You need to be at least twice that old to give up and settle for *accounting.* Even then, the clever accountants set up their lives to do what they love around their work hours. If you already know the job you're going to do, dear girl, you need to brainstorm the other pursuits that will give your life meaning. What else will you do besides accounting? Anything. Really think about it."

The truth walked out of my mouth before I could stop it. "I want to be an explorer."

"Do you now?" A gleam blossomed in his pale blue eyes.

"I'd see everything, go everywhere. I'd learn everything and help everyone and make art and take care of my mom." I paused. "Only…"

"Only what?"

"My teacher, Mrs. Sherman," I said. "She laughed and told me I couldn't be an explorer because 'everything's already been discovered.'"

"Tosh," he said, sounding more British than British, flinging a stick pretzel at me from the small snack tray beside us. "Your *teacher* has no business laughing at the dreams of a student, no matter how unfathomable they might be. I'll have a talk with your headmaster tomorrow."

"No, it's okay," I said.

He leaned forward over the board and held my gaze.

"People will try to convince you the world is getting smaller. Don't listen to them. Those people want something from you that isn't theirs to have. They want your complacency." He said it with a smirk, but behind his unsmiling eyes, I could sense a deep desire to warn me of something. "Your stagnation and lack of drive as a person. People…well…many are entirely *comfortable* with the lie that what they see and what they are told is all that there is. They wouldn't want the truth even if you offered it to them. They don't understand that if you only scratch the surface of things, you'll miss the wisdom hidden underneath…There are *so* many hidden things in the world. Mysteries, obscurities, curiosities, terrors, horrors, and wonders. They're there if you want to find them. And even if you don't, some find you anyway."

"But you have money," I said. "You can do whatever you want."

"Yes, it does help." He sighed, purging quiet desperation. He rubbed a small, curved tattoo on the inside of his wrist that looked a bit like a rough, angular crescent moon.

"But you're ten, my darling. That's much too young for that talk."

"So, it's okay to want to be an explorer?" I asked, a potential future bursting to life in my ten-year-old mind like a kaleidoscopic bomb. "I want to try everything."

He hugged me, *really* hugged me. I heard him whisper, "If I have my say, you will."

Perfection was a slippery thing. It came and went at will and slid right out of our grasp if we tried too hard to hold onto it.

It all ended one ordinary Tuesday, three days before my twelfth birthday. Will arrived halfway through my U.S. History class.

"I'm here to take you home early," he said, his normal charisma muted and a little dodgy. He peered back over his shoulder as he hustled me into the car.

"Is this okay with the school?" I asked. Finals were only a week away.

"Of course," he said. "Nat…"

His voice cracked suddenly.

"Natalie, I need to show you something I've never shown to anyone else. Something which you can *never* tell your mother about, understand?"

He flew down the highway, glancing back at me too often. I nodded just to get his attention back on the road. Two silent hours later, we arrived at the castle to find a black car with tinted windows sitting out front.

"Is Mom here?"

"No, she's running an errand. Keep up."

I followed him around to the side of the house, to a narrow corner where a gutter curved into a flower bed. He twisted the curved pipe off and coaxed the wedding band off his ring finger. This he handed to me.

"Keep it safe now."

Then he turned to the soft soil under the gutter and began to dig, piling a mountain of dirt at my feet before he pulled back and motioned for me to take a closer look. There, buried two feet down, was a small wooden keepsake box. Emblazoned on the top was a seal I wouldn't see again for another five years—the seven-pointed star wrapped in the Latin phrase I didn't know.

"I've buried this here for you," he said, producing a tiny golden key from his pocket. "Take this. Don't lose it, whatever you do, understand? This box will be here waiting for you. There will come a day when you'll have a great and terrible journey ahead of you. On that day, you'll know to come here and retrieve this, all right?"

"What's in it?" I asked, suddenly afraid. "Why don't you give it to Mom?"

"I love your mother, but she doesn't want to understand," he said, glancing behind me. "Now listen carefully. I appreciate you. That may seem so small and indelicate. Dismissive, even. It's not. I *admire* who you are. Your creativity. You and your mother both—you have been the *light* of my older life. If I could stay, I would. I would never leave you. *Never*."

"You're leaving?" My voice squeaked painfully. Before I could stop them, tears surged into the rims of my eyes.

The sound of an approaching car drew my attention away; my mother was behind the wheel of a rental. She pulled it up beside the black car and stepped out. I could see mascara staining her tear-streaked cheeks, even from fifty feet away.

"Nat, baby?" she said, her voice lilting with sorrow. "Come inside, okay? We need to pack."

Will had already reburied the box and reattached the gutter by the time I turned around, and he breezed past me with one final squeeze of my shoulder.

I followed, turning the corner of the house to see him shake the hand of a towering blue-eyed man with black hair so tousled it looked furry. Neither glanced back at me as they went inside.

Upstairs, my mom moved like a ghost between rooms. Hollow. The empty cardboard box weighed heavy in her arms as she went around packing each bauble we had brought into the house. The silence was stifling. I didn't know what to say.

"Mom?"

"It's okay, we'll leave soon."

I peered through the second-floor banister to see the furry man looming in the doorway of Will's office on the ground floor. Faint echoes of the conversation reached me like gossip on the wind.

"You're making the right decision, William," said the stranger. Will didn't seem convinced. "You're needed *at home*…and the king, well…he doesn't understand why you refuse to bring Rebecca into the fold. It's almost as if this woman has seduced you into insanity."

"Don't be ridiculous, Bruce," snapped Will. "I never wanted that life, so I went out and found one I did."

"It doesn't matter what you *want*," Bruce replied, his voice bitter with desperation. "There are simply some binds that cannot be broken."

When my mother passed by me in the hallway again, I caught her hand.

"What's happening? You can tell me."

I'll never forget the cascade of pain that washed over her face as she set the packing box down and dropped to her knees beside me, burying her face in her hands.

"I never belonged here," she said, voice muffled. "I thought we could be happy. That he loved me…but I was always just a visitor."

Pain gripped my heart. I cradled her, stroking her auburn hair, trying to comfort her the only way I knew how.

"It's okay. We had a pretty dream...and now we can wake up back home in our apartment."

It had momentarily done the trick. My mom wiped her tears and kissed my cheek.

"A pretty dream," she said. "That's lovely. Thank you, little bird. Go pack your bag, okay? You've got a week left of school, so I can drive you up every day, but next year..."

"I know, Mom, it's okay," I said, glancing back down at the furry man, still chastising Will in the office below. Of course, it was going to be okay. It *had* just been a pretty dream, and like all dreams, they eventually had to come to an end.

CHAPTER 5

After Bruce finally left, and Scarlett excused herself, I lay down with my mom on her bed. I'd missed her crying, but I'd made it just in time to hand her a tissue.

"I'm so sorry, Mom," I said.

She waved that away. "He was always a jerk."

"A colossal jerk!" I echoed. "Selfish, gross, furry little man."

My mom smiled.

"I'm sorry about Will, too," I added, watching the tears race for her eyes again.

"I let him go a long time ago," she lied.

"Yeah, but that doesn't mean you didn't still love him," I replied.

My mom blew her nose to change the subject. "What did he want anyway?"

It was the craziest thing…

"Uh," I said, unsure how to even start. I sat up, tucking my hair behind my ears. "He said…Will left me something."

She rolled her eyes and sat up beside me. "He had to spoil that, too?"

"Spoil what?"

"Will didn't want to leave you with nothing," she said. "When he ended things, he told me there would be a trust waiting for you when you got older, but he wouldn't tell me when."

"How…would that have worked?" I asked.

"Exactly. Who knows? Which is why I didn't tell you. Just in case he forgot, or it was all just a weird lie. Better you take care of yourself and be surprised by blessings than disappointed by lost promises."

"Well, it looks like Will came through," I said. "He left me everything."

Her brow quirked, begging more information.

"Bruce said everything Will had he left to me. Houses, cars, employees. To be honest, I blacked out a little after he said I was part of the nobility."

Her squeal of shocked delight was wonderful, so much better than the crying, which always made me want to cry. "What!" So was the hug she gave me afterward.

"But," I said. "He said part of the deal requires me to relocate to Scotland. He said he knows someone at the consulate. He's already started processing an expedited visa and passport for me."

"Wait, honey," my mom said. "That's so big. You can't just leave your life behind…"

She meant herself. She didn't want me to leave her behind. I could see the fear shine in her eyes, and that hurt my heart too. Like I would ever just abandon her.

"I can't relocate like that," she rushed on. "You're only seventeen. What about graduating—"

"Mom. Mom," I said gently. "I love you so much. Don't worry."

"No, honey, I *am* worried," she said. "But I can't let you give something like this up, either."

I winced. Giving it up had never entered my mind. This was too special an opportunity, for more reasons than even my mother knew.

"Well, I negotiated a deal with him," I said.

My mother's eyebrow soared high in playful disbelief. "You negotiated a deal. With Bruce. For what?"

"The summer," I said. "I told him I'd talk to you about letting me go for the summer. Then I can come back and finish school before anything else happens."

"And what did he say?"

I smiled. "Once he agreed, he told me to *inform* you that I was going."

"Of course, he did."

I hugged her. "Please let me go. It's just three months. It'll be over before you know it, and then you could retire. Move to a warmer place, maybe? Trust me, this could be amazing."

"I trust you implicitly," she said. "It's Bruce I don't trust. You have to be careful around him. He's old school."

"Old school?" I asked, pulling away to raise my eyebrow at her this time.

"Men like that cherry pick what they cherish and fight to the death for it. Usually other people's deaths."

"You make it sound like he's going to murder me," I joked.

"Just for saying that, I'll call a lawyer tomorrow," she said. "Make sure every single line is accounted for on our side before you go."

"I can go?" I was practically bouncing.

"Just for the summer," she said. "Then you're coming back to your normal life. I want you to remember who you are, okay? My kind, creative girl who cares about real things. Money is a tool, you know? I don't want you to change for it."

"I know, Mom."

At least about the money, I knew she was right. It was a tool; one we'd never had until now. It was worth a weird summer near Bruce to give my mom the life she had always deserved.

As for the "remembering who I was" bit...well, I thought maybe this would help with that, too. At the very least, it'd be a great story to write on a college application.

***

After Mom eventually fell asleep, I locked myself in my room and turned it upside down. It had been five years since that night in the garden with Will, and I had no clue where I'd stashed the key he had given me. It would have made a twisted sort of sense to remember I'd chucked it from the window as we drove away that night or boxed it away with junk or fed it to a street cat. I'd hated Will after he'd vanished from our lives like a temporary hallucination.

Luckily, even with all my talk of accounting, I'd been a romantic child. The tiny golden key Will had given me was inside a jewelry box I kept in the closet. Amongst the costume jewelry and old metallic barrettes chipped with wear, I found it, like a piece of shiny lint in the far corner of the "secret" bottom drawer. It looked simple. Flimsy. The sort of key you might get with a journal at a corner bookstore. Except this key was heavy and had a hollow end. Inside, I could see little teeth, like pyramids, running through to the head.

Honestly, I think it was quite responsible of me to wait an entire day and half a night to go find out where the key would lead me. When a whistle chirped at me from the street below, I threaded the key onto a chain around my neck for safe keeping and crept out of the apartment. Scarlett was still whistling when I jumped into the shotgun seat of her parents' Civic.

"They know you borrowed their car?" I asked, even though I didn't have to.

"Nay, my lady," she said. "Let's bounce before they do."

"Stop calling me lady."

"Would you rather I call you *Most Honorable Natalia of the Family Damarand, first of her name, mother of miniatures—"*

"Neither...unless you wanna be my lady's maid."

"Boo," she said. "How am I going to marry a prince if I'm a lady's maid?"

We were on the highway headed north ten minutes later. Nearly pitch-black farmland passed by like a dreary Möbius strip.

"So...?" Scarlett said.

"So..." I knew what she wanted me to say, and she knew I knew. She thwacked me suddenly on the shoulder.

"Spill! Who is Archer?" she said, blue eyes like little gems in the low light. "And what was the other one's name? Your other brother you didn't tell me anything about?"

"Cassian," I murmured, adding, "and they're not my brothers. I've never even met them. I don't even know what they look like, and I can't unless I accept the friend requests they sent me from their private accounts."

"How does that work? How can you know nothing about them?"

I waffled, wondering if I should explain everything—at least, everything I actually knew—or leave it to the basics. Or, easier still, just lie.

"Their dad never brought them over to visit. That's it," I said. "I didn't even know about them until after Will and my mom divorced."

That was true. It was only after we'd returned home to our empty, cold apartment in Pennsylvania that my mom sat me down and explained what had happened.

"Apparently, he'd been married twice before," I continued. "His first wife died giving birth to Cassian. A year later, he remarried and along came Archer. Ten years later, he met us."

"He wasn't, like, double married when he was with your mom, was he? *That'd* be a scandal."

"No." I shrugged. "He *did* divorce Archer's mom to marry mine, though."

Scarlett squealed with delight at that greasy little morsel of gossip.

"Apparently, they lived separately for their entire marriage, though. Again, I didn't know about any of this until *way* later."

"Your mom *is* a fox, so I get it."

A fox. Hunted to exhaustion by dogs. I thought back to how she'd crumbled onto the floor in her bedroom the night we returned to the apartment, after my dad's friend had come round with the key to let us back in. She had pulled me into her shame cuddle on the floor. Curled in her arms, I waited for her to speak. Instead, she had begun to sing:

Beyond the forest and river,
where thistle and heather hug the earth in her splendor,
a secret lies waiting for you and for me.
There's no use in waiting,
so stop hesitating,
Forever begins under the stone Alder tree.

A song I heard Will sing to her, and hum to her, and play on the piano in the ground floor salon on the rare weekend when they hosted parties. My mom *had* belonged there, in that grand hall, wearing a purple gown that brought the blue out in her eyes. And for those two years, she had loved Will more than I'd ever cared about anything, except maybe her. I didn't understand that sort of love; I'd never experienced it myself. But in the quiet moments when I watched them sitting on the porch together, her tucked into the crook of his arm, him humming the song to no one but her, love seemed worth having. Worth fighting for.

And yet, Will hadn't. We never saw him again after he left.

"Dude," said Scarlett suddenly. "Have you googled your *estate* yet?"

I tried to shove my cellphone under my body so she wouldn't be tempted. She grabbed it before I could and plonked it back into my hand.

"Google! Google-google-google it! For me."

In all the chaos after Bruce's bombshell, I had actually forgotten to google anything about the house Will owned.

"Fine."

"What's this *fine*? It's a mansion. It's yours. You're probably in line for the British throne now."

"That is where you are wrong, mi amiga. I am most definitely not."

"How do you know?"

"Bruce told me. It was the first thing he told me. Like he thought I'd murder everyone in line ahead of me to be queen or something. *Hard* pass. No freedom for the rest of your life? Everyone knowing your business? No, thank you."

I typed in *Lord William Mahon* and pressed search. The little blue loading bar moved across the top of my screen at a glacial pace. I glanced over at the screen corner; there was barely a single bar of service out here in the sticks.

"Aw, would you look at that?" I teased Scarlett. "No service. How sad for you."

"Of course," said Scarlett, grumbling playfully. "Electronics always stop working when you actually need them."

The roads were empty all the way to the lake. The narrow drive around it to the castle still looked the way it had five years ago, when we'd driven away from it in the rental car.

"Wait," I cried. "Turn the lights off, Scarlett. Stop the car."

"What? Why?"

She killed the headlights and watched me watch the house. Lights were on inside, scattered in various rooms throughout the entire castle.

"What's the problem?" asked Scarlett.

"I don't know. I didn't think that anyone would be here," I said. "For some reason, I never thought about Will selling it."

"Well, if he went back to England…"

"Scotland."

It looked like a party. Yellow light spilled out of the floor-to-ceiling windows, down onto the inky lake water below. A string of very extravagant cars lined the border of the round driveway like a hedge. Some guests were on the upstairs patio, others were in the grand salon, and at least two I could see were enjoying a tumble in some rose bushes.

"Nat."

"Hmm?"

"What do we do? Do we go home? Do we sneak in? I'm wearing jeans, so someone will *immediately* know we don't belong."

I bristled at the word *belong*. It was a cold insult, cowardly. And I'd come too far to leave empty-handed.

"Okay, here's what we're gonna do," I said. "You walk up like you're lost and got turned around heading for somewhere."

"What somewhere? What's around here?"

"Lake George, maybe?"

"You're just making up lake names now."

"Just keep their eyes off me." I quietly opened my door. "I'm gonna go dig something up in the garden."

Scarlett smiled and did a little bow. "Lady's maid at your service."

She took the road while I darted behind the tree line leading from the car to the back of the castle. Closest to the actual building, there was a short, empty expanse of grass—maybe fifty feet across—between the forest and the narrow garden bed that ran along the side of the house. Where once there had only been small flowers, now there were tall bushes crowding the corner where Will had buried the box. I forced myself into a tiny opening between two azaleas and around to the narrow corner where the gutter was. I stopped short. Someone had bolted the gutter section Will had easily taken out to the brick wall, making it impossible to remove without some sort of drill. Or a butter knife and a lot of free time. I didn't have either.

I dropped to my knees and started digging down from the side. It had rained recently. The moist earth clung to everything, and it wasn't long before the knees of my jeans were caked in the stuff.

"Gross-gross-gross," I sang to myself.

The smell almost made up for it; every till of the wet soil sent petrichor shooting into my nose like the sweetest perfume…but there was some other scent there as well. It took a moment for me to place it—the wine cellar Will kept under the castle—the scent of deep red wine left in barrels to age. It pushed the petrichor aside the deeper I dug. Although, for the life of me, my mind couldn't decide why that meant anything at all. Not when my fingers were *freezing* at the ends of my arms.

"It better still be here."

"What better be here?"

My heart practically abandoned ship as I turned and found a young man crouched behind me in the hedges.

"Whoa!" I reached for something—anything—but I didn't even have the keys to the car to defend myself. The only thing within reach was a pathetic twig, which I grabbed anyway.

"I come in peace," he said, raising his hands and face so I could see it in the light. A wave of sherry wine hit me like a freight train. He was my age, or near enough. His shoulder-length brown hair was tucked just behind his ears, caught in the collar of a crimson party blazer. His turquoise bolo tie exactly matched the aqua blue of his eyes.

And he was…Jesus, he was gorgeous. The sort of pretty you saw in agazines, not in real life. It took me remembering where I was and vhat I was doing to pull my gaze away.

"Uh," I said, trying to think of what to do. "Please don't call the cops."

"Trust me, I won't. This isn't even my house."

There was something about his voice. His American accent was southern, with a light sort of singer's twang to it. It wavered like his vocal cords were breaking…or he was drunk, doing his best impression of someone sober. But despite his wine-soaked smell, he actually seemed completely sober so that couldn't be it.

"Party's kinda lame," he added. A grin creased the left side of his face, exposing a dimple, and a brief flutter ran through my stomach. "I just saw you digging around back here and thought I'd see what you were up to."

"Okay…" I said, still frozen. I studied him, taking in all I could. He seemed relaxed, unbothered to find me here. More than that…my diaphragm tightened nervously…he was studying me, too. After a moment, he smiled again.

"Here, let me," he said, moving in the narrow space behind me. I could feel his warm breath on the back of my neck. "Excuse me."

I kept my eye on him as he rolled up the cuffs of his blazer and plunged his hands into the hole I had started.

"Come on," he said, grinning again. "I don't know what I'm looking for."

We dug together silently, our gazes dancing with one another, as our fingers fumbled over each other in the dirt until I felt something else fumbling over the back of my hand in the dark—the tiptoe of eight tiny legs across my skin.

"It's a spider!" I spazzed. "Spider, get it off. Off!"

He was there before I could even fling it away, letting it crawl into his left hand while his right held my hand steady. His skin was satin smooth and steaming hot despite the freezing earth. He set the spider down on the other side of him and turned back to me with another crooked grin. In the golden party glow, I could see flecks of black in his blue irises, little islands in tropical seas.

"You're freezing," he whispered. I froze as he enveloped both of my dirty, icy hands in his own. He leaned forward and blew warm air across them, his eyes never leaving mine. That dimple appeared again.

"Better?" he asked. One of his coffee-colored curls ha[illegible] behind his ear onto his forehead, consuming my enti[illegible] longer than I'd like to admit.

"Hmm?"

"We could go inside," he offered. "I could warm you by the [illegible] maybe make you a hot chocolate—or something stronger."

As if in response, a loud cheer rang out from inside. It sounded so warm and alive. Inviting in a way that sitting in the dirt as more mud squelched its way into my pants did not.

Mud. My eyes snapped back to the hole between us. So dark and *clearly* full of spiders. I shivered at the thought.

"This," I said, reluctantly taking my hands back. "I have to see this through."

I plunged my fingers back into the earth. To his credit, so did he. I felt my stomach flutter again.

"Wait, I can feel something," he said, a few seconds later.

"Let me get it. Do you mind?"

"Be my guest."

I had to almost press my ear to the ground to reach deep enough, but it was down there. My frigid fingers grazed the varnished surface of the box and grasped blindly, heaving the heavy thing onto the mound of soil between us.

The emerald seal, the seven-pointed star, was barely visible in the peripheral party light. The boy glanced at it, surprised and intrigued.

"What is it?" he asked.

"I don't know," I said, trying to form an easy lie. "My dad told me it was here."

"Your dad?"

"Yeah, he, um, told me if he ever died, I should come get it."

"I'm so sorry," he said. I glanced up at him. "That your dad died. How did it happen?"

I hesitated. I didn't know how Will had died. All the articles I'd read since learning of his death had called his departure "mysterious and untimely" without going into any details; Bruce had promised to tell me more about it in private when we left for Europe. So, I pulled from my own dad's death instead.

"Cancer," I said, glancing away from the intense sincerity of his blue eyes.

"Really." This time, there was an undertone. I could tell he didn't believe me. "I was expecting something…more exotic—"

"There you are!" Scarlett's voice sliced through the air like a spinning blade. Her face popped over the bushes. A coy smile crept into her eyes when she saw us. "Oh. No wonder we had to drive two hours in the middle of the night…"

My cheeks flushed with embarrassment. I grabbed the box with my still-dirty hands and waggled it at her.

"This is what we came for." I forced myself to my feet and shoved my way through the bushes onto the grass. Scarlett's eyes traveled down to the muddy, caked knees of my jeans.

Her grin got even wider.

"You're both welcome inside," said the boy, also emerging from the hedge.

"That would be *amaz—*" I grabbed Scarlett's hand before she could finish.

"We actually have to get going," I interrupted. "Finals to study for. Parents who can *never know we snuck out*."

"Yes, Debbie Downer is right," said Scarlett, ogling the boy openly. "Nice to meet you, though. I'm Scarlett."

"I'm—"

"Thanks for the help," I said, pulling Scarlett away.

We cut straight down the driveway to the car as fast as I could drag us.

"You are so strange around guys that like you," said Scarlett. "Look, he's still watching you."

"No, he's not…" I casually glanced back and the words died on my lips. He was still there, staring. He tossed out a little wave and another crooked grin, completely unashamed to watch us walk away. In the end, I was the one who blinked first, trying my hardest not to walk faster.

Back in the car, I blasted the heat and let it blow across my numbed fingers while Scarlett maneuvered the car around on the lane. My phone lit up in my lap.

"Oh no, is that your mom?" asked Scarlett, driving a little faster. She gasped quietly, "Is it my dad?"

I swiped up. The webpage had finally populated. There, chewing up the tiny screen, was Bear Glen. My house. My *estate* in Scotland was so palatial it made the New York castle look like a quaint weekend cottage. Bear Glen was so large, in fact, the layout of the estate could only be captured by drone shot. A pink gravel driveway wound through thousands of acres of pastureland until it curled in on itself in front of the house, around a fountain as large as the apartment I shared with my mom. The foundation was a garden level, half buried and made of monstrous gray blocks of stone. The three floors above that one were built from honey-colored bricks. Great rectangular mullion windows stretched from floor to ceiling on the lower two levels, while the top tier of the house was wrapped nearly edge to edge in giant oval windows.

Someone had taken the mansion's glamor shots at the height of spring; they were bursting with color. Grand yellow and purple flowers erupted from every landscaping space around the ground level, making the whole building look like a cake. Yellow blossoms overflowed from every flower box in every upper window. And at every corner, a lilac tree burst with purple petals.

"*That* is your *house?*" sputtered Scarlett, stopping the car. "It's a palace. It's gorgeous. I am *so* canceling every single plan I had this summer. You are taking me with you to Scotland!"

CHAPTER 6

"Absolutely not!"

"But Dad!"

Scarlett and I sat on the old red couch in my living room. Out of the corner of my eye, I could see the microwave clock in the kitchen read 4:07am. The soil-y mud on the knees of my jeans had hardened to rock; it felt like I was wearing knee pads. My mom and Scarlett's mom and dad were standing over us, still dressed in their pajamas.

"First, you take our car *without permission* and sneak out of the house," her father started again. He had already said this twice. "And then you won't tell us where you went. You think I'm letting you out of the country? Just disappear off doing who knows what with who knows whom?"

"It's not great, hun," her mom added, surprisingly less upset than he was. Her excessive yawn suggested she was still deeply under the influence of some sleep enhancer.

"Natalie," he said, seeming to realize I was also there. "You're better than this. What the hell were you thinking? You know how impressionable Scarlett is."

"Hey," said Scarlett.

"I'm sorry," I said, more to my mom than to them. "It was just supposed to be a quick trip."

"Where did you go?" Mom asked. "Just give us something so we know you weren't off doing drugs, or worse."

"Drugs?" asked Scarlett's mom, almost a little too excited.

I glanced at Scarlett. She shook her head slowly, purposefully. I looked away at my mom.

"Well, now you're both making me feel bad," I said.

"Don't do it, Nat," said Scarlett.

"Natalie?" asked her dad.

"We…went to our old house in New York."

Scarlett exploded out of her seat with dramatic disappointment. Her father looked practically feral with disbelief. It was easy to see where she got it from.

"New York? You went all the way to *New York*?"

"It's just one state over, chill, Dad," said Scarlett. Turning to me, she added, "Great going, ding-dong. Now they'll never let me visit."

To be fair, I *had* warned her not to tell them about Scotland when we saw her mom's car parked in the street outside. But I also knew my mom would tell them anyway.

Scarlett's parents hustled her out of the door, murmuring about groundings and revocation of her driver's license. Soon, it was just me, Mom, and the little bag at my feet, which held the box from the garden. She eyed me with patient exhaustion.

"I am sorry," I offered. "I just thought you wouldn't want me to go back there."

"I know," she said.

"Am I grounded?"

"I guess?" Mom said, gesturing vaguely. "I mean, there's a week left of school and then you head to Scotland, so is there really a point?"

"Why'd you really go to the house? You know you can tell me."

Will had warned me not to. For some reason I still couldn't explain, I obeyed. After learning of his death, I didn't know, it felt like a last request.

"I thought maybe going there would make this make more sense," I twisted. It did the trick; she seemed less tense immediately. "I just don't know why he picked me."

"Me neither, kiddo," she said, motioning me off the couch. "Maybe you can sell whatever's over there to pay for college, at least. That'd be nice, huh? No student loans."

We walked down the hallway toward the closet that held our laundry machines. She opened the folding doors and plonked the detergent into my still-soiled hands.

"Break the mud off *outside* first," she said, motioning to my grody jeans. "Then wash them with this, okay? I've got work at eight, so I'm going back to bed."

Later in my room, I pulled Will's box out of the bag and set it on the desk. Despite the time and water warp along the lower edge, it still looked brand new. The edges fit together so that you had to turn it just so to see where the lid met the box. Someone had inlaid the seven-pointed star in a blond wood on top of red and fit the keyhole at the dead center of the star. I unstrung the chain around my neck, popped the key into the keyhole, and twisted.

Shunk! Like a jack-in-the-box, the lid burst open, scattering residual dirt on my schoolbooks. I had expected...well, honestly, I had no idea what I would find inside Will's gift, but this certainly wasn't it.

The box held only a single photograph—one I recognized immediately. My mom had taken it back when we were still living in Will's castle in New York. It was a candid photo marking the monumental moment I'd beaten Will at chess for the first time. My smile was so luminous it took up nearly the entire left side of the picture. I was proudly showing off my black queen, which had toppled Will's white king and left him for dead. Will was smiling so hard his cheeks were strawberry red with delight.

As a reward for the accomplishment, Will had given me a riddle—one he claimed would take me years to figure out. Of course, I had thought he was exaggerating. I'd spent hours poring over it, asking teachers at school for help, asking my mom until she found out what the riddle was and told me it was a gift from Will that I'd have to figure out for myself. Every weekend when I went home and tried to beat him at another game of chess, he reminded me of it...until he finally left us, and I left the riddle behind me, out of spite. It was what my twelve-year-old mind considered a grave punishment for Will.

Of course, it's impossible to forget anything you obsessed over for months. So, when I turned over the crinkled photograph and saw the riddle again, written in Will's handwriting, it was like being surprised by an old friend.

A treasure beneath, a prize on high
Within stone sheath under bark of dye
Where green sentinels loom near gleam of armored show
In a sacred tomb, only the hiding one knows
The moon reveals a future bright where heads lay deep in the dead of night

...All it takes is just one bite

****

Natalie, I'm sorry.
Sincerely, William

I frowned at the bottom addition. What did he have to be sorry about? That he'd made the riddle too challenging? That he'd abandoned my mother and broken her heart to smithereens? That he'd given me the house? Whatever it was, I hoped at the very least that I'd be able to finally solve his riddle once I arrived in Scotland.

CHAPTER 7

The last week of school wasn't so much a blur as a relay race of spines and barbed wire and occasional free-write essays. Finals had students dragging bookbags behind them like sacks of iron. I was lucky, I guess. I had Will's mnemonics helping me. Every time I used one on a test, it left me with a sinking feeling that even in our "visitor's weekends" together, he'd had more of an impact on me than I'd realized.

The sudden stalking presence of one of his ghosts made that all the more obvious. For the last five days of school, I endured a begrudging and unwelcome bodyguard—Bruce. He appeared at my doorstep on Monday morning to chauffeur me to school, wearing a mostly black tartan sweater speared with lines of purple and gold, which he proudly explained was the tartan of the Mahon clan. At the school door, he followed me inside, placed me in a chair in the admin wing, and disappeared into the principal's office for nearly twenty minutes. When he and the principal reemerged, the latter looked cowed under Bruce's authoritative glare and told me that Bruce was responsible for me now. When I disagreed, Bruce implied it was a requirement to fulfill for the inheritance—one my mom's lawyer later confirmed in the fine print of the paperwork we spent an entire day going through. Another requirement was that after the summer, I'd agree to an actual bodyguard following me around my last year of school.

Bruce took his tenure as a shadow guard seriously. He followed me to every single class, looming like some great sentry robot at the back of the room, while Glam Radio gossiped that I *must* be in *dire trouble* if someone like him was guarding some nobody like me. By the end of the week, half the school thought I'd joined a mafia family. The other half thought I'd won the lottery.

Scarlett thought the whole thing was hilarious and called him Brucey behind his back. And to his face. And within earshot.

Each afternoon, Bruce dropped me off at home with a cursory warning, "Remember, we leave on Saturday. There's very little you'll need when we arrive, but whatever sentimentals you do pack, please have them outside by eight in the morning."

He said this every single day, like he was afraid I'd forget. By the third afternoon, I started messing with him.

"Best I can do is 8:15," I yelled over my shoulder as I ran up the stairs. "Maybe 8:07 if I really push myself."

I didn't need to look back to know this was driving him up a polite British wall.

I hadn't looked at the pictures of Bear Glen since that night in the car with Scarlett. It seemed too much to take in then. Too unreal. So did the fact that neither Scarlett nor my mom could go with me to Scotland.

I spent my last night at home with Mom, wearing matching llama pajamas and eating spaghetti, watching the last episodes of the Korean television show we'd started before Bruce had interrupted things.

Afterward, Mom and I stayed up into the early hours talking. I'd never gone anywhere without her before. Not really. Leaving her behind felt wrong somehow. She knew more than I ever could about Will. I had only sort of known him. I liked him, of course, and there were far worse stepfathers a girl could have, but…that seemed a weak substitute for my mom's love and heartbreak and mourning.

And yet, he'd chosen me to inherit. Over her. Over his own sons.

"Mom, did Will tell you anything about his life over there?"

"Well, some things I'll never tell anyone." She smiled. "If you mean the stuff any old biographer would know…well…he was the only child of an only child. He inherited '*all the wonderful and all the terrible*.' His words, not mine. He hated the pretense of it. He said it was like wearing a gilded, smiling mask that hid the grating discomfort underneath and crushed his reckless curiosity. Again, his words. I found him so *annoying* the first night I met him. Did I ever tell you that?"

I shook my head in surprise. His entrance had been so sudden into our lives, so wild and intrusive. Then all at once, he'd fit like a puzzle piece we never realized was missing. It felt as if he had always been there…until the day he wasn't anymore.

"My company booked this all-inclusive thing, right?" Mom said, her eyes bright with nostalgia. "That first night, we all got dressed up and wandered down to the restaurant. Complete high spirits, which were immediately dashed when they told us they could only seat eight people each at these big, round dining tables. There were seventeen of us, and they would not budge about the arrangement. Like, I was standing there with an extra chair in my hand, and they just said it wouldn't work. The restaurant was so crowded, kid. Seemed like everyone and their spouse were celebrating. I thought I was going to have to sit at the bar by myself, or order room service back in my suite, but…then, there he was. Insisting I join him."

"He was being nice," I offered.

"He was being *polite*," she corrected. "But the second I sat down, he was trying to impress me with yachts in Corsica, villas in Morocco. And then he tried to *order* for me."

I cringed; my mom hated when men ordered for her.

"He was also a total one-upper," she added.

"A what?"

"You know, I mention I have a kid, so he mentions he has two. I mention I'm a bookkeeper, and he says he has a *private* bookkeeper that *only* works for him and his various holdings. I was sick of it within ten minutes."

"So, what changed?" I asked.

"Well, I had already ordered," she said, little joy crinkles appearing at the corners of her eyes. "I was stuck there until the food came. So, I asked him what his favorite dinosaur was."

"You did what now?"

"I said you could tell a lot about a person based on their favorite dinosaur," she said. "So, I told him mine was an ankylosaurus and asked what his was."

She sipped her wine as if this answered everything.

"And?" I asked.

"I was expecting him to say a T-Rex or velociraptor, the fake kind from *Jurassic Park*. Something macho and generic and totally overplayed. But then he sat there for a long moment, and his eyes widened with this sort of…glee…that made my heart race a little. And he said *pachycephalosaurus*."

I quickly pulled out my phone and googled it. "The one with the helmet on its head?"

"He joked that it suited him. He was always running headfirst into things."

I watched my mom for a long moment; the memory danced behind her eyes.

"He was just a nerd, you know?" she said. "The rest of the conversation was about how much he'd love to find a fossil on his own, just pick one up wandering around in the desert. Then we were talking about alchemy and astronomy and a new think tank invention to clean the ocean he was thinking of funding. I loved how much he loved learning things. Surprises. Games. He might have been fifteen years older than me, but he didn't act like it."

I mulled this over, wondering if the riddle in the box was just the end of a scavenger hunt he'd arranged as a parting gift for me. A fond, fun memory to keep. Sure, he had told me where to find the box, so it wasn't technically a scavenger hunt, but still. It warmed my heart to think that the wise man with the commanding voice who had taught me to play chess was really just a big puckish kid at heart.

"Something on your mind?" Mom asked. "I know you've been quiet about all this because you didn't want to hurt my feelings, but I promise I can handle whatever Bruce told you about him."

My thoughts drifted to the strange angular crescent moon Will had tattooed on the inside of his left wrist...and the seven-pointed star on the box.

"Do you know...why he was obsessed with space stuff?"

Her brow furrowed.

"The moon tattoo he had." I pointed to the spot on my wrist. "And that star symbol on the paperwork Bruce had."

She frowned. "It wasn't space he was interested in. Will had some strange ideas about the universe, spiritually speaking. Once when we were drunk, he said it's our humanness that kills us. 'The bear follows its instincts, the human suppresses them, and the stars envy them both.' Something like that. I remember I accidentally laughed when he said it, thinking he was joking. He tried to explain, but it sounded like gibberish to me. I just sort of forgot about it until..."

Her eyes clouded momentarily.

"What?"

“I guess you’re old enough now to know. Two days before you and I finally left, I woke to whispering outside. Will was out by the lake, completely naked, with someone wearing a giant fur coat. Honestly, when he asked for a divorce, I thought he’d been cheating on me with whomever was out there, but he swore he wasn’t. He wouldn’t tell me who they were or what they wanted. He just said, ‘No one can outrun the fall of the moon.’”

CHAPTER 8

It's the littlest things you remember. Accidentally gluing my thumb and forefinger together making my first book nook with my dad. Waking to the sound of my mom's sleepy footsteps in the hallway every morning. The way rain always seemed to hit the left corner of our apartment balcony first, where we kept our wind chimes, so they sang the rain's arrival. Insignificant moments become pressed and glossed and polished like precious stones—diamonds from carbon—strung on the chain of your life.

It was raining when I left Pennsylvania; the wind chime sang me adieu. Bruce arrived ten minutes to eight to find my mom and I hugging weepily at the bottom of the apartment stairs with my overstuffed suitcase at my feet. My backpack, an old orange thing turned tabby and frayed with age, was so heavy with Mom's last-minute "might needs" that it pulled at my shoulder, forcing me into a slouch.

"You have everything?" was all he said, slipping both bags into the trunk of his Audi.

"Except my ticket," I said, turning to hug my mom. "You promise you'll come?"

"Yes," she said. "Once I know when I can take the time."

"You could probably just quit," I half-joked. "Now that I'm a marchioness."

"Yeah, sure," she said, with a playful chuff. "I've given up everything without a guarantee before, and we both know how that went. Let's wait and see."

"I'll call you the second the check clears my account," I said, again only half-joking.

"No rush, little bird," she said, giving me one last squeeze. "Enjoy this while it's happening. Don't think about school next year or college. People live in the future too much. Right now is all you have. And right now is pretty spectacular."

When she released me, the absence of her body against mine made me feel suddenly untethered. Loosed into some unknown world. *Terrified.* It took everything I had in me not to burst into tears. It was a silly fear, but for a moment, I wondered if I would ever see her again. Perhaps it would have been better if I hadn't.

***

Bruce drove in silence, glancing back at me in the rearview mirror, on the cusp of saying something that never seemed to reach his mouth. There were plenty of things I wanted to ask, but this wasn't the place or time, when I couldn't look him in the eye to see if he was lying. I resigned myself to picking at an errant thread along the seam of the leather seat beneath me until Bruce took an unexpected left turn.

"We're not going to the airport?" I asked.

"The private airfield."

"We're taking a private jet?"

"*Your* jet, my lady," he said, motioning to the right as the copse of oak trees along the road broke to reveal a private airstrip. Parked just a few dozen yards away from the small terminal, I could see a black plane striped with gold and purple—the family colors. It looked like someone had turned an obelisk on its side and strapped engines to it. "Meet Pearl, Lord Mahon's favorite plane."

"He had more than one?"

There was a valet waiting when Bruce parked. Before my Converse touched asphalt, a baggage handler rolled my bags away. Bruce motioned me quickly ahead, handing documentation and my passport to a slender woman at the only desk in sight. She smiled, almost bowing at me—yes me, the girl in an old NASA hoodie that had once belonged to her dad. Bruce motioned me to follow again, straight to the plane.

"We don't have to go through security?" I asked.

"It's handled." He glanced back at me with a cheeky grin. "Close your mouth."

I felt my jaw snap shut as a flight attendant in a Mahon tartan skirt suit met us at the bottom of the boarding stairs. She held a golden platter bursting with what appeared to be white roses until she used golden tongs to hand one to each of us; the flowers unfurled into warmed, rose-scented hand towels.

"Thank you," said Bruce. "Natalie, this is Teresa, Lord Mahon's flight attendant."

"My condolences, my lady," she said, her Scottish lilt like a morning songbird.

I followed Bruce inside, where the captain waited for us.

"Good morning, my lady," he said, his Scottish accent robust and gravelly. "I'm Ewan, your star captain today."

"I-I'm James," said a sudden squeaky English voice behind him in the cockpit. A guy who looked barely out of college, acne across his chin, poked his head past Ewan to say hello.

Ewan rolled his gray eyes. "That's James, the co-pilot."

"Lovely to meet you, my lady. We should have smooth flying today."

"That's my line, Jim," whispered Ewan.

"Are we ready?" asked Bruce.

The pilots exchanged a guarded glance.

"We're just waiting on two strays, sir," said Ewan.

Bruce attempted to hide his rolling eyes by closing them; it didn't work. He took hold of my shoulders and steered me toward the main cabin. Someone had ripped the lobby bar from an art-deco hotel circa 1923 and *painstakingly* rebuilt it here. Dark wood and red wood paneled the walls, accentuated by copper and brass finishes. The carpeted floor and painted ceiling were both the same warm, matte gray black. There were eight seats, arranged around two tables across from each other at the center of the cabin, in plush charcoal leather with marbled wood accent lines running down the sides. Behind these, there were two charcoal leather couches each larger than my bed. They flanked the hallway that led to the bathrooms and the crew area at the back.

Bruce deposited me in a seat at the right table, facing the rear of the plane, before disappearing back toward the cockpit. I craned my neck to watch him go. Now that he had completed his original mission to collect me, he seemed on the hunt for his next one.

It was strange. His cold, mechanical watch of me over the past few days had irked me constantly, but now that he'd turned away, it felt jarring. His steady, practical *duty* had muddied the hatred I'd felt for him for what he did to my mom. I still hated him, don't get me wrong, but I was starting to understand him. He didn't just serve; he was the service he provided. It was like my mom said: he picked his master and having done so, made every move and decision accordingly. It was…begrudgingly respectable from a distance.

"Champagne, miss?" Teresa appeared beside me, holding a 1947 bottle of Dom Pérignon in black-gloved hands.

"I'm seventeen," I said.

"Oh, bless you," she said, in a chipper lilt. "I'll wait until we pass into international airspace then. Where it's legal."

"As far as I'm concerned, we crossed the border on the stairs," said a voice from behind me. "A tipple sounds lovely, Ter."

My neck whipped to the side faster than I could stop it. I knew that melodic voice, had heard it only a few nights before, in fact. It was the boy I'd met in the garden at the castle. Same shaggy brown hair around his ears, eyes blue like a tranquil lagoon at midday. He had shed the crimson party blazer for a navy-blue sweater and the southern twang for an English accent smooth as a skipping stone.

"Of course, sir," Teresa said, a little brisker than she had been with me.

He eyed the seat across the aisle from my own as if it had suddenly invited him to sit. "Don't mind if I do."

"You," I said.

"You," he replied, disemboweling his carry-on in the seat beside him, organizing a laptop, mouse, mouse pad, and earbuds on the table.

I opened my mouth to speak when it hit me all at once. It felt like my mind had stepped off a street curb and leapt back as a speeding car blew past.

I hadn't accepted the friend request he'd sent me the night of my birthday. Hadn't even opened it to look at the picture. It was so obvious, in the curve of his square jaw, the shape of his ears. And that brow ridge. It was a wonder I hadn't seen it before in the garden that night. A trick of the light, or more likely my mind hiding it from me.

"You're Will's son."

“Don’t call me Archie, ever, all right?” he said. That British accent again. Where it had cracked a half dozen times in the garden with Southern charm, it now came out as a molasses ribbon, so smooth it felt as if there was a delay between what I heard and what I understood.

Confusion and anger crashed into each other in my chest on their way to my brain and mouth. “You knew it was me, at the castle.”

He must have recognized me if he used a phony accent to throw me off… He’d sent me the friend request, after all, and my profiles were public. I couldn’t help but wonder why he would lie. I looked down at his hands on the table, the graceful fingers that had cupped mine in the garden and warmed them with his own breath.

“Why didn’t you tell me?”

“Why didn’t you open the box you found?”

“It wasn’t any of your business.”

“Is it now?”

“Not now that you’ve lied to me.”

I needed air. I stood up, but Teresa was already closing the boarding door. Archer stared, studying me again. The curiosity didn’t feel friendly anymore. I turned the other way and headed for the bathroom.

I slipped inside to find an actual shower in the corner and a sink made of treated glass. I studied the short, curvy girl in the mirror, the one with a strange long tangle of hair on her head that never knew how to behave. My olive skin was always relatively clean and clear, which people seemed to admire…but I’d yet to meet a boy that thought it mattered enough to date me. And anyway, in a NASA hoodie and old jeans, my hair half up on top of my head and no makeup, there wasn’t much for doting admirers to gawk at.

I should’ve known he was playing me for a fool in the garden. I was so stupid. I’d mistaken mischief for attraction, misread everything. I felt so embarrassed I didn’t want to leave when Teresa called through the door and told me we were about to take off.

With a quick flick of a switch, I unlocked the lavatory door and stepped out into the cabin—into the chest of someone walking the other way.

“Sorry,” I said.

"My apologies," he replied, his voice silken and slightly higher than Archer's. I had to step back, almost into the bathroom again, to take this boy in. Well, I say *boy*. His porcelain skin and wiry frame suggested he was still in school, but the barely-there stubble, his staggering height, his neutral pout, and steely gaze belied someone older. He wore a blue button-down shirt, sleeves cuffed to his elbows, and wool slacks that curved with his body, made only and specifically for him. His hair was shaved close at the sides, with a jolt of golden copper locks flopping more heavily on one side than the other. His storm-cloud gray eyes dipped in my direction, seeming to absorb all of me in a split second, like a painting in an errant corner of a museum.

"You must be the interloper," he said, studying my face.

"I beg your pardon?" I said, my voice almost twanging as I recoiled at his tone.

"I don't give pardons," he said. He still hadn't moved back, essentially pinning me between the bathroom and the main cabin. "But I know we would both love an explanation."

"Okay, guy, I don't know what you're talking about," I said. I tried to set my shoulders back a little, establish a bit of space for myself, but he seemed to swallow the extra space just as quickly. He was looming over me, watching me closely. His eyes moved in microscopic intervals, like he was memorizing my face. It was disorienting.

"I think you do, Miss Damarand," he hummed, unreadable. Not angry or accusatory, but like he was trying to glean some secret I must possess. "There must be something special about you. Something Will noticed, which sets you apart. I aim to discover what it is. If you'll let me."

That flutter in my stomach.

"Ah, so thoughtful of you two to actually join us on time," said Bruce, suddenly coming between me and the ginger. "Natalie, I see you've met Cass."

As Bruce squeezed around me and sealed himself inside the bathroom, forcing me closer to the copper statue that seemed immoveable, a stone clattered its way down from my throat into the pit of my stomach. Cass. Cassian—Will's other son.

"We'll need to become *much* better acquainted before you start calling me Cass." He whispered the words at me under his breath, like he was making a promise to himself—to *me*—that we would know each other soon enough.

Then he stepped aside to let me pass. The confusion was like a fog around me as I found my seat again. In two minutes, both brothers had completely befuddled me. I felt like I had walked too far out onto thin ice I hadn't even known was there. Like they'd already judged me and found me lacking. While I had half-thought about them in the few days before leaving, I'd been too caught up in finals and Will's gift to think about meeting them. Now that I had, I didn't know what to think.

I looked up. Cassian had dropped onto the couch diagonal from me. His piercing gaze scanned my features like he was attempting to read my mind. I hazarded a glance at Archer as well; he watched me, too. I suddenly felt very out of my depth.

I looked resolutely away as Bruce joined me on this side of the aisle. Teresa strapped herself in and the plane slid forward into position on the private airstrip. Less than an hour after leaving home, we were air bound.

CHAPTER 9

I didn't sleep a wink the entire eight hours and thirty-three-hundred miles across the Atlantic. The garden encounter just replayed endlessly in my mind, steeping me in embarrassment…until I looked up and realized that whatever facial expressions I was giving off had earned me an audience. I couldn't look toward the back of the plane without finding Cassian watching me. Didn't matter if he was pretending to read, or pretending to sleep, or pretending to talk to Archer and Bruce, his eyes invariably returned to me. I felt his gaze upon my skin even when I wasn't looking, which forced me to check and made me feel creepy for looking at him. Squirreling myself away into the pretty limbo of the music in my headphones had been the only way to stop myself from looking…and to stop the little jolts of warmth that ran through me every time our eyes connected. I had no control over them, or the way they spread up from my stomach into my chest and throat and down-down-down through my lower stomach, between my…

And then somewhere along the way, the obvious hit me. He was staring because I'd unintentionally robbed him of his inheritance. Their inheritance. A strange sort of shame was attached to the thought, although I didn't *feel* shame for it. I just felt…sorry. Not that they would believe me if I said so.

While the others took strong black coffee, and I looked for anything to stave off the brutal jetlag trying to steal me from the land of waking, I slid into the seat across from Bruce then farther over to the window, where I could watch the patchwork of pastures and forests zip by below us. Mauve-gray stone jutted out of hillsides and rivers, the bones of Scotland beneath a shroud of unruly nature.

"Welcome to Ayrshire, my lady," said Bruce.

The sun had just dipped below the horizon, setting the lakes and rivers ablaze with color.

"How far away is the house?" I asked.

"About forty minutes." He took a careful sip of his espresso and added, "Tomorrow once you're settled, I'll have the housekeeper give you the grand tour. At least of the main house."

"The main house," I echoed, glancing over at Archer and Cassian, who were pretending not to listen.

"The rest should be at your own discretion," said Bruce. "One could spend a lifetime exploring ten thousand acres, especially when they have been carefully cultivated by a man like Lord Mahon. One can only imagine what you'll find."

I eyed Bruce, wondering if he knew about Will's riddle, but his gentle smile gave nothing away. Instead, I clocked Archer staring at me out of the corner of my eye. He might not have known exactly what Will had hidden in the garden box for me, but he knew enough to presume where there was one secret, there were bound to be others.

When we landed, men and women sprang forward from the private airfield office like a pit crew, unloading luggage and helping me down the stairs before I'd even fully registered the chill or the scents of petrichor and thistle saturating the morning mist. A driver as wide as he was tall emerged from the right side of a gold Rolls-Royce Phantom. He ran around the car to open the door for me like I might risk injury attempting it myself.

"Here you are, my lady," he said, his Scottish accent round and bouncy. "The name's Dave, miss."

"Thank you, Dave," I said, sliding inside.

I lifted myself across the leather seat to make room for the mass that got in behind me. I had expected Bruce; instead, I found Archer to my left. I moved to slide all the way across; the right door snapped open, and Cassian got in on the other side, trapping me in the middle. My knees came together in front of me. The scents of their respective colognes collided in my nose—sharp, dark sherry on Archer's side, earthy campfire on Cassian's.

"All ready?" asked Dave, in response to the trunk door shutting behind us. It was the only sound between the five of us.

"My belt…" I said, just to fill the emptiness. My hands dove to either side of me, between us. I felt nothing but various textures, Archer's jeans and Cassian's wool slacks, and the pressure of each of their warm legs against my hands.

"You're sitting on it," purred Cassian.

Almost before I realized, his hand had slid past my own, then under me, skimming across the rivets of the back pockets of my jeans like an albatross across the face of the ocean. My breath caught, surprised by the unexpected intimacy of it. I glanced up to meet his eyes, but he wasn't looking at my face. He was focused on the task, like a blind man sensing for features with his hands. I felt his fingers move farther under me then pull back with the belt and latch plate.

"You know what comes next, don't you?"

Without thinking, I took firm hold of the buckle on my other side and pulled it taut away from the seat, as if to ensure he could see it. I reached to take the latch plate from him, but he kept his hand under mine, moving with me, plunging the belt across my abdomen, guiding the latch plate into the buckle. I felt his fingers shift below mine, turning over so our fingertips touched, electric, his mouth mere inches from my own, while he gently pushed my fingers forward, and we listened for the click. He took hold of the small fabric tongue and pulled the belt tight against me.

Only then did he meet my gaze as he ran his gentle fingers back across my stomach and returned his hands to himself.

Just a moment. It had all happened so quickly, a dance move we both instinctively knew. I hadn't even chanced another breath yet. Then it was over, and he swiveled away to the window, as if nothing had happened at all.

I could almost hear the record scratch in my head. I had no idea what had just happened…or why.

Archer stared slack-jawed at us both, his brow quirked with confusion. My hands came together in my lap, suddenly very aware of every part of myself, hoping my heartbeat wasn't as loud as it sounded in my ears.

The rest of the trip passed in silence. Looking right, toward Cassian, felt dangerous to me. I forced myself to look only out the left window, past Archer. This seemed to fluster him, which set me more at ease. Whatever his reasoning for pretending to be someone else in the castle garden, I wouldn't have a chance to interrogate him unless we found ourselves alone. And given the nervous tilt of his head, the way his knee bounced near mine, I suspected he didn't want to have that conversation with me.

It was pitch black outside when Dave finally turned the car onto a surface I could feel and hear was gravel.

“Are we almost there?” I asked, trying to pick any distinct features out through the windows. There was a new moon; in the peripheral light from the headlights, I could just see fences to either side of the road, and beyond them flatness.

“We’re already here,” said Dave. “Another ten minutes ahead to the house, my lady.”

Ten minutes. I tried to imagine how large the estate must be if it stretched away from the house for that long.

“Home sweet home,” muttered Cassian, that intense look in his eyes again. “Dave, would you stop here, please. I’d like to walk.”

“Wait, Cassian,” chided Bruce. “At least see her to the house.”

The door was already open when the car came to a rolling stop. Cassian stepped out and shut the door behind him before I could even smell the dainty wildflowers jutting from the edges of the asphalt outside like frayed incense.

“Hold on, Cass,” said Archer, getting out just as quickly. Through the side window, I watched Archer catch up to Cassian, his mouth opening and closing quickly with a one-sided conversation I couldn’t hear. Cassian seemed to be ignoring him, plodding ahead into the darkness with his hands in his pockets.

Dave started driving again.

“It’s not you, my lady,” blurted Bruce. “The grief, it comes and goes, dressed differently for each of us. You understand.”

I nodded, eyeing the brothers for another moment until they were just shadows among shadows. Grief, Bruce called it. Their father had died only eight weeks ago for them…but for me, Will had been gone much longer than that. Add to that the plane ride, and the car, and the awkward moments with the total stranger who had inherited everything they called home…I could only imagine what that must feel like for them.

We drove the rest of the way in silence, passing meadows and indistinct shapes in the pitch black until we reached the house. It ballooned out of the darkness like a sudden giant, every single window darkened by heavy curtains with only the thinnest rings of golden light emanating from the edges. This, paired with the blocky darkened silhouette of the house, gave it the appearance of a colossal creature with night vision stalking me in the dark.

Dave pulled the car around to what I would learn was the back of the house, passing the six-car garage Bruce said had once been horse stables, long ago, before an entire new building had been built for that somewhere else on the grounds. Dave opened the door for me again.

"Thank you, Dave."

"There she is!" I turned to find an older woman approaching at a clip with a gracious, warm smile. Her voice carried like a songbird, "Welcome! Welcome, my lady."

She wore a Mahon tartan pantsuit uniform that made her look like a grown woman on her way to an all-girls boarding school. The raglan sleeves tapered at the elbow, the bell bottom-like trousers billowing at the ankles. She was certainly in her sixties, with a dandelion mane of short gray curls, but the gleam in her umber eyes suggested a much younger heart. Perhaps one that could never really grow old.

"I'm Mrs. Margolyes, the housekeeper. I tend to everything to do with the main house. It is so lovely to have another mistress of the estate. All these male hormones everywhere. You have no idea how much soap I go through."

"A little colorful, Mrs. Margolyes," said Bruce, almost blushing.

"It's been a bit gray here in recent years," she said, all but ignoring him. "Perhaps a spot of color is just what this place needs. Now, what shall I call you?"

"What's wrong with *my lady*?" hummed Bruce.

"Nothing," she said. "If you want another Mrs. Pompous running up and down the halls, barking at chambermaids and shagging butlers."

The blush on Bruce's skin deepened.

"Actually, I'm Natalie," I offered, "or Nat."

"Like the tiny flies that buzz and annoy and ruin a perfectly lovely Sunday picnic?" She patted my arm with a smile. "Come, Natalie. I'll see you to your rooms."

I would like to say that entering the Glen felt like coming home. Arriving at an unknown sanctuary, a place I could finally belong. Really, it felt like walking into a museum for ghosts. Red rope cordoned off entire sections of rooms, and mud mats covered half the floors. Distant voices of the maids and caretakers echoed down endless hallways, almost competing with one another, whispering over each other, lending the ground floor a decidedly haunted atmosphere. I heard so many people I couldn't see. Entire corridors were *wallpapered* with portraits of people in elegant finery, all of men and women I didn't know. And with years of weekend antiquing with my mom under my belt, I knew the sets of china and the Chippendale cupboards that displayed them were both rarer than some endangered animals.

In the same muted way as the exterior of the building, someone—I suspected Mrs. Margolyes—had closed all the doors along the ground floor hallway, as if withholding some extra thing here. The entire place was beautiful, dripping with prestige and style, but…it really *did* feel like a museum, stumbling upon more and more potential treasures around every bend.

Stocky Mrs. Margolyes cut quickly down the dim central hallway at a speed that left Bruce and I winded. She unlatched the red rope at the base of the staircase so Bruce and I could climb ahead of her.

"Mind the stairs," she said. "They'll kick up a fuss if you abuse them."

It was more like playing a step organ, each creaky board moaning its own particular note, combining with others in a sort of Victorian fugue.

"The second-floor promenade will carry you in two directions, toward the boys' wing and this way, toward your wing, the late Lord's rooms."

Mrs. Margolyes bypassed us on the second-floor landing and took the lead.

"I'm staying in Will's room?"

"It is customary to have the steward of the property stay in those rooms," she said in a patient voice. "All the linens have been changed, rest assured."

"Archer and Cassian won't mind?" I asked.

Mrs. Margolyes paused and turned back, glancing past me to Bruce, her eyes welling with what looked like relief.

"What a question," she said. "If the young masters had half a mind to ask anything so thoughtful, I'd die of shock… Of course, they mind, dear. Their father's body is still as tepid as old tea and Bruce has already slotted you into his place. Unfortunately, as you'll see, the other rooms need mending before anyone can have them, so it's either Lord Mahon's rooms or a room at the Guest House down the road. The latter, I would advise against unless you want to lose nine hundred pounds a night income on your first day as the Lady of a very expensive household."

Moments later, Mrs. Margolyes flung open the double doors of Will's rooms and brought us into his sitting room. This was sandwiched between double doors leading to the bedroom on the left and a short, wallpapered hallway that careened around a sharp corner to a massive bathroom and walk-in closet on the right.

The sitting room was expansive, maybe twenty feet wide by thirty feet long with soaring high ceilings. Someone had painted it a placid margarine yellow and frosted it with an intricate white crown molding. Several sets of uncomfortable, old granny couches and chairs surrounded a carved wooden coffee table the size of a small car, topped with glass. The blocky white marble fireplace was newer and stuck out like a modern sore thumb.

But it was quaint, by comparison, to the sleeping quarters. Entering the bedroom felt like slipping between centuries. One wall was almost entirely mullioned glass. The window faced the front of the house and the massive fountain at the center of the circular front drive, the outline of which I could just make out in the dark. The three other walls were windowless and busy, covered in a tapestry wallpaper of hunter green and mottled olive displaying a forest scene in which a pack of dogs had trapped a strange, unidentifiable creature in a hollow under an alder tree. Ugly men approached on horseback—and I do mean ugly. They were…disfigured? There was something…animalistic about their features. Their ears were too high, their smiles too sharp. The leader's voluminous hair began at his forehead, then swept back past his ears, down his neck, and farther into his shirt as if it continued all the way down his back. A mullet of medieval proportions.

Two standing lamps cast great golden circles upon the room's red wood floors, sparing only a little light for the bed, which made the massive thing look like it was glowing. The milky bedspread was so thick it appeared almost whipped. And the canopy bed was a piece of art in and of itself. Each of the four posts were curved, bowed slightly outward, and pointed at the top, making the bed look like it was nestled in the giant paw of some terrifying predator. The leather headboard was *completely* and *utterly* destroyed. Tatters of leather fringed the pillows in strips as if an actual predator had torn it apart.

"Don't mind the damage, love," said Mrs. Margolyes. Even though she was too short to hide the carnage, she physically stepped in front of me to block the sight anyway. "We're having it mended shortly."

"What happened to it?" I asked. "Will wasn't murdered, was he?"

I had asked Bruce about Will's death twice in the last two weeks and received the same answer each time. He completed the hat trick here. "We'll discuss that later. Once you're settled in."

It wasn't the immediate *no* I had been hoping for. Instead, Bruce changed the subject. "We should let Mrs. Margolyes leave for the evening. She stayed late for your arrival."

"It was my privilege," she replied. "There's really only one thing I wanted to get right, my dear, and that is your breakfast order. Anything special to welcome you?"

My shoulders sank. It was always awkward to tell people this. "Oh, no, whatever's easy…but I am vegetarian."

A gentle tutting smirk passed between them, like they were both surprised and bemused.

"H-How long have you been…" Bruce said it like I had been born with a chronic illness.

"Um, since I was ten?" I said. "Mom didn't understand at first either, but now she's one, too, so…"

"Not a problem, lass. Happy to accommodate. The boys eat too much red meat anyway."

Bruce flushed a reproving red. "Thank you, Mrs. Margolyes, that'll be all."

"We'll leave you to rest," said the housekeeper as silent servants swept in with my bags. She then touched a small red ribbon jutting out of the wall near a light switch. "If you need anything, simply ring this bell and someone will come running."

"Good night, my lady," said Bruce, almost bowing.

"My lady," said Mrs. Margolyes, giving an exaggerated curtsy.

When Bruce closed the doors behind them, I realized I was afraid of touching anything. I had once built my own doll house, meticulously carving little pieces of furniture out of balsa wood and sculpture foam, lovingly painting each miniature, carefully fitting each piece into place, fussing over shadow and light and texture. I'd even sourced a tiny Persian rug. I'd glued it down in front of my tiny tile fireplace with the tiny fire poker I had fashioned out of a nail I'd found in the street outside. After I had completed the thing, I had cordoned off that section of my bedroom, afraid of going anywhere near it. It was perfect and I most definitely was not.

This bedroom looked a lot like the one I had created, full of antiques and tiny imperfections of age. A frayed corner of a Persian rug poked out from under the bed. A small drawer sat askew in the end table. The crown molding on the twenty-foot-high ceiling would need to be repainted sooner rather than later. Those little wears should have set me more at ease about hurting anything, but they did the opposite. I'd never been in this room before, but I loved it just as it was. Touching it seemed a guaranteed way to ruin it.

So, I made the call I'd promised to make the second I arrived instead.

"Is it beautiful?" Mom asked after we had finished with all the necessary check-ins.

"I think so," I said.

"What does that mean?"

"It's nearly midnight here," I said. "The inside looks like Mr. Darcy's house."

"Take tons of pictures for me," she said, adding, "and have fun, okay? Be careful, but get up to a bit of trouble, Nat."

"I will," I said.

"A *little* trouble," she quickly added. "Like, just the right amount of trouble. Go to a dance, but leave before 2 a.m. Meet a boy, but play hard to get."

"Okay, Mom. Goodnight."

"Goodnight." I listened to the laughter in her voice and missed her fiercely. "Love you."

My next call was to Scarlett. She picked up on the first ring.

"I'm still mad at you," she said before I could speak, "but you need to tell me *everything*."

My head was practically drooping against the pillow tucked inside an Egyptian cotton pillowcase in white plaid, but talking with Scarlett was like dessert—I always had room for it. Before I knew it, the clock on the end table read half past one in the morning, and I told her I'd call again with updates.

There was little energy left to do much of anything; my body felt as heavy as the ocean. I picked up Will's photo and considered the riddle again. I hadn't told either of them about this, half because the ominous wording with no immediate meaning had slipped my mind, but also because neither had enough context to understand, like I did, that Will had something else up his sleeve for me.

Seconds after tucking the riddle into the garden box and tucking *that* under the narrow lip of the large standing armoire against the far wall, I set my sights on that plush white bed. All I'd need to do was brush my teeth and sweet sleep would be mine—

I paused as a sound reached me. For a moment, I thought I'd imagined it. Then it came again, a soft *tap-tap-tap* at the door. I was surprised to see there was an eyehole in Will's door and even more surprised when I saw Archer's triangular form waiting outside. He tapped again, this time in a little tune.

"I know you're there," he said softly through the door.

Embarrassment swirled through me.

“Don’t be embarrassed,” he said, a slight laugh in his voice. “Just open up.”

How did he…?

I exhaled the awkwardness as I opened the door, trying to will myself to *just be normal, for cripes’ sake.*

“Archer, hi,” I said, trying to lean against the wall in some sort of casual way. Instead, I hit the jamb with my elbow, sending spikes of TV static the entire length of my arm. “Gah!”

Archer chuckled, that dimple returning, and he took hold of my forearm, his hand massaging my elbow before I could pull away.

“What are you doing?” I said.

“Relax,” he said. “Let me fix you.”

His fingertips were velvet soft, his palms like cashmere against my skin. Paired with his furnace-warmth, the sensation scattered goosebumps up the cooler skin he wasn’t touching. I gulped. His eyes were on my arm, his focus resolute, like a craftsman taking pride in his work. When he looked up, he smiled again but didn’t pull away.

“I wanted to apologize,” he said.

I hadn’t expected that.

“I should have told you I knew who you were when I first saw you. It’s why I left the party at all. I saw your face through the window, a smudge of dirt on your cheek, fingers caked in mud, and I thought, ‘What are the chances?’”

“Why didn’t you?”

His gaze dipped again as his hands moved down my forearm to my hand, pressing on the palm, rolling his fingers in little circles.

“I wanted to meet you as you truly are,” he said. “Before all this. I honestly thought you knew what I looked like because of my friend request. When I realized you didn’t, I knew I’d never get another chance like that.”

“Uh-huh,” I said. “I’m sure you learned a whole lot.”

“Actually, I did,” he said. “But not as much as I wanted.”

I felt my eyebrows high on my forehead before I even looked up at him, but he wasn’t poking fun. He seemed to mean it.

I gulped. “What…do you want to know?”

As I watched, the softest blush colored his skin. My stomach fluttered. “You’ll think I’m cheesy.”

“Maybe,” I said. “Tell me anyway.”

His gaze traveled up my arm, my neck, to my cheek, before locking on my eyes. "I wanted you to tell me about the moment you knew you were different."

"Different?" I asked. "Do you mean strange?"

"I mean special," he said.

I felt my brain freeze inside me as I searched his face for any hint of mockery. I didn't see any...which meant it might be a compliment. But if it was, it did not compute. At least, I didn't know what to say.

"Why are you blushing?" He smiled.

"I'm not blushing. I'm not—"

"No, don't say something self-deprecating. I'd rather discover your secret for myself if I have to. I will, too. I'm very used to getting my way."

An invasive thought was suddenly there to ruin the moment. I felt myself wince.

"What?" he asked.

"Aren't you mad?" I asked. "About me being here? Staying in Will's room?"

"It's complicated," he said. "But I'm willing to give you the benefit of the doubt, if you'll do the same of me."

"Okay," I said. It sounded great to me.

He smiled. "It's a deal."

He wiggled my ring finger. It was so surprising, I giggled. His turquoise gaze skated across my face.

"Is that better?" He motioned to my arm. I could only nod. As he let my hand go, I could still feel his warmth tiptoeing across my skin. "Well, I'll bid you goodnight then. Welcome to Bear Glen, Miss Damarand. I, for one, can't wait to see how it'll grow on you."

When he finally departed, I lost time as I brushed my teeth and braided my hair so it wouldn't turn to tangles in my sleep. I had an inkling I'd toss and turn tonight. But as I slipped my shoes off and crashed onto the bed, dreams of warmth and reassurance found me instantly, and I surrendered myself to a sleep so deep it convinced me I'd never actually slept before in my life.

CHAPTER 10

When I woke, the old-fashioned corded phone on the bedside table screamed at me. The sun poured like molten gold through the windows, so bright I instantly regretted opening my eyes. I fumbled blindly for the receiver and dropped it on my ear, murmuring instead of saying hello.

"Keep your eyes closed and listen to my voice."

"Mmm?"

"Natalie, I would like permission to enter your rooms," the person said.

I vaguely registered that they were male. "Who is this?"

"I'll have to make myself more memorable. Do I have permission to come into your rooms?"

"Okay."

"Keep your eyes closed," he said again before I heard the click.

Remnants of dreams pulled at me from under the soft whipped covers until someone lifted the phone receiver still resting on my face away, and something heavy pressed into the bed at my side, in the crook between my knees and chest. Their campfire scent hit me, waking me with surprise—Cassian. My eyes fluttered.

"No peeking," he whispered. I don't know how, but I could feel his attention on me, like fingertips dancing across my skin wherever he looked. The attention dappled my temple, then my ears, my neck. Then suddenly, his hand was on my face as something dark wrapped across my eyes. His fingers trailed along the piece of cloth to the back of my head, where he took care not to catch my hair.

"What—"

“It’s just a blindfold,” he said, suddenly near my ear. I felt him tie the cloth and gently tighten. “You’re dressed under the covers, aren’t you?”

My stomach lurched as I tried to remember if I was. Yes, I hadn’t even taken off my pants the night before. I nodded.

“I’m going to guide you out of bed now,” he said, taking firm hold of my shoulders, lifting me to sit up. “I told Bruce to plan our arrival for the morning, but he doesn’t think these things through properly. Your first glimpse of what you’ve won should be spectacular.”

“I didn’t *win*, Cassian,” I insisted. He firmly slid me into a standing position. The air in the room was chilly so early. I wrapped my arms around myself without thinking as I felt him step away for a moment then return.

“Lift your arms up.”

I hesitated.

“What? What’s wrong?”

“Could this have waited for a shower?” I asked, as mildly as I could.

“It’s time sensitive, I’m afraid,” he said, tossing out a perfunctory, “You smell like tangerines.”

I must’ve looked so strange. My mouth opened and shut, without a response to give. I reached for the sky…and felt the soft lining of my NASA hoodie against my hands. He led my arms and head into the correct places and warmth descended around me like a steeping hug. Then his hand was there, delicately sweeping the hood down and coaxing my hair into some shape. His fingers patiently forked through the tendrils and across the base of my skull. I felt my lips part without my permission at the sensation, and the shiver that chased his caress across my skin.

“Thank you.”

Without mentioning it, Cassian bent to help me put on my shoes. I could feel him come around to my side. His hand slid into mine.

“We’re going to walk now,” he said. “I’m going to guide you. Trust me. Follow my instructions.”

I'd never been particularly good at trust exercises. In seventh grade, in gym class, I'd ended up with a concussion after trusting a girl who'd walked me right off the end of a set of bleachers. Since then, the only person I'd ever trusted other than my mother was Scarlett…who was so flakey in general, I granted trust to her on a mischief-by-mischief basis. Yet here I was, with a total stranger, moving through the halls of a house I didn't know, completely sightless. Yes, there were ribbons of light and shadow through the satin blindfold, but it covered my face from brow to the tip of my nose. I couldn't even see the ground below me by looking down. Each time I accidentally stepped away from him, I would feel a gentle tap from his other hand hovering around my waist, acting as a bumper.

"Two steps to your right," he said. Even without seeing, I knew he had taken the steps with me, in a dance. "We're at the stairs now."

"Cassian," I said, my grip tightening on the hand I held.

"I've got you." His tone struck like iron. He guided my free hand to the banister before moving his own hand back to my waist and holding firm there. "Step…step…step…step…step…"

His voice was as steady and reliable as a metronome. I didn't breathe the entire way down; thirty steps felt like a lifetime.

On the ground floor, his instructions began again: clear and simple and never wrong. The wood floors of the ground level hallway ached and grumbled underfoot. I could sense the passage of doors and other rooms I had yet to see…but no one else was here with us. No staff. No Mrs. Margolyes. It was early enough that the house was still asleep. A small part of me trilled with fear as I wondered if this was a setup. A ploy to walk the trusting new heiress of his family's estate off a cliff. The rest of me tingled with anticipation at what Cassian had woken early to show me.

We soon came to a door. The hand holding mine moved; he slid his fingers up my palm to loosen my grip on him before pressing my hand to the door jamb.

"One moment," he said. I heard the door open in front of me, felt the moist, biting air billow across my ankles-knees-hands-neck-cheeks. I tensed. "Are you cold?"

"I'm always cold. I'm fine."

His hand found mine again; he interlaced his warm fingers in mine, pulling my hand to his chest.

"More stairs, no railing this time," he said. "You ready?"

My immediate nod surprised even me. He guided me down within seconds, his grip tightening in response with every reassurance as I needed it, until the texture changed under my shoes from smooth stone to loose gravel.

“Just a few more meters,” he said.

It was more than a few meters; we walked across the gravel driveway until we came to long green grass, slicked with morning dew. He plunged me into the thick of it without any hesitation at all; the only thing that changed was the hold on my waist, pulling me tighter, closer against his side for better navigation. Cassian’s campfire smell was stronger than ever.

With little other stimuli, I suddenly wondered whether my mother would commend or condemn this particular type of trouble.

“You’re smiling,” he said, his tone probing and surprised.

“I’m nervous,” I replied.

“Because we hardly know each other?”

I wondered if I should mention my theory about his plans to assassinate me then squirmed, thinking it might plant the idea in his head.

He mistook my momentary silence for confirmation. “Soon, you’ll be busy with the mechanical business of running the estate. The tedium that leaches the magic out of a place like this. There may come a day when you sit in the great salon and think it’s just another stuffy room in an over-decorated house that feels nothing like a home. You’ll look at us and see us as extensions of it. Spoiled and left to rot by an indifferent father. I couldn’t live with myself if I didn’t try to dissuade you of that belief.”

“I’m not going to throw you and Archer out,” I promised. “This isn’t a Jane Austen novel. You won’t be penniless and homeless.”

“I don’t need my father’s money,” he spat. “There are far more valuable things at stake.”

“Like what?”

“I need you to,” he murmured, stopping himself. When he spoke again, his lips were almost against my ear, his words earnest and intimate like he was sharing a secret only with me. “I want you to see this home the way I do before you see it as something else.”

Eventually, he stopped me. He took hold of my waist and we pivoted together, him behind me, to face something only he could see.

“Are you ready?” he asked.

I nodded. The tie came undone at the back of my head. The blindfold fell away, revealing Bear Glen in the pink dawn light. Not just the mansion with its honey bricks, its thousand windows, its cream tiara-like trim along the roof, and its gargantuan fountain…but the land itself, sloshing away from us like a spilled bucket of green paint, around purple rocks, over mounds, and up the sides of sudden mountains in the distance.

Green was a colorblind man's approximation. Fern and moss and robin's egg and royal blue edged in plum danced in and out of sight with the breeze. Long grass and thickets of purple heather lolled gently back and forth as if invisible children were playing in it. Black currant bushes were gathered in tight brambles along a narrow groove I assumed was a stream. Several barns and other buildings dotted the landscape like scattered teeth. Hills rose some distance to the east and south, and a silver river slit pastures in half to the north of us. To the west, a thick forest wrapped around an old stone chapel, derelict with age. Another, even denser forest crowded the house from the east.

Barnyard noises played soundtrack. Sheep with white coats and shocks of black wool on their faces and shaggy red cows peered at us from a neighboring field. Here and there at varying intervals, I could see homes with chimneys smoking. A small town made entirely of gray stone was nestled across the river within walking distance, reachable over a low bridge constructed of the same stuff.

Somewhere far away, a woman sang. Her voice drifted in with the biting wind, which licked at the edges of my sleeves and pants and the collar of my hoodie ferociously. Moisture turned to ice in the corner of my eyes.

Cassian stared out across the land—his family's land—like the captain at the bow of his ship. His stony pout was still there, but he looked as awed by the sight he'd seen a million times as I was seeing it for the first time. There was love there, in the still depths of him.

An undeniable part of me twinged with desire…to reassure him I meant no harm, that I saw what he saw here and wanted to protect it, too.

Then I laughed at myself. Scarlett and my mom had always joked that I was too serious for my own good. Too sincere. It…scared people off sometimes. *Most* of the time. I'd have to keep my silly sincerity to myself for now.

"There's more here than land and money," he said.

"I know."

"What do you know?"

"I know you love this place."

He seemed disappointed by my answer.

"Yes, but I don't matter, you see. All that matters is this—what it means to our family. To the people who depend on us."

"You mean the people who work in the house?"

Again, disappointment.

"My father really didn't tell you anything, did he…" It wasn't a question. "You're just some naive girl he pulled into all this. You have no idea…"

I felt my pride prickle. I finally slid my hand out of his grasp. As our bodies separated, a coldness swept in between.

"You don't know me, Cassian."

"You have no idea what you've gotten yourself into here," he said, his voice just as cold as the wind. He wouldn't even look at me now. "You'd be better off giving it back to us. Take the cash, the treasures—whatever shiny thing you want—and just go home. Go back to your ordinary life. This isn't the place for you."

"Why? Because you say so?" When he didn't respond, I narrowed my eyes. "Yeah, I think I'll take my chances, thank you."

He winced then. Finally turning to look at me, his gray eyes appeared almost lavender in this light. "This isn't—I'm trying to help you. Your naivety could get you killed."

I backed away before I realized I was doing so, like my body was standing up for me on my own behalf. My face twisted with disdain, anger.

"I think you're wrong about me."

"I'm not."

"Let's see, shall we?"

I turned to go, picking my way back through the long grass, which suddenly seemed so full of little burrows and divots I hadn't noticed before in his guiding hand.

"Natalie, I—"

I kept walking and he didn't speak again. I glanced back only once, when I made it to the driveway. Cassian was still there, no longer looking at the scenery, but watching me walk away. His expression surprised me, though. He didn't look angry or bitter—both I would have expected to see. Instead, I saw fear.

There wasn't time to process it. I barely made it upstairs for a shower before Mrs. Margolyes barged in and corralled me toward a giant dining room built to hold fifty people, where beautiful, fluffy scrambled eggs and fruit were already waiting for me at the head of the table. No one else joined me. I ate by myself as maids scuttled about in the background, avoiding eye contact but offering a polite smile any time our gazes accidentally connected. This place was so…quiet. Empty. I didn't even have my phone to distract me, and every time I tried to leave, Mrs. Margolyes would materialize out of nowhere and tell me to sit back down.

"But I'm done," I finally said when I tried to leave a third time through a different door.

"Aye, fine," said Mrs. Margolyes, guiding me back to my seat again. "Bruce will be with you shortly, just be patient. He's got a big day ahead for you."

"Can I at least go get my pho—"

She was already disappearing back through the swinging kitchen door.

"Here you go," said Bruce. He held out my phone like a peace offering.

"Oh, you…went into my room?"

"No, no, heavens no," he said, blushing as he sat down across from me. Being back here seemed to reinvigorate him. He was warm with color, dressed in a dark green pea coat, his mussed black hair half-combed in some sort of Beethoven-esque intentional style. "Your maid found it when she went to make your bed. I'm just the deliverer."

I made a mental note to put a password lock on it later as I slid it into my back pocket and sat quietly, waiting for him to speak.

"Was breakfast to your liking?"

"Oh, sure," I said.

"The cooks can make you anything you like…seriously, anything. You need only ask. And we can buy some American things for you, too…American cheese. Cocoa puffs. Twinkies, of course, with their vital American nutrients."

"I'm good." I smiled.

"Well, if you're ever feeling homesick, we can ease it for you," he said. "We can always arrange a return trip for you, too. Just say the word."

Cassian's discouraging words came back to me. I bristled.

"I just got here, so maybe later."

"Exactly," he said. "Unfortunately, we can't chew the scenery today. Today is all business, I'm afraid."

"What kind of business?"

"To start, the tour Mrs. Margolyes has planned for you," he said. "Should only take a couple of hours."

I winced.

"It will be quite lovely, I assure you," he said.

"Oh, I didn't mean…it's fine." I forced my expression into a neutral poker face, or what I hoped was one.

"Then some tailoring. We've flown in a phenomenal stylist just for you."

"Oh," I said. Now *that* sounded very lovely.

"Shall we begin?" said Mrs. Margolyes, emerging from the kitchen with the largest binder I'd ever seen splayed in her hands like some sort of grimoire.

I glanced at Bruce just in case there was more.

"We'll go over the afternoon's schedule when you're finished," he said.

I deflated a little. An *afternoon* schedule, too?

Then I remembered the closed doors. There had been *so many* closed doors the night before. The house had seemed like one giant advent calendar, waiting to surprise me. I shot out of my seat and followed her to the far door.

Dappled light washed over me as she opened it, and my heart…began to *ache*. She had started with the best. Objectively, the best. The most beautiful room I had *ever* seen in my life.

"This is the library," she said, so perfunctorily.

A ceiling painted with a dark starry sky towered forty feet overhead, held aloft by *two stories* of shelves full of leather-bound books. A rolling ladder carved with swirls and lovingly sanded and oiled stood a few feet away. I saw another above on the balcony. Everywhere I looked, there was a new, different reading nook. Poufs by the window, a great, deep armchair at the far end of one of the balconies, a couch beside the fireplace. They'd carefully positioned the last so the rolling ladder could pass a hairsbreadth behind it. A spiral staircase and two hefty wood tables sat at either end of the main level, separated by two deep leather couches facing each other in the center. More knee-high bookshelves lined the wall of mullioned windows that faced the Eastern Wood.

Trees crowded the view, casting the room into a green twilight. These towering voyeurs huddled around a mossy, ferned hollow just outside, before muddling into a dark dense forest beyond. At some point, someone had installed a door leading directly outside to a small tea table surrounded by patterned cushions in the hollow.

"Do you like books, miss?" asked Mrs. Margolyes.

"I love them, especially in a space like this," I said, running my fingers along the edge of the nearest table; someone had painted a golden thistle border there.

"Are you a bed reader?"

"A what?"

"Under the covers and the like?"

I shrugged, nodding, just to see what she would say. A sly smile blossomed on her face.

"Well, then." She motioned me to follow her to the far south wall, where she hooked a gilded copy of *The Secret Garden* and pulled. A loud mechanical click sounded overhead, something turned, and the bookshelf popped open in front of us. I felt my knees go rubbery beneath me—it was a *secret* door.

"Are you *kidding* me?" I couldn't hide the absolute joy that filled me all the way to the top.

Inside, someone had taken a strange burrow of a room, a space between other spaces, and filled it from wall to wall with soft, plush reading lounges. It was so crowded it was more couch than room, really. The sole window looked out on an old animal trail leading deep into the forest where great oaks and birch curved to touch their tips overhead.

"This is the greatest thing I've ever seen in my life!"

"I'm glad to hear it, hen," said Mrs. Margolyes. "It'll be good to have someone else using the room, too. It can get awfully…broody in here." I glanced at her. She seemed to want to name someone specific but resisted the temptation.

"Is the rest of the house like this?"

Her smile faltered.

"Well, erm, no," she said. "I thought I'd start with the best so we could move you quickly through the rest."

Bless her and her terrible decision. She was *absolutely* right about this being the highlight of the tour, and if I had known just how right, I would have mutinied then and there. I knew better, too; I had plenty of experience with abysmal tours.

When I was a little girl, my dad had accidentally tortured me. It sounds hyperbolic, but it's true. He'd only had three great loves in his life, he told me—my mom, me…and airplanes. He'd never been able to afford the flying lessons he had so longed for, but he flew any chance he could. And no matter where we were, if there was any sort of war memorial to service pilots or an aviation museum or airfield open to the public, he made me go with him to see it. He'd always said there was something about having wings, leaving the world behind, and soaring over it that "appealed to the center of him." Not his heart, not even his soul, he said, but something down to his very bedrock.

The flying part, I understood. Even the aircrafts themselves were cool; I liked exploring the quirks of aerodynamics that allowed them to soar. And I liked imagining the inventors, the look of awe on their faces, as they watched their inventions take flight…but the *hundreds* of tours, the loss of entire days to roaming old airfields behind overly serious men with canes, had sapped any appreciation I felt for guided activities.

That's a long way of saying that as kind as Mrs. Margolyes was, and despite her obvious passion for this house and its history, the rest of her tour was torture. It was difficult to enjoy the house this way, racing between rooms I couldn't stop to admire. It felt like she wanted to keep me on a leash. Every time I tried to drift away or pause to examine some interesting detail, she was there to hustle me along, politely digging for me to keep up.

There were *seven* salons, a ballroom, and servants' rooms on the main floor, in their various nooks and wings. I discovered there was also a gift shop. Like, with an actual register and security cameras, as well as a room of security monitors and a kind old man named Harold who watched them for twelve hours before the security guard Graham showed up for the graveyard shift at 9 p.m.

"Bruce can introduce you to him later," said Mrs. Margolyes, pulling me along. "I go home promptly at six every day."

"O-kay," I said, waving goodbye to Harold.

In the great salon, she showed me an oversized guest book, even larger and thicker than her own binder, sitting on its own plinth by the door.

"We opened the house to the public for tours in 2003," she said, motioning for me to thumb through the pages. There were signatures from all over the world. "Before that, teenagers used to break in. Locals went traipsing about wherever they pleased. We even found one in the chimney once."

"A person?" I asked.

She nodded nonchalantly, adding, "When we found the one in Will's bedroom, we had to get ahead of it."

"What were they doing in Will's bedroom?" My bedroom now. That little connection didn't seem to faze her.

"Naughty things," was all she said, missing the grimace on my face. "Curiosity, dear, can be a burden or an opportunity."

"Opportunity for what?" She didn't immediately answer. "Opportunity for what, Mrs. Margolyes?"

"Relax, my lady," she said. "The tours…and the extra hotel income from the Guest House at the other end of the estate more than make up for the inconvenience."

Inconvenience, yeah, because *that* was what concerned me.

By the time we reached the servants' quarters and I met the seventeen members of staff that lived in the house in their own bedrooms and heard about the other thirteen who went home to their families each night, I felt the wear of the tour starting to get to me. They were all so cordial and formal but also obviously *so over* having to stand in a line for some new employer to pick apart.

All save one maid who darted forward and curtsied deeply at me when the others left.

"This is Mary, your personal maid," said Mrs. Margolyes.

"Hello, Miss," she said. She was only a few years older than me, her tartan uniform loose on her slim frame, her red hair braided into a chignon at her neck. "Anything you need at all, you just let me know. My room's just under yours. Day or night, you pull the velvet rope, and I'll be there for you."

I nodded, keeping a painted smile on my face as I imagined her being "on call" twenty-four hours a day, tumbling out of peaceful sleep to fetch me nonsense in the middle of the night.

"I mean it," she doubled down, almost nervous. "Don't hesitate. I'm here to serve."

You're going to get a lot of good sleep while I'm here, I thought. *I'd literally have to be dying*.

"Thank you, that's very sweet," I said, just to reassure her. She had a kind, jittery energy—what Scarlett would have called an "unmedicated ADHD-vibe," right before offering one of her own adderall.

"Back to work, Mary," said Mrs. Margolyes and away she skittered, tossing a last little wave at me. I liked her immediately.

The moment didn't last.

"Moving on," said Mrs. Margolyes, motioning me to follow her again.

My shoulders sank.

"We could break this tour up. Do part today, part…some other day?"

"Goodness no!" she said. "It's only a little longer."

"I-I don't want to be mean," I said, already hating myself, "but I could explore the rest on my own."

"Bless you," she said, laughing at me. "There will be *plenty* left for you to find on your own. Just one more wing. Best to have a chaperone for this one."

We passed more and more closed doors as she guided me upstairs. These, she said, were mine to open in time, although most would only be offices, sleeping suites, and storage.

At a cross hallway, she went left, opening a large mahogany door into yet another sitting room. After a certain point, it seemed there really was nothing more to do with space than fill it with sofas. This one was cozy despite the high ceilings. The fire blazed in the hearth, providing the only light in the room, until Mrs. Margolyes turned on a standing lamp. Thick, midnight blue curtains were drawn across the eastern windows. A desk sat in a far corner stacked high with paperwork. Beside it, a second desk was used as a printer and supply station, with just enough space left over to hold a gray briefcase, inlaid with that seven-pointed star.

On the coffee table, an Oxford mug of old tea sat beside a half-read copy of Mary Shelley's *Frankenstein,* splayed face down. It had clearly been taken from the library, its binding a brilliant green in the firelight.

I stopped breathing when I saw what was lying beside it—the blindfold Cassian had wrapped around my face this morning.

"Is this Cassian's room?"

"Aye, it is," she said sadly. "Any room as dark as this one in the middle of the day is one he's recently used."

I shrank back from the book, as if he would know I'd touched it. Given our brief conversation this morning, I was certain he wouldn't like knowing I was even in here.

"Oh," I said. "Maybe we should come back when he says it's okay?"

"Nonsense, dear. These are your rooms now, too."

I didn't like that everyone here seemed to think I was going to take over their lives, maybe even evict them.

Mrs. Margolyes didn't notice my unease. She walked to the far door and threw it open, revealing part of a large north-facing bedroom. I could just see Cass's bed, gray and unassuming in the lowlight, made with military precision.

"The Mahon family is ancient, my dear," she said. "In the old days, many moons ago, they had ten, twelve, and even sixteen children in a single generation, each child with a nursery and nanny of their own. Every room up here would have been full. Now..."

She sighed, disappointed.

"Lord Mahon was an only child and willful at that," she said. "We were lucky he had children at all."

"He didn't want them?" I asked.

"Oh, I wouldn't phrase it like that," she said. "He just...had other things he wanted to do. I've been with the family since the seventies. Even as a wee one, there were *always* other things he wanted to do. This house, the legacy of his family. A bit too much...pressure, I think. Bruce had to bully him into getting married the first time...and the second."

I blinked, absorbing that.

"When his first wife died, Master Cass fell to me," she said, adrift in her own thoughts now. "Barely two days old, the sweet little cub. The *second* Lady Mahon, don't even get me started. A lady of the gilded persuasion. Gave birth to Archer and left, lived apart from both of them for the rest of the marriage. Never explained herself...just vanished to live off her allowance until she got re-married a couple years ago."

"Was there something wrong?" I asked. She paused and turned to me. "With Will, I mean?"

I wondered if that would insult her.

"Possibly," she said, surprising me. "It's amazing how intelligent and moronic a single man can be. Aside from his boys, he didna make thoughtless choices. Just a shame he was so careless with that part of his life until it was nearly too late..."

She motioned for me to follow her again, leaving Cassian's den behind and going to the other end of this wing. Archer's rooms held a completely different atmosphere. Night and day, literally. There weren't *any* curtains in here at all and no division of rooms; he'd torn down the wall, exposing the rest of his bedroom all the way to the open door to his bathroom at the far end. His sitting area was half gym, half music studio with plush gold couches scattered with tipped over wine and whisky glasses.

Mrs. Margolyes tutted at the sight of it and rang the velvet rope in the corner. Within a few seconds, Archer's personal manservant, Rowan, who seemed intent on being invisible, entered and began tidying without a word. Didn't even glance at us, although he bowed to me when he saw me watching.

"Perhaps it's for the best," Mrs. Margolyes said under her breath.

"What is?" I asked.

"You," she replied. "We all thought the estate would pass to Archer, but you can see from the state of things…" She pointed out a stain on the floor to Rowan. "That'll need steam cleaning after we've gone."

"It would have passed to the second son?" I asked. "Isn't that…unusual?"

"Read your share of Victorian romances, have you?" she said, kindly poking fun. I blushed. "Of course, in the end, it *had* to be Archer, didn't it?"

"Had to be me, what?"

Archer entered shirtless, glistening with sweat from a run, and my brain glitched inside me. I'd never seen another seventeen-year-old boy—*man*—like him. It was as if a statue of Achilles had walked off a pedestal in a Greek museum and reincarnated. His broad shoulders and chest were smooth, supple. Brawny but graceful. By contrast, the topography of his abdomen was crowded with muscle, like a mountain range hemmed in by the deep V that disappeared into his exercise shorts, which were so saturated with moisture, they left almost nothing to the imagination.

I jerked my gaze away sharply.

"Look at this one," I heard him say. I glanced back. He was smiling at me. I couldn't help it. I looked away again.

"You're blushing *again*?"

"No!"

"Archer, behave yourself," said Mrs. Margolyes.

"Only because you're here," he replied. He was close suddenly, barely a foot away. I turned. He grinned. *That dimple*. I felt so ridiculous looking away again. Especially after his visit last night, but that had been in private. He'd been fully clothed. It was different; I was almost sure of it. "Am I making you uncomfortable?"

"N-No," I said.

"Oh, really. The ceilings are *that* interesting…"

I jerked my gaze to the floor.

"The carpet as well. It's quite soft to lay on."

"Archer!" This time Mrs. Margolyes's tone was sharper, chiding.

"I mean for sleepovers, blanket forts, midnight gab sessions, the whole lot."

I chanced another look at him. He eyed me knowingly, like we shared a secret, and he was waiting for me to realize that. Damn it all if it didn't make me feel a little more at ease. My shoulders relaxed as he backed away chuckling, and disappeared into the bathroom.

Then I chanced a look at Mrs. Margolyes, who was smiling at me, and I felt my shoulders rise again.

"That blush suits you," she said.

My hands went to my cheeks, trying to rub it out.

"I'm only having a laugh," she tutted. "And so is he."

"I know," I said, hoping they weren't so close he'd told her about last night. "I just wasn't expecting…uh…well…"

"Welcome to living with boys."

"Excuse me," Archer said, as he reappeared wearing jeans and a long-sleeved gray shirt that brought out the aqua blue in his eyes. "I'm almost a man."

He was certainly shaped like one…

I felt my cheeks flush again and pinched my leg discreetly, embarrassed at myself. I wasn't usually like this. I didn't know what was happening. I felt out of control of some part of myself. There was something in the air. Had to be.

"You'll always be my wee cub," said Mrs. Margolyes, patting his cheeks affectionately, tamping down a stray wet wave on his head. "Are you joining us for the unpleasant part?"

"What unpleasant part?" I asked. Ugh, god, there was *more tour*. I just knew it.

"Paradise has fallen," Archer said. "Mrs. Margolyes is hoping you'll save it, Miss Damarand."

CHAPTER 11

Before the sickness that killed my dad made simply existing unbearable for him, he used to spend his free time in his workshop, the little addition he and my mom had built at the far end of the ranch house we'd shared at the time. Before the medical bills bankrupted us. He called the extension *the tumor*, his sick, dark sense of humor keeping him as alive as much as the handful of meds he had to take every morning and evening. The ones that burned his body from the inside out like a mis-wicked candle, melting away what made him, *him* until you could almost see through his sickly body.

He taught me a lot of things in that workshop. But nothing, he said, was as important as the old saying *measure twice, cut once.* Life would be better for everyone, he said, if we all followed the adage.

His life had finally been snuffed out one evening in the dead of winter, under circumstances that had seemed so unreasonable to me as a kid…there one moment, gone the next. But his adopted motto survived, practically chiseled onto the crest of Family Damarand. Or would have been if we'd had a family crest.

Measure twice, cut once became *think twice, act once*, and it applied to everything. Any time my mom thought I was making a mistake, she'd simply ask, "*Have you thought twice?*" If I said I had, that was the end of it. And if I hadn't, I would. It worked both ways. When she came home with Will that first day, I had pulled her aside and asked her the same question. She'd nodded so sincerely; I never questioned his presence in our lives again. The saying became our secret code, our safety phrase.

Standing in the main upstairs hallway of Bear Glen, the phrase blared through my mind like a repeating siren. It was the only thing keeping me from freaking out.

"There's a crack there, you see," said Mrs. Margolyes, pointing to hairline fractures in the plaster on the ceiling and walls that I hadn't noticed before.

"And water damage from the last storm," added Archer, pointing to another corner. He tossed open a nearby door, revealing another bedroom currently used as storage. "It carries on into the bathroom in there as well. Don't step on the floor. You'll fall straight through."

The housekeeper led us past Will's rooms deeper into the west wing. His office was barely that; he clearly didn't like spending time here. There was only a desk and a few boxes haphazardly stacked right below a giant moldy corner speckled with black and green.

"Careful, we won't spend much time in here," said Mrs. Margolyes, closing the room off again. "Mold needs to be dealt with soon, dear."

I would have to deal with it, she meant. By the time we reached the kitchen again, they'd pointed out half a dozen rooms, including several maid and servants rooms with rotten floors, bum plumbing, and even a broken window that had been quick-patched with a watercolor sketch of an alder tree.

"Why hasn't that been fixed?" I asked about the window. It couldn't possibly be safe for whomever stayed here.

"Because we can't touch the estate," said Archer, his voice light but pointed. "It belongs to you now. The maintenance, the renovations, the expenses. All yours."

I must've blanched.

"You look like a ghost, dear," Mrs. Margolyes said. "Dinnae worry about it now. I've made a thorough list for you of everything to do."

"Great."

"See? She's up for it," Archer teased.

Not exactly, but housework was nothing new to me. I'd spent quite a few weekends helping my mom clean gutters, oil floors, and paint the stairs outside our apartment that *always* rusted with the winter snows, no matter how many layers of anti-rust paint we applied. So long as there was money, which I felt there *must* be, hopefully, none of it seemed impossible.

"Why did Will let it get this bad?" It seemed the obvious question.

"Ah, yes," said Archer. "Why didn't my wayward father maintain anything?"

"Easy now, Archer," said Mrs. Margolyes. "Lord Mahon was something of a contradiction. Always was his way. Fickle."

"Flakey," murmured Archer.

I gulped, thinking of him and my mom.

"He didn't like to be idle," countered Mrs. Margolyes. "But he didn't know when to say when. He just piled on more and more until less enjoyable responsibilities inevitably fell by the wayside."

"Like being a father," said Archer, flashing a sarcastic, manic smile, just to really drive home how little he thought of Will. It didn't really hide the hurt underneath the way he thought it did.

"Well, that concludes the tour, my dear," said Mrs. Margolyes, already speed-walking away. "If you need me, you know where to find me."

I actually didn't, I realized. She seemed to be around the kitchen a lot, but…I'd seen no office set aside for her.

I felt a sudden bump against my hip and looked up, surprised to see Archer smiling at me.

"Having second thoughts?" he asked as he popped open the red rope at the top of the stairs for me to walk down.

"No, but I am thinking twice," I replied.

"What?" he asked.

I smiled, moving on. "First things first, we need to fix that window in the maid's room. That cannot be safe."

"Cute," was all he said.

"What's cute?"

"That you care about such a small thing," he said. "You won't for long, I'm afraid."

"What does that mean?"

"A house is just a house, isn't it?" he said as we reached the west wing ground level hall and he pulled to a soft stop. "It's the secrets hidden inside that cause the real trouble."

My mind snapped to Will's riddle hidden in my room…and Cassian's accusation that I was just some naïve, young girl.

"I can handle more than you think," I said.

"We'll see," said Archer. He started backtracking toward the main hall. "I'll see you later for the hard part."

"What's the hard part? Archer! What's the hard part?"

Dear god, there was probably an entire destroyed wing somewhere wasn't there?

A door opened behind me.

"There you are." Bruce motioned for me to join him. "Come quickly, we haven't much time."

It was a smaller room, filled to the brim with bolts of fabric, facing directly west. It overlooked a part of the property I hadn't seen before and which Cassian hadn't shown me—the walled garden, which looked like a fairy tale come to life.

I was so entranced with the view I completely missed the woman kneeling in the corner of this room, by a dress form manikin.

"Judy," Bruce said with a grandiose wave.

Judy popped into view with a smile, her cat glasses askew, tangled in her long, dark hair, which was piled in a messy bun on the crown of her head with a gold scrunchie. She was wearing—I kid you not—the most elegant black jeans and peacock-tail geometric shirt I'd ever seen. They molded to her body like fondant.

"Hi-hi!" she said, running forward to shake my hand. "Lovely to meet you, Lady…"

"Just Natalie," I offered.

"Eh, Lady Damarand, Judy, thank you," corrected Bruce.

"Right, yes, well," she said, breezing on in an accent I'd later learn marked her home as South London. "My name is Judy and I'm here to fit you for your wardrobe, my lady."

I glanced down at the NASA hoodie I had been wearing for the last two days. My *house clothes*, as my mom called them. God, I must've looked like a mess next to this woman.

"Let's take your measurements and discuss your tastes, all right?"

I hadn't even spoken again before my hoodie came off and a lick of chill blew across the black camisole underneath. I stepped onto a square platform as a tape measure wound around my waist. She kept a tiny square stack of yellow lined note paper tied to her wrist like a watch, where she discreetly jotted the numbers. "Who would you like to be, love?"

"Uh…" *That* was a massive question.

"Your clothes, love," Judy said smiling, measuring my chest. "Not your life, I'm not your therapist. Although, fashion is a sort of therapy."

"Elegant, refined, I think," answered Bruce when I didn't.

"Of course, sir," she said, still looking at me.

"She'll need looks for day and night, and three sets of clothing for royal occasions to start—you know the kind."

Royal occasions?

"I'm not Kate Middleton," I joked. I glanced at him, expecting a smile. He was entirely serious, pulling "elegant," dowdy fabrics from Judy's assortment, bending them in the light to examine the finer details.

“What about your casual looks, love?” she asked me. “Girl’s gotta have her fair share of comfort in this world.”

“Nothing too…foreign,” said Bruce. “A healthy integration of the styles here and at court. Little affectations of her former life are fine. Nothing too…rock and roll.”

He whispered the last bit, like saying it too loudly would summon Nirvana in a puff of black smoke. I couldn’t help it; my eyebrow quirked high onto my forehead. My face split with a grin I usually reserved for Scarlett when she said something ridiculous.

“Rock and roll?” I asked.

“Like the Rexhas and Diddys. Exercise pants that are too tight. Or too loose for that matter. Or *whatever* they’re wearing to the Met Gala these days.”

Cringe. Cringe! CRINGE! He had said it so unironically, too. My skin began to crawl with secondhand embarrassment.

“Bruce,” I blurted. “I don’t think you need to be here for this. I’m more than capable of dressing myself.” I watched him open his mouth and spoke before he could, “Yes, I know I can’t wear a NASA hoodie everywhere.”

“Look, if this helps, I’ll turn away to give you privacy.”

Like a grandparent, I watched him just pivot on the spot to face the wall. Honestly, it baffled me. Shocked me stupid; I didn’t even know what to say.

Thankfully, Judy saved me. She suddenly produced a set of keys from her purse.

“Do you know what? I left my ribbon bag in the car. Bruce, would you be a dear and fetch it for me?” He blinked, surprised. “I’d ask the help, but I trust you.”

Her smile was already wide; she widened it again to comical proportions to set him at ease. It worked like a charm.

“Oh yes, of course. Be right back.”

Judy waited until the door closed behind him before turning back to me.

“Don’t let him get to you, love,” she said. “He’s a fuddy duddy old man. Institutionalized. Cloistered up here in this great big house with two boys who don’t listen to him. He thinks you will, but you don’t have to, you know.”

"I know." But did I know? Really? Had I even thought about it? I mean, the money was mine, the house was definitely mine if I had to arrange all the work on it. I could technically fire Bruce if I wanted, which—not going to lie—filled me with a cozy sense of potential schadenfreude. Being able to punish the guy who did my mom wrong was like having a wishing penny in my back pocket.

Then again, I didn't want…to be that person. I didn't want to be the "interloper" as Cassian had called me. Or, at least, if I had to be, I wanted to wield that power wisely. Use it when it really mattered. There'd be no coming back from that.

"Excellent!" Judy said, pulling more interesting, patterned fabrics from her pile. "Give me a style icon. Anyone you like."

"Does it…" I blushed, realizing how stupid I was about to sound. "Does it have to be…a fashion person?"

"A fashion person? Do you mean a model or a designer?"

I blinked. She laughed.

"Name a person you admire. Real or fantastical, I don't mind. Or a type of person. A movie, even. Let's let *your* style shine…while also satisfying Mr. Pompous-what's expectations, all right? He may be guiding you through all this, but you have to live in it, so whose style do you like?"

"He'll probably hate anything I choose."

"He's a bloke. He won't remember what he told me to give you. And he won't care what you wear so long as you look spiffed up and ready for display. Besides, I don't have a ribbon bag. He'll be out there looking for ages."

I grinned.

"You're going to make fun of me," I said.

"Promise to Cher, Twiggy, and the Hepburns, I won't," she replied, leaning in. "I'd swear on Coco Chanel, but her ghost talks to me every day. I'd never hear the end of it."

I told her the first—and only—image that had sprung to mind the second she had asked in the first place. "Could you do…a vintage aviator explorer vibe?"

If it was possible, her smile grew three sizes bigger, this time bursting with genuine excitement.

"*Ooh*, could I ever!"

Over the next hour, I realized Bruce had undervalued her. She wasn't "just" a stylist; she was a designer. She drew several dozen looks I could only dream of owning. When I said so, Judy told me sometimes dreams come true.

Bolts of beautiful forest greens and goldenrod yellow and roycroft copper red were pinned to my body in shapes I could only understand once she explained them to me. Every shade made my skin luminous and brought out the low reds in my awkward dark hair. But I still didn't believe her when she said an entire collection of tailored dresses, pants, shirts, and skirts would be delivered to my rooms in a few weeks. She'd even sketched a ball gown, which Bruce insisted I'd need when he returned empty handed. He spent the next twenty minutes apologizing profusely for not being able to find the bag Judy wanted in her car…until our time was finally up.

"It's almost time, Judy," said Bruce, tapping his watch.

"Right-o," she said. She removed the last shape of fabric from my body and flicked through several black garment bags hanging from a nearby rack. "Not exactly your aesthetic, love, but this'll have to do for now."

She grabbed a bag stamped *Burberry* and unzipped it carefully, removing an emerald green A-line dress with beautiful, braided detail. Goosebumps rose on my arms.

"Is this…for me?" I asked.

"Of course, it is," she said, glancing at Bruce, who was also admiring the dress. "A little privacy, Bruce?"

He blushed several shades of red as he backed out. "I'll call Jemina in."

"It's just a loaner," said Judy, "Unless you love it, in which case I can send my friend your measurements and bring the real deal with me when I drop off the other pieces."

I didn't know what to do with the dress. It was too much. Too delicate for someone like me.

"What's the matter, love?" she asked.

"I can't wear this."

"Whyever not?"

My mind flipped through the series of hand-me-down and thrift store dresses I'd worn to all my school dances. The embroidery my mom had hand-sewn to cover a stain on one.

"It's too nice," I finally whispered.

"Stop that," she said sternly, unzipping it for me. "I don't want to hear anything like that again. Men never wonder if they deserve what they have. Why should you? You deserve the world. Say that."

"Say…?" I asked, putting it on.

"I want to hear you say you deserve the world. Go on."

"I…deserve the world."

"Damn right, you do. Again. Louder!" She tilted her head back as she shouted, "I DESERVE THE WORLD!"

"I deserve the world!"

"Again!"

"I DESERVE THE WORLD!" I howled.

We said it again together and again as Bruce entered the room with a stylish British woman of Indian descent. I snapped my mouth shut mid-howl.

"What's going on in here?" asked Bruce.

"Just havin' a howl, love," said Judy, as if that explained everything. "Nothing to worry about. Jem and I will get her spiffed up."

"We only have twenty minutes," said Bruce.

"Then better leave us to it," said Judy.

I watched her and Jemina eye him until he retreated from the room. The second the door shut, they laughed between each other.

Judy gestured me into a nearby chair as Jemina snapped a salon apron open. I blushed, smiling at her.

"Hi," I said meekly, a little embarrassed.

"Hello, my lady," she said.

She glanced at Judy; they both tilted their heads back, "I DESERVE THE WORLD!"

I felt the sound reverberating in my bones. When their howl ended, the tension broke like a wave.

"Are you going to straighten my hair?" I asked. Every social function that had required a trip to the hairdresser had ended with some sort of flat ironing of my wavy hair.

"Hell no," said Jemina. "Lovely waves like that? You're gorgeous already. I'm just here to make you shine."

Jemina worked her magic on my unruly hair, smoothing the briar into something as soft as wavy feathers that cascaded over my cheekbones and framed my face in a way I'd never seen before. I could barely look in the mirror when she handed it to me; the reflection showed the version of myself I'd only ever seen in dreams.

Her doing my makeup became the quickest tutorial I'd ever seen. Just the softest foundation to even my olive skin, a gentle smokey eye, a little lip stain, and Jem's promise that she'd be on hand for any public appearances in the future all but convinced me I must *actually* be dreaming.

Until I thought twice.

"What public appearance?" I asked.

"Just remember," said Judy, her hands landing on my shoulders. "The press in this country, their job is to create drama and engage eyeballs any way they can. It's no reflection on you, all right?"

I realized why they were dolling me up. The dress, the haircut. *A public appearance.*

"But I'm not…today, right?" I asked, hoping they would reassure me. Judy and Jem simply eyed each other and patted my shoulders again.

"You look incredible," was all Jem said. "It's all right to say you don't know something."

I felt sick as Bruce opened the door and motioned me out of the chair. In the hall, I noticed my hands shook.

"Bruce?" I said, steadying my hand by clamping it on his arm to get him to stop. "Where are you taking me?"

"The ballroom. Hurry, we're already late."

I eyed him pointedly.

"Late for *what*?"

His mouth opened in surprise.

"Cass was supposed to tell you this morning…" He set his jaw. "I'll have to talk to that boy… Look, don't worry. It's just a television interview."

"I'm going to be sick," I said. All the joy Judy and Jem had steeped into me like calming tea drained away into the creaky boards under my feet. I leaned against the wall, rubbing my neck, trying to will air through my closing windpipe.

"You're fine," he said, shifting. "The boys will be there, too. You won't be alone."

In no way did I find that reassuring.

CHAPTER 12

"Welcome to BBC Tonight, I'm Ed Winstead. In the next hour, we'll speak with the American teenager who suddenly found herself the newest Marchioness of Ayr when she inherited Bear Glen, the largest privately owned estate left in the United Kingdom after those owned by the royal family."

I was distinctly aware of my toes, tucked inside the half-size too small little black pumps Judy had fit onto my feet while Jem did my hair. I couldn't stop tapping them. It was the only thing that grounded me in that chair. That, and the dark, gnawing feeling in my gut that I had been led here like a lamb to the public slaughter. Dolled up and docile and clueless. The camera's terrible dark eye watched me, unblinking. Beyond the camera, I could see half a dozen faces in the semi-darkness, including Bruce and Mrs. Margolyes.

They had tucked me in the center seat, between lanky, serious Cassian on my right and athletic, coiffed Archer on my left. I felt about two feet tall. Even smaller when I noticed Mrs. Margolyes waving at me to mimic the way her legs were tucked under her seat. Before this, no one had ever looked at me twice; sat between the boys, I felt more on display than I ever had before in my life.

"Lady Damarand."

I turned my attention back to Ed.

"All of this must seem overwhelming to you." I smiled politely. "Is it true you only found out about the estate very recently?"

"Yes," I said. "It's been a little over two weeks."

"Wow," he said, his face exaggerated with surprise. "Is there a reason you haven't visited Lord Mahon's grave yet?"

The question reached my brain and popped like a bubble. Were they having people watch me?

"Uh," I stammered. "I only arrived last night. I plan to visit as soon as I can."

"As I mentioned in my introduction," he breezed on, unabated. "This is the largest private landholding in the entire United Kingdom, after the royal family's. It encompasses four townships, five hundred thirty-seven rental properties—all of which are occupied, which is quite a feat in and of itself—and two whisky distilleries."

He paused, as if waiting for a response, but then surged ahead before I could speak.

"You seem surprised to hear that," he said.

I was, but he didn't need to know that.

"I'm waiting for a question," I said.

I watched a recalculation happen in real time behind his eyes, like he hadn't expected me to have a response.

"Were you surprised Lord Mahon selected you over his own sons?"

"Of course, but—"

"Do you have any idea why he would?" he asked before I could finish my thought.

"We certainly don't," said Cassian.

"Yes, it was very surprising," added Archer, his voice deeper and more serious than I'd heard before.

"Our father was under an enormous amount of strain in the end," said Cassian. "One has to wonder if he was thinking clearly."

And there it was. I felt the bottom drop out of my stomach—the way it had all the way back in Tommy's Pizzeria when Glam Radio made fun of me. Only ten times worse and on national television. I felt a raging blush of humiliation spreading.

"There *was* a previous version of the will, wasn't there?" asked Ed. It wasn't really a question—or rather, it was a leading one. He already knew. It was like he was teeing up prepared conversation starters for them.

"Yes, there was," said Cassian. "It named my brother, Archer, as the main inheritor."

"And you were all right with that, Cassian? As the older son? Surely, you'd expect at least half the estate to go to you."

"I've made peace with it," he said.

My hackles rose. He was lying. I could feel it. Anger spread like ink away from my right shoulder, which was just touching his. I shifted so I wouldn't feel him there.

"I'm well squared away at Oxford," said Cassian. "My path is set…but Archer was being groomed to take over. The estate is almost nine hundred years old. It's been in our family since the very beginning. Why would my father give it away now? And to a child who isn't even blood related? A foreigner, too."

Cassian turned to me then. His dark pupils had shrunk to pinpricks, turning his gray eyes almost silver with focus. "Don't *you* think the estate should have gone to family?"

Silence fell over the room like a wet blanket. This was the reply they were waiting for. I guessed it was the reason for the interview at all. Catch the new, naive owner admitting that she was going to return the estate to them. If I were honest, yes, that made the most sense…It had always been their home. It had never been mine. It would be the easiest path forward for everyone to just give it back to them and move on, return home with enough cash for college and a bit more breathing room to pick something I *actually* wanted to study. I had already won the lottery. I'd never have to be an accountant at least.

But…Will had brought me here for a reason. And I hated the thought of letting someone self-righteous like Cassian win.

"My stepfather saw me as family," I said finally, when I could feel the wet silence starting to chill the room. "We were kindred spirits, in a sense… He was a complicated man who saw the world in his own way. But he wanted me to take over for him—Will explained everything to me in a letter—so that's what I'm going to do."

"There's no letter." It escaped Cassian like a gasp.

"Enough, Cass," said Archer, suddenly.

There was another heavy silence as Cassian eyed him *over* me. I couldn't look at either of them. Instead, I glanced past the camera at Bruce and Mrs. Margolyes; their eyes were latched onto Cassian, clouded with simmering disappointment.

"Our father must have had his reasons," Archer said, turning to Ed. "And I trust his instincts. Natalie will make an excellent caretaker for everything our family has built here."

"You sound quite sure of that," said Ed, wearing his carefully practiced mask of unimpeachable objectivity.

"Just this morning, while we were giving her a tour of the house, she showed great concern for the safety of a maid. I hadn't expected that."

"What had you expected?"

"A dilettante," he said, his voice breaking with honesty.

"You've only known her a day," said Cassian, still looking over me.

"Exactly," said Archer. "We shouldn't speak of her character until we know her better."

"That's very gallant," said Ed.

"Or naive," Cassian murmured loudly.

I couldn't help it; I chuffed with laughter.

"You have a response to that, my lady?" asked Ed.

"No," I said, smirking. "Cassian just loves to overuse that word."

I heard a light chuckle, barely a squeak, and glanced past the camera to see Mrs. Margolyes hiding an incredulous little smile from Bruce.

"See? She's holding her own already." Archer leaned forward enthusiastically. "I've been preparing to take over for my father as head of Bear Glen my entire life. We can hardly hold her to the obligation and sacrifice it requires on her first day. And I'll be here to help her every step of the way."

His blue eyes dipped to meet mine, and he nodded at me before glancing away again. The discomfort twisting like a rubber band in my stomach eased a little until I glanced over at Cassian to gauge his reaction. I had expected to see anger, indignation, contempt. Maybe even more of the disdain I'd seen on his face when he led me outside this morning, which seemed like a different life ago now. Instead, Cassian looked like…a stage director watching from the wings. What Archer had said seemed to both pain and reassure him. I was also pretty sure he was fighting for his life trying to avoid looking at me; he finally set his eyeline on something near Ed, where he stared until the interview was over.

The tension spilled over into less volatile topics after that—plumbing issues forcing them to tear up entire sections of the estate, the effect of rent control on their various properties—and I was left thoroughly in the background for all of it. The only questions thrown my way were about my Americanness and how I planned to fix it as I acclimated.

When the giant lights shut off, I could barely muster the stomach to shake the reporter's hand. It felt slick when I pulled away, and I was grateful Judy had warned me. I wanted to leave the room immediately. I wanted to cry out the embarrassment, maybe take a walk and call my mom.

I was halfway to the door when a hand landed on my arm.

"Are you all right?" Archer asked, his voice quiet, his turquoise eyes almost glowing in the low light.

"I'm fine," I lied automatically.

"Cass was unforgivable," he said, rubbing my arms. "Would you like to talk about it?"

"Not right now." The emotions welled up inside me. If I didn't leave soon, I'd start to cry. And I did *not* want either of them to see me cry. "I'm just going to go for a walk."

"I could accomp—"

"You weathered that admirably, my lady," said Bruce, appearing beside us, his paternal energy bristling with thinly veiled anger. He turned a steely eye on Archer. "You and Cassian, with me."

"I was just—"

"Now," Bruce said, and that was the end of it.

I watched Bruce lead them out, his hand firmly on Cassian's arm like a vice. Mrs. Margolyes was overseeing the camera crew as they broke down their equipment, chiding them any time they came close to hitting a wall or piece of furniture.

Alone in a crowd of people, I exited through a different door, on borrowed time to get somewhere private before the waterworks began. I took my shoes off in the hallway, leaving them where someone would find them and return them to Judy.

It was twenty quick steps to the library, which was rich with shadow so late in the afternoon. And so quiet. I fell onto one of the couches facing the window.

But a sound reached me only a moment later. Bruce's muffled voice drifted into the room from somewhere on the second floor. Barking at the boys. It was just sharp enough that I understood the emotion, but not clear enough for me to hear what he was saying. It became distracting once I heard Cassian's dulcet reply, which I also couldn't understand. The temptation to eavesdrop would get the best of me if I didn't get away. I pushed out through the glass door that led to the seating area outside and through the green hollow, into the forest beyond.

Alone, surrounded by nature, I finally let the tears out. It was so stupid, though. I felt so dumb for crying. But also like I'd explode if I didn't. I'd been in-country less than twenty-four hours and I'd already been embarrassed on national television. Just some stupid American intruder interfering with ancient traditions, stealing heirlooms, ruining families. I couldn't even call my mom or Scarlett. I'd left my stupid phone in the dressing room.

After the tears came nausea and little lightning flashes of residual embarrassment striking different parts of my body as I glanced down at the green Burberry dress. Other types of people wore this sort of clothing, not me. I must've looked like a porcelain clown doll. I certainly felt like one.

And after the shame lightning receded, anger descended. *That absolute prick, Cassian.* I wanted to punch him in his stupid, smug nose. I wanted to put a snake in his bed. My head filled with all sorts of devious payback schemes. My original kind idea to try and integrate peacefully felt like it was off the table now. Maybe I could expel all of them. Literally move their trash out on the street and lock the gate. The place was already falling apart; let it go to ground. Better yet, sell it without them knowing it. Shatter them into a million pieces when they woke up to moving vans and a clueless family arriving to take their place.

Ooh, if I were only a terrible person, all the fun I could have.

Being in nature helped…a little. I found a soft divot by a creek where deep, earthy soil and sweet basil perfumed the air as thick as fog and sat until the anger left. By then, hours had passed, and the golden-green dappled light had deepened and desaturated to a sort of lavender twilight.

When the last strings of light abandoned the animal trail I had walked to get here, I stood up and set off for the house. I hadn't eaten since breakfast. My stomach cawed with hunger, and I'd never needed an emotional support hot chocolate more in my life—

Crack!

I came to a soft stop, listening. Another twig snapped. I'd mustered a spark of bravery for the interview ambush, but that was long gone now. Standing in the near-dark, I tried to summon any subconscious knowledge I had of Scotland's wildlife. Rabbits? Deer? An appalling image leapt into my head without my permission—the mural in my bedroom. Those horrifying monsters on horseback.

The murky forest loomed suddenly darker. I'd always had impeccable eyesight, better than twenty-twenty, but not during magic hour. Natural details by day became organic forms, shapes, *figures* in the gloom. They were leaves and rocks, I had to tell myself. Even if they were clumped together like something crouched and watching.

I took a step back and heard another twig snap. My eyes darted to a rustling bush in the far distance, just beyond a tall sycamore, and I *bolted.* Something growled behind me…then to the side of me. I glanced that way only once to see something rustling through the brush, keeping pace with me as I ran. I picked up speed, sprinting, feeling the soil and rocks and painful ragged edges of fallen branches slamming and scratching and tearing at my feet. I wasn't a runner. This was painful, sore in my ribs, a piercing hitch in my diaphragm.

I had to slow to catch my breath when I reached the green hollow where soft golden lamp light from the library splashed almost the full length of the open space between the house and the tree line. I turned to face the forest, taking small backward steps, watching for flashes of movement.

I didn't need to. Two green eyes glowed in the pitch blackness. Staring. Glaring. Watching *me.* I could make out no other features, which made the fact that they seemed to hover nearly six feet above the ground—taller than *me*—terrifying. My breath caught in a whimper, then a yelp as my back hit something hard behind me. The house. I'd reached the library door. I nearly broke the handle off as I wrenched it open and pulled the door shut behind me. I flicked the flimsy lock with my thumb, hearing the mechanism turn with a slight *snick*, as I peered back into the forest. The creature was gone if it had ever actually been there in the first place.

I breathed an audible sigh of relief anyway, just in case.

"Did you see something?"

I whirled around at the voice, half expecting a nightmare. And I was half right. A crown of red hair lit by lamp light caught my eye on the balcony. Cassian was reading or had been before I entered. Now his silver eyes were fastened to me, as unflinching as whatever had been in the forest.

His unreadable expression brought me back to the reality of what had happened this afternoon. That ambush. That *staged* ambush. Angry bile began to rise in my throat again, but I squelched it immediately. I didn't have any more tears in reserve. If I got angry now, I'd have to hurl something heavy at him. So, I said nothing. I headed for the door.

"What did my father's letter say?"

I stopped again, wondering if I should tell him I had lied about there being a letter. Maybe he'd get off my back if he knew about the riddle.

"You should let me see it," he said, his voice low and thoughtful, his mouth set in stone. What had Mrs. Margolyes said? *It could get awfully broody in here*.

"Is that right?" I said, prickling. "You should learn how to ask for things instead of demanding them."

He pressed his eyes, which only exaggerated the snark in his voice. "*May* I see it?"

"You can't," I said, happy to meet his rudeness with a bit of my own.

"Why not?"

"Because I burned it."

A new expression slashed across his high cheekbones, something between devastation and indignation. "You *what*? Why?"

Because I don't want you going into my room to look for it, I thought.

"To punish you," I said, turning and leaving without another word.

I felt a sickly sort of pleasure leaving him uneasy. I doubted he'd be able to solve the riddle even if I showed him. And why would I? The handsome ginger twerp had embarrassed me on purpose and left me confused otherwise. Both brothers had. And I hated how intensely it occupied my thoughts. I was still thinking about it when I reached my rooms and found my phone and a steaming bathtub waiting for me, the bath full of flower heads and soap suds. Only when my body hit the warm water did I realize how cold the entire day had left me. I leaned my head back against the curved neck of the tub and called my mom so I could cry again, more constructively.

CHAPTER 13

I dreamt that two great green eyes floated down from the trees onto a fallen log in the moonlight; its branches stretched and curled into claws, its trunk opened on a jawed hinge, exposing razor sharp fangs, and it came for me where I sat at the foot of a massive alder tree. Right before it swallowed me whole, I heard Will tell me to *run*.

I woke in the bathtub as the sunrise spilled over the mountains to the northeast. The water was still sudsy, still warm. The waterlogged flowers and buds from the night before sat gritty against my body in the bottom of the bath, while new blossoms bobbed and floated around me, now intermingled with little bundles of sweet basil and lavender tied with purple ribbon.

I immediately realized why. The door cracked open softly, and Mary tiptoed in carrying a plush green towel in one arm and an outfit dangling from a hanger on the other. My tatty six-dollar thrifted jeans, orange sunburst shirt, old bra, and boyfriend-cut panties looked almost offensively out of place carefully arranged like that, as if they'd been flown in fresh from the fashion houses of Paris. The Burberry dress that I had taken off the night before was gone, as were the dirty footprints I'd left on the floor, intending to clean them up in the morning.

"Mary?" I said, watching her freeze mid-step. Her brown eyes widened as she turned to me. "Have you been changing my water?"

"I can be very quiet with a bucket when I need to be."

"That's not…I'm naked, Mary."

I felt *so* very naked. And I winced, wondering if she'd replenished the water more than once, or even through the entire night. Competing with the embarrassment was guilt. I'd sworn to myself I'd never wake her for unnecessary things.

"It was no trouble at all," she added. "I'm an early riser."

“Oh, Mary, that’s not the prob—”

“Besides,” she cut me off pleasantly. “We all have to get up early with guests coming.”

“Guests? What guests?”

“For Master Archer’s party, of course,” she said. “It always takes at least three full days to prepare every time.”

Her eyes widened again, realizing I had no idea what she was talking about. She set the clothing and towel down and backed away toward the door.

“Well, I’ll just…let me know if you need anything, my lady…I’m only a bell away.”

I was starting to understand that this family thrived on managed chaos. Bruce met me halfway down the hall, waving a leather binder with that seven-pointed star at me like it would dispel the negative energy of whatever he was going to say next.

“I don’t want you to be surprised,” he started.

Too late.

“I’ve heard about the party,” I yawned.

“The…?”

“Is it Archer’s birthday or something?” I asked as I lifted the red rope at the top of the stairs.

“It most certainly is not,” he said. “Oh, we should go another way.”

“Well-well-well, what an absolute treat!”

Bruce and I turned at the sound, realizing there was an entire tour group in the main hall at the bottom of the stairs. The tour guide, a pleasant, fluffy woman Mrs. Margolyes had introduced to me as Sophie, waved up at us.

“Everyone wave hello to the new Marchioness of Ayr herself, Lady Damarand,” she crooned gleefully. A dozen cameras rose to faces. Flashes blinded me. I tried to smile like a normal person, but I had a sneaking suspicion I looked like an awkward little kid sitting for school pictures.

“Just wave,” said Bruce, already doing so.

They were gone soon enough and I’ll admit it felt sort of nice to hear little snippets of their conversations as they moved on, “What a lovely girl!...So down to earth…*love* those jeans, them!”

“Maybe I could get a schedule for tours?” I asked Bruce as we walked into the east wing. “As well as, you know, a general schedule for everything else?”

"Of course, my lady," he said, turning to a maid in passing, "Archer has started preparations for his party."

I watched her startle like a little creature caught in the long grass then burst toward the kitchen ahead of us like her tail was on fire.

"So, it really does take three days to prepare for one of these?"

"I'm afraid so," he said. "I thought we might get a break with your arrival, but they're part of Archer's routine. Diversion. Frivolity. Blowing off steam. It's how he decompresses before the full—"

He cut himself short. I watched his baffled expression as he tried to come up with a convincing alternative to whatever he was going to say.

"Don't hurt yourself," I said, too tired and hungry to really care. "It doesn't last like a week or something, right? He isn't starting a cult. It's just a party."

"Oh, no-no," he said, "They'll all be gone by the end of the weekend."

So, it'd be a weekend of room service for me, then. That seemed all right, all things considered. Maybe after a wild bacchanal, they'd realize I wasn't here to stage a coup. Maybe I could take a hike, explore the grounds while they were off with their friends, and try to figure out Will's riddle—

Bruce stopped me around the corner from the corridor that led to the dining room.

"The party wasn't the surprise to which I was referring," he said. His eyes darted toward the hall and back to me like someone around the corner might hear him. "We have a special guest."

"For me?"

"Yes, miss," he said, eyeing my ensemble. "I should have asked you to change…uh…maybe you should rush back up and do so. I can have Mary prepare something before you get there."

"Bruce, I'm not changing," I said, brushing past him. "It's not like the king of England is here."

I turned the corner and stopped like a cartoon, my sneakers squeaking against the hardwood floor as I pulled to a short, hard stop. Two British guards in full regalia stood to either side of the dining room door. A woman in a blue suit paced the far end of the hall, whispering into a cell phone. Mrs. Margolyes appeared through the kitchen door at the far end of the hall. Just for a second before the door shut behind her, I could see an open outside door and beyond that the unmistakable shape of a helicopter on the back lawn.

The woman stopped pacing and eyed me from toe to crown. Mrs. Margolyes blanched and hurried forward.

"Bruce, what do I do?" I whispered, panicked.

"He's just a man," said Mrs. Margolyes, tutting as she judged my clothing. "A very posh man. Just remember to always call him *your majesty,* and you'll be fine. Also, no swearing, of course."

"Okay. I hadn't planned on it," I said.

"She should change, Mrs. Margolyes," said Bruce. I'd never seen him flap before; it was sweet...and disconcerting. "But what *is* there for her to change into? Judy was only here yesterday. Nothing's ready yet!"

"Dinnae bother," she said. "Strike the right tone from the start. Don't give him any unreasonable expectations, I say."

"Expectations of what, Mrs. Margolyes?" I was getting tired of not having all the information I needed to make my own decisions.

"He's just here to talk to you," Mrs. Margolyes replied. "Just a talk."

"Lady Damarand?" It was the woman in the blue suit. She zipped forward to shake my hand.

"Yes, hi," I said.

"Hello. I'm sorry to rush this, but his majesty has to be in Aberdeen in an hour. Could we?"

"Of course!" Bruce and Mrs. Margolyes yelped together, each placing a hand on my back and ushering me forward. The dining room door opened ahead of me, and they shoved me inside.

It was funny. Seeing the actual *king of England* seated at the head of the table only sort of registered for me. He looked so much like a cardboard cutout. Until he moved, it was entirely surreal. What *really* registered was the fact that there was no food on the table, only tea and coffee. My stomach warbled its loudest protest yet.

"Hello, my dear," he said as I approached.

"Hello, your majesty," I replied, thinking that I had absolutely *nailed* that one rule I'd been given...until I realized no one told me whether I should curtsy. So, I tried, wobbling into a half crouch in jeans. Did it count? Did I look as ridiculous as I felt?

He seemed to think so. A shy smile broke across his face, his eyes crinkling at the corners, and he laughed.

"No need for that," he said, motioning me into the seat beside him. He studied my face for a long moment. "So. *You* are Natalie."

"You've heard of me?"

"Of course, I have," he said, sipping his tea from a cup decorated with one of those weird monsters on horseback from the mural in my room. "Whom do you think William spoke to about your arrangement here? A most unusual request, bequeathing a title and property to someone…outside the normal spheres…but I owed him a favor, and he was singularly devoted to the idea of your installation here. He was adamant that you and you alone could fill this position."

"Thank you," I said, genuinely touched to hear it.

"However, the question remains, do *you* want it? This is a grand responsibility. It's not a job, nothing so crass. It is a life's commitment to serving your people. When they come to you for answers, you'll need to supply them. When they beg for your help, it'll fall to you to muscle through. Heaven help you if you fail, they'll rip you apart, although it's been many years since they did so literally. Like Atlas, on your shoulders be it."

He waited for some response from me. What could I say to that?

"I understand."

"Do you?" he asked. "This family's secrets…the rituals…they only compound the responsibility, don't they?"

Archer had mentioned secrets, but *rituals* were a new one. I met the king's eye and nodded, hoping he'd believe I had any clue what they were.

"And yet," he plunged on. "They're not *your* responsibilities yet. They never have to be if you entertain my offer."

"What offer is that, your majesty?"

His blue eyes twinkled with mischief.

"I'd like to buy the estate from you. Today, tomorrow, yesterday—whichever is most convenient for you. And I'd pay more than fair market price for it. Far more."

He certainly didn't mince words. The offer hung in the air between us like a bubble until a sound nearby popped it. The swinging kitchen door moved an inch on its hinges. It could've been a draft, but I was pretty certain someone was listening. No doubt gossip was already spreading through the house like a virus.

"That's very generous," I replied when the door settled.

"I can be *very* generous." He slid a tiny piece of velveteen paper across the table toward me. "Don't look at the offer until after I've gone, but it has the private number of my secretary on it, if you'd like to accept. You could return to your own life a very rich young woman."

It was tempting. But of course, so many things here were.

"Can I ask a question?"

"Of course, my dear."

"What would happen to the staff?"

"The…staff?"

"Bruce tells me I have over four hundred employees. I couldn't leave if it meant they'd lose their jobs."

"Most magnanimous of you," he tittered, but not sincerely. The words fell out of his mouth like he always had to have the last word. It dawned on him more slowly than I liked that I was serious. "Oh, of course, they would remain at their posts. I have no reason to dislodge them."

No reason now, I thought.

"I have another question," I said.

"Of course!"

"Why do you want it? I'm sure you have plenty of land, and now that I've seen the state of the rooms upstairs, I'm sure you have grander houses, too." I could guess it was because he wanted to "collect the set," so to speak. Maybe this land was between two other pieces he owned. Maybe he wanted to tack his family's crest to a patch on a map that taunted him.

His answer actually surprised me.

"Goodness," he said, laughing. "To finally have a great house? What I wouldn't give to rule a kingdom twice over."

I didn't understand but smiled politely as if I did, and it seemed to do the trick. He patted his knee and rose to stand. I leapt to my feet, too.

"Well, you have my card. I *will* be checking in again, Lady Damarand. Once you truly understand the sacrifices you'll have to make for this place, this family, I think you'll find my offer even more appealing."

He shook my hand, which I had expected, but then he *bowed* at me, leaving me well and truly shaken. Did kings bow to commoners? I didn't think so. When he finally walked out, I turned over the velveteen paper. There were more zeroes at the end of his offer than seemed fiscally possible. It was the entire GDP of some countries.

A shiver shot up my spine and exploded into fantasies in my head. My mother would *never* have to work again. Neither would I. Neither would my kids or my kids' kids. Hell, neither would Scarlett or her parents for that matter.

It was winning the lottery. *Several* lotteries.

But of course…I'd already won the lottery.

My belly growled again, and I tucked the paper away. I wasn't deciding anything on an empty stomach. Unfortunately, I never made it past the swinging kitchen door.

Someone taller and stronger pushed from the other side, propelling me backward, matching me step for step, dancing me suddenly to the side, then up against the wall. A crest of red hair fell like a short curtain above me, and I peered up into silver eyes framed by long, wine-colored eyelashes.

"What did he want?" Cassian's words weren't threatening at all—more desperate—but he was invading my personal space again, leering over me like a giant. My breath caught as I realized his wiry arms had me pinned against the wall.

"Could you step back, please?"

"I will once you tell me what he said."

"This is inappropriate. Back off, Cassian."

"He wanted to buy Bear Glen, didn't he…" It wasn't a question. I could see from the scattered look in his eyes that he might not have heard what I said at all. He appeared genuinely terrified. When he spoke again, his soft voice pleaded, "He can't have it. You can't give it to him. My father turned him down hundreds of times. Did you hear anything I said during that interview yesterday? It's been in our family for *nine hundred years.* Can someone like you even comprehend that length of time?"

"What is wrong with you?" I tried pushing against his hard stomach. He didn't flinch at all. He grabbed my hand and brought it to his warm, trembling chest, pressing my palm tightly against it so I could feel his raging heart. I was surprised to feel calluses on his fingers, the slightest tension as he held his hand against mine, keeping it in place. His face dipped to within an inch of mine, flooding my senses. He'd taken a bath with bundles of sweet basil, like me, but his potent campfire scent cut through it—intoxicating.

"You'll sell it back to *us.* You won't get as much as you will from him, but we'll cherish it with our bodies and souls. We'll *break* ourselves for it. My father died protecting it!"

"What do you mean Will died protecting it?"

"You couldn't…" His eyes tightened in pain as he swayed closer, pressing his forehead to mine for the slightest second, surprising me and scattering sparks through me. "Please, my lady. This has been our entire lives. My entire existence until you arrived has been spent protecting this place."

"I'm not selling—"

"Just think about it." His voice was like a hungry purr; the fingers holding my hand to his heart squeezed. His silver eyes appeared stormy this close, little threads of bruised purple streaking through the clouds, rain threatening to fall. For a long moment, I was lost there, in fields of heather under a growling, angry sky, waiting to see how it would break. "I'll give you anything you want. Name it and it's yours."

Something searing hot shot straight down through my body from heart to toes, warming recesses in between. For the very first time ever, I knew exactly what I wanted...and what I wanted made absolutely no sense at all. I wanted this. I wanted him. Perhaps it was his fingers on mine or the pronounced Cupid's bow on his upper lip. Perhaps it was that his penetrating gaze belonged entirely and only to me in a way no one else's ever had. Like he had fought an army of his own demons to reach the very depths of me, pulled the stake with my name on it from the soil, and planted it in his own barren fields. Like he was returning with his own named stake, offering it to me. All I had to do was take it.

"I've done terrible things to protect this place." He looked away and all I wanted to do was cup his face and force him to look at me again. "I've ruined lives for it. Tell me what you want so I don't have to ruin yours."

"You couldn't ruin my life if you tried," I snapped back.

"And yet, you don't have to try at all to ruin mine."

I could feel my stupid heart shedding layers: first surprise, then anger, then admiration, then desire, then resentment, then confusion. There was *beauty* in his passion; I felt such things knowing it was directed at me—*wishing* it was directed at me differently—and so much frustration that it was also against me. Why didn't he understand I wasn't his enemy?

"You know it doesn't have to be like this, right?" I asked. "I don't want to hurt you."

"Nor I you," he said. "But the fact that you're even necessary pains me. I want you to leave. Go home. It'd be better for all of us. You included."

I yanked my hand out of his grasp and pushed down the strange sudden sense of *loss* that replaced his touch.

"You can't bully me into doing what you say!" I laughed with frustration, ducking out and under his arms. With distance came rational thought. The power of his scent lessened. "I'm not a tough-love person, Cassian. I don't respond well to threats or shame or peer pressure. You would know that if you tried to get to know me *at all*."

He growled in desperate frustration. "I'm not threatening you. I'm trying to warn you."

Exasperation filled the space between us. "Warn me of *what?*"

His pouty mouth opened and closed, as useless as a broken radio.

"You're such an idiot," I said, surprised by the disappointment I heard in my voice. I escaped the room, inhaling deeply in the hall like I'd escaped a burning house.

"Is everything all right?" Mrs. Margolyes scurried toward me, her eyebrows bowed with concern.

"It's fine, I'm fine," I said quickly.

"Did the king say—"

"I'm not selling, okay?" I was tired of people asking questions and demanding answers while they pretended to be deaf to what I asked. "Could you please ask the cook to prepare a packed lunch for me in a backpack? Nothing too intense. I need to get out for a while."

"Where will you—"

"Wherever I want, thanks."

This was Cassian's fault. The adrenaline from…whatever had happened in there was still raging through my body like a storm. The *hairs* on my arms stood on end. My skin boiled, my heart tugged like a dog at the end of its leash for me to return to him, all while the sour embarrassment of being attracted to someone who had humiliated me and wanted to get rid of me curdled in my stomach. What was wrong with me?

Whatever it was, I wouldn't figure it out here, while I was still hungry and still clueless about whatever made Bear Glen the sort of place some people would spend entire fortunes to own, and others would ruin lives to keep.

CHAPTER 14

The heavy backpack full of food tugged at my shoulders as I emerged onto the back lawn, picked a direction, and marched ahead, like I had any clue where I was going. I had briefly visited my room to put on hiking boots and grab the photo of Will and me with the riddle on the back. By the time I returned to the kitchen, someone had prepared an entire feast and packed it away in someone's green backpack, which looked so brand new I was convinced someone had sprinted the two miles to the village and back while I was upstairs to purchase one for me.

It probably belonged to Cassian, I assured myself, *and he refused to use it. After all, it wasn't in the Mahon tartan, so it was too beneath him.*

Luckily, the house had been practically vibrating with party-prep activity, so no one batted an eye at me in passing as I slipped away. I wanted to see how far away from people I could get in a place like this.

Being out of everybody's hair would be a good change of pace, and it felt *so* good to be outside in the sun. Dew dappled my legs as I trampled through the long grass past the lawn, past the place Cassian had brought me, and beyond. I figured I'd walk until I reached the bridge that led to the village then turn with the wind and continue on into eternity—or until I reached the mountains in the distance. There was no way my scrawny Pennsylvania legs could best those yet.

The earth smelled sweet as I walked. Mossy and floral notes took turns drifting toward me on the soft breeze, intercut by some pungent stench that almost made me gag when I stepped on a patch of small white-yellow flowers. I could appreciate that; who wanted to be stepped on?

Eventually, I found a thin animal trail slicing through the meadows to a stream that carved through the land for several miles and brought me to the far northeast corner of Bear Glen. I hadn't expected to recognize the estate's edge when I came to it, but the ten-foot-tall sandstone pillar was hard to miss. It looked like a gravestone or chest piece set atop a tiny hill. Upon closer inspection, I found crumbling mortar and a few gray stones attached to the south and west sides of it, suggesting it had once been the corner of a massive estate wall, which seemed impossible; this place was just too expansive to contain.

It was incredible to imagine this place nine hundred years ago. Will had told me a little of his family history on stormy weekends when there was nothing else to do. The Mahon's, he'd said, had been cultivating this western coastal land since Vikings looted the kingdoms to the east and Scotland united to drive them away. One great uncle had died fighting the Kingdom of Norway during the Battle of Largs; another great uncle had perished in the Battle of Culloden. And a several-times-great grandmother had lured a British battalion into her kitchen and poisoned them with stew. Even before that, ancient Romans had occupied the land. Will had kept a collection of the Roman coins he'd found wandering as a boy and promised me that there were plenty more to find.

He'd been proud of his heritage, proud of the ancestors he'd never met. Sort of, anyway. He seemed to prefer the fanciful version of events rather than the dry dates and real details. The exaggerated tales of triumph. The great heroes. The valiant skirmishes. How the family's fortune had been built on the broad backs of Ayrshire cattle, a herd of which he—and I guess now I—still kept somewhere on the property.

But sometimes, when a mood struck him or the night was too dark, he would lapse into strange palls and his stories took a darker turn. Tales of relatives lulled to their deaths by sirens and selkies. Revenge between houses. And a village massacre that had resulted in the hunt for something he called *The Great Beast of Falkirk.* Will claimed sixty men had died hunting it and one of his own captured the beast before it was burned at the stake.

The worst of Will's stories, though, had scared me more than even that creature in the East Wood could. A famine had plagued Scotland at the end of the seventeenth century. Crops died. Men and women and children shrank to bones. But not the Mahon family or the four hundred families living on their lands at the time.

"They made a choice, you see," he'd said as he sat in an armchair by the fire, rolling a whisky glass in his hand at an angle on the chair arm so it caught the firelight. "A terrible, unforgivable choice. *Real* rabbits reproduce spectacularly fast. They make an ideal food source in times of need. But they can be tough to catch alive...unless they see you as one of their own. So, my kin waited until those poncey rabbits from the clan in Troon met under the light of the full moon and gathered them all into cages. Then they set those near *real* rabbit dens and collected all who wandered out to investigate.

"In a single night, we had an entire stock of breeding rabbits, didn't we? When dawn broke and some of the rabbits changed...well, unlucky for them...my kin kept them to use again when the meat ran out. Not a single empty belly from here to Prestwick."

Something about the way he'd phrased it, the cold, calculating way he differentiated them—the *real* rabbits from whatever qualified as poncey ones—had set me on edge. For months, I'd had nightmares about rabbits and men coming to collect them, cage them, cook them.

Will had had a darkness in him I never fully understood. All I knew was that my mother's love had tamed some part of him—or at least danced it away from the edge. And here I was, wandering across the open fields of a valley I now owned, thanks to a man who'd filled my head with scary stories. In less than a month, I'd left home, traveled to another country, and was now exploring a land that had only slightly changed in a thousand years. Sure, I could see the occasional car passing along the far road to the west that connected the driveway to the stone village, and electrical poles sprung out of the ground like wild hairs every so often, but this place seemed to exist in its own dimension, excused from the goings on of the rest of the world.

Some yards away from the property's cornerstone, the sound of draining water caught my ear. It was a hollow, manmade noise. Unnatural. From where I was, all I could see around me were tufts of meadow grass and a small, overgrown bulge. I stepped over and around it until my boots squelched in water and bent to investigate. Drawing the long grass aside like a curtain exposed a beautiful carving—the form of a bear on all fours, leaning forward to stare me down. It had to be ancient—the stone was half crumbled and broken where water had frozen and expanded, splitting edges of the drain apart—but the bear remained intact. My neck prickled with joy.

There was nothing else here, and although the bear was beautiful, I wondered if it had anything to do with the riddle Will had left me. I pulled the photo of Will out of the backpack and turned it over, reading the riddle again:

A treasure beneath, a prize on high
Within stone sheath under bark of dye
Where green sentinels loom near gleam of armored show
In a sacred tomb, only the hiding one knows
The moon reveals a future bright where heads lay deep in the dead of night

…All it takes is just one bite

This might qualify as a stone sheath, and maybe if I returned after dark, the moon might reveal something I couldn't see in the light of day, but…it seemed like a stretch.

I pulled out my phone, lifted it until I found just enough service, and placed a pin in this exact location on my map app, so I could return later once I knew more.

The rest of the day passed in a stomping, tromping romp across the countryside, which I enjoyed more than I'd ever expected. The sight of that silly drainage ditch decorated with the ancient carving of the bear had invigorated me. At the very least, it confirmed for me that one part of Will's riddle was true—there was treasure here. I just had to figure out what kind and where.

The snacks the cook had packed—Tunnock tea cakes, something labeled a *rumbledethumps pie*, Scottish butter fudge, and an "Edinburgh rock," a stick of chalk that crumbled to peppermint candy in my mouth—kept me hiking until the evening, and I returned to find a beautiful lentil shepherd's pie waiting for me at the dining room table. I called Scarlett and told her everything, while listening to a discordant, inconsistent knocking and banging coming from various areas in the house. Hammers and nails, and at one point, the voices of several staff going, "*Oy, Oy, Oy!*" in a harried, panicked tone actually ejected me from my seat with worry before I heard deep, joyful laughter a second later.

By the time I headed for my own rooms, the hallways were partitioned off in places by large floor-to-near-ceiling dividers fashioned from bedding—sheets, quilts, comforters—stretched taut between wooden stands. I could see shadows behind them, but when I tried to pass, someone would make excuses about why it was too dangerous for me to walk that way.

"Don't worry, we have the party preparations well in hand, my lady," said one girl named Kenna as she passed me carrying an industrial-sized box that seemed to weigh nothing at all.

I was fairly certain Archer would tell me what the party was if I asked, but to be honest, I had plans of my own to keep me busy. In my rooms, I cleared a narrow side table to use as a desk and pulled it away from the wall. It was just early enough in the evening that I didn't feel bad about asking Mary to fetch me the biggest piece of paper she could find, along with some colored pens.

"We have paints if you prefer, my lady," she said, arriving with what I'd asked for, along with an artist's kit that someone had assembled in a worker's toolbox.

"Thank you, this is great," I said. "Eventually, I'd love to move all of this into a studio if I can."

Shc giggled. "Of course, you can! Nothing but space in this place. Just have to clear it out first. Do you mind if we wait until after the party, or…do you need it now, my lady?"

"Later's fine," I said. "Thank you, Mary. Does Archer keep you all up working late when he throws one of those things?"

"It's all right," she replied, which wasn't the answer I was hoping for. "Bit of fun, isn't it? Gives us something to look forward to."

"Okay, but get some sleep," I said. "It's just a party."

Mary gave me a coy smile. "Master Archer's real excited about this one. He says it's for you, miss."

I quirked my brow and eyed her, expecting a joke; she wiggled her eyebrows at me instead.

"What do you mean?"

"He's asked us to take great care with the decorations. Wants them to be perfect. Usually, he's on and on about which famous chef we can get to cater, the guest list…the who's who and such. But all he cares about is what you'll think of it. I caught him combing through your socials, pulling reference photos and everything."

"Oh." I looked away just in case I was blushing. "Thank you, Mary."

I suddenly regretted *not* peeking behind the dividers downstairs. Thoughts popped off in my head like fireworks, wondering exactly *which* pictures he'd seen. I went through passing phases like everybody else; one summer I'd gone batty for costume jewelry, and poor Scarlett had had to cut me off to keep me from spending all my babysitting money on shiny baubles I never had an occasion to actually wear. My room looked like a disco ball for the next six months until I got over it and gifted it all away for Christmas. Then there was the year I'd fangirled over athletic Michael Phelps so hard Scarlett nicknamed me Phelpie…

I pushed the thought from my head. I was sure I'd find out what the party was on the day. In the meantime, I had something else to obsess over. I pulled out my phone and dialed Bruce's number.

"Is everything all right, my lady?" Beyond him, I could hear the white noise of what sounded like a pub halfway through a bar fight, which probably meant there was a football game on. I was just surprised to learn he actually left the estate at all.

"Hi, yes, sorry to call, but do you know the dimensions of the property off the top of your head?"

"Erm, well…" I listened to him bumble for several seconds as he stepped out of the pub, and quiet descended around him. "It's not a square, my lady."

"Is there a map somewhere I could use?"

"I could find one tomorrow," he offered.

"Please, thank you. What about general dimensions?"

"It's thousands of acres," he said. "Some here, some elsewhere, half the property's on the islands off the coast, my lady. Is there something specific you're looking for?"

I wondered how truthful I could be.

"It's something Will asked me to find."

"Oh?" he said. "Can you tell me what it is?"

"Not yet."

He was silent just long enough I wondered if I'd have to look up the dimensions myself.

"Well, if it has anything to do with Will, imagine the house at the center of a map and go ten acres in any direction. When he was here, he mostly kept to that square."

"Thank you, that's great," I said. "Have a good night."

"Are you sure I can't—"

I hung up on him. The artist's kit contained a ruler, which I used to mark large squares on the piece of paper, one for each square acre to search. I drew a little house at the center to mark the manor. If Will really stayed that close to home when he was here, then I had my treasure map. All I would need to do was thoroughly search each section before moving on to the next, and I was sure I'd find the answer to Will's riddle soon enough.

The next day, I woke before dawn and dressed in layers. I tucked my makeshift grid-map into my backpack, along with a hardback day planner I'd found in a drawer that I could use as a writing surface in a pinch.

I stole down to the kitchen and packed myself a couple egg and cheese sandwiches for the road and a water bottle before I stepped out the back door and headed across the driveway toward the walled garden. I could walk through that then head at a northwest diagonal until I reached the far corner of my search area. I would start there with the first square and work my way toward the east until I reached the corner pillar I had visited yesterday. Anything unusual or worth further investigation I would mark on the map.

It sounded easy in my head…of course, I had underestimated the obstacles that laid before me.

I cannot stress how much I wanted to *loiter* in the walled garden. Acres of walkways branched away from the main stairs, leading to a central fountain shaped like a thistle, and beyond to brick pergolas and glass greenhouses rendered jungle-like and green by the sheer amount of foliage visible through the windows. Past that, I moved into the orchard where delicate pink apple blossoms crowned one row of trees, and lux white plum blossoms crowned the next. There were already tiny pears taking shape in the final aisle. Floral honeysuckle scent sat so thick around me the air looked textured, and my brain buzzed with lightheadedness. I wanted to lay down like Dorothy in the poppy fields and sleep in this aromatic orchard forever. Instead, I took a shortcut across a beautiful carved bridge, across a manmade pond, to the far exit where I lingered, staring wistfully back at the garden until I remembered I owned it and could return whenever I wanted.

From there, I made my way across more meadows and the main village road until my phone told me I had traveled far enough to reach the northwest corner of Will's territory. There was no standing pillar here, but there was a badly crumbled gray foundation stone where a pillar once stood.

It was at this point, of course, that I realized I should have brought some sort of rope or spray paint to mark off the corners of each acre as I searched. But, I figured, maybe that was just something you saw on home improvement shows for the drama…or murder mysteries. At the very least, I knew I could split the distance between where I stood and the walled garden and use that to gauge my search quadrant. That would have to do.

I made quick work of the first few acres. The only neat things I found were a piece of pottery and a fifty-pound note that had clearly flapped its way out of someone's car in passing along the road. But I made a point to draw any distinctive detail on my map. If this entire search turned out to be pointless, at the very least I'd have a neat illustration of the area to paint and hang as art on the wall.

By the time I reached the northeastern pillar again—an entire twenty-five percent of the way through my search—I was pretty sure I'd made a terrible mistake. I'd burned through the egg and cheese sandwiches by lunchtime, leaving me feeling hollow and painfully hungry as I began the schlep back to the house at dusk. Because I hadn't brought any music, I spent the entire trek listening to the annoying empty bell that was my water bottle clanging against my backpack. Mocking my dehydration. And somewhere along the way back, I entered a thicket of stinging nettle, which bedazzled my bare right thigh and calf with a constellation of painful red hives. That was on top of the rubberized jelly that had replaced my legs. I must've looked like a newborn foal wobbling around on them. I took a breath when I reached the gravel drive, mustering what little dignified composure I could on the walk back to the house, but it didn't matter.

As I rounded the driveway circle, I caught Cassian staring at me from his upstairs window, hands buried in his trouser pockets, wearing that deep-set look of concentration that knitted his brow together *and* produced that thoughtful pout. Ignoring him would have been easy, but I wanted him to know I could see him. I raised my hand and waved, adding a little sarcastic flick just to see if he would realize it was creepy to watch people from on high like a gargoyle. It broke his spell at least. He shifted his weight, glanced away, and—miracle of miracles—raised a hand from his pocket in a half-hearted return wave.

"There. Was that so difficult, you damp saltine?" I said through an exaggerated smile.

Since our strange encounter in the dining room, my thoughts had cooled considerably. Overpowering scent and passionate rhetoric aside, he hadn't tried to speak to me since. Or apologize.

Somehow, Mrs. Margolyes heard about my injury by the time I reached the house. She sprinted toward me down the hall like some sort of manic mouse, fussing over my swollen leg, calling the nearest maid to drop the party supplies she was carrying and go "*find some calamine immediately! Our lady is hurt!*" She had another servant fetch a chair and another a crystal glass of iced lemon water. I felt like I was being swarmed by a flock of birds as they maneuvered me into a seated position in the main foyer.

Then, as quickly as it had started, the swarm ended. They were just…*gone*. One moment I was surrounded by servants, and the next I was completely alone. Even odder, they had left the calamine lotion and cotton balls on a gold platter just out of reach of my chair. I was honestly so tired I almost left it, but the unpleasant sting nudged me forward.

"Let me get that for you…"

A gentle hand landed on my shoulder, as hot as summer sand, accompanied by that delicious sherry scent. My gaze traveled up the full length of Archer's brawny arm before locking onto his turquoise eyes and those little black islands in the blue lagoons.

"You don't have to do that, Archer, really."

"Nonsense," he replied, pulling the platter closer, kneeling at my feet. "I'm the only athletic person in the house. I've had my fair share of run-ins with the local wildlife."

His warm hand wrapped around my calf, scattering more goosebumps where the skin was chilled, as he lifted my leg onto his knee. A few dabs of pink calamine on the cotton ball and his hand was once again on my skin, methodically applying the salve where the nettles had stung hardest.

My mind blushed, a feeling completely foreign to me. It spread to my skin, raising the temperature across my face and neck totally without my permission. I clapped my hands to my cheeks to cover it, which of course only drew his attention to it.

"Are you blushing again?" he said, that dimple appearing on his left cheek.

"No. It's nothing. I swear."

He frowned a little and turned back to the task at hand. "It'll feel better tomorrow. Unless…"

"Unless what?"

"It's nothing," he said with a playful smile.

"Could it get worse? Archer, what were you going to say?"

He eyed me pointedly. "What were *you* blushing about?"

"Oh, come on," I said, feeling the flush deepen, spreading to my chest. "It's nothing, really."

His smile widened. "I was saying you'll be fine tomorrow unless you have a nettle allergy like Cassian. Property's wild with the stuff, which is why he's such a *lord of the castle*. Has to defend it from within."

The thought of Cassian walking me outside in the early morning came back to me. Seemed strange he would take me out there if he was so allergic…

"Geez," I said.

"It's only one of his many…physical deficiencies," Archer murmured to himself. "But never mind him. I shared, so now it's your turn. Why are you blushing?"

He waited, his stubbled face quirked in a goofy grin.

"Don't make fun of me, okay?"

"I won't."

"Promise?"

"Okay, now I'm *really* curious," he said, adding, "I promise, I promise."

"It's stupid, but I just realized the only people who've ever touched my legs are my doctor and my mom. And Scarlett…but she's trouble, so it's always suss when she's near me."

He chuffed pleasantly. His sherry wine musk rose into my nose, cutting through the calamine.

"Is she your best friend?"

I nodded, missing her. She would have been standing behind him right now, shooting me exaggerated lovey-dovey glances and thumbs up and other inappropriate gestures it would have embarrassed me for him to see.

"Why didn't she come with you?"

"Her parents grounded her because we went to the castle."

"The castle?"

"That night in the garden…"

He glanced away, smiling, as if pleased by the memory. "Ah yes, the great heist. Plundering my family's treasures before you even got here. Are you sure you're not British?"

I must have grimaced because he curled his forefinger under my chin before I could register it, pulling my attention back to his blue eyes.

"I'm joking, I swear," he said. "I know you didn't know any of this was coming. My father was…"

He brought his hands back to my leg, lifting it gingerly to reach the rash on the other side.

"Mysterious?" I offered.

"Unreliable. Unpredictable…"

I didn't know if I should ask. "What else? What was he like?"

"You and I saw very different sides of him, I suspect. He was damn near gone my entire life, reappearing when and how it suited him to…*correct*…unbecoming behaviors in my brother and me. Always with words, of course—we *are* posh—but words can cut as easily as any blade, can't they? I honestly think you saw the best of him, Natalie."

"I'm sorry." And I was. I'd lost my father when I was little and it'd broken me, broken my mom. For months, I had entered their room in the mornings to jump them awake, only to see the empty space he'd left and burst into tears, forcing my mom to wrap her arms around me and sooth me through tears of her own. I couldn't imagine what it would be like if he had *chosen* to leave us, over and over again.

"None of that pointless sorrow," Archer replied, setting my pink, sticky, mottled leg down, but leaving his soothing, warm hand on my knee. "You're a wonderful thing."

I felt my cheeks flushing red again, damn biology. My hands flew to my cheeks once more.

"And I love your blush," he said, cupping my hands and pulling them away. "You shouldn't hide it."

"Easy for you to say. You don't turn into a strawberry when you're nervous."

"Oh, you'd be surprised what I turn into."

A faint sound drifted to us. We turned and found Cassian on the stairs with his foot firmly planted on a creaky step, wearing a coat and carrying that briefcase I'd seen in his room.

"Don't mind me."

"I was just seeing her sorted," said Archer. "Since you can't."

Cassian walked the length of the room past us to the front door along the far wall. As if there were some sort of invisible aura around us he preferred not to touch.

"Going somewhere?" asked Archer. "Burning the cubicle oil?"

"I have business in Glasgow. Bruce and I will be back in a few days."

"Well, don't let us keep you from it, brother," said Archer.

Cassian paused with his hand on the door. His gaze turned to my tender leg then rose to meet my eye, concern clouding his steely gaze before he eyed Archer. "Remain the gentleman, Archie."

This time, it was Archer's cheeks that flushed beet red.

"All right, Granddad," he said, flapping a little. "Jog on."

After Cassian left, Archer turned to me, still flapping. I couldn't hide the huge grin on my face.

"Are you *blushing*, Master Mahon?"

"No," he said too quickly, backing away. "Be careful out there, and I'll see you for the party, all right?"

"Maybe," I said playfully. His eyes widened with concern. I doubled down. "I don't know if I'll be in the partying mood. Tomorrow, is it?"

I knew the party weekend started tomorrow.

"Yes. If you could return to the house around eight tomorrow, that'd be ideal."

"Well, we'll see." With that, I turned and strode up the stairs to my rooms to call Scarlett and tell her everything.

CHAPTER 15

The next day brought one more chance to search the property before there'd be people roaming everywhere asking me questions I didn't really want to answer. Sure, everyone would be busy with the party…but there was no chance people wouldn't talk the second I mentioned I was on a treasure hunt. That's classic party banter. At least, I figured it was.

Archer had been right; the hives on my leg had all but receded by the time I left, but I still wore long pants anyway. I'd asked Mary last night to get me a pair of heavy-duty gloves, too, just in case I had to touch anything, and they were waiting on my backpack when I woke.

By the time I reached the kitchen to make myself something, the cantankerous cook—who I'd learned was named Gordon—was already there doing the dirty work for me. Clearly, Mrs. Margolyes had told him my wake-up times. The bags under his eyes almost fluoresced blue, dark and deep set, against the red of his nose.

"Oh, you didn't have to get up early for me."

"It's my job, my lady," he grumbled in a chiding teacher's tone. "Just a few minutes, if you please."

"Thank you."

He snorted at me, which I interpreted as *you're welcome, but don't ever touch my knives again.*

I rationed my water this time, even though the backpack was practically bursting with food today, and the extra weight made me want to drain the bottle just to lighten the load. I began my survey in the area just above and behind the walled garden with plans to stop where I'd found the drainage ditch with the bear carving.

Just as I'd done yesterday, I drew details as I found them. The entrance to the Western Wood, the long-condemned chapel with the collapsed roof, as well as a small grave plot. Every grave was old and crumbling, save one—the gravestone for Cassian's mom, Amelia. A new message had recently been carved into the stone, "Missed *every day*." Poor Archer had half a parent and Cassian had had none at all. I caught myself thinking it explained a lot, but that wasn't fair. I didn't know them well enough to say that.

Unfortunately, the macabre memorial to Amelia was the most interesting thing I found between that square and the one with the drainage ditch in it. I was thorough—I genuinely thought I'd searched thoroughly, at least—but this stretch had been more or less a meadow obstacle course, with me weaving between patches of stinging nettle and those pungent white-yellow flowers. Surely if anyone in the house glanced out at me now, they would think I'd gone insane, walking back and forth across random patches before moving onto the next random patch of land and doing the same.

When I reached the bear carving on the drain, I wasn't ready to return home. Couldn't. I hadn't found anything yet. But…I didn't want to move into the next search quadrant, either. This one, and the few after it, were in the Eastern Wood, which hugged the library, kitchen, and the upper wings Cassian and Archer occupied. The memory of those green eyes in the dying light hadn't left me since that night. Scotland didn't have any predators that stood six feet tall anymore—the last wolves had died out long ago—which meant the thing must've been a deer or one of those Ayrshire cattle Will had loved. Those were the only things big enough, unless…

Unless it was human…or something else. I didn't like either option. Whatever the creature had been, it had followed me back to the house. Watched me from the wood. Disappeared when I locked the library door behind me.

The prospect of searching the woods and focusing all my attention on the rocks and soil and water while something unseen watched me awoke some ancient biological terror in me. But it was only two in the afternoon. The sun was high in the sky, roasting the back of my arms. If I was ever going to search the woods, this was the best time to do it.

At the edge of the forest, all I could hear was my heartbeat pumping panic into my ears and the wind crashing branches together overhead in terrifying encouragement. That, and the soft prayer I whispered to myself before stepping in. "What would Scarlett do?"

Foliage thick with spring growth completely veiled and erased the open grassy meadows as I entered the forest. Petrichor saturated the air. The mechanical clashing of tree branches softened to something like forest chatter. I could hear animals I couldn't see. I could read moisture in the air through my skin, a new extrasensory type of braille that told me the stream I'd once sat beside laid off to the southwest about five hundred yards or so. Even though I couldn't see or even hear it, I knew it was there.

The forest *glowed.* Dappled light walked through the forest ahead of me, patterning the ground with its footprint. Mushrooms and flowering vines clung to tree trunks in splatters of colorful life, breathing and swaying. But, of course, that was impossible…wasn't it? Unless some hallucinogenic mushroom had released its magic into the air, accidentally poisoning me with beauty.

When the trees and bushes around me began to move, I started to believe my own story about airborne hallucinogens. The forest came alive in a way that was hard to explain and even tougher to believe.

SQUAW! The largest golden eagle I'd ever seen sat a few feet ahead and above, watching me.

Woo-WHO! On another branch, a barn owl. Beyond it, I could see two dozen other birds perched on high.

A flicker of movement caught my eye, and I looked down to see a squirrel…and a rabbit…and a badger as they emerged onto the soil at my feet. They paid each other no mind, focused entirely on me. As if in echo, *several* branches broke deeper in the wood ahead of me, parting as an enormous red deer pushed them aside with its antlers. Its black eyes met mine with tranquil acknowledgement.

"What the…"

Brrrip? The final guest to the party—a sleek, majestic red fox—stared at me from atop a fallen tree trunk nearby. Unlike the rest, it seemed confused by the presence of the others. Its head tilted, its paws recalibrated, watching me. Watching *us*.

I didn't know what to do. Leaving felt impossible; the ground around me *undulated* with movement from tiny feet and swishing tails. More animals were arriving every moment I stood there. There was even a tiny, round mouse touching the toe of my boot.

"I don't…What do I do?"

I'd only said it to fill the air, maybe to talk myself through this strange, fairy tale predicament I'd found myself in, but the swell of life ebbed in response. The animals parted along the edge of a narrow animal trail leading deeper into the woods and stood watchful, patiently waiting for me to understand. I *did* understand, but it didn't make following the path the animals had chosen for me any less ridiculous. I should have been petrified, but the sensation was exactly opposite that. Curiosity filled me like molten sunshine, splashing up into my head and down to my finger and toe tips. I inched forward and the deer's antlers swung, motioning me along.

Each step I took deeper into the wood was shadowed by some sort of tiny creature, their brown or gray or golden eyes glued to my smallest movements. All save the fox, who I caught glimpses of through the underbrush as it followed me.

Around curves, over rocks, and under fallen trees, there was nowhere to go but forward. Soon, I found myself in the purple tender darkness of dense forest, where the trees crowded out all but the softest light, and the forest floor between them was carpeted with neon green ferns. Crisp dampness clung to my skin with an icy tartness that made me feel entirely awake. As if everything I'd ever known before was the dream from which I was only now waking. No place I'd ever been before had looked this lovely. The Pennsylvania woodlands were and are gorgeous—especially when bedding down for the winter—but they'd lost their wildness long ago. This place thrummed with it.

The animals, I realized, hadn't followed me down into the gully; they stood along the rim above me like a silent audience watching some play unfurl. Even the fox had joined them, venturing no farther than the lip of the animal trail I'd stumbled down to get here.

But…it seemed an odd place to bring me. Aside from the palpable electricity in the air, the zing of something I didn't understand, there wasn't much here, except the old growth towering overhead and the young growth cushioning me from below. Maybe there was something under the ferns—

Oh, there definitely was. One moment I was perfectly upright, the next, I hit something unforgiving beneath me. My foot caught on a stone, and I face-planted on a large, overgrown granite slab, scattering the birds above me. I turned back to watch my flock of guardians erupt up and out of the trees in a massive swirl of wings and squawks. The other animals bolted, the littles disappearing into the underbrush with tiny chittering squeaks as the deer clattered away on its thunderous hooves. The spell—or whatever it was—had broken.

I picked myself up, minding my bruised pride and the dull ache in my left knee where it'd hit the stone. At least no one had been there to watch me fall. That tempered the embarrassment…a little.

The ferns had taken hold here a long time ago. So, too, had the trees. The roots of several clung to the stone in a death grip where they had tried to penetrate before growing around. Despite that—and the Scottish winds and rains and snows that had tried their hardest to wipe this thing from existence—it was remarkably well preserved. The corners weren't crumbled. The edges were still straight and relatively clean where it protruded from the moist soil. Someone in the recent past had clearly been tending to the stone. No, not a stone, I realized—a stone container. A crypt.

Gloves on, I ripped up clods of dirt and ferns by the root until I could see the mammoth thing in its entirety. Until I could examine the carving on top of an alder tree mighty and swaying, reaching toward the heavens. But this was no ordinary tree. The trunk, the branches, the roots—they were carved with animals. Each bump in the bark, each knot in the limbs, each gnarled tendril reaching into the soil was something different. Birds and rodents and…I blinked. There were even dragons there, hidden among the more normal creatures like horses and seals.

Beyond the details, though, I'd…seen this tree illustration before, the shape of it in another form; I was absolutely sure of it. I just couldn't remember where. What I *could* remember was the song Will had sung to my Mom, and my Mom had sung to me.

Beyond the forest and river,
where thistle and heather hug the earth in her splendor,
a secret lies waiting for you and for me.
There's no use in waiting,
so stop hesitating,
Forever begins under the stone Alder tree

Excitement scurried up my spine. This *had* to be it, didn't it? This had to be the thing Will wanted me to find. My mind flooded with possibilities of what could be inside. It'd clearly been here a long time—a *long* time. Maybe Will had been the one keeping it up all those years.

I knelt at the corner and tried to shove the container lid, moving it not a single inch. I tried again, only exhausting myself before backing away. I'd have to return with…I didn't know. A pickax seemed too cruel. Some sort of machine?

No!

Another burst of excitement crawled across my skin as I realized there was a keyhole at the center of the great slab, right in the very heart of the tree trunk in the middle of a seven-pointed star.

There was no doubt in my mind that this was what Will sent me to find. It was *meant* to be opened. By me. I just had to find the key.

I could've flown back to the house on the high of my discovery. My toes barely touched the ground as I walked the trail to the edge of the forest where I had first entered, emerging to the sight of a violently pink sunset spreading toward me from the west.

I blinked with confusion. I'd only been in the forest an hour, if that, and yet it was almost sundown. I checked my phone, too—sure enough, it was almost eight o'clock at night. Somehow, I had spent *hours* in there. I hadn't just run away with time; it had run away with me.

It also meant Archer's party was about to begin.

CHAPTER 16

I stepped into a madhouse. Bedlam on steroids. The set of some elaborate one-take shot for a movie where the assistant director had long ago given up any semblance of control.

Two servants I hazily remembered were called Pete and Harry opened the rear French doors ahead of me, spilling noise like a tsunami across the back driveway. British pop crashed against my ears and hit my equilibrium like a mallet slamming into a gong. Dua Lipa jump-scared the soul out of my body.

The main hall swayed with chaos. Teenagers were everywhere, on everything, *in* everything. Running, playing, tossing priceless vases between them one-handed while sipping from red solo cups. Whatever the party punch was, it was doing its job. I watched in slow motion as someone splashed sticky purple across the robe of a guy who stripped it off and flexed before running up the stairs on all fours. And every single guest was wearing white pajamas. Nighties. Negligees. Tighty whities. A guy with hair so red it looked like he was on fire wore a white kilt…and nothing else. Literally nothing, I realized, as he suddenly leapt over the back of a sofa to join a game of darts against the far wall. At least there, I could see they'd put some sort of plate glass cover across the paintings. Priorities, I suppose.

Of course, they were technically *my* paintings now, weren't they? It was a privilege that belonged to the very rich and very poor alike, I realized, to destroy things that only held symbolic meaning for them. I wondered if I should worry about the value of their carelessness…but I was more worried about the loss of the art. Someone had spent their time, poured their soul, into those pieces. For some, it might be the only thing they left behind. The thought saddened me.

"There she is!"

Archer walked down the main stairs, arms outstretched. The deep V of his white robe framed his bare chest before plunging into a knot at his waist just low enough to disguise whether he was wearing shorts underneath or not. When he enveloped me in a hug, pressing me into his chest, I was even less certain either way.

"You like?"

"They definitely like," I replied.

"Come on, I'll get you a drink and you'll fall right into it."

With an indulgent smile, Archer clapped an inviting hand on my shoulder and nudged me forward into the fray. I'd never call myself a prude—mostly because I didn't have enough experience to qualify—but his guiding hand was a godsend in the pandemonium. Just enough reassurance to keep the introvert in me at bay.

But it didn't last long enough. He swerved me into the doorway between the ballroom and the main salon before leaning into me, his lips on my ear. "Take a look, I'll be right back."

"Oh…kay…" And he was gone, taking my dram of courage with him. I could feel its absence like sudden hypothermia in the back of my stomach. I'd been to my fair share of ridiculous, over-the-top parties—or the high school equivalent anyway—but always with Scarlett by my side. In a sea full of unfamiliar, raucous strangers, I felt completely adrift.

But…in a weird way, this felt like my time. To do the things I'd never done before. After such a magical day, I wanted…more. I just wasn't sure how to go about getting it.

In the ballroom, someone had lowered a *wall* on a drop swing, exposing a *massive* speakeasy bar. Like, an actual bar that you could walk behind to serve from a twenty-foot-high wall of liquor bottles. A maid—I'd been trying to learn all their names…Ella, I think her name was?—was serving drinks with flair. Two more teenagers hung from the chandelier overhead while a ground team of servants—John, Rory, Duncan, I think—stood underneath carrying a life net stamped SCOTTISH FIRE AND RESCUE SERVICES. They moved it incrementally as the two boys swung so they could catch them if, or more likely *when*, they fell.

I realized the servants were also wearing pajamas, although theirs were in dark Mahon tartan vests and loose trousers. They were also wearing small eye masks in Mahon tartan, which didn't so much hide their identities as make them look like Scottish Batman sidekicks.

"Mary?" My mouth dropped.

“Welcome, my lady!” my maid said. She curtsied at me with a full tray of drinks in her hand, her bramble of red curls bouncing. “Can I get you anything?”

“Do you have a diet coke?”

“That is too cute.” An elegant waif wearing a white tartan teddy and shorts that barely covered anything was suddenly beside me. “You must be Natalie!”

I smiled awkwardly, craning my neck to look her in the eye. She must’ve been five-ten on a slouching day. Her blonde hair curled at the ends like wild wheat, tickling her collarbone.

“Hi, yeah,” I said.

“Lovely to meet you, I’m Maisey.” She enveloped me against her tight body, my head hitting her chest like a crash-test dummy. “I’m Archer’s *friend*.”

Oh. Her euphemism didn’t escape me.

“Come meet the rest of us!”

Her hand was in mine, drawing me away before I could even say goodbye to Mary. Along the way, we passed Gordon, the harried cook, behind a small buffet of snacks set out in the hallway, and Graham, the night guardsman, watching the merriment like the evening’s satyr. He actually tipped his cap at me in passing.

Just as quickly, we reentered the thick of things in the library, and I pulled up short in disbelief. Someone had transformed it. They’d fit a giant, semi-transparent paper moon over the chandelier and trailed dozens of string lights of stars away to the high corners of the room. Some sort of gossamer material in pearl and butter and lavender had been braided around the balcony handrail and each individual spindle before trailing over and down along the balcony’s edge. Plush white covers transformed every seat in the room into clouds. Tables in white became altars laden with drinks and fruit.

“Incredible, isn’t it?” asked Maisey. I glanced over to find her studying my face. “My favorite weekend of the month.”

I blanched, remembering what Bruce had said. This was Archer’s way of blowing off steam *every* month.

“And it’s only just starting,” she said, leading me to a group of people gathered on chaise lounges. “Guys, she’s here!”

“Brilliant!” said a gangly one with thick, square glasses.

“Aces, man,” said a shirtless guy who never seemed to stop flexing.

“Has he told her—”

"God, don't be a bore and ruin everything," Maisey cut him off with a scathing stare.

"Told me what?" I asked.

"Archer's being entirely mysterious," said another girl, whose dark purple hair matched her eyeshadow and the snobbish perma-pout on her lips. "Said we had to wait for you. Welcome you properly or whatever."

"It's fine, we were happy to wait," said Maisey, the corner of her mouth curled in a way that set me on edge. I had a feeling I was about to be hazed, which was...*fine*, I guess? I'd never been much of a joiner. And I pretty much collected strays as friends, so this would be new. "Shall I get you a drink?"

"No need, no need, dear friends," Archer said, appearing with a tray of drinks and a theatrical grin on his face, stretching that dimple on his left cheek to its breaking point. He bowed to me. "I have arrived, my lady has arrived. The festivities can begin!"

As if some unseen theater manager had heard their cue, the lights overhead snapped out, casting the entire mansion into twilight as the music pumped on, never ending. Overhead, the chandelier festooned with the paper moon began to glow, all but transforming into the real thing. The stars and banister decorations glowed silver in the dim light. And fog crept out of vents near the floor, trailing along the wood and carpet around our feet, before filling the first level of the room, plunging us all into the clouds.

My skin prickled as I felt Archer's head land on my shoulder, his stubble tickling my neck, shivers like roots burrowing deep into my skin. "Welcome to heaven."

Archer's group raised their cups, almost crushing them together, before downing them in one gulp. I took a quick breath for courage and swigged my own drink back, grimacing as the bitter, *bitter, BITTER* flavor hit my tongue. I couldn't get it down fast enough.

"That's disgusting," I said.

"Tell me about it." This girl had dark, thick braids down to her waist. She giggled, producing something dark and round in the low light. There was a small *snick* sound and the glint off a blade as she cut the ball in half. She handed me half. "Chase it with this. Use your tongue."

Anything to get the bitter taste out of my mouth. Halfway to my face, I realized it was a passionfruit. The tart tang neutralized the worst of it.

All around us, the guests began to howl. Servants appeared carrying silver platters of white animal masks—rabbits and birds and bears, horses and wolves and dogs and bats. Before I could pick one, Mary's form materialized through the fog with her own tray holding a delicate golden mask clearly meant for me. Archer plucked it from her tray before I could see what it was and brought it to my face. I traced the bottom line of the mask—which fell just above my mouth—around to Archer's hand as he tied the ribbon against my hair with a feather-touch caress.

"Is that all right?" he asked, coming around to admire me. "Looks perfect on you."

He removed the other thing from the tray for me, too, holding up my costume for the evening. My stomach rolled; balled up in his hands, it seemed like so little fabric. Archer gave a gentle smile, leaning into me so I could hear him over the howls and music. His warm breath curled up my cheek, behind my ear, sending shivers.

"I mentioned the party and Judy sent it for you. You can change in the bathroom over there. Mary will take your clothing and things to your room."

I think I glided to the bathroom, sealing myself away still in darkness, afraid to turn on the lights, catch sight of myself in the mirror, and realize how much none of this suited me. I didn't go to all-but-adult pajama parties or dress like girls who looked like Maisey. Past humiliations by girls who only dreamed of looking like her left me shivering with doubt. My immediate instinct was to slip out and away to my rooms before Archer realized.

But again, I didn't want the day to end like that. As terrifying as it was to be so far from any comfort zone I'd ever known, this all looked so *fun*. It was strange to admit, but…I wanted to be the sort of person who had these types of experiences. Or at least to know I didn't like them because I had tried them. Besides, both my mom and Scarlett had commanded me to try out this exact sort of thing. Okay, maybe not half-naked pajama parties, but…when in Scotland.

I flicked on the bathroom light like ripping off a Band-Aid and studied myself in the mirror—Archer had placed a bear mask on my face. Its sharp teeth pressed into my cheeks, its ears rose round and textured from my head, and I felt…powerful. Beautiful. Behind this mask, I could be whoever I wanted to be, even if only for the night.

Judy hadn't done me wrong, either. For one thing, she'd given me pants. They and the camisole fit me like a glove, not too revealing but hugging landscapes I never knew I possessed. For the first time in my life, I felt made anew. Anything was possible. Cassian's face drifted into my mind for a moment, but I put him away just as quickly. I couldn't have him. He wasn't even here tonight. Even if he was, he'd made it clear he wanted me gone. But the girl I saw in the mirror didn't need to worry about him; she could have anyone, if she was open to it.

I emerged from the bathroom excited about the night to come. Mary's beaming grin as she took my things gave me an extra dash of courage, which was only emboldened when I saw Archer in his own bear mask standing with rabbit-Maisey. His mouth dropped open at the sight of me in the fog.

He left her, making a beeline straight for me.

He took my hand without a word and guided me into the thick of things, making space between others who were already dancing.

"Won't Maisey mind us dancing together?" I asked.

A baffled, half-grin bloomed on his face. "*Maisey*? Why would she mind?"

"She said you two were…*friends*." I hoped I wouldn't have to spell it out for him.

"*Blech*," he said. "It'd be like kissing my sister. She's just a friend from school. And she couldn't hold a candle to..."

His hands found my waist and he met my giggle with his own as I wrapped my arms around his shoulders. He was too tall to dance with like this. I tried to step back, but he only moved with me, his eyes unwavering, his hands pulling me to him, almost off my feet.

"Ready for the roar?"

I nodded, unsure. Still holding me, he leaned back and roared in a way I'd only seen footballers from New Zealand do it when they did the haka. It was guttural, powerful, pulled from the abdomen. He was glorious and shining. I joined him, then so did the rest of the dance floor, their masked faces tilted back. Deeper in the house, echoing down the halls, I could hear them all responding in the silver shadows.

Archer did it again, this time to me, watching me as I growled, matching him better this time. His proud, beaming smile was as intoxicating as his scent. Even hidden by the mask, he felt like the boy I'd met digging in the garden that night.

The smile on his face shifted then. The cocky bravado collapsed. The gleam in his eye retreated behind sudden shyness. His grip on my waist softened with…fear? Caution? Anticipation? He looked nervous, staring at me like I might disappear if he blinked.

I'd never been kissed before, but I'd seen and read enough to know he wanted to.

"Kiss me," he said…and I went for it, rising onto my tiptoes and pulling him down toward me in the same motion. Our lips met like a spark; we had barely parted again when he wove his fingers around the back of my neck and drew me in again in one explosive moment, almost knocking me off my feet…save for his hands, which stabilized me until the initial exploration of each other's lips subsided. When I pulled back, I half expected that arrogant playboy smile from the stairs to greet me. Instead, I found his cautious gaze racing across my skin, examining my features for signs of rejection. He didn't find any. I was on tiptoes a second later, meeting his lips again, this time longer, deeper, hungrier. His tongue slid between my lips like a secret, grazing my canine tooth as it retreated again. My abdomen squeezed with longing as he suddenly drew back.

"I'm sorry," he said.

"Why?"

"I don't know." His happy laughter was everything.

In a flash, he took hold of my legs, guiding them around his waist for purchase, lifting me off the ground. I squealed with surprise.

"Archer!" I whisper-shouted. "What are you doing?"

"Admiring you," he said.

I glanced around nervously. The fog around us was so heavy I could barely see the nearest dancers. We were cocooned from prying eyes. Suddenly, Archer's hand was cupping my face, drawing my attention back to him.

"I'd never want to make you uncomfortable. Say the word and I'll put you down," he said. Then a grin broke across his face as he leaned toward my ear and purred, "*Please* don't say the word."

My stomach curled with joy as I watched him wait patiently for me to make my choice. I believed he would do exactly what I asked, either way, and that pleased me.

I willed myself to relax, letting my fingers skip across his skin like water dancing across the surface of a searing hot pan, then around to the nape of his neck, into the soft depths of his silky umber hair.

When the bear masks collided awkwardly between us, we guided each other's up onto our heads. I was entranced by the greedy desire in his eyes, his sweet breath against my skin. And there was something delicious in the fact that he could carry me so easily and still raise his warm, soft hand to sweep my hair behind my ear and pull me in for another kiss in the same movement. My legs squeezed around him—I think surprising both of us. The next kiss was soft, gentle. A peck. The next, our eyes were open, smiling. These staccato beats, the electric strikes of our tongues seeking each other in the darkness, were a kinetic conversation neither one of us wanted to end.

"You smell incredible."

I blushed, pulling back. In response, his hand went to my back to support me.

"What?" he said, breathy and nervous. "What's wrong? What did I say?"

"Well, I've been digging around in the forest all day. Didn't have a chance to shower. I probably smell awful."

"The forest?"

I nodded in the direction of the window, but I couldn't see four feet away from me in the fog. He seemed to understand anyway. His smile faltered as he lowered me to the floor, which felt hard and unforgiving under my bare feet. And without the warmth of his blazing skin, the camisole did nothing to keep out the encroaching chill.

"Is something wrong?" I asked.

"No, of course not." He was lying. The smile on his lips didn't reach his eyes. "What were you doing out there?"

It seemed strange to hide things from him now. Didn't it? I could still feel his kisses on my skin, the surprising caress of his fingernails along my scalp where he'd run them through my hair. Then again, we were the same people we had been five minutes ago before we'd lost ourselves in the moment. He was still the boy who ran hot and cold as it suited him, like right now, but if the truth chilled him, then it was good to know.

"I was just looking for something Will asked me to find."

"Something to find? In the woods? Natalie, all you'll find out there are bugs and more stinging nettles."

"And creatures," I joked, thinking of those terrifying eyes…thinking of that bizarre configuration of beasts that had found me this afternoon and led me into the forest. Of course, there was no way he'd believe me if I told him that.

Archer smiled and playfully pulled my bear mask down over my eyes again. "No bears, I hope."

"No, just a deer, some eagles, a fox—"

The last vestiges of his dimpled smile disappeared so suddenly he looked like he had seen a ghost.

"A fox, did you say?"

"Yeah. Beautiful, red."

His head pricked toward the east windows. He even squinted his eyes as if he could see perfectly well through the fog. If it was possible, his open robe stretched even tauter against his chiseled frame.

"Is something wrong—"

"You careless child!" A dark figure cut between us like a sudden closing gate. In the fog, it took a moment to recognize Cassian in his dark, serious clothes.

"Give over, Cass."

"*What were you thinking!*" It wasn't really a question. There was so much disdain and disappointment in his voice it wasn't even a stern reprimand. It was a missile. "You said it would be a normal party like all the others, not…an initiation."

A cruel sneer split Archer's mouth. "Jealous, brother?"

Cassian didn't reply, but through the haze, I could see his body shaking. His fist hung in a tight ball by his side. He deigned to look at me for half a second, and I saw what looked like genuine pain there.

My brow furrowed. I wanted to laugh in disbelief. There was no way they were talking about me. And there was definitely no way high and mighty Cassian, who thought of me as nothing more than an encroaching dilettante, would be this upset about a kiss.

"It was supposed to be her *choice*," said Cassian after a moment. "That may not mean much to you, but it will to *her* when she can't take it back."

I wanted to laugh again, to ease the tension with a little harsh honesty. What choice did he think I had? Until a few minutes ago when Archer's mouth had met mine in an unexpected frenzy, I hadn't even thought *he* was a real option. Hell, I *still* didn't think so. Not once the lights cut back on and he saw someone like Maisey again, "just friends" or not. Never mind her, someone like him would forget about me after turning his first corner in any major city. This was just a fun, meaningless moment for him and a new experience for me.

Laughter punctured the wall of fog around us. For a moment, Maisey and the others were visible, plainly ogling us from the far couches. Even with crossed arms, a scowl, and bunny ears, Maisey looked gorgeous. I felt my skin flame with humiliation. It *had* just been a bit of fun, right? Or had it been a bit of fun at my expense?

"Nothing happened, you dramatic idiot," said Archer.

Cassian motioned to the paper moon overhead. "Nothing."

"It's just a bit of paper! And it doesn't matter anyway," he said. "We have bigger problems."

Cassian tore off Archer's bear mask and shoved it into his chest. "You think?"

"She saw a *fox* in the Eastern Wood."

Once again, the air went out of the conversation, but this time, it went out of every conversation in the room. Everywhere I looked, a group had stopped whatever they were doing to stare.

Cassian turned his silver eyes on me. "Where?"

"O-Out there," I said, gesturing vaguely toward the wood. "So what?"

"It means a change of plans." Archer grabbed my hand and squeezed. His eyes shimmered with mischief as he turned to the other guests. "Seamus, sound the horn. We're going on a fox hunt."

CHAPTER 17

"Out of the question," said Cassian. "She stays with me."

Everyone—including the servants—had assembled in the hollow outside the library still wearing their party negligees, as if it wasn't fifty degrees out here. Only a handful of us, including Maisey and me, had scrounged up coats, and I'd tamped down the *strong* desire to go find my real pants wherever Mary had taken them. The rest of the party had only put on their shoes and most held full party punch cups. Gathered together in such a strange, tight cluster of blinding white in the darkness, fitted with flashlights and masks, we looked like a cult preparing to swarm some unsuspecting township. The entire group was in a starter position, preparing to sprint off into the darkness on a "fox hunt." They'd been holding this position for the last two minutes while Cassian and Archer argued…about me.

"Are you serious?" asked Archer.

"You don't appreciate the full weight of what this will mean. Not even for yourself, let alone her."

"She can decide for herself."

"When? After?" Cassian leaned into Archer. He seemed to think—incorrectly—that this would mean I couldn't hear him. "You can't control yourself and she doesn't know any better."

Archer looked sick of it. "Can't you embarrass me on a weekday?"

"Fine, but she's coming with me."

"I'm not going with you," I said finally. "Or you, Archer. Go be territorial somewhere else."

"Don't be ridiculous," said Archer. "You can't wander out there by yourself."

"You're right," I said, improvising. "I'll go with…Maisey."

"Hurrah," she said, her tone just sarcastic enough I took it at face value; she was stuck with me.

"But—"

"No. This is a party, isn't it? You've got everybody in limbo waiting for you. *I'm* freezing. Let's *go*."

A deep cackle sounded from near the far door to the library. Graham's wicked smile lit up the night as he lifted a starting pistol. "You heard my lady. Let the hunt begin!"

BANG!

The hundred or so people sprinted into the forest in a breaking swell of whoops and howls and screams. Maisey motioned for me to follow, and I did, not bothering to look back until we were several hundred yards into the forest, on the threshold where the house lighting faded away to absolute darkness beyond. When I finally looked behind me, I was surprised to see it wasn't Archer who had followed us, but Cassian. He wore his gloomy seriousness like a shroud. When he saw me looking, he set his eyes on his feet and continued his trudge.

"Great," said Maisey, spotting him, too. "We've been fully regulated to the loser group."

"What do you mean?" I asked.

Maisey turned to say something, glanced back at Cassian, and changed tact. "Let's just say the cool kids don't need chaperones."

"I'm sorry," I offered. "I didn't mean to lump you in with me."

She sighed then motioned for Cassian to come forward to help her over a fallen tree. When she was over, he offered his stiff hand to me. Our eyes locked on each other for a long moment, and I tried to read his thoughts; he looked so…disappointed in me.

"I'm not lumped in with you," said Maisey. "You're lumped in with me. You're the luckiest girl in the world."

"No," I said, shaking my head.

"You are—you just don't know it yet. You have your entire life ahead of you. This house. Master Archer, if you're so inclined…"

She smiled at me as we walked over a small bridge, dancing her fingers across the railing.

"Maybe this boy as well." She tossed her head toward Cassian, who had returned to his distant sentinel post behind us.

"Cassian can't stand me," I said. She chuckled. "I'm serious. He called me stupid the other day. He embarrassed me on TV. He—"

"Pulled your plaits on the playground?" asked Maisey.

I blushed, trying to think of something else to talk about.

"Is this sort of thing normal?" I gestured as a burst of flashlight beams and howls sprinted past us through the thick foliage.

"The hunt?" she asked. "Not really anymore. Foxes know better than to come here. Most do anyway."

"Maisey." Cassian's quiet voice was firm, and surprisingly loud considering how far he was behind us.

"It's not a…*real* hunt, though, right?" I asked. Some of the howls had taken on a sharp, serrated quality. Others flat out raked across my skin like steel wool. "We're not *trying* to kill an actual fox."

"They really didn't tell you anything, did they?"

"Damn it, Maisey, are you really this thick, or does being around Archer turn you into an absolute plonker?" Cassian was beside us with surprising speed. "Go join the others."

Maisey pouted cruelly at him. "If second fiddle says I must."

She turned and disappeared into the forest so silently it was like she'd never been there at all.

"What'd you do that for?" I asked. "I told you I didn't want to be out here with you."

"I heard you," he said, motioning me forward down the trail.

"I don't want you behind me, either," I said, wrapping the cropped coat I'd borrowed tighter around myself.

"As you say." In a millisecond, he shed his coat from his person and dropped it—and its luscious warmth—over my shoulders.

"I don't want this."

Before I could take it off, his hands were on my shoulders, keeping the coat in place. "You'll wear it and stop being combative for no reason."

"I'm only combative because you don't listen. You think so little of me."

His jaw tightened. "Likewise, Miss Damarand."

Those words actually hurt me to hear. It wasn't true and I wanted to tell him so, put the past behind us. But after this entire weird day, and his continued arms-length approach to friendship with me, he'd probably just insult me some more. Instead, I shifted focus.

"There's something that's really been bugging me," I said, watching him shift in preparation for whatever I asked. As if he already expected an accusation. "Are you really allergic to nettles?"

He blinked with surprise. "Oh, uh. Yes."

"Then why did you take me out into the meadows that first morning?"

"To show you—"

"I could've seen the land from the driveway."

"Yes, well, I didn't think—"

"*You* didn't think? I don't believe that."

He cleared his throat.

"I didn't get the chance to thank you for taking me," I said sincerely. "So, thank you. Now if we can just get you to stop treating me like an invading conqueror—"

Before I could finish, something large, hard, and white hit me like a speeding train, almost teleporting me to the ground at Cassian's feet before I even felt it. It was the kilt guy wearing a seal mask. I heard a retreating "Sorry, love!" as he bounded onward into the forest.

"Are you all right?" Cassian found purchase on my arms and brought me to my knees, eye to eye with him. "Were you scraped? Cut at all?"

"I'm fine."

"This is serious, Natalie. You need to check."

"I'm okay, Cass..." My voice trailed away. Under his hiked-up pant leg, I could see savage blotches of red nettle rash splattered across his shins like raw, fresh burns. The thought of the pain crawled into my heart and tore. "You need a doctor."

"It's nothing," he said. His hands cupped my face as he tilted it cautiously, studying my neck and chin. "You've got a small scratch here along your jawline. I think it's just from where you hit the ground. We'll go back and see to that."

We never got the chance. A sudden *drumming* shook the ground around us. I heard a wall of howls, yips, and barks as the stampeding feet of a dozen people kicked me off the trail. I was suddenly sliding, then falling down a slope in the pitch black, every rock, every twig, every pinecone scraping across my body. I hit something big, tearing along my rib cage, before rolling to a soft stop.

For a long moment, I lay there, allowing the pervasive pain to settle where actual damage had been done. I was *shaking*. Both coats and the golden bear mask were gone.

When I sat up, blood trickled from a gash along my ribs, soaking the beautiful satin cami and pants Judy had made me with hot crimson. Otherwise, the rest seemed cosmetic. More bruises across my legs and arms and a "road rash" across my hip that actually stung worse than the wound in my side.

I forced myself to my feet, using the fallen log that had punctured me to pull myself up. The forest was quiet here and lit faintly by the crescent moon. It was another place that felt like it was holding its breath.

And everywhere, a sickly floral scent of violets.

"NATALIE!" It was Archer; he sounded half crazed. I could hear others murmuring around him.

"Archer, I'm here! I'm hurt!"

"We're coming! Just stay there."

My flashlight had fallen a few feet away. I limped toward it, holding onto any sapling for dear life...but when I reached it, bending my torso seemed impossible. Spined arrows of blinding pain migrated into my arm and shoulder. Instead, I had to fiddle my foot out of my shoe and roll the flashlight up my leg. I hoped it'd be worth the effort to signal the others.

"Here. I'm here!"

I waved it frantically in one direction, swiveling to wave another, when something small and frantic caught my eye. The beam of light landed on a furry red creature like an old-timey prison spotlight. The fox froze in place, staring at me, in the closed jaw of something that looked like a miniature bear trap without teeth. It was the sort of thing that squeezed rather than cut, but the fact that this trap was gumming its leg rather than tearing into it didn't seem to matter. I could see fresh blood matted along the limb where it had tried to pry itself free.

Even worse, I could see a set of proud initials prominently lasered into the metal trap—*C.M.*

When the initial shock of my presence wore off, the fox began to whimper and gnaw at its leg, spilling more blood. There was already a black pool of it beneath its feet. It was horrendous.

"No-no-no! It's okay," I cooed, forgetting my own problems. "It's okay. I won't hurt you, I swear."

I edged forward and held out my hand about two feet in front of its face, wiggling my fingers to draw its attention. Then, in one sudden movement, I latched onto the scruff of its neck. *Her* neck. She screamed, writhing, but I held on, avoiding her claws and fangs to trigger the trap's release. The terrible contraption fell away with a dull *thunk*, and she stopped fighting.

"Please don't bite me..." As gently as I could, I tossed her away toward the brush. I could hear the others bearing down on us. "Go! You'll be okay. Hurry!"

But she lingered. Her golden eyes studied me. After what felt like an eternity, when the whooping howls of the others bored down on top of us, foghorn loud, she finally slipped away. Sweet relief flooded through me when she was finally safe, followed swiftly by cold, simmering rage.

"Natalie?"

"I'm here." I waved the light again and Archer was there, kneeling to scoop me into his arms. He didn't notice the thing I was bringing back with me.

"Careful, it hurts."

"We'll call the doctor right away."

Masked faces peered at us in passing, but I didn't see Cassian.

A few moments later, we arrived back in the library, and the house staff scattered like barn mice to fetch the doctor, fetch some water, fetch some painkillers. I was coddled onto one of the couches after Archer swept a mountain of red solo cups into the sea that littered the floor. The main house lights were on again. In the normal golden light, the party decorations looked extravagant and gaudy and the masks cheap. The guests were just visible at the far end of the hallway, in the main foyer, all save Maisey, who whispered at Archer in tones I couldn't hear. Her exaggerated frown probably worked wonders in normal situations; she probably had men falling over themselves to make her smile again. But now, it was the frown of a little kid wondering if she'd be punished for leaving me.

Archer finally left her to kneel before me.

"I'm so sorry, Natalie. I am *so* sorry."

But I didn't need his apologies.

"Where's Cassian?"

"Cass? Why?"

"He was there when I fell. Did he come back?"

"Yes, but—"

"I need to talk to him now. I need to talk to all the staff."

"Can't it wait until morning? The doctor is on the way."

"No. Right now, please."

Archer shifted awkwardly before leaving, Maisey trailing behind him. Then it was just me. With the fog gone, I could see my reflection in the window; I looked so wrecked it was almost funny. There were still branches in my hair, leaves hanging out of my bra. Twigs at high speed had scraped their way across my cheeks, leaving bloody whiskers. A rock had stained my collarbone with bruised purple. My pants had ripped, exposing a corner of my purple underwear. A color theme was emerging, and I laughed at the dark thought, wincing where my lip had split. Cassian had been worried about a *scratch*, but that little wound had been long erased by the rest.

"Natalie?"

Cassian entered, pressing a massive ice pack to the back of his head. Little nicks and bruises peppered his face as well. Archer and Maisey loitered by the door as Cassian came to me. His expression was the most readable it had ever been—I'd recognize that sort of self-loathing guilt anywhere.

"Please forgive me," he started. I didn't need his apologies, either. "I got knocked out in the fray, and someone carried me back. I would *never* have left you—"

"What is this?" I cut him off, holding up the trap with his initials on it that I'd taken off the fox. "It's a bear trap, right?"

"Not likely," snorted Maisey. Archer cut her off with a shushing sound.

"Then what is it?"

"It's a leghold trap," said Cassian. "It catches the animal's leg so the pelt remains unspoiled."

"For foxes?" I pressed.

"Yes," he said. "Whatever's the matter?"

"How many are out there?"

"I don't know. We don't keep track."

"So, they're everywhere?" I asked.

"In the woods… Did something happen?"

"You need to remove them, Cassian." He blinked. I turned to Archer. "Are there monogrammed traps out there with your initials on them, too?"

"Natalie, you're hurt," Archer murmured. You're not thinking clearly."

"Don't tell me how I think," I said calmly.

The staff began to trickle in behind him as Mary appeared. "The doctor's here!"

I held out my hand to Cassian. "Help me up."

"You shouldn't—"

I shook my hand until he took it. Archer leapt forward and supported my back as I grunted through the pain, shaking. I turned to the staff. "I want all of these gone. Go out in pairs tomorrow during the day and get them out of there. Every single one. I don't want to see these anywhere."

The staff's eyes wandered to Archer and Cassian, waiting for confirmation.

"Don't look at them. I'm telling you to do this. I don't want any traps like this used here. They're cruel and painful. Something was trying to gnaw its leg off to get out of it when I found it."

The boys practically leapt forward. "Was it a—"

"No, it wasn't a fox. A rabbit or something. It got away before I could see. The point is no living creature should get trapped in this and left to die. You got me?"

I waited…for literally any sign that they, in fact, were listening to me at all. I didn't want to play the part of *Mrs. Pompous-what*, as the housekeeper had called it, but I would. The rage I'd felt in the forest had congealed to bitter disappointment. The accident was what it was—I'd have a scar, some pain, whatever—but we'd stopped the fun, silly, warm party to go hunt something to death in the freezing forest like a pack of crazed zombies.

I put on my strongest American twang, raising my voice like a drill sergeant. "*Do you got me?*"

"Yes, my lady…Yes, ma'am…Will do, my lady…"

I tossed the trap to the floor, happy to be rid of the weight, and stumbled toward the door, moving around Archer's outstretched arms to keep him from helping me.

"Natalie, you don't have to be…silly about it," Archer said.

"Oh, but I *want* to be silly. Absolutely goofy. Real slippery banana about it."

"Huh?"

I paused just long enough to look back at both of them, catching the tiniest smile on Cassian's face.

"No. Traps," I annunciated, smiling incredulously. "That's all I'm asking. It's not that hard."

With that, I turned and let Mary wedge her shoulder under my arm and help me toward the doctor I could see waiting in the hall. The boys and staff followed at a distance like a flock of ducklings.

“Hello, my lady, I’m Dr. Martin, but you may call me Alice,” she said. “I’ll examine you right in here and see if you need to go to the hospital.”

“Lovely to meet you, Alice,” I said, pausing to motion back to Cassian. “You’ll examine him afterward, right?”

“Y-yes of course.”

“Great. He’s hiding an allergic reaction on his legs, just FYI. Maybe he thinks it’s manly to repress it or something, but it’s not. It’s dumb and it needs to be dealt with…I’ve never lived with boys before.”

The doctor smiled. “Of course, my lady.”

The last thing I saw were two chastened boys watching me close the door on them.

CHAPTER 18

"You *kissed* your stepbrother!"

"Gross, Scarlett, don't say it like that."

"Talk about burying the lead. You should have started with that."

It'd been three days since the party. Mom and Scarlett had taken turns being my constant phone companions since the doctor bandaged me up, prescribed me bedrest and loopy painkillers, and left me to listen to the party continue on without me for the remainder of the weekend. It had been three days of thudding bass and giggling, howling teenagers rampaging through the halls. I didn't hate them for it, but let's just say the roiling envy in my stomach had simmered low and slow to something syrupy and sticky against my ribs. Mercifully, it had finally ended all at once on the fourth day. I'd cricked my neck from my awkward spot in bed while I watched Archer wave away a fleet of retreating cars.

"I mean, I've been perving on their socials, and they *are* hot, so…no judgy…but…"

"But?"

"I watched that heinous BBC interview," Scar said. "Why do they have British accents if they're from Scotland?"

"Ask our European History teacher," I said. "The kiss just happened. I didn't think about it."

"I am living vicariously through you, girly," Scarlett said, her voice high with excitement. "I just like hearing it happened at all."

"Well, I'm glad *you* liked it—that's really all that matters."

She snorted before taunt-singing at me, "You liked it. You like him. You're living a fairy tale full of forest animals and hot guys clamoring for your attention."

My heart sank a little. Archer hadn't visited once since that night, but that might have been because Bruce had rushed back home the next day to check on me and take the boys for yet another closed-door chiding. Random shouted words had reached me from down the hallway—*unconscionable...dangerous...wanton disregard for decorum.* Ah yes, because decorum mattered so much when your ribs were bruised.

But I knew that Archer cared, at least. Every morning around four-thirty, when the last of the party music finally died, steady footsteps would walk up and down the hall outside my rooms. Approaching the door, retreating, approaching, creaking the floor so loudly he couldn't help but know I could hear it. Almost like he wanted to come in but couldn't.

Mary had flitted in and out, day and night since. Making a loud ruckus in the other rooms. Fluffing pillows. Bringing me snacks. Helping me bathe. Reapplying fresh bandages. All while refusing to look me in the eye. I didn't know if it was out of guilt or resentment for telling the staff to go pull all the traps out of the forest. Mrs. Margolyes, on the other hand, stormed in each morning like a headmistress to lay a warm, concerned hand on my forehead and tell me the to-dos of the day. Each time, she gave me a play-through of the daily scolding she gave the boys. And each time, she almost begged for me to forgive them, as if she thought I'd hold it against them forever.

"I've given Archer a good talking to," she said. "But go sweet on the lad, he's gallus and glaikit, that yin."

I appreciated her visits as vocabulary lessons. *Gallus,* mischievous. *Glaikit*, foolish. But also because she was actually willing to tell me things. When the nightly processional outside my door had started, I had asked her about it.

"The poor boy feels just awful about what happened to you, my lady," she said.

"Could you tell him he can come in?"

"Of course."

But Archer didn't come to see me even then. I didn't know why I didn't tell Scarlett that the rejection sat bruised and tender inside me and hurt worse than the scrapes. The only sign I'd had that he cared at all was the giant heap of disarmed fox traps that greeted me the second morning when I looked out my window. I'd watched a garbage truck arrive to haul the things away.

"What are you going to do now?" asked Scarlett after the conversation had lulled.

“You mean when I’m allowed to move again?” I asked. “I’m gonna find that key.”

I’d begun my report to Scarlett at the very beginning. With my search of the grounds and the strange encounter I’d had in the forest, finding that great stone carving of an alder tree made of animals with the keyhole at its center. I’d also told her Will’s riddle for the first time, fully prepared for her to make fun of me for it. Instead, she’d sent me a video of her bedroom whiteboard at home, where she had written the riddle and started deconstructing it, swelling my heart with gratitude and love.

“If I think of anything, I’ll let you know,” she said before I heard a door open on her end. “Gotta go! I’ll talk to you later. Feel better. And, you know, if the fun brother backs off, try the other one on for size. Brooding can be sexy, too.”

“GOODBYE, Scarlett!” I said, ending the call to the sound of her cackling laughter.

By the fifth day, the cozy comfort of my room had become its own prison. I mean, I was an introvert, happy with a picturesque reading corner and a good story. But I could only watch so many movies, read so many books, and stare at so many tiny torn edges in the tapestry wallpaper overhead before I wanted to *get out*. Especially when every day began with watching the sky outside my massive window flare to life in a blaze of color. Bushes and trees were in full bloom across the property; and the flowers…the beds on the front lawn and the borders of the driveway were alive with golden, purple, and *black* flowers in the repeated Mahon tartan pattern.

By the seventh day, even the beauty felt tedious. Mocking. The early morning footsteps outside my door had lost their romance, too. Why wouldn’t Archer just *come in* already? The party had ended days before; he had no excuse now. Not to mention, someone had been rooting around at the far end of my rooms. I could hear things being brought in, but trips to the bathroom revealed nothing was out of place or different and when I asked Mrs. Margolyes, she only said I’d see for myself once I was “in working order” again.

Plus…something had changed in the last twelve hours or so. Something in the movement of the staff. Mary had finally begun chatting to me again, but she was jumpier than I'd ever seen her. Distracted and giggly, like her mind was away wandering. Mrs. Margolyes had trundled in as prickly as ever, apologizing that she had *so much to do today* and *couldn't stay long*, even though she always only stayed a few minutes.

Through my window, I could see other staff members hurrying around, pulling things off large trucks that trundled into view at the crack of dawn and woke me from my half slumber.

"Not another party…?"

Perhaps it was a fear of missing out, or an excuse to leave this once-comfortable bed that had started to feel like a torture device, but I forced myself to my feet. The pain in my side whispered now, rather than shouting. A cursory glance in the mirror revealed the scratches and bruises had faded as well.

The house clattered and crowed with activity. Just stepping into the hallway brought the harried noises of movement rushing at me like I'd entered a construction site. Each staff member I passed nodded politely at me, wearing the same distracted expression as Mary and Mrs. Margolyes.

"Ah, my lady! Good to see you looking so well this morning." Bruce barreled toward me out of the boys' wing, wearing his own brand of preoccupation.

"What's going on?"

"General repairs," he said, obviously lying.

"Did someone crash through a wall?" I joked.

"Good one, my lady," he said, blowing past the question entirely. He wrapped an arm around me and turned me back toward my rooms. "I was actually on my way to see you. I think, given everything that's happened, you should get away for a bit. I've arranged a wonderful weekend adventure to Edinburgh for you so you can see the sights, meet the people. Just enjoy your new adoptive home for a bit."

"Oh," I said, surprised.

"No need to thank me," he replied. "Mary's already prepared a bag for you. All you need to do is get dressed, and we'll be on our way."

"We're leaving today?"

"Right now, miss. No better time for an adventure, I always say." He had clearly never said this before in his life. "But wonderful news. Judy's pieces arrived last night for you. Truly spectacular. Mary's arranged them in your walk-in wardrobe, so feel free to wear whatever you like."

With a gentle pat on my back, he delivered me to my rooms and physically waited there until I'd closed the door on him. Honestly, his strange mood aside, I wasn't in a position to argue, nor did I want to. The thought of an entire weekend in one of the most beautiful cities in the world sounded like heaven to me.

Mary was already waiting for me in the wardrobe when I entered, but I barely noticed. I was struck entirely frozen at the *sight* of the clothing Judy had made for me. Every hanger and drawer was filled with dazzling colors and patterns that connected in a palette I couldn't understand but *adored*. Mary had already arranged several outfit options and left them to hang at the ends of shelves for me. Every. Single. One was a revelation. Judy had taken my vague request for a vintage explorer vibe and elevated it to goddess-tier. I couldn't take it in all at once. Masculine shapes with feminine fabrics. Feminine shapes inspired by things I'd only seen on men before. Plaid capris and skirts in Mahon tartan. Cashmere sweaters in earth tones. Cream tops with lace touches. Patterned blouses that looked like Moroccan tiles and stained glass. A cinch-waist top made by layering a sheer steel-blue fabric hand-embroidered with the moon and stars over champagne satin. Something a note from Judy said was a Parisian belle epoque Montmartre striped jumper. A black puff sleeve top that totally modernized some ancient style I'd seen in one of the downstairs portraits. And several svelte sweaters that fit me to perfection, like I had slipped a bodysuit on. She had even made me multiple sets of "house trousers," as Mary called them. Comfortable blue jeans and linen shorts I was clearly only meant to wear where no one else would see me. Most of the pants were long, loose trousers that clung to my hips like a mold before elongating my legs in flowing drapery and coming to a soft stop at my ankles so I could wear flats with them. Although, I suspected they wanted flats to be the exception rather than the rule. Judy had only sent two pairs—a set of sneakers embroidered to high heaven with woodland imagery and perfunctory black ballerina flats decorated with golden thistles. They sat on the *literal wall of shoes* that crowded one end of the closet.

Along the opposite wall, lit like works of art, three formal gowns hugged headless dress forms exactly my size. The first, a V-neck, long-sleeved, golden knee-length dress made with sparkling lace, wrapped at the waist with a faux leather and rope belt. The second, a green one-shoulder gown saturated in Swarovski crystals, with a dramatic single sleeve that dove past hand-length almost to the floor.

The third was *different*. Almost impossible to describe without pointing out how much it resembled...well...a wedding dress. Champagne elegance. A sweeping, dramatic silhouette that swelled into a *gorgeous*, ethereal bramble-thorn collar that was almost Elizabethan in proportions, rising above where my head would be. When I looked closely, unusual details popped out at me. The sleeves were lined in a delicate, soft brown fur with a texture I'd never seen before. Tiny golden thistles and white bells of heather were affixed to the collar like pearls. Strangest of all, I thought I could see the initials *N.M.* discreetly woven into the stitching on the bodice.

"Bit formal for Edinburgh, my lady," said Mary, after I'd stood gaping at the last gown for what seemed like ten minutes.

"Where would I even wear something like this?"

"Bless you, I don't know," she said, laughing. "But that Judy sure is an artist, isn't she?"

"She really is."

Another ten minutes of perusing found me in one of those velvety-soft pairs of black trousers and a green sweater that slid across my skin like a cloud. The shoes—the lowest-heeled, non-flat pair I could find on the wall—would take some getting used to.

Mary sat me down at the vanity and transformed my wavy tumbleweed of bed hair into a beautiful, just-messy-enough braid. Then, to complete the look, she handed me a pair of vintage jeweled earrings she told me had once belonged to Cassian's mother.

"I don't think I could—"

"I've already asked him, my lady. He said you were welcome."

When she helped me stand up again, I took in the whole look in the full-length mirror and my stomach clenched with excitement. For the first time in my entire life, I looked like the version of myself I'd always seen in my head. The bright-eyed exotic dreamer girl sipping tea on the veranda of a safari lodge before catching a cab to the airport to fly to any cosmopolitan city I wanted.

"Lovely, miss," said Mary. Her scattered look from earlier had vanished, replaced by a smile so sincere I felt like a bride.

Even more so when I emerged into the hallway. A passing worker wearing a toolbelt paused, his eyes widening as he stepped to the side of the hall to let me pass, even though the hall was several times the pair of us in width.

Walking down the main stairs and through the foyer brought the same reaction from passing maids and servants. They paused to watch me leave, beaming, curtsying to me with hushed *my lady's*.

Bruce met me on the front stairs with eyes so wide I thought he was having a stroke for a second.

"A vision, my lady," was all he said.

He offered me his hand to help me to the driveway, where the driver, Dave, waited by the car with a wide grin that squinted his eyes half to closing. Together, they fed me into the backseat of the Rolls Royce like a delicate piece of fine china.

"You brought your pain medication, my lady?" asked Bruce.

"Yes, thank you."

"Any discomfort at all, you just let me know," added Dave.

The door shut me in, and I inhaled deeply before they could take their seats up front, dreaming of some peace and quiet alone in the city.

At least until the door opposite me opened unexpectedly and Cassian swept in wearing a midnight blue peacoat around his shoulders like a cape, apparently embracing his inner supervillain. The scowl on his face, like he was calculating some life-or-death math problem, only exaggerated the effect.

"Morning, Miss Damarand," he said, not bothering to look at me.

"Oh," I said, confused by his presence. He didn't seem to want to be here, and I didn't want the weekend ruined by a reluctant companion. "More business in the city?"

"Bruce asked me to accompany you. Show you around."

"Well, if you have other things to do, I love exploring and...I don't need a chaperone."

"The incident at last week's party would suggest otherwise."

My eyebrow rose high onto my forehead. Did he even know how to speak without being insufferable? It was enough to make me laugh—at him, of course.

When he began to shift, searching for his seatbelt past the thick wool folds of his coat, I couldn't help myself. I reached over and pulled the buckle out so he could see it.

"You know what comes next, don't you?" I teased.

His stormy eyes met mine, defensive and suspicious.

“I don’t need a mother, you know,” he said, taking the buckle from me and clicking himself in.

“Great. I don’t want to be one.”

I turned away to look out the window. I knew he was staring; not only could I see him in the window’s reflection, but I could feel his gaze locked on the back of my neck, my hair. When his gaze reached my ear and he saw I was wearing his mother’s earrings, I heard him inhale sharply and almost turned…but I resisted the temptation. If he was going to be a broody bore from the get-go, I’d happily have the last word and leave him to it.

But in the temporary silence, something else drew my attention. My mom liked to say that people went loony sometimes; some days just…brought it out in them. Today seemed to be one of them. The same restless energy that had distracted the staff was everywhere around us as we drove away. The air had gone strange, like the world was electrified somehow.

If it hadn’t been for that mad charge in the air, I might not have noticed the peculiar woman standing at the edge of the Eastern Wood at all. She caught my eye as Dave turned off the long driveway onto the main passing road. Hair like rusted bronze. Eyes bright and focused on our car. So rigid, so still, she seemed more statue than human. I watched her watch me until our car passed out of view, and an uncomfortable shiver squirmed through my neck.

Bruce seemed to sense my pensive mood.

“I’ve arranged a fabulous itinerary of the city and made reservations for dinner tonight at Timberyard. Vegetarian for you, of course. If there are any sights you’d like to see, just let me know and I can arrange private viewings of those as well.”

We arrived at the Edinburgh city limits before Bruce stopped talking, and even then, it was only to point out some new, more beautiful urban detail. The entire place was a gothic relic, modernized. There was no mistaking how it had inspired the world of a certain boy wizard, either. Magic permeated every square inch of it, from cobblestone to tower. The fact that it was rainy and gray—what Bruce called Edinburgh’s *formal uniform*—only elevated its beauty. And it *was* beautiful.

Dave drove us right into the heart of it, giving me a little tour, past the Castle, past the surprising spire of the Scott Monument, and around to Moray Place, a circle of exquisite Georgian townhouses wrapped around a central park, before pulling to a stop on Ann Street in front of a four-story Georgian terraced house born of golden bricks and the golden ratio. Symmetrical mullioned sash and case windows drank in the natural light; flowers festooned every inch of its sizable front garden.

The others abandoned the car before I could ask them where we were, but it became apparent pretty immediately. Bruce opened the front door for Cassian, who stormed past without a word, before lingering to hold the door open for me.

"Welcome, my lady."

"Is this—"

"Your house. One of twenty-three, last time I counted."

"I might need a map of those, too," I said, a little shaken.

"Of course," he replied.

I entered with a single thought parading itself around in my head—the foyer was almost the size of my mom's entire apartment in Pennsylvania. Each room we encountered afterward only compounded that thought, their size exaggerated by the original, foot-thick crown moldings gilding the walls of every single room like frosting, while a black marble, double-facing fireplace ran from roof to foundation like a dark minimalist spike, staking the building to the ground. And all four stories centered around a spiral staircase, which was wrapped around a circular single-person elevator that looked like it had been torn from some historic art deco building and put to use here.

But the sheer size was nothing compared to the *atmosphere*. Only the house's facade had remained faithful to some bygone tradition. The inside had been renovated into livable art. I'd seen places like this in architectural magazines or behind models in high-end photoshoots or in the movies of fantastical worldbuilding directors.

The walls were textured black over some dark metallic base that caught the natural light like hidden gold. Pops of black and white and patina exaggerated the curved, irregular furniture, which had clearly been custom designed to fit the space, yet still appeared decadent and loungeable. Even though this house "only" had thirteen rooms, each had its own distinct flavor. The upper two floors were all bedrooms and bathrooms, one blue, one green, one gray, and one a yellow that looked out over the back garden and matched the yellow vining flowers curled around the windows' edges. I took this last one as my bedroom before venturing down to the garden-level kitchen, which looked like someone had splashed oil everywhere before flash-freezing it into countertops and islands with waterfall edges. This flowed into the forest green dining room where a stocky hand-carved table sat beside a serving bar that ran along the fireplace mantel. Bruce explained it used the fire to keep food warm. Beyond that, I found my favorite spot in the house: a glass solarium that intruded into the garden like a submersible surfacing in the flowerbeds.

"Is it everything you thought it'd be?"

I turned away from the dazzling blossoms to find Cassian staring at me from the doorway.

"I didn't know it existed, but…" It was hard to take my eyes off the garden; with everything in full bloom, I felt like a fairy hidden in a bouquet.

"But?"

"It's the sort of place you dream about, growing up without money," I said finally. "A wish you make, never expecting it to come true."

"A wish only made possible by my father's death."

Annnd he ruined it.

"Could you just be nice, maybe?" I snapped. "I didn't kill him, you know. I didn't ask for any of this. I'm just as surprised as you are that he named me, and if it's not too much to ask, I'd like to enjoy this in peace, okay?"

Cassian nodded before stepping backward through the doorway and disappearing like a ghost. I lowered myself onto the couch, wondering if I'd have every little joy soured by a rich boy's jealousy. But then, like a balm, a soft rain began to fall overhead, pinging the glass in a melodious patter, cocooning me in the fantasy of the garden again. Warmth billowed in from the fireplace as I heard someone build the fire. I leaned my head back against the couch's delicious pillows, and dreams came with the rain, washing worries and frustrations straight down the gutter.

Bruce woke me hours later and helped me off the couch.

"Almost dinner time, my lady," he said.

"I can't believe I fell asleep."

He smiled at some private thought.

"What?" I asked.

"William used to nap here, too. I didn't visit him here often—this was his own private sanctuary, where he came to escape, even from me—but when he allowed it, I'd always find him snoring away 'under the flower veil' as he called it."

Cassian was already waiting in the car by the time I changed into a lush cream sweater dress Mary had packed for me. Again, he didn't look at me, didn't acknowledge my presence, as Bruce helped me lower into the seat. Cassian just stared out into the purple twilight like some sort of undead sentinel brought to life by a cruel doctor.

It was a little more than a mile to the restaurant, which was deceptively low-key for being one of only five Michelin-starred restaurants in the city. I'd assumed I'd experience black tie sumptuousness and waiters in coattails and chandeliers made of some sort of crystal and built by blind nuns in the Swiss Alps or something. Instead, Dave delivered us to a black-framed, three-paneled red door that looked like the opening to a garage. There wasn't even a line.

The car door opened beside me, but I was surprised to see Dave wasn't the one who had opened it. Cassian stood there, holding out his hand for me to take. I glanced ahead. Bruce was quite settled in the front seat.

"You're not coming with us?"

"Business, my lady, and I'm afraid Dave and I *are* running late." He lifted his eyes to the sky, to the last pink line of light standing between us and sundown. "But don't worry. I've spoken with Cass. He's promised to take great care of you tonight."

But would he be fun? I didn't ask that.

I took Cassian's warm hand, watching for signs of resignation, maybe disgust. Instead, his eyes were on the wounded area on my abdomen, and his other hand was acting like a bumper again, to prevent a potential fall.

I was learning quickly that this city guarded its best secrets in unexpected ways. The host bowed to me as we entered and turned a corner into the main room where people were already dining under naked dangling light bulbs and giant, aromatic dandelion-shaped bursts of dried flowers.

"The Shed is available, if you would prefer to dine privately, sir," said the maître d.

"No, our table is fine, thank you, Sam."

I followed them to a small table in the far back corner, which seemed to be a place of high honor in the restaurant, lit by its own string of lights and perfumed by fresh flowers instead of dried ones.

Other diners eyed us as we sat down, their smiling whispers a burbling stream of noise around us. They seemed to be staring at *me*...maybe they'd seen the BBC interview and thought they were in for a show. *Embarrassed heiress eats too much at dinner—more at 11.*

Or maybe they were looking at Cassian. My mind knew it made an obvious sort of sense. He was absurdly attractive; he'd probably brought dozens of girls here before to show off, as any rich Oxford boy would. My heart, however, *hated* the thought of it. Them. Girls I'd never even seen, whom he obviously liked more than me. It was a ridiculous, random, intrusive thought, but knowing that didn't soften its effect. The jealousy sat rancid inside me, poisoning my self-esteem.

"Come here often?" I asked.

"Not really," he said. "My father helped finance this restaurant. It's pretty good."

"Oh yes," I said playfully. "Pretty good. Only the one Michelin star so far."

"I didn't mean—"

A dapper waiter appeared with a giant platter of various breads and compound butters, cutting off Cassian's retort.

"Welcome, welcome!" he said, his Scottish drawl slow and deep and friendly. "Can I get you anythin' to drink, sir? My lady?"

"I'll have a MaCallan," said Cassian.

"Of course, sir."

"And perhaps a soda for the lady," added Cassian.

"Perhaps not," I said, putting on a sweet smile. "Could I have a Meadowsweet, please?"

"It'd'a be my pleasure," the waiter replied with a deep trill of joy. "Now the chef *is* out tonight."

"Of course," said Cassian.

"But *Michael* is filling in. He's prepared five fabulous courses for you."

"Excellent. Although this one," Cassian said, nodding at me, "is a vegetarian, so…"

"Not a worry, lass, Michael loves a challenge."

When he darted away, silence descended as I waited for what I knew was coming.

"Do you think drinking alcohol is wise?" Cassian had his nose buried in the menu, even though we'd already ordered.

"What, because I'm a naive girl eating with a stranger in a city I don't know?" I replied, smirking.

He finally looked up, catching the smile on my face before turning away again. "Just never heard of alcohol and painkillers mixing *well* before. A secret of American healthcare, I presume."

I laughed, realizing he hadn't meant anything with his warning. "I haven't been taking the pills, actually. The stitches only hurt when I get up or sit down."

He hummed in response, his fingers moving across the menu to give him something to do. I smiled again. Maybe this was the moment to set things right between us. Maybe I could break through that strange shell he wore like a straitjacket.

"Can we clear the air, Cassian?" I asked.

"The air is plenty clear, Miss Damara—"

I reached over and lowered the menu he obviously wasn't reading. His silver eyes rose to meet mine nervously.

"I mean it," I said. "Please? I don't want you to hate me. Or scold me. I swear I'm a pretty fun person to know when you let me know you. I'd like to be your friend."

I knew it was silly to do, but without an olive branch to offer, I held out my hand instead. I watched his Adam's apple rise and fall as he swallowed, studying my hand like a puzzle, before he placed his own in mine and shook.

"All right."

"All right," I said, feeling that strange sense of loss again when our hands separated. It evaporated immediately as I watched him rub the hand I had shaken across his red sweater…in some sort of ham-fisted attempt to wipe it clean? I forced myself to let it go—couldn't very well give up the tiny morsel of civility he'd offered me.

Thankfully, the waiter returned with our drinks and our first starter—a basket of flaky, golden St. Andrew's gougères with a mustard mornay dipping sauce.

I couldn't help myself; despite the name, it seemed so unpretentious. "Cheese puffs?"

The waiter beamed. "Aye, exactly, my lady. Fresh from the oven."

Buttery, airy pastry melted to cheesy heaven in my mouth, putting to shame every other piece of cheese I'd ever had in my life. I was already halfway through my second when I looked up and saw Cassian watching me, a glass of some amber liquid in his hand.

"What did you get?" I asked, motioning to the glass. "A MaClagan?"

The first smile I'd seen since that night in the library appeared on his face. This one was just large enough to reveal that he had a dimple, too. "MaCallan. Whisky. Good whisky."

"Really embracing that inner fifty-seven-year-old, I see."

"Excuse me, Miss Meadowsweet. You ordered an alcoholic child's drink."

I took a sip and coughed immediately as the brandy fumes flamed through my sinuses. His smile broke even wider as he laughed, the baritone sound rich and genuine.

"Are you all right?" he asked.

"It tastes like grass. Like someone mowed the lawn and chucked it in my drink."

"That's the meadowsweet."

"And…apples. Mint comes through right at the end," I added, taking another sip. "It's good."

"Only good. That's the one Michelin star for you." I relaxed a little, relishing how it felt to hear him volley my own joke back at me. "Do you like it?"

"Yes, it's strong, though."

"You want strong?" He pushed his own glass toward me across the tablecloth. I reached for it, accidentally grazing his fingertips in the process. I took a sip and grimaced. He laughed again. "Your first whisky. What a milestone."

"It's…well, it's…"

“An acquired taste,” he said, taking the glass back. I watched in confusion as he discreetly turned the rim where I had sipped *toward* him and sipped from the same spot. So bizarre. Drinking from the same glass was okay, but shaking hands wasn’t?

“You’re only a couple years older than me,” I said.

“Three…and a bit.”

“Right, so we’re basically different species, then?” I joked.

The light in his eyes shifted away momentarily, as if I’d said something inappropriate.

“I should have let Archer introduce you to it,” he said.

“Why?”

“Well, at the party,” he said, pivoting. “I thought you two…shared a moment, or several.”

Oh.

“Oh,” I said. “Well, I wish I could say the same.”

“What do you mean?”

I shrugged with embarrassment. Of all the people in the world to talk about this with, he wasn’t it. “Archer didn’t come to see me after, so it probably didn’t mean anything.”

Cassian frowned, his mood sobering.

“I could hear him walking the hall outside my room every night, which was really sweet,” I said, glancing down at my napkin when I realized Cassian was listening with rapt attention. “I probably liked it too much, really. But I told Mrs. Margolyes to let him come in, and he never did. I mean it’s been a week and he hasn’t said anything to me.”

“It’s probably nothing, really.”

“You don’t have to make me feel better. I shouldn’t have mentioned it.”

“No,” he said, sitting forward, the light catching on his red hair, revealing just how much of it was tempered with gold. “He’s just not used to making the next move. He was giving you space to recover. I heard him talking about you to everyone at the party after you left. Really.”

“Why do you care?” It seemed strange, given how the party had gone.

“I care…about Archer. He means well and he cares for you. Just give him a chance. You’ll see.”

There was a quiet, wild need in his eyes, which I didn't understand, but I half-smiled at him anyway. Hearing that *did* make me feel a little better. In the lull, the waiter reappeared with our next course, duck and pork belly for him, a *divine* poached egg, morel mushroom, asparagus dish for me.

"Speaking of truth," Cassian said when we were alone again. "You misunderstood me in the solarium. When I said the house was a dream only made possible by my father's death, I wasn't accusing you of being insensitive. I…My father was a ghost in our lives before he died. When he was home, he was off doing strange things on the property, in the forest, in the meadows."

I froze, thinking of the riddle and that crypt in the forest.

"But he lived here in the city when he could get away with it. In that house. *His* house. Archer and I were never permitted to go there. I figured that's where he met all of his—"

He cut himself off with a self-chiding glance in my direction.

"Lady friends…" He took a sip of his drink, blurting, "Not when he was with your mother, I don't think."

I shrugged. "It's okay. They divorced. He could do what he wanted after that, couldn't he?"

I looked askance, embarrassed that after all these years, I still felt a little bitter about how he'd left us. I'd once woken up at 3 a.m. and tiptoed down to find them dancing in the castle salon, completely enraptured with one another. Him humming his song, her smiling up at him with nothing but trust in her eyes. It had taught me something, some core desire for my own life. A future great love.

"But," I said, grasping at straws. "It's not like he had a choice."

"What do you mean?"

"Will was happy with us," I said, feeling a twinge of guilt as a flash of sorrow danced across Cassian's eyes. "Then Bruce came and everything changed. One night we were family, the next we were asked to leave."

"Don't blame Bruce," he said, turning his glass of whisky round and round, scattering refractions of light across the table. "And don't make excuses for my father. It was just another terrible choice he made in the string of thousands throughout his life."

I glanced away, wondering if we were about to slip back into calling me one of Will's mistakes.

"If I knew a love like that—a love worth upending the foundation of my life for, worth dying for—no god or goddess would be able to tear me away."

Death? I was sure my mom's marriage had caused headaches, maybe even humiliation among these blue bloods scandalized by the wrong dress worn to the wrong occasion, but *death?* I looked back at him, prepared to poke fun at his melodrama, but his attention was still on that glass, still on its ripples of light.

No, not on the ripples themselves, but on where they fell. As I watched, he moved the glass so the rings of light washed over my fingertips on the table.

"I'd give anything for something so true. To know absolutely that I was loved by someone and to give myself completely to them in return." His eyes met mine before darting away again. Quietly, he added, "My father *let* Bruce take him away from your mother."

I bristled at the thought. The memory of burying the box in the garden with Will came back to me. He didn't want to leave; I was sure of that if nothing else. And Bruce, well. In the little time I'd really spent with him, he'd shown a penchant for putting people in their places through brute, selective honesty. He was like a divining rod for human emotion, locating the vulnerability that would produce the result he wanted and pressing. He'd done that to Will, telling him whatever would scare him home again.

But I couldn't tell Cassian that. Bruce was, as far as I could tell, his most consistent parental figure, so I shrugged it away with a platitude. "What do adults always say? It's complicated."

"That's just something they say when they're afraid. We build our lives through our choices, Miss Damarand. Every decision places another stone in the foundation of who we are. We choose every day who we want to be."

"If you have the luxury," I replied. "It's a little different for us lowly peons. Our foundations are supported paycheck to paycheck, accident to accident."

"But you see that's the point, my lady," he said, raising his silver eyes to meet mine. "My father had every luxury."

My heart broke a little thinking about it. He was right; Will had power, money…and he'd been entirely too comfortable leaving his kids to be raised by staff. Nothing short of a reckoning could have forced Will to do what he didn't want to do.

"William was a solitary animal…" The bitterness I heard in Cassian's voice was surprising.

"You loved him very much." I felt my mouth close around the words I'd uttered without thinking.

"What makes you say that?"

"You have to really love someone to be that disappointed, I think."

"He was a great man, my father. Just a shame he waited until the end to be a *good* man."

I wanted to ask what he meant, but the waiter cut us off again with our next course, and afterward, Cassian moved the conversation on to less touchy topics. Like the fact that he had never—in his entire life—been dancing. Seemed unfathomable to me. I was on my phone before he could protest, searching for the nearest place that might let a seventeen-year-old in. Every website returned the same answer—the Black Orpheum, right off the Royal Mile.

Cassian's face colored with surprise when I mentioned it. "Interesting choice."

"Can we go after dessert?" My leg was already bouncing under the table.

"Bruce left a night tour itinerary for us, you know."

I smiled, sensing how much he *didn't* want to do that.

"That gives us something to do tomorrow. I'll even buy the first round."

"Fair enough. I should warn you; I won't dance and I *will* drink you out of house and home."

"I thought they taught better priorities at Oxford."

"What do you mean? Those *are* the priorities."

Less than an hour later, after I'd found the new love of my life in a dessert of oats, honey, bee pollen, and parsnip, we were stumbling around Johnston Terrace, wrapped tightly in our coats and craning our necks skyward to study Edinburgh Castle. That looming fortress that appeared carved from Castle Rock itself. When I realized the road inclined before reaching Edinburgh's bustling city center, we hailed a cab.

The warm darkness of the taxi soaked into my bones, curing all manner of ills and the twinge in my side where the stitches itched ferociously. Cassian suddenly leaned across me and pointed out the window, perfuming the air with that smoky campfire scent.

"That is where Bruce once fought a pine marten when it tried to grab his slice of pizza." His silver eyes scanned the buildings as we passed, absorbing violent pops of color with each neon sign. "And that is where Archer insisted on having his first legal pint of beer."

Drunk men were gathered outside the open wooden door of a windowless bar, whooping and hollering as loud as a freight train.

Cassian smiled. "It's a hooligan bar. It was the last night of the World Cup."

"Was there a fight?"

"Would've been damn disappointing if there wasn't one. Of course, Archer made friends with them all by the end of the evening. Never seen a cockier idiot in my life."

It was strange, admiring him in the comfortable lull of the conversation. He was inches above me, his presence saturating my senses, his piercing eyes searching the world for more to show me.

In the interim, I glanced down. Leaning forward this way had raised the ankles of his pant legs; the nettle rashes were gone and his legs had healed nicely. A strange, joyful pride rose in me. He hadn't been too pigheaded to let the doctor tend to him, and the thought that he had listened to me and *let* her treat him made me happy. It'd taken a couple weeks, but like a house cat introduced to a new pet, he was finally starting to come around to me.

A smile crept onto my face before I realized.

His eyes swiveled to me immediately. "What?"

"Nothing," I said, turning away.

He'd think it was weird. Well, let's be honest, he *already* thought I was weird. It was the sort of thing you told a friend, not someone who might someday be one.

I pointed to a random building. "Let me guess. That's where you won your first game of higgledy piggledy or something."

"What?"

I pointed to others. "First game of football…first place you bought a tie…your first date, maybe?"

His eyes dipped to mine, and I watched in real time as some cold wind blew shut whatever had opened in him. He pulled back to the other side of the cab.

"You don't want to hear about that." He motioned to a passing artisanal-style store with a flippant point. "Bought socks there once."

"Cool," I said dryly. Once again, I felt his glances on the back of my neck like stardust.

“But this place,” he said, motioning to another random building I saw in a blur. “Archer once purchased a watch there from a reclusive Romanian royal everyone calls the Dragon of Bucharest. And over here, Archer…”

Thankfully, we arrived at the Black Orpheum a few seconds later, saving me from more of Cassian’s weird desire to sell Archer to me like a black-market diamond. I spilled out of the cab into a throng of teenagers so thick it was possible to lose sight of the actual buildings from inside it. I lost sight of Cassian, too. The human wave undulated around me while empty tin cans and glass bottles played percussion underfoot. I found it was easier to slide my shoes forward without leaving the ground than to take a step. All around me, that same manic energy I’d felt at home was feeding off the crowd, nourishing it, spreading it.

“All right, ya heathens! Inside all of ya!” It was a voice I assumed belonged to a bouncer, a referee for whatever…*event*…was happening here tonight. The teen tsunami surged toward the open venue door, moving me along like a piece of debris. At one point, shoulders smashed into me on either side, and my legs left the ground. I landed several yards later when the crowd finally split and something took my breath away, stopping me cold. I’d become a rock in a fast-moving river, bodies streaming to either side of me, oblivious to the impossibility I saw before me.

She was *here.*

The bronze-haired woman I’d seen only this morning standing at the edge of the Eastern Wood was *right there*, skirting the crowd with a slight limp in her step. I let myself enjoy the thought of it for a moment, the fun serendipity of seeing a stranger for the second time in a single day. But I realized it was no mere coincidence as she moved toward me suddenly in the rabble.

“Miss Damarand?” she said, eyeing the crowd around us nervously. “You’re in danger.”

"Excuse me?”

“I cannae tell you more here, but if you’ll follow me, I can show you what the Mahon’s have been hiding from you. I’ll even tell you what lies in the crypt you found in the forest.”

I blinked, absorbing her words, as she suddenly backed her way through the crowd and disappeared around the far corner.

Stragglers darted into the venue, and the bouncer muted the crowd's mighty roar by shutting the door. Cassian was nowhere to be seen. Perhaps if he had been there, in all his stoic, pragmatic brooding, I would have remembered to think twice before acting. I'm ashamed to say it never even occurred to me. I had to know who she was and hear what she had to say.

So, I took a quick breath for courage, wrapped my coat tighter to stave off the night's chill, and followed her into the dark.

CHAPTER 19

Perhaps it was the weekend crowds or the bright evening lights of a living, breathing city, but I was several streets away from the Orpheum before I realized shadowing a stranger was a terrible, dangerous, silly thing to do.

She didn't turn around once, didn't pick up her pace. She *strolled* through the city.

Soon, I was trailing this woman down darker and darker avenues. Before I knew it, we had turned a corner and arrived back at the foot of Castle Rock. The full moon had risen. Its brilliant silver light dusted the top of Edinburgh Castle like fine salt while the castle's ghoulish green base lighting clawed at it from below. The few surviving black shadows between wrote in an ancient cuneiform script across the stones; it looked like a spell to summon some beast.

In the distance, something *howled*, and the woman paused, turning her head just slightly. "A little farther now and I'll explain everything."

She opened the small, squeaky gate ahead of her and disappeared down the stairs beyond.

Half of my mind told me to turn and run, to seek out brighter lights, other people, even Cassian if he hadn't just given up on me entirely and returned to the house. The other half was too eager to know what she had to say.

I hustled across the street and slipped through the iron gate after her. A few dozen rough steps took me into the heart of a graveyard, where trees and high walls kept the modern city at bay and the pungent stench of musk tore visitors from the modern world. This was a secret place.

I found her leaning in the shadow of a small, ancient mausoleum half eroded by wind, rain, snow, and moss. I paused far out of reach, with my hand clamped to the stair railing, and waited.

"I'm impressed you came," she said. "Do you know who I am?"

I shook my head.

"Do you know…*what* I am?"

This was stupid, *stupid.* My mind screamed inside me like a panicked captive begging me to let it go if I wasn't smart enough to save myself.

"You've come this far," she said. "I only ask that you stay once I show you. I have much to tell you. Don't be afraid."

She took a step forward into the open between us and lifted her head to the sky.

At first, nothing happened. An active nothing as noise seemed to fade away and the world seemed to hold its breath.

And then…

The full moon's softest glow brightened to molten silver, thickening until an actual *beam* surrounded her. A waterfall of light. Pain swelled across her in a terrible tsunami; her whimpers of agony sounded…like two voices crying out in the night. Her flawless pale skin rippled. Her teeth sharpened. Her brown eyes lightened to gold. The hair on her head began to spread, across her cheeks, down along her neck as she melted away in front of me, until all that was left was a jumble of dark fabric and red fur on the ground. My mouth fell open as the scream in my brain reached my mouth and emerged as a mind-bending yelp.

The bundle of clothing *moved.* I could see skin, like some terrible shed glove, on the ground beneath. A flash of red, then black, then white whirled in the jumble until a new face appeared, belonging to a massive, gorgeous, *impossible* red fox.

Her golden eyes met mine and held. She emerged from the clothing and leapt onto the nearest gravestone, curling her white-tipped tail under her paws. She was easily three times the size of any fox I'd ever seen, more like a coyote or dog. And there was an unignorable but subtle pattern, a swirling of black-tipped red fur across her coat, like a mark of magic. The moonlight curved through her fur, hugged her body, and rose from her skin like an aura.

"Incredible." The fear in my mind fell away, replaced by *wonder*. I stepped forward. "*Incredible*."

Then I saw it. Yet another detail I hadn't expected. I'd *met* this fox before. Along her right back leg, I could just see a tender cut I recognized immediately.

"Are you…the fox I saved during Archer's hunt?" Of course, the fox didn't answer, and I felt silly even thinking it. "No, couldn't be, that one was *normal*."

With a final soft eye blink, she suddenly disappeared behind the gravestone. There was a terrible *crunching-clicking-squelching* sound and the very human howl of a woman in pain before the human she was and had been emerged naked, dripping in blood and fur. She limped to her clothing then pulled back into the shadows between the mausoleums. Once there, she avoided the narrow strips of moonlight creeping between the buildings like they might scald her.

"Are you okay?" The words sounded as stupid to me as they must have to her because she chuckled.

"I will be once I alter again," she said. "But first, there are things I need to say. Would you come a little closer, please?"

She shivered her way back into her clothing, which clung to her human skin in red blotches where the blood was still wet, and cradled herself, studying me.

"You're right, you saved me that night," she said finally. "Without full moonlight, not so impressive."

"*Plenty* impressive," I countered. It—all of it—was the coolest thing I'd ever seen in my life.

"You seem surprised," she said.

"I am. Why wouldn't I be?"

"I thought they would've told you by now," she said. "Would've thought they would've given you an earful when you set me free in the forest."

"No, I gave them one. Made them remove all the traps." I backtracked. "Wait. Why would they have told me about you?"

She exhaled then; I could hear the disappointment and anger in it.

"My name's Marix," she started. "Probably means nothing to you, but it's like to put the fear of god in them. Those traps weren't meant for just any animal. They were meant for *me*."

"Why?" I asked finally. "Because you're special?"

She laughed again, this time with deep sorrow. When her eyes met mine, I could see tears brimming. "Suppose I am now."

She dug into her coat pocket with shaking hands and held something out for me to take. A photo she'd clearly pulled out a thousand times before, to the point of tearing. Beyond the harsh folds and delicate creases, I could see the face of a beautiful young woman, maybe my age, maybe a little older, with black hair, red-brown eyes, and a wild, lovely smile.

"My daughter, Mael," she continued. "Light of my life. I used to think…" She whimpered, biting her lip to keep from crying. "I used to think the fact that she had black hair would keep her safer from predators. That it would hide her better."

I realized she meant as a fox. But maybe as a human, too.

"But it didna do anything. It didna protect her from them."

"Who?"

"The Mahon's, girl! Why do you think I'm talking to you?" she snapped then seemed to recalibrate. "I'm sorry."

I had so many questions burning on the tip of my tongue. But I knew she had come to tell me things; I just needed to listen.

"Mael used to spend time in that house," she finally continued. "She went to Archer's parties. She was one of their friends. *More than that, too…* When she came home pregnant, I thought at least that they would help her. Do right by her."

I could feel my blood run cold inside me. Archer's kiss on my skin, his warm breath in my hair, his fiery hands caressing my back—the memories were as fresh as if those moments had happened yesterday.

"She went to tell them…and she never came back."

"What do you mean she never came back?"

"I've gone to the authorities; I've demanded answers myself. Nothing but excuses. A slap on the wrist. That was months ago. I've been searching the property ever since, looking for signs of her. At least a body I can lay to rest."

"Maybe she left."

Her eyes shut, splashing tears down her bloody cheeks. "She didn't leave, pet. She's gone. I'd feel her if she were still alive."

"There must be some other explanation," I said, trying to make sense of it in a way that didn't suggest the boys I'd been living with were capable of something like this.

"If there was, why wouldn't they tell me where she went?" she asked. "Why set traps to keep me out of the woods? Why sic the party on me that night?"

"Why would they set the traps for you unless…"

It hit me all at once. The animal masks at the party. The giant paper moon in the library. The fox hunt that sent a hundred people yipping and careening through the forest like blood-hungry psychopaths. The fox traps would only make sense if they *knew* she could turn into a fox, but why would they know that unless…

"They change, too."

She stared at me, unblinking, in silent confirmation. A sullen, spiteful scowl crept onto her blood-red lips. "Bear Glen isn't just a pretty name."

My mind unfolded like a pop-up book, springing a bear to life with it. Not just any bear—potentially one *three times* the size of a normal one, if Marix's fox-form was anything to go off of. Wrapped in magic and bathed in moonglow.

"It's the first night of the full moon, lass," she said. "At this very moment, Master Archer prowls the Eastern Woods. He's frenzied by his animal urges. As divorced from his humanity as a man can get without...crueler choices. His scent is irresistible. It calls to the humans like a nectar of the gods. Beckons them to their own deaths. If you were to visit the stone village tonight, you'd find it all barricaded, less to keep him out than to keep them *in*. If they met him on the road, they would *offer* themselves to him without a second's hesitation, and the young master's not experienced enough yet to resist."

I didn't know if I should ask. "Do you think that's what happened to your daughter?"

Marix shrugged. "But they can't risk deadly charms on you. That's why that manky butler brought you here to keep you safe. That's why he's not here now. Alters know better than to come into the city during the three nights of the full moon. It's forbidden to our kind."

"You're here," I said, uncertain whether I wanted to know why.

"Aye, I am," she said. "I had to risk it. I need your help to find my daughter."

I felt the blood leech out of my face as a cold shroud replaced it.

"What can I do? I'm nobody. I'm not an animal. I don't know anything. I just got here."

"You really dinnae ken, do you?" she said. "Lord Mahon dinnae just give you a house, girl. He gave you a *crown. You* are the ruler of the Eighth Kingdom. *You* have a seat at the Gathering Table. From Cornwall to Ceide, from Kerry to Shetland, there isn't an alter who disna bow to *you*. And *you* can get close to the boys. If anyone can learn the fate of my child, you can."

My mind stretched like taffy, almost to tearing. The alteration of this woman, the suggestion of a great, wide world of people just like her capable of transformation, the revelation that I could be living with murderers, the somber mission she had just laid at my feet—it was too much. All of it. I couldn't go back now; was she *insane*? All the thinly veiled double-meanings of everything Archer and Cassian had ever said to me suddenly made sense. I'd have to stay out until dawn, then drive to the house for my passport, and fly home before they knew I knew.

I was already wondering if home would be far enough to run when she took hold of my hand, smearing still-warm blood across my fingers. Drawing my attention back to her eyes, shining wet pearls of sorrow. I didn't have the heart to pull away.

"I know it's an impossible ask. The chance you'll find anything to help me is so slight, but... maybe there's something of hers in one of the boys' rooms. Or Lord Mahon's. Maybe she's in that grave in the forest you found. Just look for her, please, while there's still time."

"Still time?"

"Sweet child," she said. "Bear Glen's a dangerous place. Especially for those who threaten the Mahon's power. I wouldn't ask for your help if there were any other way but…you're my last hope."

So, she *did* understand what she was asking of me. That made it so much worse. It was easy to say no to someone who asked unreasonable things of people without thinking about it. It was impossible to say no to a mother almost on her knees in front of me begging me for answers. I thought of my own mom, how far I knew she'd go if anything ever happened to me. It would define the rest of her life. I could return a ghost ten, twenty, *thirty* years after my death, and I would still find her pawing through the pile of corpses she'd sliced through looking for me.

And I knew this because she already had…not corpses, but close.

"I'll help you," I said finally, peace of mind finding me when the tears washed across her cheeks and caught on the corners of her trembling smile.

"Thank you! Thank you, my lady!"

She bowed to me, kissing my hand over and over. Then she stepped back to the very threshold between darkness and moonlight.

"Wait…er…ma'am…" I called. "How do I find you again?"

"I'll be searching the woods, my lady," she said. "Call for me, and I'll find you."

She stepped out of the shadows and *altered* again, shedding her humanity like a winter coat and silent as fallen snow. With that, she disappeared in a flash of orange fur slicked with moonlight, just another ghost in the graveyard.

CHAPTER 20

A few months after Will had moved us to New York, and everything I'd ever known—my room, my clothing, my school—had changed overnight, something peculiar happened. I'd always been a sound sleeper, easily woken by unnatural noises, but otherwise quick to succumb to pleasant slumbers. Until one night, my subconscious ran away with me. I crawled out of bed, entirely asleep, and walked away into the night, into the frigid winter forests surrounding the castle wearing nothing but a sleeping shirt.

Aside from the icy chill streaking up into my body through my bare feet, nothing else pierced my dreams that night. I never found out what happened when I sleepwalked. I only remember what happened after, when I woke as Will laid me down on the ambulance gurney, surrounded by police officers and what seemed like a hundred people with their flashlights out. They called it a miracle. I had survived a night of sub-zero temperatures without a single scratch or frostbitten toe. And in the end, it was Will who'd found me. Saved me. Carried me six miles to safety snuggled in his arms.

My mother…had been *inconsolable*, they said. She had trudged nearly forty miles back and forth through the forest ahead of the rescuers, over icy streams, under fallen trees, and through giant, unmistakable bear tracks in the snow, howling my name like it was the only sound she could make. And when Will found me and brought me back to her, she had *wailed* with relief. She had collapsed over me sobbing, releasing the venom pooled in her before it could spread. Even as a ten-year-old, I knew that if I hadn't come home that night, she would have been a beast apart, unshakable in her resolve to find out what happened to me.

I'd seen that venom in Marix tonight. That harsh, painful *ache* of true suffering. Raw emotion translated through flesh into the grating desperation in her voice, the tension in her hands on mine. It was the only part of the experience that rang absolutely true. Whether she was right about the Mahon's and what she suspected had happened to her daughter, Marix's *emotion* was real. Her daughter had gone to Bear Glen and never came home.

I thought back to what Cassian had told me when he cornered me in the dining room.

I've done terrible things to protect this place. I've ruined lives for it. Tell me what you want so I don't have to ruin yours.

I'd have to leave, sooner rather than later. But not before keeping the promises I'd made to myself, Marix, and my mom. I would solve Will's riddle, look for Mael, and make sure my mom never had to struggle again. The boys could have the rest of it—the fancy houses and dinners, the cracked walls and weird parties, the *title*—if they were willing to kill to protect it. It wasn't worth my life…and it wasn't worth the life of the girl in the photograph.

"Are you insane?" I was only three feet into the Ann Street townhouse when Cassian rushed toward me in the foyer. "What were you thinking, disappearing like that?"

"I didn't disappear. I just lost sight of you."

"I looked everywhere. I thought something terrible had happened to you."

His hand landed on my shoulder, pulling me toward him, while the other snaked its way around my throat, feeling my neck as if he expected to find a braille tattoo there.

I tensed under his touch, backing into the wall.

"You're stiff with cold," he said, pulling me toward the roaring fire in the living room. "But you're all right otherwise?"

“I’m fine,” I lied. It was incredible how a single conversation had soured his touch for me. His calluses raked across my skin now. His smokey campfire scent scared me; cascading waves of adrenaline coursed through my body in white rapids. I tried to tell myself that maybe there were circumstances that would contextualize Marix’s story. Maybe it’d been an accident. Maybe Mael really *had* run away. If I could just ask him what happened, just have an honest conversation with him…but how could I risk it? I was alone in a house with a boy—a man—a *stranger* accused of disappearing a girl barely older than myself. And if it wasn’t Cassian, it was Archer, it was Bruce…it was Will.

It’s all of them. The entire household staff had been at Archer’s party. They’d joined in the fox hunt. I wondered how many of them knew…how many of them could change, too.

“I feel a little sick,” I said, dropping into the chair by the fire, shoving off my coat. I brought my hands to my face to steady the sway of my head; it felt like my entire body had been replaced by a loose guitar string.

“You’re hurt!” His hands were on mine, turning them over. Marix’s now-dried blood almost glistened in the firelight. “Natalie, please tell me what happened.”

“It’s nothing,” I said, trying to conjure a convincing lie. “After we got separated, there was a guy who ran by and knocked into me. I think it’s his.”

I’d never been a good liar. I didn’t like how it felt in my mouth, dry and heavy on my tongue. Heavier on my mind.

“Don’t move,” he said. I watched him disappear into the bathroom and return with a black hand towel wet from the sink. He dropped to his knees before me suddenly; this time I could feel his hard stomach against my leg and through that his raging heartbeat. I watched as he delicately wiped the blood away finger by finger, meticulous and *so* gentle. “I don’t see any broken skin. I think you’ll be fine, but I’ll call Dr. Martin in the morning to examine you.”

Something *twinged* inside me. A suspicion.

“Why don’t you call her right now?”

His silver eyes rose to meet mine. “It’s after midnight. I’d hate to wake her.”

A lie. I could see it so plainly.

“She’s paid to be on call, isn’t she?”

"Y-Yes, but…she might be busy." Busy roving the countryside as a giant elk, perhaps? Or slinking through the water as a seal swirling with magic. Who knew how far this went? "If you're truly worried about it, the hospital's just up the road."

"No, that's all right. It's not important," I said, thinking of another test. "Maybe we should just go home early. It's been a strange day."

His mouth opened then shut without a sound. Again, I could see his eyes *scanning* for the right combination of words to say. "Bruce arranged an entire tour for us. I hardly think something this small demands a hysterical reaction."

It was funny. I could see him trying to change the beat of the conversation, to distract and provoke me, using a word like *hysterical* to get under my skin. But where it would have worked only a few hours ago, it now held no power whatsoever.

"Like fussing over me on bended knee?" I said softly. My eyebrow rose in gentle derision. Surely, he must see the irony here. Surely, he knew how strange his behavior was.

Then again, maybe he didn't. Even though the blood was long gone, he still held my hands in his own. In the heady silence, he glanced down and suddenly…slowly…drew his fingers across my palms, tracing lines, exploring nooks. My breath caught with confusion and curiosity. Through my knee against his chest, I could feel his breath hasten, his heart pound, his muscles hitching in anticipation. His fingers slid through my own, around them. There was a pulse in the skin, a tugging charge like magnets brought within range of each other, a *hunger* that radiated away from our connection and spiraled into a fiery knot in the pit of my stomach. No, not my stomach. Lower.

When he finally lifted his gaze to meet mine, I could see he was having some sort of internal argument with himself. One he seemed to be losing. A breathless, aching growl escaped him, as soft as a breeze, as loud as thunder in my ears, and he plunged his hands into my hair, tugging me closer.

Our lips collided like someone had let the magnets in our skin go. They fused, pressing, then parted as if we could breathe through each other. His tongue slid across mine like a question, curious, then dove deeper for the answer. Slowly. Teasing. Tossing kindling on the fire in my belly. When he retreated, I half expected to see surprise on his face; surely, he could see it on mine. But that's not what I saw when I looked at him. I was met only with hazy, *hungry* desire. His eyes locked on my lips and he chased that magnetic charge back to me, wrapping his arms around me as he moaned against my mouth. I could feel his heart pounding against my chest as his whole being enveloped me, pulling me into him like it might break the barriers between our bodies, merging us into one.

It was ages before either one of us came up for air. Even as I turned away to catch my breath, his lips were on my chin, skating across my cheek, frolicking along my neck. Tasting. I felt his teeth graze my ear; fireworks exploded far below, rippling up through my abdomen, into my throat, and out through my mouth as I moaned involuntarily. It only emboldened him. He nibbled again and his fingers flexed. He drew them slowly down my back, met the crest of my hips and rounded them before yanking me that extra inch closer.

"Cass."

"My lady."

His lips were against my ear; his voice was soft and deep, patient, tickling, scattering sparks along my neck as he nibbled again.

It was…nothing like Archer's kiss, which had been light and playful. Curious. And for all intents and purposes, outside of me.

Cass's touches were an exquisite torture. Intoxicating. Tantalizing parts of me that had lain dormant my entire life until now. I *shivered.* I was suddenly a passenger in my own body, my own pleasure controlling it…and his… My right hand was inside his shirt, exploring between the buttons, grazing soft skin and softer hair on his chest. My left fingertips, my nails, were tracing circles along his scalp as I listened to the soft moans he delivered to my ears like secrets. Nothing else existed in the entire world.

Until Mael's face surfaced in my mind like flood debris.

"Wait," I said.

I was surprised how *immediately* he pulled away and relieved that he hadn't gone very far. His trembling lips hovered an inch from mine, on standby. He was hanging on my every word. I could have asked for anything…and there were plenty of things I wanted to ask for…

“I can’t.”

It was the least convincing lie I’d ever told. Even now, my fingertips were still exploring his skin without me. But they shrank back as Marix’s glistening eyes met mine in memory, and I cringed. I watched his heart break a little in response. Mine *ached.* Regret burned through my everything; there was a part of me almost screaming that I was wrong to resist this. Especially as he suddenly leaned in, drawing his lips within millimeters of mine so I could feel them and not feel them, right there to take. He was holding up that stake with his name on it again.

“Of course,” he said. His hands released me as reluctantly as a lifeline, sliding across every last excruciating inch of my clothing until he had to leave it behind.

This time, when he pushed away and rose to stand, the *loss* I felt was immense. Like someone had stolen the air from my lungs. I had to force myself to take in a breath and only drowned myself in his smoky scent.

“My apologies,” he said, his fingers on his lips, his gaze clouded with thought. “Good night, Miss Damarand.”

CHAPTER 21

I'm sure Edinburgh is a beautiful city, full of rich, historic corners to explore, but I wouldn't know. I spent the next two days in a fog in the back of the car, sitting a foot and a half away from a man who I desired almost as much as I feared him, while Bruce and Dave played tour guide in the front seat.

I couldn't even tell my mom or Scarlett about it. Him. The desire and the fear belonged to me and talking about something I might never have again seemed like a guaranteed way to make sure I never would.

In the end, the fear won out. Each night while in town, I sealed myself inside the yellow room upstairs, above the room I knew he'd taken for his own, and locked the door. Then I wedged a chair under the handle just in case.

The first morning, I'd woken to a tray of toiletries outside my door containing a *pungent* sea salt and lemon bath wash, as well as a handwritten letter from Cass, written on actual stationery. An apology for coming between me and Archer. For impugning my honor. For not asking permission to touch me.

Of course, it had only made me want him *more.*

Which only heightened the fear I felt every time I thought about Marix's request. What I was returning to the house to do. To find. I'd never seen a dead body before. I didn't want to now. Definitely not one tied to either of the Mahon's.

Shame found me then, when I'd hoped for half a second that *Will* had done something to her. At least then it wouldn't be them.

Stupid. Pointless. I needed to get my priorities straight. Nothing could happen with either of them until I either knew Mael was alive and well or dead by accident. I still had a riddle to solve, too. And in the end, the only thing that truly mattered was my own safety…and leaving if I discovered I was living in a home full of people I couldn't trust.

Cassian and I didn't speak again, even when we reached Bear Glen. As we pulled up to the front stairs, the door opened beside me to a gargantuan bouquet of calla lilies, red hyacinth, tiger lilies, and nasturtiums, which swooped away as Archer bent to help me out of the car.

"Hello, gorgeous," he said, offering me his arm. "These are for you."

"What for?"

"I owe you a monumental apology, explanation, the whole lot…and a real date, if you'd like to join me for a picnic this beautiful afternoon."

I was blindsided a little, realizing I'd forgotten Archer's weeks of silence—and any thought of him—when Cassian touched me. I needed to think.

"Maybe some other time—"

"Oh please, let me dote on you a bit. There's so much I need to say."

His charm aside, I didn't think I could say no. Mrs. Margolyes and Mary had come to meet us at the car. They, as well as Bruce and Dave, just stood there, watching. Waiting for my answer. Cassian looked at everything *but* us, but I could feel his attention on me like a heat lamp regardless.

"Sure, that would be nice."

"Wonderful, shall we?"

Archer led me through the house and out again, across the back drive, into the walled garden where someone had laid out a Mahon tartan picnic mat and half a dozen cashmere blankets and throw pillows on the gentle slope by the thistle fountain. Beside that, the chef had laid out an entire buffet table of afternoon tea snacks, as well as an ice bucket with chilled champagne.

"Sit, sit, please," he said, drawing me down onto the blanket. His hands landed on my knees and swirled in little circles. "Is…everything all right?"

It was an intimacy I hadn't expected after two weeks of *zero* communication, made more complicated by what I'd learned in Edinburgh. What I'd *done* in Edinburgh.

"I guess I'm a little surprised by the attention—"

“Maybe I should just start my apologies?” he said, offering me his most theatrical pout. “Natalie, I cannot imagine what you must think of me. I am so sorry I didn’t come to see you after your accident.”

“Thank you.” I wanted to believe him…

“And I know now that I should’ve sent the guests away. Believe me, Mrs. Margolyes gave me a right talking to about it. I’m only lucky she can’t spank me. I think I’d be a bright aubergine.”

Damn, he couldn’t help but be charming, could he?

“Only don’t hold it against me,” he said, darting forward, touching his nose to mine. “You’ll make fun of me for the truth.”

“Which is?”

“I’ve never actually had a g-girlfriend before.” He even stuttered on the g-word. “Gosh, I haven’t lived, have I?”

It was difficult to imagine him doing anything terrible to anyone; then again, it was difficult to imagine that a creature lurked just under his chiseled, athletic form. He was certainly larger in general than any seventeen-year-old boy I’d ever met, save a few football players, but a *bear*? Out of pure curiosity, I brought my hand to his arm, undid the cuff button, and rolled up his sleeve. The skin along his strong, wiry arm was softer than the cashmere. Was I only imagining it, or was it brand new, too? Even his hair, wavy without a whiff of product, looked downy fresh.

I blinked, realizing he’d fallen silent as I explored. His shallow-shore eyes watched me curiously. The hesitation in the set of his jaw and mouth, the heat *radiating* off his skin, nevermind that intoxicating scent—I could see how a girl could get lost in this. If I wanted to kiss him, a simple flex of my wrist would have brought him right to me. And suddenly, I couldn’t think of anything else. The way he’d lifted me into his arms, trailed his tongue along my canine, toyed with the tip of my tongue.

I blinked, shaking my head a little just to clear it. I wanted…I needed to keep them at bay if I wanted to know the truth. Close enough not to arouse suspicion, far enough not to arouse…well…

I smiled brightly and shifted to lay down on the blanket beside him and admire the lovely spring blue above me.

“Well, we have that in common,” I said. “I’ve never had a boyfriend.”

“Drink?”

“Please.”

He retrieved the champagne and poured me a mimosa.

"I think you're lying," he said as he handed me the drink.

"Lying?"

"About having a boyfriend," he said. "You are way too chill to have been single for long."

"Okay, Party King."

"Party King? Moi?"

"Oui. Weekend bacchanals *every month*, surrounded by beautiful girls like Maisey and the one with the braids."

"Rhona? We've practically known each other since birth."

I thought of Mael.

"There must've been someone else," I said.

"Well, I'm not exactly a monk. I enjoy many finer things and I've known many fine women."

"That does not surprise me, but it's also not exactly the flex to me that it is for you. You're my age."

"It's been an eventful few months since puberty hit. What can I say?"

"I'm sure one of them must've wanted more from you," I pressed.

I inhaled sharply as his hand slid onto my stomach, across to the tender spot where the branch had pierced me.

"None of them ever took a stake to the heart for me…may I?"

May he what? I shuddered, which must've looked like a nod to him. His soft hand went to the hem of my shirt and brought it up above my healing wound, to just under my bra line. There was no bandage there anymore. I craned my neck, surprised to see there was just a pink line swaddled in dots where the stitches had already begun to break down. Dr. Martin wasn't just a doctor; she was an artist with that line. Another few months, there probably wouldn't be a scar at all.

Archer brushed his warm thumb across the spot thoughtfully. He bent down and kissed it. I shuddered again.

"Your skin smells like sunlight," he whispered.

It was too corny. I laughed. "And what does that smell like?"

"Like the possible heat death of my world." His eyes studied me again, that same look of curiosity as before.

"Archer, I have to tell you something," I said, sitting up to clear the air. "Cass kissed me in Edinburgh."

"He what?" I expected anger, shock, disappointment. Instead, Archer's face twisted with disbelief. He looked almost impressed. "That's rather bold. Didn't know he had it in him."

"I didn't stop him. But also…"

"Also, what?"

"I think he only did it to distract me in the moment."

"Distraction, eh?" Archer's lips found mine and pecked. He pulled back with a smile then plunged in for a second lightning round, tickling my neck. "Dangerous thing, being so easily distracted. I'll have to remember that trick."

I caught him before he could kiss me again. "Archer, this isn't real, right? This is just a bit of fun."

"I'd like to think it's both. And if you don't believe it is, allow me to prove it to you."

All thought of looking for clues of Mael's fate, for the key, went out the window for the rest of the afternoon. Not because I didn't want to look, but because Archer was *e.v.e.r.y.w.h.e.r.e.* I went. When he fell asleep on the blanket, I returned to my rooms, only to emerge a few seconds later to find him waiting for me. Lunch was served for two in the dining room. And the door to the secret room in the library was left conspicuously open when he pulled me along, showing me his favorite pieces of old history they kept in little lockable glass boxes scattered around the room.

By nightfall, there wasn't a hall we could enter where staff didn't retreat behind doors at the first sight of us. And there didn't seem to be a room unprepared for us. A chess board was set up in the salon. The bar was open in the empty ballroom where someone had set a James Blunt record playing on a loop. Gordon had even left hors d'oeuvres in the kitchen for us. Either Archer had held a staff meeting about the pair of us, or something else was going on. I mistrusted the strange, manicured quality to it, like I was suddenly living in a house full of wingmen, on call to help Archer flex and impress me.

But I also knew pointing that out wouldn't help. Picking things apart had a way of ruining them, and I didn't need his suspicion. I needed him none the wiser as I continued my search for answers.

When all the staff had finally gone home, I made excuses for sleep, and he escorted me to my door, kissed my hand, and retreated slowly in reverse down the hall, as if waiting for me to call him back and keep the evening going.

Instead, I shut the door and retrieved Will's riddle from where I had stashed it in the bed's headboard.

I would sweep the house for the crypt key first before searching outside again, starting with the far northwest room where Judy had once styled me. It was empty now, thankfully, which made the search much easier. I ran my hand over every surface, pressing lightly, lifting paintings and rugs, rattling wall outlets. Anywhere that might hold a key. The next room was a bust, as were the three after it. I skipped the staff's rooms entirely; I couldn't go in without annoying or alerting them, and I had a feeling it was the last place Will would have thought to hide anything.

I moved along the ground hallway, scouring room after room, until I reached the main entry, and my eyelids began to mutiny. I'd have to do the rest of the downstairs tomorrow, which would leave only…the boys' wing.

I gulped at the thought of it, wondering how I could get them out of there long enough to search. Ugh, I'd just have to burn that bridge when I came to it.

I went to sleep and dreamed of creatures watching me open the crypt in the forest…and woke to Archer's weight landing on my bed.

"Good morning, gorgeous."

My eyes cracked open like rusty garage doors then slammed shut against the bright morning light. Archer gave a soft chuckle. I heard glasses clink against one another as he maneuvered a serving tray onto the end table. Then his toasty hand landed on my cheek. He brushed the hair out of my face, and his thumb traced the helix of my ear.

"What are you doing?"

"Breakfast in bed. Gordon's made you French toast with a pomegranate glaze—fruit of love, you know."

"And knowledge," I murmured.

"And lust."

My eyes sprang open then. His sharp, mischievous grin greeted me as bright as any sun. His dimple might as well have been a canyon. I pushed myself to sit up and his hands were on my knees immediately, his sherry scent overpowering any pomegranate I was likely to taste. Marix was right; it was actually hard to…think with him here. It was like being haunted by something you crave, unable to escape it, and not wanting to. The only thing that kept my head above water was *knowing* I craved him because I couldn't help it.

"Figured you for a night owl," I said.

"A nighthawk at least, give me *some* credit. Actually, I'm sort of an early to bed, late to rise sort of guy."

"Except when there's a party."

"Oh no, *especially* when there's a party. I don't get up before noon."

"But…I heard you outside my door at like four-thirty every morning."

"That wasn't me, I can assure you."

That did not assure me in the slightest. The only other person who felt like they might do that was Cass…

"I'm sort of lame actually," he plowed on. "When the house is full, I'm a master of ceremonies until I reach my limit, then I give them a big send off and leave them to it mostly."

"You…weren't outside my rooms?"

He shrugged; he clearly had no idea what I was talking about.

"I thought we might go riding today. There's something important I'd like to show you."

I blinked. He wasn't the sort of guy to throw around the word important.

"Like what?"

"Finish your breakfast and come find out." He gripped my face full of French toast between his giant paws and pulled me in for a kiss, taking half my slice of toast with him as he leapt for the door.

"Hey!"

"Delicious! Toast, too."

Thirty minutes later, the servant, Duncan, was holding my foot in his hand, helping me into the saddle of a chestnut-colored highland pony called Hinnie, who had a silver mane plaited into a spear along her back. She skipped below me, chittering.

"O..kay," I said, holding on for dear life.

"Don't worry, love," Archer said. He was there beside me on his own jet-black horse in an instant, maneuvering him like they were one. "She knows who you are. She won't falter."

I doubted "who I was" would stop her from falling off a cliff, but I appeared to be wrong. Hinnie was a gentlewoman, following patiently as Archer led the way into the hills around the estate. She seemed to know how I was feeling before I did, skirting fallen logs and slowing on inclines, attuned to every slightest discomfort in me.

She must've been a nervous wreck by the time we reached Archer's destination. It was a narrow lip of rock, barely three feet across, overlooking Bear Glen. From here, the entire area looked like a giant meteor crater, created when the gleaming golden house crash landed in the square center of the verdant valley long ago. He dismounted his horse in a single flourish then lifted me off mine like I weighed nothing at all.

"It's just over here," he said, pulling me along to the very edge. "Are you scared of heights?"

"No, actually," I said, which was true. "Just the fall."

"That's not the sort of falling I have in mind…come look, it's right here."

The stone's chill shot through me like an ice bolt as I sat, and the breeze chased itself up the legs of my pants when I set my legs to dangle. I took hold of a belt loop on his pants firmly and leaned to see the thing he was pointing at, wondering what could possibly be worth all of this. It was a pictograph. A painting on stone, in a shocking blue color, protected from the ravages of nature and erosion by a narrow lip of rock that took the assaults in its stead.

"Your family's crest…the seven-pointed star."

"That's right. A heptagram. That's how long we've been here."

"This is nine hundred years old?"

"Even earlier. The very dawn of man."

There was some strange intonation to the way he said it. That turn of phrase meant far more to him than it did to me.

"It's beautiful, Archer," I said.

He turned back to me, beaming with pride, and took my hands in his, blowing warm air across them like he had done in the garden the first night we met.

"Once upon a time," he said. I laughed. "This bit is very serious. Once upon a time, the world as we know it was born. The wild magicks of this world folded in on themselves, creating the rocks and rivers, trees and flowers, sun and moon. It crashed against the shoreline. It exploded from the ground in great fiery fountains. It slithered underfoot so small it would take a mad inventor thousands of years to create a machine powerful enough to see it."

He reached for the strings of his and my hoody and began to tie them together.

"There was only one problem. The magicks had tied themselves so tightly in knots they couldn't undo themselves again. Their frayed ends snapped back and forth like live wires across the surface of the Earth, trapped, desperate to be free. Until one day, the animals came. They roamed, curious and hungry. They bled and breathed and bred with relish.

"The magicks conspired to ensnare them, learn their tricks, steal their very souls if they had to, just to be free. But the animals knew better than to venture near the magical wellsprings of the Earth. All save the humans, those foolish, hairless apes who thought themselves too clever to be caught. The magicks appealed to their bottomless appetites. They lured them in. Took hold of their souls. Changed them to suit their own untamed desires."

A lick of wind tore up my spine.

"Of course, the magicks never suspected the foolish apes preferred it that way."

Archer suddenly pulled on our knotted hoody strings, bringing our faces together. His kiss bounced playfully across my cheeks and nose.

"You goof," I said, genuinely tickled.

"Do you like that?"

Then his thumb was on my lower lip. His fingers slid like satin feathers around to the base of my skull. His lips skimmed my lashes and the apple of my cheek. Each dappled touch a delicate spark.

I was in danger. His…everything…was overpowering. I could feel his caresses across my body, the sparks skipping across my darkest, most private pools, before sinking into them, setting them to froth and bubble.

To my surprise, when he pulled back to study my face, I saw the same shy glint in his eyes that I had seen at the party. I couldn't help it. I grimaced playfully.

"What?" he said, laughing.

"You're dangerous," I said.

"Me? Dangerous?"

"Since I got back from Edinburgh, you've been weird. The whole house has been. Trying hard…but I'm not sure why."

"Well, it's simple really," he said. "I've never been in…"

He suddenly stopped himself, eyed me, then looked away, which was almost impossible to do with our hoody strings tied together. I pulled them myself this time. He laughed as his face swung around back to me, planting another kiss on my forehead before starting to untie them.

"Been in what?"

"You know, been…*in like*…before."

My eyebrow arched. "In like?"

"I've never had a girlfriend. I don't know how to do it yet, but I *am* trying."

"So you involved the staff?"

He finally got the strings undone but held onto them, playing. "Are you kidding? Half of them have been married longer than we've been alive. Surely they know a thing or two about lov—"

Again, he caught himself. He glanced at me sheepishly and pulled me into the crook of his arm. If this was a game, he was even better at it than I imagined.

"About being in like," he whispered. His eyes darkened then as he stared off across the valley. "Can't learn anything about it from our parents, unfortunately."

"You're surrounded by people who care about you, Archer."

"Because they're paid to," he said. "I drove away the ones who were supposed to actually care."

That broke my heart a little.

"The last thing I ever did to my father was try to shame him for being a good man. For doing the right thing, even when no one was watching."

"How did he die? Bruce never told me."

A sigh seeped out of him, slow and low. "Heart attack." Archer glanced down at me; I must've had some look on my face that suggested I needed comfort. He hugged me tighter. "I know. It was a shock to me, too, that he even had one."

Give me a thousand years and I might have been able to come up with some poetic description of the pair of them, Archer and Cassian. Something about onions or cakes and their various fine layers. But it would've been a description written in hindsight, after the finer details had been polished away. The brothers were like tattered, soggy newspapers left to dry on worktables. They had layers, stiff and brittle and hard to read. The headlines blazed in bold fonts while the substance inked away into the paper, setting the whole thing off color.

Archer had finally been real with me and in the process burned his whole family. Will had been a good man without a heart. No. Not quite. He was a heartless man trying to be good. That didn't fit right, either. Yet the truth was written between the lines, not just about Will, but about who Archer was.

I wondered if the same was true about their connection to Mael. Would I have to read between the lines there, too, if I ever found out what happened?

It was well past dark by the time we returned home to find a feast set out on the dining room table for us and two seats wedged against each other at the head of the table. It was ten before I made excuses and sent myself to bed so I could sit on the couch and wait until I heard him retreat to his own wing.

I was in the kitchen a few seconds later, opening drawers, lifting loose tiles under the trash can, removing racks of preserves from the pantry. In the dining room, I crawled under the long table then lifted the edges of the Persian rug all the way around. I thought about unpotting the tall plant by the window for half a second until I remembered dirt had a way of propelling itself across rooms if you didn't lay something down underneath first. No way they wouldn't notice that in the morning.

The other rooms to the southeast of the library took no time at all—an office and a moldy room used for storage of antiques that had fallen out of fashion, both empty.

It was the library, I knew, that would take me all night. Not that I minded. In the darkness, lit only by the peripheral path lighting outside, the giant room with the frescoed ceiling seemed…otherworldly. Especially now that I knew there really was more to this world than I'd ever imagined.

Not to brag, but I made it a quarter of the way through the ground floor bookshelves, pulling each book down, fanning through it, and replacing it, before I sneezed for the first time. I caught it in the crook of my arm before the noise could get away from me.

But I grew too cocky as I edged toward the fireplace. I caught the fourth sneeze…and lost the book I was holding, freezing as it struck the floor with a single resounding clap. It was so loud I could still feel the silent alarm going off around me long after the clap faded. I waited like a startled cat on the balls of my feet until I heard the click of a lock, the turn of a knob.

I pressed myself as far against the wall as I could, but it didn't seem to matter. Feet suddenly appeared on the spiral staircase, and Cassian's eyes met mine in the dark before he even reached the ground floor. Like he knew exactly where I was.

My breath caught at the mere sight of him, which was as silly as it was involuntary. That part of me that had screamed not to resist him suddenly opened its door again inside me. When I tried to shut the door, it stuck its foot out, holding it open. Archer was irresistible, sure, but Cass was…undeniable.

"Is there something I can help you find?"

"No, I'm fine." I retrieved the book from the floor, shook it at him a little. "Couldn't sleep."

"So, you came to do a bit of light reading," he said, taking the book from me and holding it at just the right angle so I could actually read the cover in the low light. "Nothing like a little seventeenth century calculus to put you right to sleep."

I took the book back, feeling the reluctance in his hand to let me have it. "Sounds like I made the right choice…goodnight."

"Goodnight, my lady." I cut a quick pace to the door. "Unless you're open to suggestions."

I turned, surprised to see a glimmer of anticipation in his eye.

"If you hand me fanfiction, so help me…"

He motioned for me to follow him up the staircase to the balcony, to the reading area he liked. His chair, a sort of plush mid-century modern leather recliner, looked like a nest. Blankets had been packed into the corners, along with an Oxford mug and a slim four-by-five leather-bound book warped around an old pencil. It was a tiny, damaged thing. Yet he handed the book over with two hands. It was…precious to him.

"Careful, the pencil's there for structural integrity at this point."

I could just make out the first few lines as I nudged the edge of the book open.

"Poetry?"

"Riddles. My father used to do them before bed. He said nothing would exhaust the mind faster."

"Thank you, I'll return it in the morning."

"Take your time. I've done all I could do. As you'll see, that wasn't much."

I held out the calculus book with a wry smile. Here I was trying to *solve* a riddle and he'd handed me a compendium of new ones.

I moved toward the spiral staircase and paused. There was no point going back downstairs only to go up again. I turned back.

"Actually, would you mind if I cut through your room?"

"Uh, it's not prepared for guests."

I smiled. "Think of me as a ghost then."

The secret door in the bookcase was partially ajar; it was a marvel of engineering I hadn't seen the seam before. As I passed through now, I noticed the book chosen for the secret handle was a midnight blue leather edition of *Cyrano de Bergerac*. I wondered if it had always been that book or if he had chosen it.

I drew to a soft stop as I entered his sitting room. It was *far* messier than it had been during Mrs. Margolyes's initial tour. The couches had been pushed back into a corner and covered in drop cloths—the rest of the floor, too—to make room for a massive canvas, which was angled toward the roaring fire. Great big orange buckets were stacked alongside a table littered with putty knives and paint scrapers.

I glanced at Cassian. He was busy staring at his feet.

"What's all this?"

"Nothing."

"That's a lot of nothing," I said, tilting my head toward the canvas. "May I?"

His back stiffened, he plunged his hands into the pockets of his sleep pants, and he shrugged a nod at me, his eyes round and shiny with terror.

I'd expected a painting. Who am I kidding? I'd expected some severe self-portrait in blacks and grays and blues. Something that already looked five hundred years old. Instead, I found a porcelain illusion. Gobs of plaster had been heaved onto the canvas then rounded and smoothed meticulously to unearth a three-dimensional face buried within. It felt as if I had crashed into a pool of milk and looked up to see a giant's face peering in at me.

Despite the sweltering heat, I wrapped my arms around myself. Goosebumps were every second spreading across my skin as I gazed upon the face. Just the gentlest smile. Sweet, peaceful, curious eyes. He'd captured something akin to déjà vu. Whoever she was, she knew me. She *wanted* to know me.

Out of the corner of my eye, I could see Cassian watching me, watching her.

"It's…"

"No, don't tell me," he said. "I'm not prepared for kindnesses."

I smiled; there was nothing more terrifying than sharing what you made with people. Some core part of it ceased to be entirely yours. And then you had to dissect polite compliments, looking for the cruel truths within them, only panicking *more* if you didn't find any. Self-flagellation at its finest.

"Darn it, I'm fresh out of insults," I said.

I stepped away to leave; he matched me step for step before his hand landed on the doorknob ahead of mine, and he opened the door for me still wearing that sheepish, wide-eyed expression. In the full golden glow of the hallway lights, I could see plaster bits in his hair and along his cheek.

"You should wash that out before it hardens and you have to cut it out. Trust me, I know from experience."

"Do you...plaster?"

I laughed. "Hot glue for the miniatures I make. Bangs sit differently when you *have* to have them. Fringe, I mean."

"It's just a bit of fun, you know," he said. "Once I thought my life would be filled with responsibilities. Before I knew it, I'd missed my entire childhood preparing for a job I didn't know I'd never have. I don't really know what to do with myself."

"You're looking for a calling."

"What do you mean?"

"After my dad died, my mom took me to a therapist. She was scared I wouldn't recover, I think, but...the therapist gave me this really extensive personality test, sort of as a way to suss out what I would need from her. She told my mom that after trauma some people need friendship and a strong family foundation, others distraction, and so on. What works for one person won't work for another. You strike me as someone in need of a calling."

"Great," he said, laughing. "Easiest one, right?"

"Sweet dreams, Cass."

"You as well."

As I walked away, I could feel his dappled attention follow me to the corner...and right before I turned, I heard him say something under his breath. Words that surprised and confused me as much as they tickled some secret part of me.

"Haunt them anytime, my lady."

CHAPTER 22

There was no putting it off any longer. I *had* to get into the boys' rooms to search for clues to Will's riddle and the crypt key. It'd been three days since my incomplete rummage of the library. Since then, I'd woken with the sun every day to find an ethereal figure staring at my window from the far tree line—Marix. Her teary, expectant eyes were inescapable, even from so far away.

Archer was just as persistent. Every day, he was either at my bedside with breakfast and a kiss, or he was outside my door with some new distraction at the ready. Driver's lessons in a golden jaguar, his *second* car so it was "okay if something happened to it." A tour of the stone village that ended with an afternoon tea at a cafe where the waitresses bowed to me, and the owner barreled out of the back room to snap a picture of us for his wall. Badminton on the back lawn with some of the kids from the party, including Maisey, who insisted on sunbathing in a bikini and staring daggers at me through her translucent green sunglasses any time Archer kissed the top of my head.

Of course, Cassian was there, too, in spirit. Gargoyling from on high, pretending to read in a chair by his window.

The one time I tried to head out on my own for a little hike, just to recharge my social batteries and catch my breath for god's sake, Mrs. Margolyes called out to me to wait before practically grabbing Archer by the scruff of the neck and shoving him out after me.

I didn't know how I was going to do it. How could I search for anything when they were *always there* now? It was like they were trying to smother the *me* right out of me.

I was being dramatic. It felt…lovely…to be so included. And super weird. I just wasn't used to it. And, of course, there was the teensy-weensy detail that they were all lying to me. Hiding Archer's secret from me. Maybe Cass's too. Sure, he hadn't changed in Edinburgh that I'd seen, but it wasn't like I knew the rules for any of this. With each passing day, it felt more and more like they were plotting something. Under better circumstances, it would've been a surprise party, but Marix's warning had disenchanted me. There was definitely no party, and I genuinely feared the surprise that might come when—if—they told me the truth. Revealing a secret, especially a big one, was really a burden for the person hearing it; they became responsible for it. And they would be the one endangered by it if it came to that.

I had every reason to be concerned. I'd scoured the internet for any information I could find about someone named Marix and a missing girl named Mael, but there'd been nothing. *Literally nothing*. Until I finally accepted the boys' social friend requests.

Doom scrolling through their pictures, scrutinizing them like crime scene photographs, had brought Mael into sharper relief than Marix's folded image of her. Mael was in the background of half a dozen of Archer's parties from last year. And before that, her unmistakable red-brown eyes followed mine from the edges of other photos. Never tagged. Always at the periphery. Stranger still, there wasn't a single photograph in which she was actually talking to Archer, or Cassian, or Will. She never paid them any attention at all, no matter who was taking the photograph.

But she'd known them, or been around them often, until February of this year. After that…she was gone. Dropped off the face of the earth.

I didn't know if finding the key to that crypt in the forest would answer her mystery or mine, but it would narrow the possibilities. I could give Marix something, at least. I just had to get them out of their rooms…

The opportunity arose with a ring of the front doorbell, a loud chime that could be heard all the way out on the field where we were playing Badminton.

"Is the pizza guy here?" It was the gangly teenager from the party—Tom—who had turned out to be a stiff, vain priss.

"Don't even joke about that," said Archer. "Gordon would skin you alive."

"I'm hungry," pouted Tom.

"He can make you a pizza if you want."

"Maybe…" said Tom. "It's always a little Scottish for my tastes."

"You're Scottish, mate."

"Natalie, look out!" Rhona, the girl who had shared her passionfruit with me, pointed as Maisey tapped the bird over the net. I barely caught it in time.

"Thank you!"

"Kiss-ass," escaped Maisey like a hiss.

Rhona replied with a feisty meow.

"Archer, the next one's yours!" I said, letting the birdie fly over my head.

It landed like a lead shot in the grass at his feet. Archer was distracted, discomfort stretched thin across his tight jawline. I turned to find Mrs. Margolyes solemnly staring at us from the mansion's open back doors. There was no mistaking her body language, either; whoever was at the front door, they brought bad news.

"Ooh. Somebody's in trouble."

"Shut it, Tom," Archer snapped. He turned to me and held out his hand, more serious than I'd ever seen him. "I think we have company."

The others remained behind as Archer hurried me through the grass to the gravel driveway.

"Is something wrong?" I asked.

"No-no…well," he said, inspiring zero confidence. "But we'll need to change."

"It's not the king again, is it?"

Mrs. Margolyes hustled me up the stairs to my rooms, where Mary was already waiting with a simple black A-line dress with thistle embroidery around the hem. Her hand shook as she tried to apply blush to my face.

"Do you know who it is, Mary?"

"No, my lady," she lied.

Mrs. Margolyes proved just as taciturn. She just *kept moving*, holding her hands out behind me like a snowplow driving me where I needed to go. On this occasion, it was the great salon; she simply opened the door and shoved me in. I hadn't been here since the ambush BBC interview, but the atmosphere was still thick with passive animosity. Bruce, Archer, and Cassian eyed me from their seats like hostages trying not to make any sudden movements. The only one comfortable in the space was our guest. With bobbed chocolate-brown hair dipped in wheat, her suit just a deeper shade of the same, and muscles that rippled with each graceful movement she made, she reminded me of a character come to life. Pulled straight off the pages of a graphic novel or fashion magazine. Her perfume—some overwhelming floral note—hit me with an open hand...but under it, only barely disguised, was the unmistakable stench of rot. Sulfur.

"You must be Lady Damarand," she said, her voice raspy, her accent foreign. Scandinavian, maybe, but that was a pointless descriptor, like saying someone had a North American accent. "Please join us."

There was only one empty seat left, between the boys. As soon as I sat, Archer's hand slid into mine and squeezed, stifling the noticeable tremor in his body.

The visitor relished this intimate gesture, her lips curling into a crescent smile full of...accusation.

"So wonderful to see you all getting along so well." Her hand slid into her pocket, produced a cigarette case, and lit one before she felt the need to speak again. "It is lovely to meet you, my lady. You may call me Eike."

"Nice to meet you," I replied.

She chortled, a strange, hollow snort. "I forgot you are American. Lord Mahon was full of surprises."

Bruce sat forward suddenly. "Honored djat, perhaps we could speak privately—"

"In time." Her eyes never left mine as she blew a thick cloud of smoke between us. "What do you make of this arrangement, my lady?"

"Will's gift to me?" I asked.

"Gift, sure."

"It's growing on me."

"Does it *suit* you?"

I sensed no malice in the question, only an underlying test I didn't know I was taking. The boys did, though. They leaned forward in unison to either side of me.

"We're introducing her to everything slowly," said Archer.

"It's a lot to take in all at once," added Cassian. "Our father sprung this on all of us."

Eike's eyes swiveled to Cassian, nonplussed.

"She must be very special," she said, "if your opinions have changed so drastically since that melodramatic interview you gave."

"They have," Cassian said. "She is."

"And yet…" Her eyes swiveled to Archer. "You have not presented her to his majesty."

Bruce, Archer, and Cassian were silent. Of course, since they already knew I had met the king, this royal must be someone else.

"We expected proper introductions, but you keep her all to yourselves… I mean I can see why. She is intoxicating. Just being this close, I want to leap over this table and tear her clothes off right here, you know."

I felt an icy explosion go off in my stomach as I digested her violent words delivered with such a casual tone. Archer squeezed my hand again…and Cassian's hand slid into mine on the other side. Both of them were almost panting beside me. Archer looked like my hand was the only thing holding him back from hulk-smashing Eike through the far wall onto the gravel beyond.

Eike absorbed all of it. Another crescent smile broke across her face as her cigarette dove between us into some unsuspecting antique bowl on the coffee table.

"Master Archer," she said, relishing her own slow cadence. "Do calm down before you go feral. Lady Damarand, do you know who I am?"

"No," I said.

"I can see in your eyes you know they are hiding things," she said. "Why do you let them keep you in the dark?"

"Please, djat," said Bruce again. "A little privacy, I beg you."

I wanted to escape this room as badly as they wanted me to leave it. I didn't know who this person was, or who she thought she was, but my internal warning systems were on high alert, rubbing against my insides like sandpaper.

"Fine," she said, standing. Bruce, Archer, and Cassian lurched to their feet as well. "My lady, it was a pleasure we're sure to repeat shortly."

The boys followed Eike out, all but corralling her to the door. I waited until I couldn't hear their footsteps anymore and leapt from the seat. I'd have to leave today. Forget riddles and missing girls. If I wasn't careful, I'd become both.

I closed myself inside my rooms and locked the door, wondering if Marix knew about this, about that person, her strange authority over the family. If Eike could threaten to attack me so casually, it seemed all too possible the same could be said for Mael. Perhaps Eike was a lead Marix could follow for answers after I had left.

My feet stopped me there, in the dead center of the room. What was I talking about? I couldn't leave like this. For one, there was no way I could escape from the house without one of them noticing. For another, Eike was right. I *did* know the Mahon's were hiding things from me, and I'd let them continue to think I knew nothing so I could snoop around. I'd played the spy, dammit. Too well to give up now. The answers—to Will's riddle and Mael's disappearance—were *right here*, I just knew it.

Didn't stop me from feeling monumentally *stupid* as I slipped my shoes off and tiptoed out of my own room, down the empty hall to Archer's door, and pressed my ear to the wood. I only heard silence; wherever they'd gone with Eike, it wasn't here.

The doorknob turned so easily in my hand. The massive bedroom was just as bright and inviting as it had been on my first visit. A five second tiptoe brought me to the open bathroom door to check, but there was no one here. The search itself took me about as long. Everything was so new in here—the couches, the weightlifting equipment, the karaoke machine he put here instead of just *cleaning* one of the many free rooms elsewhere—I was basically done once I felt the walls, opened drawers, and tapped on the tiles in the bathroom. The most scandalous thing I found was in Archer's bedside dresser and didn't surprise me much.

Moving down the hall to Cassian's room was a different experience entirely. I realized this felt like a bigger betrayal somehow. I'd already barged into his rooms once, seen things I wasn't supposed to. But the temptation was too great; his door was right *there*. I'd never stop thinking about it if I didn't open it now.

I crept in like a shadow. The sitting room was empty and the secret door to the library was closed. I slipped quickly to the door to his bedroom and peeked in there, too, just to be safe. Once I knew I was truly alone, I felt my way around the walls, leaping past the windows, which looked *directly* upon the Badminton court in the back. But I looked back almost instantly as I realized that all of Archer's friends had vanished from the back lawn. I moved every picture frame, lifted every lamp. I avoided the bed; there was no way to check under it or behind it without wrinkling the military-neat sheets and comforter. Not to mention it seemed like a strange place for Will to hide a key…or a body, if it came to that. I did it all again in the bathroom, lifting and shuffling, then resetting everything exactly as I found it. It was the one saving grace of a perpetually cleaned house; there were no dusty spots to give away what I had moved.

Cassian's desk was a different monster. There were old teacups and mugs stacked in cairns along the edges and precarious piles of papers that would *never* sit right again if I touched them. The drawers were fair game, although they seemed to contain only the barest necessities…at least until I came to the last. It was so dark inside I almost didn't notice the strip of fabric at first. It was tattered, torn…and discolored. Barely more than a rag, browned and misshapen by whatever liquid had soaked into it.

Blood, I realized, as I lifted it from the drawer. The unmistakable splatter pattern of long-dried blood.

Something inside me wanted so badly to rationalize it—*it could be from a nosebleed or sports injury.*

Something else asked, *then why keep it*?

I didn't know what to do with it. Leaving it here made the most obvious sense, but I'd promised Marix answers and maybe with her heightened senses, she could tell whose it was. I plucked a few tissues from a box nearby and wrapped it before stuffing it in my pocket.

Clunk. Creeee-k.

I froze, listening as footsteps fell somewhere nearby. A second set followed close behind the first. I was already in some sort of sprinter's starting position, ready for the turn of a handle to run for Cassian's bathroom. Maybe I'd get lucky. Maybe I could stay hidden.

"What are we going to do?"

My heart jumped then relaxed as I realized Archer's voice was coming from the library. I stepped toward the secret door on silent toe-tips.

"Calm down, we can deal with this."

Cassian. They were downstairs, not on the library balcony. I was safe for now.

"I thought you said we had time."

"Never enough, unfortunately."

"Are you seriously making a joke right now?"

The library door creaked open below as a third person joined them.

"Cassian, what the hell is going on?" Bruce's gruff, paternal anger sounded strained. Forced. He was…terrified. "I thought you handled this."

"I tried to. I petitioned the king for additional time."

"And?"

"He must've denied it."

"Oh, you think? Eike's not a carrier pigeon. She's a goddamn attack dog."

"I know." Cassian sounded so anxious. "I thought we'd have enough time to…"

"To what?" Neither brother responded. "What did you two do?"

"Don't look at me," snapped Archer. "It was his idea."

"You know how much women love Archer. He's like a walking cloud of pheromones. I thought it'd be best for all of us if Archer just…won Natalie over. There'd be no need to *force* the alteration on her if she fell in love with him. My mother, Archer's mother—they were human. The treaty says the rulers of the Great Houses must be bound by blood *or* marriage to their house. I thought in a couple years, or even sooner, they could wed, and then we could give her the choice to change or not."

"Oh, Cassian," said Bruce. His voice was heavy with contemptuous pity.

"I know," replied Archer. "Who *wouldn't* choose to be like us?"

"Maybe someone who understands it's a choice they can't take back," said Cassian.

"Children, the pair of you. Just wait until Mrs. Margolyes hears about this."

"She already knows," said Cassian. "She's been…helping him romance her."

My mind was a blizzard of competing thoughts. Pain, sure. Embarrassment, too. I'd known, at least since returning from Edinburgh, that Archer's attention was…superficial somehow. Practiced. And I couldn't say I'd been entirely authentic with him either after meeting Marix. But his first secret visit to my room? That first kiss at the moonlit party? They had seemed real…or so I thought, until now.

"Did you really think the king would give you *years* to win her heart?" asked Bruce.

"I don't need years," said Archer. "I just need this one not to snog her while away on weekends."

There was an awkward silence, yet through the wall, I could sense Bruce's head turning in surprise to stare at Cassian.

"She told you about that?" murmured Cassian.

"Immediately, you wanker," snorted Archer. "She was asking questions you couldn't answer. I'd compliment you on the improvisation if it didn't make me want to punch you in the face."

"Yeyeye," said Bruce. "Aside from the horrendous moral implications of this scheme of yours…do you think she cares enough to marry you, Archer?"

"It's too soon," said Cassian.

"It's too late, as far as I'm concerned!" replied Bruce. "Eike's booked a room at the Guest House. She thought she was coming here to greet the new Alter Supreme of Bear Glen, not some clueless human teenager. Eike's not going anywhere until we make our choice."

"What choice?" growled Cassian. His voice thrummed with concern. "What choice, Bruce? We're forbidden to tell her anything about our world unless she alters, but she doesn't know enough to choose it for herself! So, either Archer seduces her into the family, or he forces the change on her, or we let that…that…*creature* at the Guest House *assault* her. Natalie deserves better than that."

"Why don't you marry her, you love her so much?" quipped Archer.

"Do you *really* care so little for her?" asked Cassian. "Let's just tell her. We can explain everything to her and let her choose."

"You literally *just said* why that isn't possible."

"It is if we accept the king's punishment," said Cass.

"What, a thousand lashes?"

"I can take it."

"Are you mental?" shouted Archer. "It'd kill you!"

"Enough!" Bruce's voice carried like a foghorn. "We are changing her now and that's the end of it."

I heard the sudden screech of a chair across the hardwood floor. The *slamming thud* of a body hitting the bookshelves.

"Cass!" said Archer, his voice tight with concerned surprise.

"You touch her and I'll kill you." Cassian's voice was raw and low, almost a snarl.

"Son, everything I've ever done was to protect you and your brother. This great house." Bruce's voice quivered with surprise. "And I will continue to do that even if you're blinded by pheromones. Even if you broke the covenant and told her, if she didn't submit, she'd die anyway."

"Archer can't control himself!" said Cassian. "He'll kill her."

Bruce hissed, annunciating every syllable, "That is a risk we'll have to take."

"Please don't make me hurt you, Bruce," said Cassian.

"It's already done, Cass." Bruce's voice was soaked in sorrow.

"What's done?" asked Cass, his voice trilled with fear.

The library door opened for the final time as the last player entered the stage. Even through the wall, and the space between us, I could smell that pungent floral rot smell. Eike.

Long gone was the protective growl in Cassian's voice. "Please."

"Shhh," replied Eike. "Sometimes, it's better to beg forgiveness than ask for permission. The girl knows that better than anyone. She's there, listening right behind that wall."

All at once, I could sense four sets of eyes turning toward me through the plaster.

I turned to run…but there was nowhere *to* run. Two men I'd never seen before were standing at the exit, staring at me.

There was a sudden crunch and creak as the secret door to the library swung wide on its hinges revealing Eike on the other side. Before I could take a step back, her hand shot out, and I felt a terrible electric bite in my side as she cast me into utter darkness.

CHAPTER 23

I woke in the arms of Eike's men as they carried me down the main stairs.

"Let me go!" I screamed, squirmed, and yanked indecorously in their tight grasp, until they set me down and then pulled me to standing so I could walk…while they kept their hands clamped to each of my wrists.

Before I could try to tear myself free again, a terribly calm voice reached me.

"Don't fight this, child," said Eike.

She stood at the entrance to the far hall. Behind her, Bruce and Archer held Cass much in the same way the men held me. But he'd been fighting longer. Bruce had a black eye, Archer a busted lip. When Cass saw me, his own guilty, impotent terror amplified my own. I felt my body beginning to quiver out of my control.

"Please just let me go," I said. "I…can sell you the estate. It's fine. Take it. Cass, just take it. Archer?"

Archer couldn't look at me. Bruce wouldn't. The mood was so somber I felt like I was walking to the gallows.

Only Cass, with his shining eyes, met my gaze, and in it, I saw a thousand competing things. Promises. Apologies. That warning he'd been trying to give me in the most ham-fisted way possible. As I watched, he tore futilely against their hold on him; terrible bruises formed on his arms where he strained.

"Natalie, I'm sorry!" he said.

"I just want to go home now," I tried. I hated the fear in my voice…and I hated the indifferent, patronizing grin on Eike's face. "Just let me go home."

"You *are* home, my dear," she said. "Where, Bruce?"

"The second salon. It's due for renovations anyway."

Due for…

"You asshole!"

I dropped my weight into my toes, leaning back as far as I could in their grasp, forcing them to drag me there. I thought of screaming, but there seemed to be nobody here. For the first time since I'd arrived, the servants were nowhere to be seen.

The door opened ahead of us, exposing a dark *hole* of a salon. One I'd never bothered to spend much time in. There weren't any windows; there wasn't even any wallpaper. Just a water stain on the ceiling, broken crown molding, and wood floors that turned to painful splinters under my bare feet as they tossed me in and shut the door.

"Let me out!" I wailed on it until the side of my fist turned purple. "Archer! Bruce, you coward!"

When that didn't work, I turned to the room itself. There was *nothing*. Not even a vent. Until I saw the tiniest lip of wood extending upward along one of the floorboards. I knelt beside it, clawing with my nails at the smallest hope that I could pry it free.

I just…barely…had the lip. I wiggled it to loosen the ancient nails. I pulled the plank slightly up and to the side.

The door opened suddenly and I rose to hide what I was doing, expecting to see Eike and Bruce. Instead, Eike entered with Archer, who swayed rudderless, torn, like a little boy waiting for a parent to come clean up after him. His gaze wandered to my feet, then away, then back again.

"Archer?" I asked.

"It'll be over before you know it, Natalie," he said. "I'll make it as painless as I can."

I recoiled, looking at Eike, who seemed disgusted by his placating.

"Darling," she said. "Don't make promises you can't keep."

Archer did a double take. "What do you—"

There was a sudden blue flash of light so bright I had to jerk my gaze away. When I looked back, Eike was gone, the far door closing behind her. And Archer began to shake. He looked back toward Eike's retreating figure with a look of genuine surprise and fear.

"Archer?"

I didn't know what to do. I couldn't go to him; I couldn't run. I could barely breathe. I was hiccupping whimpers.

"Please don't hurt me."

The words were barely out of my mouth when Archer's muscles suddenly bulged to incredible proportions. I couldn't tear my gaze away as the skin split, exposing a darkness within.

I stepped back instinctively toward the plank on the floor and hefted it into my arms, ripping the last nails out.

His shirt ripped first, then his pants, as the boy I'd known became…something else. There was a terrible rupturing sound, the wet rending of flesh, and a bear tore from him as big as an elephant with paws the size of rakes and claws the size of sickles.

It—*he*—grumbled, shaking bits of Archer from his muzzle, before turning his clouded, uncertain gaze to me. The boy I knew, the boy I'd kissed so many times—and liked despite his airs and strange manipulations—was gone, but the turquoise eyes remained. Cold and observant.

He reared back onto his haunches, hitting his massive, woolly head on the chandelier. His roar cleaved the air between him and me into pieces, disorienting me. Then his paw was there, tearing the entire fixture from the ceiling. Crashing it down between us in a jumble of glass and metal that drew his terrible attention back to me.

He lunged so fast I screamed and struck before even registering. The plank of wood broke across his head, and I broke for the door, throwing my entire weight at it.

"PLEASE! LET ME OUT!"

His shadow fell across me, and I ducked just in time as his gargantuan body *slammed* into the spot where I had just been. He missed me by inches.

In the settling dust, I realized he had broken the wall and door, opening the whole thing like a can opener. Beyond, I could just see the others recoiling and coughing on plaster dust.

It was my only chance, and I took it. As the bear swiped, I ducked and crawled through the space under the door.

Where once the halls of this house had seemed too big, too extensive, too winding, they were now claustrophobic, tightening, collapsing in around me. The floors were flypaper; they stuck under my feet, holding me back, slowing me down.

I hit the far corner as the rest of the salon wall exploded outward in a firestorm of wood and plaster shrapnel. The monster gripped the hallway walls and dug in, heaving itself out after me. I raced for the staff wing. Each door I tried was sealed tight, but beyond them, I could *feel* the pregnant, scared presence of someone silently begging me to leave their door alone. In the hour Eike had been here, the staff had battened down the hatches, barricaded doors. Prepared for this.

At least here, I could turn off the lights. I'd seen Mary and Mrs. Margolyes do it. I slammed my hand down across the entire row of switches, plunging the hall into darkness.

A round giggle caught me off guard. I pressed myself to the wall and listened.

"Sweet child," Eike said, her voice distant but clear. Unharried. "Bears adore the darkness."

I rushed on, down another long, turning hall of bolted doors, leading right to a dead end, where a massive, unopenable mullioned window looked out across the back expanse. The sun had set; the badminton court was still well and truly deserted. Of course, I had no illusions that any of Archer's friends would help me, but it hit home all the same that I was *alone* here. Truly alone. Mere inches from freedom.

Another roar barreled down the hallway toward me as loud as a train. My brain foundered in response, texturizing the darkness in horrible shades of fear. Beckoning me to unconsciousness. The monster was there, observing me in the dark. I just knew it. If I didn't do something *now*, I'd collapse and awaken as its fangs pierced my soft flesh and tore.

But there was *nothing* here, except a pair of dark curtains and a massive vase of roses on an end table.

All at once, the fog in my brain cleared. The only thing between me and freedom was a thin pane of glass. I turned the roses out on the floor and hefted the stone vase into my hands. My grip firmly around the pedestal base, I closed my eyes and smashed, obliterating glass and wood frame. I dove through headfirst, ignoring the scrapes of broken glass along my legs, tipping myself forward and foisting the rest of my body out and down as a massive claw swiped through the broken window. My lungs purged as I crashed onto the compacted garden soil ten feet below; it was several seconds before I could breathe again. My vision swirled. I heaved myself to my feet and turned back. The giant bear was there, a menacing silhouette with glowing turquoise eyes.

I bolted across the back driveway toward the village in the distance. My legs were on fire beneath me, straining. I realized this was a terrible idea almost immediately. The wide stretch of meadow long grass caught and snared my feet and hid holes that my ankles hit at bruising, spraining angles.

As terrible a terrain as it was for my clumsy human body, Archer's bear was built for it. I heard his growl again, punctuated with gruff puffs of exertion. Eike and that *coward* Bruce had opened the back doors for him. The bear sprinted across the driveway on all fours. He hit the meadow grass with a bounding grace and speed that only increased as he set his sights on me.

Horror didn't come close. He was a nightmare come to life.

He was there.

Behind me.

Almost on top of me.

There was nowhere to go.

I couldn't outrun him.

As he lunged, I did the only thing I could think to do—I ducked, dropping to the ground in a ball, my hands wrapped around my neck, covering my head.

His body soared over mine, a looming shadow of raw, undisciplined might. Archer's claws raked up my back, tearing flesh, spilling warm, thick blood across my body. With it spilled memories, worries, fears. My mother's sweet face. Scarlett's mischievous one. And Cassian's, trying to warn me.

I heard Archer's monstrous form tumble to the ground nearby like a felled tree, heard his snuffling as he regained his feet and charged toward me again.

This was it. Each thunderous step was another note of my death knell. Each growl a eulogy. I could barely see for the veil of blood. I could barely hear for the ringing in my ears. At least, it would bring sweet relief to the searing pain that was at every moment wriggling through my body like thorned roots.

Then…I felt a soft hand touch me and darkness carried me into a future not of my own making.

CHAPTER 24

The darkness was textured. Soft below me. Chilled above me. And everywhere across my skin, a dappling of snowflakes at all times.

Sometimes, calluses, soothing across my arm.

And occasionally, a gentle voice, though I couldn't for the life of me understand what they said.

The pain waxed and waned every few hours in a stormy tide across the battered shore of my back. Dreams and nightmares ebbed with it. There was no such thing as time. The images lived around me, enveloping me in a landscape I didn't recognize, but that felt ever and ever more familiar. Even though I was aware of the dreaming, I couldn't control it. It took me where it wanted me to go, chasing me through the darkness in the form of a monstrous bear.

Until…

All at once, a soft light blinked into existence overhead and some dark, comforting thing soared across it, calling to me.

My eyes opened one at a time, swollen and dry. I winced at the bright daylight streaming in through my room's windows and hid my face in the warm embrace of my pillow.

I was face down on my bed with something tight and unnatural draped across my back—a bandage. Or several. Trailing from neck to hips. Another unnatural thing poked indelicately into my hand—an IV, the thing that must be delivering sweet, glorious pain relief.

"Thank gods, you're awake!"

I heard a chair push back and soft steps creeping toward me. Calluses scraped across my arm as Cassian knelt by my side, haloed in the afternoon sun.

I…I didn't know what I had expected, but my body recoiled instantly. A lightning bolt of fear streaked from the crown of my head down to my toes, and darkness fell again as swiftly as it had risen.

With it came more dreams. Revisionist memories of different choices made. What would have happened if I'd found an open room to hide in. Or an unlocked exterior door. Or…if I'd gone home when I knew it wasn't safe anymore before all of this had happened. The woulda-coulda-shoulda's stampeded through my head, trailing guilt behind them like tin cans singing, *this is your fault.*

The next time I awoke, it was long after dark, in the quiet hours when the world was still. And yet…I wasn't alone. I turned as much as I was able, flinching through the pain that movement caused, and found Cassian dead asleep in a chair at a desk that had been brought in and placed by the window. Already, there was the scaffolding of a soon-to-be tower of coffee mugs and teacups by his side as well as a cricket bat half the length of his body propped against the door frame behind him. How long had he been here?

Seeing him brought the same fear as before, tempered slightly by the fact that he was asleep, but anger filled the space that the retreating fear left behind. I hated them all. I wanted to leap out of bed and use that bat on him, then find something sharp and creep along to Archer's room and punish him, too. Bruce would come next then Eike, who I knew was still skulking around here somewhere. I wanted to slice her back open, see if she liked it.

I wanted my mother. I wanted Scarlett. I wanted someone I could trust.

When sleep swallowed me back into the abyss, it answered my request with a new memory. I was in the meadow behind the house again; the behemoth bore down on me. Only this time, I watched from a distance. I looked so small trying to outrun the monster.

This memory didn't end when I hit the ground. With blessed detachment, I watched the bear's claw pierce my skin like a rake splitting soil. I saw the blood spill across the fine tatters of the dress Judy had made for me. I saw myself go limp, stranded on my stomach, awash in blood and fear, unable to help myself as the beast turned to strike again.

I should have been petrified. This should have felt like a nightmare. But instead, relief pattered across me like warm rain, melting away the guilt I'd felt. There was no escape, nothing more I could've done. I hadn't *done* anything wrong to begin with. This wasn't a mistake *I* had made; it was a brutality that had been done *to* me.

Then…the memory surprised me again. I saw a figure dashing across the meadow—Cassian, his flop of red hair sailing behind him as he ran into the fray. He was beside me, then in front of me, warding Archer off. The monster hesitated, drew back, and swiped. The powerful claw struck Cassian's shoulder and he fell across me, curled around me, shielding me with his body as the beast struck again, crushing, shoving, pulling, trying to remove him to get to me.

I heard a great shout, saw a brilliant blue light, and the vision retreated into the darkness.

This time when I woke, I could feel the dappling of snowflakes across my skin, the calluses on Cassian's fingertips gingerly brushing hair out of my face. He had a sling on his arm; a sore blue bruise peeked out of his gray shirt along his shoulder and collar.

"It's all right, you're safe, I promise," he pleaded…he *lied.*

Tears spilled down my cheeks, unstoppable. Pathetic mewling whimpers crawled up my tight, hitching throat from deep within me. His eyes were glassy with tears, too. He crawled onto the covers beside me, wove his arm under my head, and pulled me in, pressing his warm cheek to mine.

"I'm sorry," he whispered. "I'm sorry. I'm so sorry."

I was a torrent of emotions, a broken dam unleashing sorrow upon the world. I cried not out of pain or fear or anger, but *loss*. Who was I now? What had they made of me?

***

Cass remained long after the flood subsided. It was hours before either of us moved. Even then, he only pulled back until he could lay comfortably beside me to sleep. His watchful eyes were the last thing I saw as mine closed and the first thing I saw when they opened. His silver eyes fluttered wide as he felt me waking. Night had fallen again, swaddling us in shadow.

We lay there, studying each other in the dark. There were too many questions fighting for places in the queue, all pushed back by the prevailing rage inside me.

"I want to hurt you," I said finally.

"When your strength's recovered, you should," he said.

"Has Archer been here?"

Cassian blinked with surprise. "Do you…*want*…him here?"

I wanted nothing less. My head was already shaking before the words spilled out of me, jagged and desperate: "I'll kill him if I see him."

"He won't come in."

"I mean it, Cass."

"I swear it." His hand grabbed mine tightly. I hated the touch as much as I needed it. "I'll *never* let him hurt you again. His damage is done, all right?"

I sincerely doubted that.

"That means you can tell me everything now, right? No more secrets. No more lying. Promise me the truth always."

"It's all I ever wanted to give you," he said, squeezing my hand.

I searched his eyes for deception, but I didn't see any there.

"What'll happen to me?"

"You're going to…change. We call it the Alteration. It's a process by which your human body falls away, replaced with its animal form."

"A bear?"

Cassian nodded.

"And I'll…just mindlessly attack people?"

"No. No!" he exclaimed. "Not once you have control of your alteration. It's a long process, but with time will come discipline. Power. Control. I can help you. I trained my whole life for it."

"You can change, too?"

His eyes softened with self-pity. "Unfortunately, I can't. I know it doesn't feel like it to you, and won't for a long time, but…it's meant to be a gift."

I thought of Marix, her change in the graveyard. How amazing it had seemed then. But the violent images of a bear chasing me into the darkness hit me like a slap to the face. I shrank physically from them as if the bear was right there in the room with us.

Cass began to move, drawing my eyes open again in a panic. I was a trainwreck of competing emotions I didn't fully understand. Where before his mere presence had driven me into unconsciousness, I now couldn't bear to be parted. As he moved to stand, I clung like he was the only lifeline keeping me from drifting away into a deadly, tumultuous sea.

"It's all right," he said, squeezing my hand. "Let me just show you, then I'll return to you."

I released him so reluctantly. Golden light splashed across the room as he turned the bedside light on. With care, he removed his arm from his sling before removing his shirt.

I let out a wounded sigh. Beyond the fresh, tender, purple bruises scattered everywhere, his chest and abdomen were a battlefield of torn cuts, bite marks, claw scars. He turned slowly, exposing the war-torn landscape spread across his back as well. One mark in particular—deep parallel valleys running across the left side of his waist—looked healed but recent. He completed his turn and met my eyes again.

"Don't pity me."

I reached for the cuts and waited for him to decide if this was okay. Eventually, some resistance in him broke and he leaned into my hand. My fingertips slid across the raised edges of the gashes, and the tension in me eased a little more. If he could heal from that, then I could heal from this.

When I pulled away, he slipped his shirt and sling back on and returned to the bed just like he'd promised.

"You chose this?" I asked.

"I tried to," he said. "When I turned sixteen, my father tried to force my alteration. His mother had forced it for him by biting his arm while she was still human. He thought that would work on me…now I just have a permanent reminder of one of the few times my father showed me affection. After that, I tried to force it every way I could think of. You can't imagine how many people I've asked to…"

A vivid, unwelcome image of Cassian invaded my brain, howling in pain as Will bit into his shoulder, as one stranger tore into his arm, and another sliced into his stomach.

"None of it worked. Not even when Archer tried."

My body involuntarily shuddered at the thought, even though I knew it wouldn't have been an attack, vicious and unrelenting, like mine had been.

"Does that mean it might not work for me?"

"It already is," said Cassian.

"How do you know that?"

"You have to trust me for me to show you," he said.

I expected to hear a disgusted laugh echo in my head, incredulous and angry. Instead, my mind whispered to itself the softest concern. The murmur of mistrust was there, but so was *actual trust*. Nascent and fragile, but sincere. I nodded for him to go ahead.

Cass rose again.

"Roll onto your side," he said, his reassuring hand on my arm then my legs, guiding them to dangle off the edge of the bed as he helped me sit up. "What do you feel?"

"Should I feel something?"

"No pain, right?"

I realized there wasn't any. Just a faint tingle along my spine and the discomfort of the bandage's adhesive rubbing against my back.

"Painkillers," I said, waving the hand with the needle in it at him.

"That's just for hydration," he said. "Stay there. I'll tell you when to look."

He darted around the bed, and I heard something shake as he dragged it across the floor. There was a *thunk*, a breathy gasp, then nothing.

"Are you okay?"

He crawled across the bed to sit behind me.

"There's a mirror just there. May I lift your shirt?"

My nod surprised even me. Touch delicate, his fingers dove under the hem of the tank top someone had put on me and lifted, exposing the fresh bandage. Slowly, he peeled this away, too. I glanced over my shoulder at the full-length mirror he'd moved from the corner, expecting to see torn flesh and horrid scar tissue where Dr. Martin had sewn the wounds. But there were no stitches and no ugly tatters, either. Only five nearly healed claw marks, a white tattoo of guitar strings down my spine.

"How long have I been asleep?"

"A week."

"That's impossible."

"That's the alteration," said Cass, returning the bandage to my skin and lowering my shirt. "Increased healing is just a fringe benefit."

"And the PTSD is just a fringe drawback?" I joked, letting it fall flat between us.

"It's *magic*, you know? I've been a part of this world my entire life, and I don't even know all the possible gifts and responsibilities you're going to receive now."

"Responsibilities, right," I said, thinking of what I'd overheard Bruce say before the attack. "I'm the Supreme of Bear Glen…"

"Alter Supreme, but there's plenty of time to explain what that means."

It would have to wait anyway, as another more painful thought ripped through my heart, and I grimaced with panic. If it had been a week since the attack, it meant it had been a week since I last spoke to my mom. She was probably going insane.

"What's wrong? What's the matter?" The worry in Cass's voice was lovely.

"I need to call my mom. She's probably freaking out."

Cass got up and retrieved my phone, but when I reached for it, he clung softly.

"Natalie, I know you have very little reason to trust me, but *please* don't tell her what happened. It's dangerous."

I balked, but…I knew he was right. The attack had been coordinated, even if they'd rushed it. Eike was an experienced attack dog; our brief meetings had shown me that. If I ever told my mom, it would have to wait until I was fully rested and prepared for the consequences.

"She doesn't know," he continued. "Bruce told her we took you to view the island estate."

Island estate. Sure, that might as well be a thing.

"I'll keep it short," I said, swiping away nearly fifty missed calls and dialing as he released the phone.

"Natalie! Baby?" She didn't even wait until the second ring. "Are you okay?"

"I'm okay, Mom," I fibbed. "It's been a busy week. I'm sorry I didn't call."

"What's going on? Everyone's treating you okay, aren't they?"

"It's great, here," I said lifelessly.

"You sound tired."

"I am *so* tired," I said. Cass squatted beside me, obviously listening. I thought of something to say. "This place is like a contractor's dream."

She laughed, and the sound filled me with longing. I needed a hug. "Falling apart, huh?"

"Yeah," I said, my voice breaking. "H-Hey mom? Can I call you back when we return to the mainland? I'll tell you all about it then."

"Of course, honey, I'm just so glad to hear your voice. By the way, I think I found a time I can visit soon. I can't wait to see you."

"Me too, Mom. I love you."

"I love you so, so much, little bird." Her trust in me made the lying so much more bitter.

I let Cass take the phone from me. Sleep was singing her siren's song inside me again; a wide yawn split my cheeks almost to breaking. Cass guided me back down and lay beside me, taking my hand again as it came between us.

"You'll still be here when I wake up?"

"In so many ways," he whispered.

For the first time since the attack, I slept soundly, shaken by neither nightmare, nor dream.

In the morning, I woke to the sound of an argument between Cassian and Mrs. Margolyes.

"Yes, thank you, I'll take it."

"Sweetheart, you really must come out of there. The king's djat is demanding to speak with her—"

"Now's not the time," Cass replied.

"She's losing her patience."

"She should've thought of that before the ambush. I must go, ma'am, Natalie doesn't want to see anybody. Who could blame her?"

"But—"

I heard the door shut and something click into place. Then Cassian was there with a tray and coffee. I rolled over and pushed myself up, feeling the movement along my back. Still a tingle, still no pain. I realized Cass had removed my IV as well.

"Good morning," he said. "Hungry?"

The tray he carried was piled mountain-high with the largest full Scottish breakfast I'd ever seen—streaky bacon, half a dozen eggs served sunny side up, tattie scones and mushrooms, and roasted tomatoes…and a literal tower of black pudding. The smell didn't creep into my nose; it hit like a battering ram, disturbing my to-this-point hibernating stomach.

"I know. A lot of meat. Bears…aren't exactly vegetarian."

"Maybe later," I said.

"You'll need it," he warned, setting it aside. "Your metabolism is going to skyrocket, especially in the days leading up to the full moon."

The full moon. I'd forgotten the connection. My uterus winced at the thought of having a *second* monthly ritual to endure, this one even stranger…and much bloodier.

"I want the food, it's just…"

"Just what? Do you feel all right?"

I could sense a hot blush across my skin, only doubling the embarrassment.

"I," I said, dropping my voice to a whisper, even though we were alone, "*really* need a shower."

A smile crept onto his face as he came to my side. "Well, I wasn't going to say anything."

"Hey!" I laughed.

"I've already drawn a healing bath. Would you like me to carry you?"

I shook my head. I wanted to walk on my own, to know that I could…if I needed to run.

Muhammad to the mountain, I placed my hands on the edge of the bed and coddled myself forward, feeling the cool hardwood under my toes as I summoned the strength to put pressure on them. My calves quivered like jelly. My back stretched as tight as old, chewed gum. And my neck strained in opposite directions, toward my arms, like someone had overworked the interconnecting muscles.

I collapsed almost immediately.

And Cass caught me.

"Oh."

"It's all right, you're doing great."

"I'm just sore."

"I've got you."

The steaming tub looked like some sort of elven pond. You couldn't even see the water through the floating chamomile flowers, juniper berries, boughs of pine needles, sage, and mint leaves. Cass lowered me onto a small step stool where a towel had already been placed for me and slowly began peeling away the bandage on my back. All save the very nape of my neck, where he said the deepest cuts had yet to heal.

"If you need anything, I'll be in the next room," he said, backing away.

The bracing warmth of the water enveloped me like a buzzing, soothing hug. Where the water's additives touched my back, there was a pleasant numbing fizz. I fell into a lulling doze as I organized the thoughts and questions that had scattered my mind since the assault. This bath—these rooms—were a temporary sanctuary from the terrors awaiting me outside. Separate and protected from who I would be, who Cass was when surrounded by the others. He might be able to keep the others at bay for the next few days, but eventually I'd have to face Bruce, Eike…and Archer again. And under their influence, it was only a matter of time before the guilt Cass felt for what happened to me would fade. The *responsibilities* of this "great gift" they'd forced on me would influence the information he shared with me freely. I needed to use the time I had.

"Cass?" I finally said.

"Hmm?" He hadn't even made it to the next room. I could just see the edge of his foot and leg, the soft red fuzz along his pale skin, where he was sitting on the floor right outside the bathroom door.

"What will the alteration be like?"

"I told you—"

"No, I mean *how* will I change?"

"Each month, when the sun sets on the three nights of the full moon, your body will…molt. The form you've known your entire life will become another, your back will break and realign, your nails will sharpen and stretch, your ears will relocate. Fur will spread and your human mind will recede. Archer says it's like falling down a well into a world soaked in moonlight. You hear your humanity from far away, but it doesn't have control."

Even in the hot water, I shuddered.

"But Bruce and Mrs. Margolyes say that eventually the well shrinks. Your human brain melds with your animal soul, giving *you* control again, among other things."

"Do they—?"

"Yes," said Cass. "A cantankerous badger and bossy hedgehog, respectively."

As much as I despised their part in this, the image of them transforming into woodland animals swirling with moonlight made me smile. Cass had been right—it was *magic*, pure and simple.

"If it's only at the full moon, then how did Archer change to hunt me?"

"Eike has something in her possession that allows her to temporarily force the alteration. Just one of many unscrupulous tools she's used to rise in our world. Wolverines aren't exactly *noble*. Especially when they're used as a gun-hand for the king."

I didn't care about this king or his bloodhound. If I never saw Eike again, it would still be too soon. But I did care about the pain of my body ripping itself apart.

"Will it hurt?"

"No!" His response wasn't just immediate—it warbled with desperation. "We have strong painkillers to give you. My father believed that a peaceful transition made regaining control of your humanity easier in the long run. With a lot of training and concentration and discipline, you'll be able to transform at will, full moon or not."

That explained Marix on the night of Archer's party, trapped in the snare. I tried to imagine wielding that type of power, but I still felt wholly and only human. I took hold of the tub's rim and strained, shaking, to stand in the tub so I could study my human body in the mirror. Everything looked the same as it had before—I was still a strange, curvy, short thing with olive skin and wavy hair prone to tangle—although I noticed the milk chocolate of my hair had deepened in the interim to dark. The only true difference, aside from the myriad bruises, were the claw marks, the white violin string scars running along my spine from head to tail. Ugh, god, would I have a *tail*?

"Are you done?" asked Cass. "Are you covered?"

I reached for the soft towel and wrapped it around myself like a strapless dress.

"Do we have another towel somewhere for my hair?"

Cass entered bashfully, eyeing me like a curious animal. He pulled another towel from a nearby cupboard and approached, smiling.

"What is it?" I asked, ignoring the stupid flutter in my stomach that had hurt me more than it had ever helped me.

Cass plucked chamomile flowers and juniper buds from my wet hair.

"Are they everywhere?"

"Yes. Suppose I didn't think about where the loose pieces might go."

I peeked down the towel dress instinctively then met Cass's wide eyes as I glanced up again. I watched his Adam's apple rise suddenly and crash and felt a delicious pulse ripple through my abdomen in response.

"What's the matter?" he asked, his voice as soft as a morning breeze.

"Nothing," I lied, doubling back immediately as the truth forced its way up through my throat. "Thank you."

"You don't have to—"

"I hate that you lied to me and tried to manipulate me, and I loathe that you kissed me insincerely…but thank you for saving my life."

"I was just trying to do the right thing," he said.

"Well, I know I'm biased, but I think you did."

His Adam's apple rose and fell again as he held out his hand and helped me from the tub. I took several wobbly steps to the closet door with his help then watched him retreat only to reappear again.

"For the record," he said, his eyes bright and hopeful, "it was never insincere for me. When I learned you'd told him you thought my kiss was a diversion, I didn't deny it…only to protect my brother's feelings. In truth, from the moment I met you, you have been my constant distraction."

CHAPTER 25

My dad's old NASA hoodie gave me courage as I toddled my way back to the sitting room; it also hid the blush that had ravaged my body in the few seconds since Cass had last spoken.

"I understand that, ma'am, but she doesn't want to see him…"

Cass was at the door. Just beyond, I could see Mrs. Margolyes's dandelion mane of brown curls. I skirted the long couch at the center of the room, out of her eyeline, listening.

"Really, sweetheart," she said, her voice aflutter with worry. "This isn't healthy—for either of you—to stay so long locked away. There are so many arrangements to be made before her alteration, never mind her presentation to the peasantry."

"I'll discuss it with her," he said, pulling back with a full tea tray in hand.

"When can I see her? I think it's important I explain what happened."

There was a second figure in the doorway. His long, brown hair was oily from lack of washing and the circles under his aqua eyes were so deep he looked like he hadn't slept in a week.

Archer.

An invisible pressure rippled across my body like a shockwave, tightening my muscles almost to tearing. Unconsciousness yanked abruptly on my mind, like pulling a leash. But rage—that roiling flame that had been waiting just under the surface of my skin since that night—burned the leash away and set my feet on fire.

"Just give her more time, Archie. Be patient."

"Give *her* more time or you?" said Archer. "I can smell her all over you—"

I had traveled the distance between the couch and the door in the blink of a wrath-blind eye, and my hands were under the tea tray in Cass's hands before Archer even registered I was there.

"Natalie, I—"

"Get away from the door, Archer," I said, my fingertips *blazing* with the heat from the tray.

"You must know it wasn't me," he sputtered.

"Go away!"

"I swear I didn't mean to hurt you!"

My hands exploded toward the tray and hurled it at him. He ducked aside as the entire arrangement crashed into the far wall with the crunch of ceramic, splatter of jam, and tinkling rain of silverware.

"That was an *antique,*" Mrs. Margolyes said a moment later, when Archer had turned back to face me, looking far more hurt and surprised than I had anticipated.

"Stay away from me," I snapped at him once more for good measure before slamming the door in his face.

I shook as I watched Cass fit a chair under the doorknob just so, barricading it, before turning his curious eyes on me.

"I know I shouldn't have reacted that way," I said, shaking the adrenaline out of my arms; they were *buzzing* with the stuff.

"It's okay," he said.

"It was that or-or faint again."

"Do you feel better?"

"No."

"What can I—"

I wrapped my hand around his neck and pulled him toward me like a rushing tide. His soft lips responded to my unspoken question, matching my frenzy with patient desire, calming me. His uninjured arm enfolded me in his embrace, his fingers caught on the folds of my hoodie and held me fast. When we came up for air, his red lashes skimmed across the quicksilver pools behind them like sparks dancing.

Just as quickly, the joy in his eyes fizzled with pain.

"Is this…okay?" I asked.

He kissed me again and again, his morse code clear without translation.

"They'll come eventually," he said.

I dove into his chest and whined—I didn't want to think about that.

"I'll be with you the entire way, teapots at the ready."

It was a lovely thing to say, especially accompanied by the brush of his fingers across my forehead, playing with a loose wave of my hair. But I would need more than that if I hoped to stand on my own here. If I hoped to get ahead of the plans other people had for me.

"I need you to do something else for me," I said. "There must be books, guides, papyrus scrolls about all of this."

"Of course," he said.

"Bring them to me. I want to prepare."

"Oh, gods." A smile broke across his face, bypassed his dimple, and crinkled the corners of his eyes. "A nerd after my own heart."

"I hope that's a compliment?"

"More of a silent prayer."

He slipped out into the hall with a mischievous glint in his eye and returned a few moments later carrying a stack of old, *thick* tomes. As I opened the door to let him in again, I could see a smattering of staff—including Mrs. Margolyes—gaping at him from down the hall.

"Heavens help us," she said, staring at me. "Is he *smiling*?"

Door barricaded again, he saw me nestled on the couch and called out the fragile, ancient corners of the first volume, saying that it would come apart in my hands if I wasn't careful. Then he kissed my forehead, handed me the book, and slid into his own chair nearby with a novel in hand.

"Cass…"

"Hmm?"

"You don't have to stay for this," I said.

"Believe me, I know." He smiled. "I learned all of this ages ago. Just think of me as a handsome search engine on standby. Or an inspiring work of art, in a pinch."

The heavy tome's gold filigree title, *The Age of Animals*, had worn away over time, leaving the shadow of a brand across the fabric face. Only the letters *Anima* retained some sparkle of their former elegance. When I cracked the cover open, I was surprised to find it began with the very origin story Archer had told me on the ledge overlooking the valley—the magicks of the earth twisting themselves into unbreakable knots, forever trapped within and forging the physical confines of the Earth. Jealous of the animals' freedom to roam, the magicks had conspired to ensnare and possess them…but only the early humans had been naïve enough to venture within reach. The magicks reimagined them. Improved them. *Altered* them.

Cultures all over the world had myths of their own to explain why some of their kinsmen were able to change their form, but it happened wherever humanity and the wild, frayed ends of the creation magic mixed. And it continued happening throughout the centuries until every single loose thread of magic had been pulled.

With time came a sense of community as alter families found each other, drawn together by their scents and their collective "murmurations" under the full moon. With time came mistakes, poor choices, and the insane few whose alteration awakened terrible darkness in them. With time came fear…and hunts among the humans to rid the world of the strange monsters who devoured their children while they herded sheep on the hillsides.

The book contained drawings of these incidents. Too many of them, as if at one point the information had to be digestible to an illiterate audience. Gruesome and gory, their colors bright and fresh, as if they had just been painted—

When my stomach mutinied and waves of nausea rolled through me, I wedged a bit of paper in as a bookmark and shut the book. I was barely a quarter of the way through, but I'd seen enough for a lifetime.

"You all right?" I looked up and found Cass watching me. Then I blinked, realizing he was haloed by the setting sun.

"How long was I reading?"

"Nearly four hours."

"Time flies when you're making yourself sick."

"You reached the highlight reel, I gather." He put his book aside and came to me. My stomach fluttered as he lifted my legs and draped them over his lap, then sat almost flush against me, like it was the most obvious place for him to be.

"Highlight reel?"

He grabbed *The Age of Animals*, opened it to my bookmark, and hummed playfully. "This is only the thirteenth incident of hundreds."

My stomach rolled again. "Hundreds."

"Over thousands of years." He smiled at me. "I can move your bookmark past that section, if you want."

"No," I grumbled. It was tempting, but the entire point of this was to know what I'd been forced into. "I just need a break."

"Ask and ye shall receive." He leaned forward over my legs and deposited the book on the coffee table with a delicate thud, and his hands settled on my knees before I could blink. He leaned back with a lovely, contented sigh and his brow furrowed. "You're much too far away though."

I wiggled closer, savoring the ripple of joy through my body as he closed his eyes and pressed his forehead to mine. He was beautiful like this, with the storm clouds lifted off his shoulders, his hair a disheveled wave of fire, and his stubble such a beautiful dark contrast, like burnt jasper. And there was a spot just between his chin and cheek that looked so kissable. Even his pale complexion, no doubt a result of *brooding* in dark rooms, had gained some color, which seemed silly considering he'd only traded one room for another.

Gah, how he had *ever* thought I could concentrate on Archer with him here was beyond me. Honestly, him coaching Archer into a relationship with me should have angered me, but it just left me baffled.

"Are you staring at me, my lady?"

Ugh god, I was. How embarrassing.

His eyes remained closed, but the corners of his mouth quirked upward playfully. Before I could retreat, he lifted his hand to the neck of my hoody and hooked two fingers into it, tugging a little to keep me close.

I sucked my teeth, letting the fluster and excitement of being caught mellow before speaking. "Maybe."

"Well mindreading *isn't* one of our perks. What are you thinking?"

Ah, but that'd be even more embarrassing…

No, I was honestly curious about it, and had been since I'd eavesdropped on them through the wall.

"How…" Was that the way to start this question? "Why did you try to *Cyrano de Bergerac* me and Archer?"

His eyes opened with a mixture of amusement and fear. Like he couldn't decide if I would hate him for the truth or find it funny. Or maybe like he'd known I would eventually ask but had been dreading it.

"Now *that* is one hell of a question." His tone was murky just like his expression. I raised my eyebrows at him for more. "He's the alter, Natalie. The natural choice. And obviously, girls flock to him so I thought you would too. Not to mention that if you had married, he could have represented our kingdom and you would have been able to remain human."

I shuddered at the thought.

Almost to sooth himself, he reached for the arm cuffs of my hoody and slid his hands into them, stretching them, until he could wrap his fingers around my bare forearms inside. "I set that in motion before I knew you. Before I knew he couldn't give you what you deserve."

My heart fluttered. From his tone, Cass thought *he* could.

I couldn't help it; I had to ask. "And what exactly do I deserve?"

His eyes widened for barely a heartbeat before his grip on my arms shifted. He drew me toward him and punctuated each statement with a kiss. "Right now? Comfort. Joy. Rest. Maybe a night of distraction?"

My eyebrows rose. "Show me what you got."

With a heart-stopping glint in his eye, he untangled himself from me, and pulled me to my feet. "Go into your bedroom and I'll call you out in a few minutes."

As soon as I entered the bedroom, he shut the door behind me with a smile. I felt a rush trying to keep myself from peeking, and I turned away completely when I heard him moving things around out there and the urge became too strong. The desk by the window where he'd been working while I slept was littered with things I hadn't noticed until now. He'd purged it of the cairn of teacups at some point and replaced those with textbooks. *Law and Armed Conflict. The Making of Global International Relations. The Logic of Violence in Civil War.* All of these sat at the edges, forming a nest around two smaller volumes. One I recognized immediately—the book of riddles he'd given me, now feathered with scraps of paper. The other was thin and sapphire blue and *mangled.* Clearly folded lengthwise and carried in a back pocket, although I'd never seen him with it.

My fingers slid in between the delicate, warped pages and peeled them back in a flutter. The entire interior was an inky tartan of black and red and blue and green. Handwritten words were scribbled everywhere, on every inch. On pages where he'd initially left margins, he'd gone back and filled them in, writing sideways. It was a journal. No, I realized. It was something more intimate.

It was poetry.

I saw only a single line before I realized what it was: *I shall devour you at the end of every day like the ocean devours the sun.*

I snapped the cover shut with a gasp. Then I panicked when the notebook's warped U shape leapt open at me again, like it intended to give my snooping away.

It wasn't the snooping I was worried about, though. Or even the way that single line of poetry had instantly rekindled the fiery knot in the pit of my stomach—no, *way* lower—that I'd felt the first time Cass and I kissed. It was the juxtaposition of everything on the desk that scared me. He had accidentally splayed himself out on the table, revealing everything I knew about him was just a rough sketch of who he actually was. Meanwhile, I was a silly blank girl who couldn't even summarize herself for a college application.

To add humiliation to panic, I was struck by the intrusive memory of telling him he was looking for a calling. Him! The talented, beautiful man who'd saved my life.

I suddenly felt about two inches tall.

And it was suddenly too dangerous for me to be left alone with that blue notebook. The first peek was almost accidental; the next million wouldn't be.

I backed away from it just as the door opened behind me and I whirled around, trying to disguise the frozen panic I could feel on my face.

"Natalie, it's ready." The warmth in his smile was gloriously beautiful. So was the furrow of his brow a second later. "Everything okay?"

I nodded and forced myself to take his hand when he offered it, ignoring the little inner voice calling me an imposter, which only got louder when I stepped into the sitting room. He had *transformed* it in the fifteen minutes I'd been in there. The staff had obviously helped, but that didn't change the fact that the vision was entirely Cass's.

The furniture had been moved aside to make room for a cozy Bedouin tent so marigold yellow it looked as if Cass had plucked the setting sun from the sky and wrung the color out of it. He'd arranged a large television on the coffee table at the entrance and filled the interior with a mountain of pillows I'd never seen before, along with a platter of cheeses and fruits and crackers.

A blanket fort. This man had built me a blanket fort.

The breath went out of me. My heart jackhammered inside of my ribcage.

"What do you think?"

What did I think*?* I thought he was a mind reader, a wizard, and entirely too good for me. I also thought it looked like something a child would love…god, this is how he saw me. Like a whimsical simpleton. And he was right! It was *gorgeous*. Exactly what I wanted. Just looking at it set me at ease, then backfired as my panic level soared inside me.

It was like a kaleidoscopic bomb went off in my brain, robbing me of anything but insecurity.

"It's too nice, Cass," I whispered.

His brow furrowed again as his lips parted in alarm. His grip on my hand tightened, pulling my stiff body toward his, as his other hand cupped my cheek and pulled my attention away from the fort.

"That's mental, Natalie. This is barely enough. If I'd had an hour—"

"If you'd had an hour, I'd be having a panic attack." I already was.

"No, hush." He pulled me toward the tent, then fell into it pulling me with him. Before I could stop him, he reached up and turned on golden fairy lights.

"Oh my god, Cass!" I didn't mean for it to come out accusatory, but it definitely did. "Twinkle lights too."

"Absolutely twinkle lights." Still nudging, he laid down on the pillows and guided me into the crook of his arm. "And next time, real stars."

"This isn't funny," I said.

"No, but I am enjoying it a little bit." He leaned over and planted a kiss on my temple.

"Cass." I sat up then, just to breathe, and he mirrored me, crossing his legs and planting his knees against my own. His hands held mine firmly, activating that magnetic charge just under the surface. "You need to tell me about yourself."

"Anything in particular or just stream of consciousness?"

"You go to Oxford, right?" Those books *would not* leave my mind.

"I do."

"What do you study?"

"International Affairs. Although, I took a trimester off when…" He winced. "To deal with my father's passing."

"Did you *always* want to study that?" Was that a dumb question? Yes. What I really wanted to ask was *were you always fifty seven years old*?

"Yes," he said with a smirk. "Finally feels like I'm studying something I want to. I much prefer it to my first degree."

“First degree?”

“Oh, you would call it an undergraduate degree, I think.”

I blinked. “You already have an undergraduate degree?”

“In history. I hated it. Never been so bored in my life. But if you want to change things, it helps to know how they got that way.”

“So you’re getting your master’s,” I said, just to make absolutely sure of my own inferiority. “At twenty.”

“Most degrees last three years here.”

That did nothing to assuage how I felt…and he seemed to sense it, as a gorgeous smirk stretched his cheeks again and he kissed me.

“I told you I’m a nerd,” he said, nipping at my jawline.

“That means you started college at sixteen.” He nodded against my skin, tickling with his stubble. “You study. You write poetry. Next you’re going to tell me you play the viola and won an international tennis tournament or something.”

He pulled back with a light in his eyes and a slow smile that tightened that knot in my stomach. “You read my poetry?”

“Accidentally.” His hands squeezed mine. “And I suddenly feel completely undressed.”

His eyebrow rose.

“You know what I mean,” I said, feeling a blush beginning to spread. And I couldn’t even cover it while he had hold of my hands. “You’re…” *Lovely. Amazing. Too much.*

“Natalie. Do you remember what I told you at dinner in Edinburgh?” He blinked softly at me. “We choose who we want to be.”

“And you chose *all the things*,” I said.

“I did,” he replied. “I was a spoiled rich kid. I had the time. The breath of mind to take my time. I never had to work at a pizzeria after school and *then* go to a second job.”

I did a double take. “How did you know about that?”

It was his turn to blush. “I stalked you on social media. Public profiles, remember.”

It shouldn’t have set me at ease, but it did. “That’s how you knew I liked blanket forts.”

He smiled again. “I love having an excuse to make one. And someone to make one for.”

And I loved someone making one for me.

"My point is I *know* I'm lucky to have the resources I do. I don't take them for granted. I don't take anything for granted. Neither do you. And now you have all the resources in the world. I can't wait to see what you'll do with them."

That sounded lovely. And humongous. And terrifying. And like he was offering me a challenge. Might be silly that that's all it took to calm me down, but it did. It didn't just calm me; the possibilities thrilled the fear right out of me.

"You're not *that* spoiled," I said after a long exhale.

He ran his thumb across my hand and that heart-stopping smile reached his eyes. "Yes I am."

Twenty minutes later, we were on our stomachs lost in an animated movie, his hand draped over me, his fingers tracing imaginary figure eights across my back, careful to avoid the scar along the spine. And when we went to bed, we fell asleep holding hands again.

The next day, I woke to a feathered kiss across my forehead as he rolled out of the bed and went to get breakfast. By the time he returned, I was already in the tent reading, pushing myself through the *hundreds* of reports of what *The Age of Animals* called aberrant alter behavior. Entire sections read like rudimentary police investigations as small bands of alters hunted their own most wayward members, desperate to save the herd at the expense of the *feral*.

This last word caught my particular attention. The book seemed to talk *around* this phenomenon, almost fearful of it, even though it seemed to happen more regularly than the author wanted to admit. As far as I could tell, it happened when the animal form overpowered its human, with terrifying deadly results. But there were no details about how someone went feral, or why. Only accusations. Any time there was an attack on humans, the hunting party tacked it on as the only possible explanation. *Except* when the crimes involved dragons. Yes dragons, which the book treated as commonly as it did bear and seal and rabbit alters. Like dragons were everywhere, and constantly doing nefarious things. They seemed to survive *solely* on human prey, but save one specific incident in London in 1888 and another in the 1400s involving someone called *the Dragon of Wallachia*, they were never called feral. In fact, the book said they exhibited enviable restraint which *prevented* them from going feral.

Unfortunately, by the time I finished the gruesome historical records of attacks, the book offered no more details about the phenomenon…and I was starting to feel sick again. The pictures had only grown *more* detailed and grotesque as the history progressed toward the modern age.

"Cass?"

I looked up and blinked rapidly to alleviate the strain that had crept into my eyes. It had been hours since I'd started reading, and Cass was nowhere to be seen. I forced myself to my feet, stretched feeling back into my feet, and found him at the desk in the bedroom hyper focused on Will's book of riddles.

"Oh no," I said, admiring him. "You're so bored you're solving riddles."

"Or trying to." He hooked his hand inside the pocket of my hoodie and pulled me in, blinking contentedly. "I've almost got this one."

He'd scribbled, erased, and re-scribbled notes along all four margins of a full-page riddle called "A Tower, A Man." But he seemed to have stopped vandalizing the book in favor of scribbling on a piece of paper nearby.

"I've at least figured out it's a two-way riddle."

"What's that?"

With a flick of his finger, he slid the piece of paper over to cover the right half of the riddle. Like breaking an optical illusion, the remaining visible words formed a new, more digestible puzzle called "A Tower."

He slid the paper over to cover the left-hand side of the riddle, revealing a second puzzle titled "A Man."

"I...didn't know there was such a thing."

"My father used to love them," said Cass. "He said if you only scratch the surface—"

"You miss the wisdom hidden underneath," I finished. A caterpillar of excitement crawled up my spine.

"That's right," he said. "He said these sorts of puzzles rewarded a second look and a skewed perspective, something which he probably admired a little too much."

Knock-knock. Someone was at the door.

Cass rose like a shot, kissing my nose in passing. "I'll get that."

Will's riddle was still hidden in the backpack, which had gotten shoved into a corner in the nearly two weeks since I'd traipsed across the estate looking for the riddle's answer.

As I flipped the photograph over to study the riddle again, Will's *I'm sorry* at the bottom came into sharper focus than it ever had before. But so, too, did the split narrative hidden within the riddle:

A treasure beneath,	***a prize on high***
Within stone sheath	***under bark of dye***
Where green sentinels loom	***near gleam of armored show***
In a sacred tomb,	***only the hiding one knows***
The moon reveals a future bright	***where heads lay deep in the dead of night***

...All it takes is just one bite

As embarrassed as I was not to have realized, seeing Will's split riddle so clearly now made my heart soar, and it *was* clear.

I was certain the left side referred to the crypt, the stone sheath which I'd found deep in the forest under towering green sentinels, which meant the right side was a clue about where to find the crypt's key.

Bark of dye—a drawn or painted or colored tree.

Armored show—sure, it might be actual armor, but a show suggested pretense to me, as well as representation. A piece of art again, depicting the *pretense* of appearing strong and capable.

Only the hiding one knows—it was a given the thing was hidden...but "hidden" wasn't the word he'd used. Hiding was active. *The hiding one* was probably a visual clue about what to look for.

Where heads lay deep in dead of night—pillows. A bed!

No, it couldn't be. My heart leapt in my chest as I stepped closer to the tapestry above the very bed I'd been sleeping in. I studied those weird, misshapen armored hunters on their horses surrounding the creature hiding in its den under the alder tree.

"You have to be kidding me," I whispered.

It was there. *Right there.* The key had been right under my nose this entire time. Or rather, right above it. There was an almost invisibly fine seam in the tapestry wallpaper at the heart of the alder tree.

"Natalie?" called Cass.

"Just a second."

A new voice replied, "By all means, take your time."

Eike. My heart lurched at the sound of her arrogant, apathetic voice and plummeted into my feet as I approached the sitting room doorway and saw not only Eike, but Bruce and Archer lurking in the far doorway. Their expressions were a caricaturist's buffet of impatience, indifference, and shame. Eike eyed the marigold tent with a disdain that bordered on revulsion.

Cass stood in the no man's land between us, his back to me, and my heart flinched, wondering if this was the moment. The moment they called him back to them, bursting the little bubble we'd shared in here.

"Cass?"

He turned and I saw the cricket bat in his hand, his white knuckles tight against the handle, ready to swing.

"It's all right," he said, backing up to join me. His hand slid into mine and squeezed again, administering courage.

"It really *is* quite all right," said Eike, rolling her eyes. "Why are men always so dramatic?"

"What do you want?" I asked.

"To talk, darling child." She eyed Cass like a gnat. "Alone, preferably."

"I'm not going anywhere," snapped Cass.

"Ugh, saving this one won't erase your past failings," said Eike, her nose almost curling with contempt.

"Shut up."

"Cassian!" Bruce's face paled instantly. "My apologies, djat. He's not thinking clearly."

"A good poke in the eye might fix that."

I could feel Cass's heartbeat quicken through my palm. It wouldn't do. There wasn't time for more medieval cruelties and thinly veiled threats. I didn't want these people in here any longer than they had to be…and the thought of that tapestry waiting to be peeled back, exposing the treasure within was boring a hole in the back of my head. Quickly, I wrapped Cass's hand in both of mine and drew his attention away from them. I shot him a gentle, reassuring smile.

But I couldn't maintain it for long. When I turned back, Archer stared at me. He wore shame like a shroud. He still hadn't showered. Or shaved. And his knuckles were freshly scabbed where he'd split the skin.

"I'll ask again, honorable djat," I said. "What do you want?"

“To be friends, of course,” she said. “Once we’ve gotten the unpleasantries out of the way. The only reason I’ve remained so long in this dreary place is to confirm your mark. I’m dying to see it.”

My brow furrowed in confusion.

“They want to see your back,” Cass whispered to me.

I gritted my teeth and turned, pulling up the shirt for her to see. Eike’s hollow hoot of a laugh broke the silence as she approached. She pressed her cold fingertips to my skin and ran them the length of the scars. The pain I felt at her touch was violent, spiritual pain though it was; I had to squeeze Cass’s hand for more courage.

“Lucky girl. So elegant. Imagine if he’d caught your face or something more delicate.”

I turned to face them again and absorbed the new variety of expressions I found. Eike was amused, Bruce relieved. Archer looked like he was going to be sick…which suited me just fine.

“Now that you are *truly* one of the family,” said Eike, “we may speak freely.”

She strutted to the couch and sat, draping today’s costume—a blue, single-shoulder pant suit under a cape—across the seat before settling, scattering her sulfur stink into the air. She motioned to the loveseat across from her, and I pulled Cass to it.

“With a little less than a fortnight until your first change, you haven’t given us much time to satisfy tradition, but it is of little consequence. Your presentation to your people, the coronation, your cataclysmic suffering—these pale in importance compared to your royal oath of allegiance. After your true nature has claimed you and returned you to your human form, I will take you to the palace at Hrafnagud to see the king. He is just *dying* to meet you. Of course, he thought it would have happened sooner, but he forgives the slight. You were…uninformed.”

Bruce cleared his throat. “Yes, it was a most unfortunate misunderstanding. We sincerely apologize.” He was talking at me, but not to me. “We’re thankful for the chance to set things right.”

“Wonderful,” replied Eike, again looking at me, but not speaking to me.

Their dance curdled my stomach.

“I have a question, Eike,” I said finally, trying to keep the acid out of my voice. “Why the attack? I’ve read about other alterations. Some only took a scratch. Will’s mom altered him with a bite on his shoulder while she was still in human form. Would allowing me to change with dignity have been too much to ask?”

"Dear child, it's not your loyalty alone that I was sent here to test."

I glanced at Archer again. Shoulders dropped, head bowed, exhausted, and deflated—he looked so…small now.

Eike rose from her seat with the same sharp, disconcerting elegance as she did everything else. Cass's firm, guiding grip pulled me up as well, just in time. Eike bowed low to me, kissing my hand. "It has been my honor, my lady."

Cass, Bruce, and Archer all bowed to Eike in passing, but I couldn't bring myself to do the same. After she departed and the air cleared, her slick kiss still sat on my skin like a cold, slimy territorial mark.

Then it was just me and the Mahon invasion of my personal space again. Bruce and Archer loitered by the door, shifting uneasily as I stared. I wondered if they truly understood the new nature of our relationship.

"I hope you understand that it wasn't personal—" Bruce tried.

For Cass's sake, I tempered what I really wanted to say. And even what I said…probably not reassuring for anyone, but it was the best I could do. "Bruce, the only reason you're not choking on your own blood is because Cass has already lost a father."

Bruce glanced at Cass. I could sense his attention but didn't look at him.

"All the same. We must discuss the schedule, my lady."

"Slip it under my door."

"And your responsibilities—"

"OUT."

Bruce went willingly…but Archer lingered, wringing his hands like a little thief trying to curry favor from a cold, uncaring judge. I pointed after Bruce.

"Natalie, please," he said. "Eike forced me to transform. I would *never* hurt you. It was her. She made me—"

"Just go, Archer."

"Can't you hear me out?"

"No."

"Why not?"

"Because it makes me sick to look at you!"

His eyes glassed over instantly as he turned to flick away a tear and hide the quiver in his lip. Then he went through the door, closing it behind himself. In the vacuum afterward, I didn't know what to do. I turned to find Cass waiting, watching with a hound dog expression of his own.

“I wanted to say worse,” I said, rubbing my face.

“I know,” he replied.

“But you should talk to him,” I said. “I know you want to. And he needs you.”

“Will you be all right?”

I nodded, letting him pull me into a hug.

“I’ll bring back tea as well.”

After Cass left, I returned to the task that had been five years interrupted. I entered the bedroom, shedding the unpleasantness of the last few minutes from my person like a bulky bag of homework.

This…well, this riddle was for me. I had finally solved it.

I stepped onto the bed to reach the tree in the tapestry and slid my fingers across the textured expanse, feeling the threads, the grooves, the minute tears in the plaster until I felt the small square seam in the heart of the alder. I ran my nail along the edge before I felt the plaster give a little under my fingers and pressed. The tapestry dented a solid quarter inch before I released, and a small door popped under the fabric. Slowly—carefully—I cut the tapestry and left the piece to hang, swinging the tiny door open to reveal my prize within.

CHAPTER 26

I blinked in confusion, absorbing the narrow, pitch-black cubby before me. Anticlimactic was an understatement: it was empty. And from the heavy black snow of dust along the bottom, it had been ages since anyone had used the cubby at all. I reached in all the same. My fingers slid through the gritty layer of dust, searching blindly, until they hit something smooth and metal-cool in the darkness.

Holding my breath, I seized a corner of the thing and pulled, catching the skeleton key in my open hand. The sheer weight of it scattered goosebumps up my arms…or maybe that was the strange vibration I could feel resonating through the metal into my flesh. It was the *most beautiful* thing I had ever seen. Under the cobwebs and dust bunnies, the brass shined as bright as a new penny, weaving in and over itself along the throating, collar, and shank before billowing into a strange, angular bulb at the end. The bow was hollow; inside, a tiny, many-sided die made of obsidian rolled freely within its ornate cage. At the other end, instead of exposed teeth all pointing down, they alternated strangely, nestled inside an oversized, rounded pin.

"No, that's amazing," I whispered.

From head-on, the key looked like a bear head, with its mouth full of teeth, its pin a rounded nose, and the strange shape of the bow at the back rounding up and out to form the ears.

It was almost too beautiful to hide, but I would have to for now. I fed the glorious thing into a small groove in the torn headboard, and carefully sealed the secret cubby shut again as best I could, wetting a tiny corner of the old adhesive to put the tapestry back.

I heard Cass come in and stepped off the bed to admire my work—the tree was a little wonky now, its trunk a bit more wrinkled than before—but it would do until I could source some actual glue. If Cass found it beforehand, well…it was the sort of puzzle that would reward a second look and a skewed perspective.

What mattered now was tying up loose ends before the rising tide of this new life overwhelmed me. I needed to find Marix and open that crypt in the woods. If Will's riddle led me to it, then it likely didn't have anything to do with Mael's disappearance, but it might at least give Marix peace of mind to know her daughter wasn't here.

"Tea." Cass wrapped a warm arm around me, resting his chin on top of my head. "I've always hated this tapestry. Morbid even for me."

"It tells a story," I replied.

I woke the next morning with his arm still around my waist and a crisp piece of parchment resting by the door. It simply read *Tour ~ 9:30* in Bruce's unfussy handwriting. Beside it, someone—Mary or Mrs. Margolyes—had arranged an outfit for me. One I hated as soon as I held it up to myself. One Cass told me I was expected to wear.

"*This*?" I was gob smacked. "Are they serious?"

"Tradition calls, I'm afraid."

The cream pants were fine, flowy things, comfortable as clouds and architectural marvels that knew my body better than I did…but the shirt. Judy's careful touches were everywhere apparent across the *backless* copper blouse, clearly designed to expose—nay, *showcase*—the scars up my spine like they were some masterpiece in a fine arts museum. I tried to imagine what the garment would have looked like if he had ripped off my face or torn open my leg instead. My resentment was only tempered by the sheer care Judy had shown in the front bodice, which supported and hid the rest of me with grace.

"You look like a queen, my lady," said Cass when I'd finally put it on and turned to judge it in the full-length mirror.

More like forced to imitate one as I set the final piece, a golden tiara, upon my head and felt the small, golden tines dig into my hair to keep it in place.

At nine-thirty on the dot, I took a deep breath and let Cass open the door to the hall, where Mrs. Margolyes and Bruce waited. Their gentle, excited smiles scared and saddened me—a single, selfish choice on their part had soured this. There was a very nearly identical version of this moment in which I would have welcomed their excitement and joined in it. A respectful bite instead of a hunt. A conversation instead of a crime. It would have felt like a dream come true.

Worst of all, I could see on their faces how badly they wanted me to *get over it*. Not spoil their fun for them. I was the Most Honorable Ninth Marchioness of Ayr, after all. From what I knew of Will, his flights of fancy, his grazer's personality, they'd never actually had a real head of the house to flaunt. Now they had one; they didn't seem to care that she was damaged and scared and barely old enough to drive a car. It set my teeth on edge, made my skin crawl. I thought I'd known hatred when Will left us, but I had no clue. Now I did. They had all known this was coming. My imagination ran wild, wondering if they'd still be smiling when I shed my humanity and came for them under the full moon with sharp claws and sharper wrath.

Their desire for normalcy became even more apparent as they guided me through the house. It wasn't just the staff that bowed at me; it was the paying tourists that had returned to their regular visiting schedules while I was indisposed. I didn't need to fake a smile for them; their camera flashes set my teeth on edge, cementing the smile in place like a mask. Emergency repairs had been made to the salon Archer destroyed, and when we reached the far hall where Archer had cornered me and I had bashed the window out in a futile bid to escape, I found the mullioned glass entirely intact again, not a cracked pane or noticeable new paint stroke to be seen. As if it had never happened.

"This is very important, my lady," said Mrs. Margolyes, pulling a massive key ring from her pocket. She found a key without even looking and plunged it into a nearby door. "The dungeon is where you and Master Archer will begin the night of the full moon. Please excuse the mess. We hinna had time to repair the rooms from last month yet."

We stepped into a bombed-out shelter that had been ravaged by velociraptors. Strange mats along the walls had been reduced to tatters by claws. Broken, wet straw covered the floor in clots, hiding several industrial drains. And strewn amidst the wreckage, like a bizarre piece of modern art, a white Dior robe marred by a massive, bloody bear print.

"These doors," she said, motioning to a pair of cellar doors, "will be open and lead directly into the Eastern Wood where Master Archer will take you for the duration."

"Take me where?"

"Archer can show you later," said Bruce. "Closer to the day."

"Cass will show me," I replied, broaching no negotiations.

"Yes, of course."

"The rest of the doors to the house will be locked for the protection of the staff that remain behind. Those who live in the village and beyond will leave promptly at four-thirty on the day and won't return until the full moon has passed, but food will be laid out for you both near the tree line."

Like a zoo animal, I thought to myself.

"Master Archer prefers pork," she added with an annoying smile. "Shall I bankrupt the local farm of its entire stock of berries, or will pork work for you, too?"

I couldn't rise to another vegetarian joke.

"Where will you be?" I asked Cass as we ascended the steps back into the house.

"There's a panic room."

"Of course, there is…" They'd thought of everything. Tomorrow, Dr. Martin would arrive to draw blood and prepare the right cocktail of painkillers for me. Day after that, they'd put me on the diet both Archer and Will found worked for their burgeoning metabolisms—I could only foresee more black pudding towers I wouldn't eat.

And, of course, because absolutely *nothing* had changed, there was another weekend-long party set to assuage Archer's anxiety before the full moon. I wondered if now was the time to press my authority and cancel it, rub it in his face…but then I thought again. I could use his party to do something for myself.

"Well, since I won't be attending that," I said, stopping the tour cold in the foyer, "I'd like to make arrangements of my own."

"Of…of course," said Bruce. "W-What did you have in mind?"

"I want to see my mom and Scarlett."

All three leapt forward at once, talking over each other. "That won't be possible…perhaps another time…it's such short notice."

"Why not? They're only a private flight away," I said, forcing the answer I knew they didn't want to give.

"We…" started Bruce. "You must understand there would be terrible consequences if you spoke with either about—"

"You sicced a bear on me, Bruce," I said, staring him down. "Archer would have killed me if Cass hadn't intervened, and you would have let him. Do you think I would do *anything* to risk their safety?"

"No, my lady," he said, cowed. "But I *have* been routinely updating Rebecca on your good health and happiness here during your recovery."

"Yes, you're a very good liar," I replied. "And now that you've altered my life forever, I'd like to say a proper goodbye to the old one before everything changes. Can you understand that?"

"Yes, my lady," he said. "I'll arrange the flights."

"This way, my lady," said Mrs. Margolyes.

She motioned ahead of us toward the front doors where two footmen waited to open them. Sunlight poured in, shining down across the front drive and the convertible Bentley waiting at the bottom of the stairs for us. Four Mahon tartan flags embroidered with a bear head at the center of the seven-pointed star flew from the corners. Surrounded by flowers and greenery and the cream finishes of the front fountain, the all-black vehicle looked like a strange gothic missile.

Even more off-putting, Archer was already seated in the backseat, clean and dolled up like his old self, his long brown hair fluffed and swept back, his eyes a blazing blue against the dark sapphire of his suit. He was a picture-perfect prince.

I stopped on the spot, and Cass answered my unspoken question.

"I can't go with you for this. It's—"

"Tradition, I know," I said, already physically recoiling from the thought of being within scent range of the man who had marked me.

"Just remember," he said. "The people—the alters—don't know how you came to be. They only see their kingdom's sovereign. Your poise and strength will inspire the same in them."

"Then why does he have to come?"

Cass's pale skin flushed red, worrying me. "After Archer's party, gossip spread. They'll...like the thought of you two together. It's been centuries since our region was ruled by *two* alters."

"It was just a kiss."

"Not to them." He squeezed my hand. "Forget him. You know how strong you are. Show them."

The absence I felt as I let go of his hand this time was akin to a kite snapping free of the line tethering it to the ground. But I knew it was necessary. I'd have to face this alone, just like I'd have to face the alteration alone. I forced myself down the twenty steps to the car, breathing through my mouth, and climbed in, the disgust like a magnetic aversion against my skin.

"Comfortable, my lady?" asked Dave.

No.

"Yes."

"This is only the first quarter of our grand tour, my lady," said Bruce, once again playing the tour guide in the front passenger seat. "Today, Scotland, and eventually the whole of the British Isles."

Bruce made sure to call out every single site as we passed so he could inform me whether or not I owned them. Apparently, one of the Mahon's had gone mad buying old church ruins once upon a time. They were beautiful, but it was the villages I cared about more. Ayr and Turnberry, Givan and Ballantrae, Cairngaan and Whithorn. I wanted to understand this strange world and how I fit into it. Did they actually care about me? Or was I just a figurehead who could skulk off into the shadows at the first opportunity and live a life of distraction like Will had?

The actual answer proved surreal. As our car pulled into Ayr, dozens of people emerged from shops and offices to watch me pass, waving and smiling like I was some movie star coming to momentarily grace their streets. The other people—the *humans*, as I realized they were—crowded the parade more out of solidarity than understanding. But the alters…they cared. Singletons, packs of strange siblings, and entire families with tiny children loitered excitedly on sidewalks, waving until we were out of sight. "Bless you's!" and "my lady's!" filled the air like sound confetti.

By the time we reached the next town and the next, the local alters were already waiting for us along the main street to make our trip easier. Some even waved small banners of their own, displaying their animal—rabbits, seals, horses, deer.

More surreal still, *I could tell them apart* from the humans. Perhaps it was the bouquet of competing smells, so distinct between families, but there was something in their manner and in the air around them as well. It was difficult to take in all at once, but I felt my mind expanding with each new scent.

"Something on your mind?"

I turned to find Bruce eyeing me quizzically.

"The smells, they're…"

"Be grateful you rule in an era of good hygiene," he said.

I hadn't thought of that, but sure.

"How does the smell stay so…" I searched for the word. "Specific?"

"Specific?"

I pointed as we passed. "Why does everyone in *that* family smell the same?" I pointed to a group of couples. "Why do the pairs smell the same?"

It was unmistakable. I didn't know which smells belonged to which animal, but I would have staked my life on the fact that the mated pairs—was *that* what they were called?—transformed into the same animal, if they were both alters.

"Oh," Bruce said, waving it away like it was the most obvious thing. "Like goes with like, doesn't it. Can't very well let a horse marry a snake, can we?"

Smells repeated between towns, some soured by sea salt, others deepened by moist earth, and occasionally, there was a rare scent from a visiting foreigner—tiny glimpses of those other cultures, perhaps more exotic animals. Even they seemed to respond to my presumed authority, even they rejoiced in my attention.

By the time we reached Eyemouth on the east coast, where only three families came running to wave us through, I could individuate among family members—which were alters and which weren't, which children would someday turn and which were carriers of the genetic magic.

It was, in very real terms, like there was a secret world hidden in plain view all around us. One infinitely more complex and vaster than I had imagined. And I'd found myself at the pinnacle of it all, by chance. Sure, I was sitting next to the monster who had put me there, but still.

"Natalie?"

Speak of the devil. Somewhere outside Edinburgh, Archer begged my attention by nervously tapping my knee with his finger.

"Can we talk?"

There was nowhere to go and no way to pretend I hadn't heard him. I hadn't even grabbed a pair of headphones. I shrugged. Honestly, I was amazed he'd stayed silent as long as he had.

"Is there any chance you could forgive me? I meant what I said. I *never* meant to hurt you. I thought I would simply bite you."

I prickled. *Simply* bite me.

“Then that stone came out of Eike’s pocket, and I barely remember anything after that.”

“You sliced me open like a piece of meat,” I said.

“I-I know, but…”

My eyebrow rose in disgust, waiting to hear what he could possibly say to excuse it.

“It was going to happen anyway. It was either that or Eike would have killed you.”

“So…better *you* kill me?” I fixed a cold stare on him, watching his gaze flit around the edges of my face instead of meeting my eye. “I’m only alive because Cass stopped you from tearing my body apart.”

“No, you’re alive because he hates himself after...” His voice died like a gunshot.

“After what?”

“After he got our father killed,” he said.

My mouth opened and closed in confusion. His curled into a petty, angry grin.

“Didn’t tell you about that, did he?”

“You said Will died from a heart attack.”

“He did, in a manner of speaking. Took a silver bullet to the chest.”

More twisted words. More subterfuge. He seemed to sense my rising disgust again, and his haughty air faded.

“Look, I *am* genuinely sorry, Natalie,” he said. “I’m sorry my father got you mixed up in this. I’m sorry it hasn’t been easy for you. I’m sorry my brother lied to you.”

“Are you sorry you attacked me?”

“I already told you. I couldn’t help it once my bear form emerged.”

Disappointment leached into me like a vapor; he really was just a little boy unwilling to take responsibility for his actions.

“You know,” I said. “Before the attack, I had decided to return everything to you. After the attack, I wanted to kill you. But this feels like a more fitting punishment.”

“What does?”

“To watch me live well despite what you did. I mean, because of you, every alter in our kingdom sees me as their lady now. And I have every reason to embrace it since I can’t give it back…Who knows? Maybe one day, they won’t remember you at all.”

It was almost nightfall when we reached the house again. Archer left the car in a sullen huff, drawing Bruce and Mrs. Margolyes along in his wake, leaving me at last in blessed silence as Dave pulled the car away. Upstairs, I could see the lit windows of my room and a flicker of ginger hair.

I needed a walk. I needed a breath. I needed to find Marix.

I walked the edge of the house, past the dungeon cellar doors, around to the small green hollow outside the library, then headed into the forest, down the animal trail where a dark creature had once chased me home.

I'd expected quiet. Solitude. But this place had never been louder. A riot had replaced the once-gentle conversation of the wood. The birdsong was now overlaid with the percussion of hooves, the harried sniffs of tiny noses, the *digging* of creatures underfoot. Through it all, I heard her coming, her soft padded feet bounding over rocks, her fingernails digging into logs for purchase. A branch snapped a hundred yards away, as loud as a ringing phone. I knew where Marix would emerge before she did…and knowing that set my brain on fire with joy.

I waited, wondering if she would sense the change in me.

"My goddess, I couldn't stop thinkin' about you. Are you all right?" she asked, rushing forward to wrap her arms around me.

I hadn't expected the hug, but I fell into her warm, soft kindness like I needed it. Tears fell on the white shoulder of her blouse in dark smears.

"I saw the whole thing," she said. "I was halfway across the meadow coming for you when I heard you scream. There was this…bright blue light…dunno what it was, but my body just collapsed. I couldn't get to you. I'm so sorry."

She released me and turned my body so she could see the scar. When she turned me back, I expected pity, but found only wisdom.

"My nan, she used to say you could tell a lot about a person's wyrd by the look of their mark."

"Wyrd?"

"Their destiny," she said. "*You* have a song to sing, strings to pluck."

I smiled. "An instrument was the first thing I thought of when I saw it."

"Everything's made of music, love," she said. "You've got your entire life ahead of you."

"What was yours?"

"My what?"

"Your mark. What did it look like?"

"Oh, I never had one. For those of us born of this, it's more of a spiritual mark. Ancestral, I guess. And what was there is gone now anyway."

For a moment, I watched her gaze glass over with tears and memories of the past. A twitch of pain turned to sorrow. I could practically see Mael's smiling face in her eyes.

"I found the key to the crypt, Marix," I said.

The clouds vanished from her eyes. "The…are you sure?"

I nodded.

"This is incredible. You don't know how long I've waited!"

I winced. "You know there might be nothing in there, right? I don't want you to be disappointed. I found the key following a riddle Will gave me years ago. It might not have anything to do with Mael's disappearance."

She wrapped me in another aching hug, dismissing the thought with a soft *tut*.

"It's all right. I already know who's responsible."

"Who? Did you learn something while I was away?"

She reached into her pocket and produced something I didn't recognize outside the context of Cass's bedroom. A slip of wrinkled, tattered fabric, soaked through with brown liquid and never washed—the blood-splattered cloth I'd found in his desk.

"After they took you inside, I found this where you fell," she said. "It's her blood. My wean, sweet baby."

Her tears hit the dried blood, rehydrating it to its original crimson, as a hairline crack ripped across the surface of my heart.

"Are you sure?" I asked, hoping she was wrong.

"See for yourself," she said, handing it over. "You're one of us now."

It was a strange sensation, like reading a map of blood and sweat, scents clashing across the fabric in the heat of battle. The blood smelled like Marix, floral violet and musk. The invisible stains of sweat along the edges smelled like…campfire.

Cassian's rich cedar campfire scent.

A sick rot swept into my stomach. The bile climbed up my throat and evacuated my body as I turned away.

It wasn't just that it smelled like him. The odors were *interwoven*, inseparable; any longer steeped together and they would have formed their own perfume. And the emotions…the blood was tainted with agony, the sweat with fear.

"She spent her last moments being torn apart. My sweet kit didna deserve that." I felt Marix's body shudder as she let out a ragged sigh. "They'll pay for it. If it's the last thing I do. And you can help me."

I hesitated. As much as I hated what Archer had done, as much as the sight of him robbed me of my well-being and my mind sometimes ran wild with ways to hurt him, hurt them all, actually *doing* it was different. The glee in Marix's voice didn't help, either. Unless she knew more than she was letting on, neither she nor I knew what had really happened yet. The torn, bloody rag couldn't tell us that. Only Cassian could.

"We can punish them together for what they've done to us."

The glint in her eye gave me pause, too.

"Natalie!"

Bruce's voice cut through the thick greenery and my crushing thoughts like a machete. Marix leapt to the balls of her feet beside me.

"Find me when you can—you know where I'll be," she whispered.

I blinked…the forest was huge. I had no idea—

"Time to come in."

I couldn't help snapping at him. "I'm not a dog, Bruce!"

I turned for half a second. Marix was gone when I looked back, her soft footfalls muffled by the forest chatter.

Bruce held the library door open for me as I approached, searching my face for answers to his questions.

"Who was that out in the forest? Who were you talking to?"

I ignored him. The train of my mind was on a runaway track tonight, tearing rail toward the man who had saved my life.

CHAPTER 27

"What's wrong?"

Cass was fresh from a shower; a single wet curl dangled over his furrowed brow as his hands slid along my waist and pulled me into him. His lips pattered my forehead like marshmallow rain.

"You don't have a fever. Are you feeling all right?" He felt along the bandage on my neck. "You need a fresh one of these. Come sit and tell me how the processional went."

As he disappeared into the bathroom, I tried to organize my thoughts. Mael was most likely dead, and Cass had something to do with it. He'd told me he had ruined lives to protect this place—was she one of them? Was Will another? Had he really killed his father, as Archer had suggested?

But that didn't make sense… Bruce was Will's best friend. I couldn't believe he'd protect Cass for doing something like that, let alone *care* for Cass like a son after the fact.

And yet…Will had left me everything over his own sons, a bizarre choice on a bad day, but one that made perfect sense if he thought his sons would kill him.

"Natalie?"

Cass's hand caressed my shoulder. He sat close behind me and undid the neck clasp on the backless blouse so he could reach the bandage. There was no ill-will I could sense in his touch. No ulterior motives, no malice. He'd *saved* me for goodness' sake. Saved me when it would have been better for all of them to let me die.

Something fluttered down in front of me, lifting me from the quagmire of my thoughts. A tiny, downy-soft black feather.

"Where did *that* come from?" I asked, admiring it.

"It was in your hair," he said. "Slight pinch."

The bandage came away from my skin without any resistance at all as he delicately, slowly, meticulously slid his finger along the edges to release it.

This was the hand of a killer?

"What does it look like?"

He was quiet a long beat before I felt a fresh bandage land and his hands gently rub it into place.

"Still healing," he said when he was finished, leaning in to kiss the nape of my neck before reconnecting the clasp. "Are you sure you're okay?"

"I'm not," I finally said. "I need to talk to you about something, but I'm scared of what you'll say."

"There's nothing to be scared of—you can talk to me about anything."

If only that were true…

"Hey. Look at me, Natalie."

I turned on the couch to face him, but I couldn't even do that. Even when he tilted my chin upward, it took the last of my resolve to meet his gaze. My diaphragm twinged with longing, confusion, fear, desire. It wasn't just that I liked him, or I owed him, or I actually trusted him. Until twenty minutes ago, it had felt like I *knew* him…or I was starting to, at least. And I…I loved what I thought I knew.

"I will always tell you the truth. Ask me anything."

"You'll hate me."

"Impossible, but also irrelevant," he said. "Don't think of my comfort; think of yours."

"I'm afraid you'll…hurt me…even though I don't believe you will. I *really, truly* don't believe you're capable of that."

A wave of disappointment washed over his features, wounding me as badly as a knife. He took a breath and shook whatever he was feeling away.

"What do you need from me? Do you want to tie me to the bed or something?"

Oh hello, *what* did he just offer?

"No, of course not…"

I hesitated.

"Maybe." The corner of his gorgeous mouth quirked suggestively, robbing me momentarily of anything but the fantasy he'd just planted in my head. "Definitely…Later."

This was stupid. No matter how I questioned him, I'd still be trapped in this house afterward. If I wanted answers, I'd have to embrace the risk that I had accepted when I let him stay in my rooms—that he might choose his family over me. After all, I was nobody. A random teenager injected into their lives against their will. An interloper who'd driven a wedge between them. I stood up from the couch and paced, summoning my courage.

"Oh gods, it's something big, isn't it?"

I forced myself to meet his eye. "How did Will die?"

I watched his face crumble, little micro expressions collapsing in on one another like a house of cards until he looked scared to death. But…he didn't look away.

"He was murdered."

"By whom?"

"An alter named Marix Cernu from the Lesser Sionnach family had him killed."

Marix? I felt my brow furrow in disbelief, which he seemed to mistake for confusion.

"I can explain the titles later. It's more important *why* she killed him."

"Why did she kill him?"

"Because I killed her daughter."

My mind bled white with despair.

"Why?"

"It's a long story. One you won't entirely understand." I opened my mouth to protest. "Not right away, but I'll explain. I promise."

Cass stood. He began filling the far half of the room with moseyed ramblings as he spoke.

"In the millennia since the first alters united as a community in Europe, regions have almost naturally fallen under the rule of eight great families. Ours is one of them. One of the perks of being a ruling family has always been access to a Cure."

"For changing?" I asked.

He nodded. "Centuries ago, it could be found everywhere, available "over the counter" as you Americans might call it. Nowadays, it's much rarer. Almost impossible to find, in fact."

"Do you know why?" I asked.

"I think the plant used to make it went extinct in the wild some time ago, or the recipe went to somebody's grave, but in either case it meant that once it was gone, there was no receiving more. So, what we had we saved for emergencies. On the night Marix brought her daughter to our doorstep, there was only a single vial of the cure left in our stores."

I watched his shoulders slump as some terrible memory took over his mind.

"Her daughter—Mael, she was called—was pregnant. But she couldn't control her alteration yet, and the baby wasn't…like her. She was like me."

My stomach sank.

"It was tearing her apart from the inside. Her fox form couldn't take it—there was blood *everywhere*. So, Marix carried her to our house on the first night of the full moon and begged for the cure. My father and brother had already turned and left for the woods. Archer had barely started altering himself. At that stage, he was little more than a feral plague that needed to be kept from humans, alters, and animals alike, and I was alone at the house."

"And you didn't give it to them."

A terrible shade of self-loathing crossed his features. "I didn't."

"Why?"

"I-I…"

"Was the baby yours?"

His head swung suddenly to look at me, mouth laughing with anger and bewilderment.

"Gods no," he said. "I've been with my fair share of people, safely, but those are shameful stories for another time. Nor was it Archer's. Mael ran in different circles. We knew each other certainly. I'd seen her around at Archer's parties from time to time. But…she *was* a citizen of our kingdom. We were meant to be her guardians."

"So why did you say no?"

"I wasn't…" he said. "I'd tried everything—*everything*—to force my alteration. Then Archer was blessed with his naturally, upending my entire life in a single lunar cycle. I could show you pictures you would think were photoshopped—that's how quickly Archer grew into the man he is today."

"He's still a boy," I said.

"Not in our world. When Marix arrived with Mael, I was waiting out the sun in the panic room. Mael's screams of pain, Marix's screeching panic—I opened the door. I found blankets for her. Mopped up the blood around her. I even offered to fly in the nearest doctor who knows our secret, but...Marix begged for the one thing that would allow her to take Mael to a human hospital. I didn't think I had the right to give it to her. It belonged to Archer. He had to make the decision to use our last cure."

"What happened?"

"I ran into the woods to find him." He gulped. "But I never did. By the time I returned to the house, Mael was lifeless...and Marix, well..."

He lifted his shirt, exposing the slow-to-heal gashes along his waist.

"If Bruce hadn't returned at that moment, she would have killed me right then and there. Instead, she took us to court."

It was such an abrupt segue, I almost laughed.

"The Court of the Raven King in Denmark, our highest rule of law on the continent. As the Ruler of the Eighth Kingdom, my father chose to stand trial in my stead. It was the strangest, and kindest, thing he ever did for me. Marix, of course, was furious. By taking my place, my father had robbed her of any chance at justice against me. And she went to Denmark for blood."

"Could the king have killed Will?"

"With a snap of his finger."

"But he didn't."

"No, it was the maddest thing," he said, his eyes bright with surprise as he remembered. "King Rav ordered us to pay her a million pounds and sentenced my father to suffer through a single brutal alteration. By our standards, practically probation."

"You said Marix had him killed?"

"That very first night we returned to Bear Glen was a full moon. My father chose to serve out his sentence right away and imbibed no medication for the pain. Bruce said it was so excruciating my father collapsed before he even left the dungeons. Once they were out in the open heading for the woods, he said my father caught the scent of something. Without the stimulants he normally used to transition peacefully and retain his human mind, there would've been no stopping his hunt."

Cass shuddered.

"Bruce said they rounded a tree and a human hunter fired a silver bullet into my father's chest at point blank range. Bruce killed the man and then did the only thing he could think to do—he gave my father the cure."

"So, he could take him to a human hospital…"

Cass nodded, his jaw straining through some emotional pain he didn't know how to handle.

"He was gone before the helicopter arrived to fly him to Glasgow Royal. As for Marix, there was no mistaking her involvement. She scented my father's body after he died so we would know she was responsible…and not just for his death, but for the loss of the last cure in our entire kingdom."

He ran his hands across his face and when he pulled them away, crescent tears split his silver irises in half, making them look like a stormy sea below a seething gray sky. In them, self-loathing drifted like hurricane debris.

He was telling the truth; I could see that in his pain. Which meant…that Marix had lied to me. Not about the loss of her daughter, but about how it had happened. And what she had already done to the Mahon's to retaliate. Which meant the only reason she was still here was to punish them further.

"Cass," I said.

"I ruined everything. I'm the reason she lost her child. I'm the reason my father's gone. I'm the reason you were attacked and why I can't give you your old life back—"

"That's not true! It isn't."

Whatever magnetic charge had repelled me from Archer, the same force sent me hurtling toward Cassian now, enveloping him in the warmest hug I could muster. I believed every word he said, and I needed him to know that. But…he didn't want to give this to me.

"Don't," he said. I held him anyway. "You should hate me."

I ran my fingers through his wet hair, pulling him gently against my chest, hoping he could feel my beating heart, how badly it wanted to be there for him.

"Please, don't push me away," I whispered. "I want all of you."

It was absolutely true. Even if the circumstances of Mael's death were his fault, his guilt, his humility told me he'd learned from it. And whatever it said about me, his honesty struck a match against that fiery knot low in my belly, which I was starting to realize wasn't just desire, but something more complex. Something essential.

Like a dam bursting, I heard a ragged sob escape, his hot breath reaching through my blouse to the skin underneath. His arms came to my waist, almost pushed, then yanked me down onto his lap and held me as I held him.

"You'll change your mind," he said.

"What if I don't?"

"Then it'll be the end of our lives as we know them," he said. "The beginning of the one we build together."

His hands ran up my back into my hair, guiding me toward him. His kiss was tender. Lonesome. When he pulled back, it was only to select the next corner of my face to kiss. Delicious explosions of delight spread across my skin as somewhere below I felt his…rising delight as well.

But it would have to wait.

Would it?

No, yes, it would. I could feel myself losing the thread of my questions.

His lips were on my neck, dancing. My toes curled. Our blind hands roamed each other, reading the braille across our skin. I knew if I let him reach my ears, my body would do the rest of my talking for me. And oh, the conversations it wanted to have…

But there were things he needed to know. He seemed to think the choice of us rested only with me. Not only did I not want that to be true, it couldn't be until he knew everything.

"Cass."

"Yes, my lady?" When he pulled back this time, his grip was immoveable upon my hips, as if they'd fused there. Somehow, it grounded me.

"I've met Marix," I said.

I felt a sudden charge of fear run through him as his hands flexed. "When?"

"The first time was in Edinburgh. She's why I wandered away. She told me I was in danger here. That her daughter came here and never made it home."

"What…did you think?"

"At first, the way she explained it to me, I thought someone here had done something to her."

"That's why you were in my room the night of the attack," he said, almost with relief.

"You're not mad?"

"It undoes a mystery. After the doctor came and went, after you were safely in your rooms and the others had stopped trying—at least for the moment—to make me leave your side, I returned to my room for a few supplies to hold me over in here. You haven't noticed yet, but I've claimed a section of your closet as my own."

I laughed, pulling him in. "Really?"

"I knew I wasn't going anywhere." I pulled back as a shiver ran up my spine. "I noticed you'd taken the cloth from my desk. As it's the reminder of my gravest mistake, I didn't know what you had made of it."

"I knew it was blood," I said. "But until tonight, I didn't know whose."

Cass winced. "More fringe benefits kicking in."

"Marix had the cloth," I said. "She found it after the attack."

Cass's pale skin lost its last remaining color and his hands pushed, coaxing me off and up. He rose with me; his attention snapped to the window.

"You talked to her tonight?"

"I did."

"Where?"

"The Eastern Wood."

I felt that strange absence again as his last hold on my body disconnected, and he suddenly disappeared into the closet. Within seconds, he reappeared wearing something I'd never seen him wear before—a simple pair of jeans.

"She wants revenge, Natalie."

"She thinks I want revenge, too, against your brother."

He paused, searching my eyes. "Do you?"

I hesitated.

"I wouldn't blame you," he said, forcing on his socks then his shoes. He was up again, darting for the bedroom, running his hands across the desk in there, before he reappeared with the cricket bat.

"Where are you going?" I sounded so simple. I knew where he was going and I hated the fear I heard in my own voice.

"She'll need to be dealt with, as soon as possible," he said, already heading out. I intercepted him at the door. "She could have killed you. If she knew I was here with you like this, she would have."

"You can't go out there alone."

“I won’t be alone. I’ll have to tell Archer, Bruce. Half the staff are alters as well, the rest come from alter families. They understand how dangerous she is.”

It was strange; she had lied to me, manipulated me, misled me…except where it mattered most. Her pain, her grief, had been entirely real. It made her an exceptionally dangerous victim. My mom had almost gone mad at the possibility of losing me; Marix had actually lost her child—she was capable of anything.

“There has to be some other way to handle this. You can’t hurt her.”

“I couldn’t hurt her even if I wanted to, which I don’t.”

He *did* want to do something. I could see his solution stamped in the guilt across his face. A cold bubble of anger rose in me. “You can’t sic Archer on her either.”

“You are *days* away from your alteration,” he said. “I’ll do whatever it takes to get you there.”

His last kiss landed like a lead weight on top of my head. Then he was gone, running down the hall like he’d found his terrible calling.

I didn’t see him at all the next day, or the next, or the next. As much as I understood why he was doing this, I felt abandoned regardless. I’d been left to mark the progress of the moon through my window alone, become the gargoyle he had once been. I watched half the staff arrive at the house with weapons, traps, and dogs. They plunged into the forest like a murderous, suicidal search party—one I was prevented from joining upon pain of being tied to a chair. They did everything but…including posting guards at every door and locking every window. Mrs. Margolyes and Mary never left my side, nor did they really talk to me, too preoccupied with the sudden baying of hounds in the distance, the shouts and appearances of men and women as they trickled in and out of the tree line.

My mother and Scarlett’s visits had been *indefinitely postponed* until the threat was neutralized, which was code for Bruce hadn’t arranged their trips in the first place, only fueling my desire to amputate him from the estate at the first opportunity. And Archer’s party had been called off for the first time since he first altered.

Doctor Martin was ushered into the house like we were under fire—even she seemed to understand the significance of the hunt. When she handed me the pain pills she had specifically calibrated to my body, she described their purposes in terms of what I would and wouldn’t be able to do while taking them.

"You'll have your full strength for fighting, but you may get dizzy, so I would advise remaining in the dungeon until your bear form has manifested entirely and you're quite invincible. Your usual prescription will include a muscle relaxant but given present circumstances, I thought it best to forego that so you'll have full dexterity and reduced chance of fatigue."

In the end, it wasn't Cass or Archer who escorted me into the Eastern Wood to the resting place where Archer would lead me when I changed, but Bruce who walked with a twelve-gage shotgun resting against his shoulder. As if that was going to reassure me. He guided me deep into the forest to a stone hill that appeared ancient and solid until he pulled back a curtain of morning glory vines to reveal the mouth to a man-made grotto Will had built decades ago. This inner sanctum had already been prepared for our full moon arrival; cashmere and silk throw rugs draped every corner of the grotto's floor that wasn't water. Seven pools—three chilled, three heated, and one painted with darkest black—surrounded a central lounging plinth.

Bruce pointed to a projector bolted to the ceiling overhead. "Cass controls the remote for that. He usually picks something animated, but he takes requests."

The lulling sound of water, the open ceiling overhead that peered up through a clearing at the sky, the video on demand—it was meant to inspire confidence. And it would have succeeded...if it weren't for the *thousands* of claw and fang marks along the walls. Old, faded tapestries and vines covered much of the destruction, but not all. The marks were *everywhere*, reaching as high as twenty feet in some places. It looked like the grotto had been wallpapered in carnage.

"Why do you change in the dungeons if you have this place? Why not just do it here?"

Bruce blinked with surprise at the question, as if it had never occurred to him.

"I never asked Will that," he said. "A 'don't explode where you sleep' policy, perhaps?"

Explode?!

"Sounds like we need to build an antechamber out here," I said, swallowing my sudden nausea. "One that can be hosed down."

"Excellent idea, my lady," he said. "That's the sort of inspired thinking we need around here."

I scoffed, unsure whether it was a compliment or some underhanded insult.

"I-I mean that, you know," he said quietly.

"I don't believe you."

"All the same, I think Will knew what he was doing when he chose you."

Will. That jerk. Couldn't even be bothered to leave me a beginner's guide to shifting, which was especially cruel considering he knew I'd be altered at some point after arrival. Half of his riddle all but confirmed that.

In the mayhem since I'd told Cass about Marix, there'd been no chance to seek the crypt…and no way to contact Marix, either. A person was present in every single room I walked into, and at night guards were posted at my door. Every time I told them to get lost, they were back within a few minutes or lurking like shadow creatures at my periphery wherever I went. I felt entirely impotent, babysat, and distracted, while the boys played monster hunters in the woods. I had half a mind to pin a giant hand-drawn sign to my window so Marix might see and know to run and, more selfishly, so she wouldn't think I was behind the hunt. As much as I had needed to tell Cass the truth after he told me his, it was still a monumental betrayal. If she wanted to take a shot at me with a silver bullet now, I'd totally understand.

I hoped she was running.

I hoped she was okay.

I hoped—if she *didn't* run—that it wasn't because she had some darker plan in play.

Since I wasn't allowed to do anything, I spent the rest of my time in the days before the full moon finishing *The Age of Animals*. The rest read like the zoological report of someone who'd never written a layman's cliff notes in his life. I'd seen furniture instructions more digestible than certain sections.

It was also entirely Eurocentric…and rife with the misogynistic, racist, and xenophobic "common sense" of previous ages. In one part, an entire section had been ripped out of the book and replaced with a scribbled note that read *America rebelled; attempts to quash revolution thwarted; census and nomenclature no longer relevant to the Eighth Empire.*

But I kept reading anyway for courage. With each passing hour, I felt subtle changes across my person that only made sense in the context of alters past. Like an undiagnosed illness finally making sense after obscure research.

In the days prior to Prima Mutatio, child may experience racing heartbeat, hot flashes, sudden aggression, and inescapable nightmares.

In the hours prior to Prima Mutatio, child may witness false moonlight caused by the moon's appearance in the sky before nightfall.

If child is not exposed to direct lunar light immediately on the night of the full moon, delayed alteration may result in sudden, agonizing, explosive alteration later.

That word again—explosive. I was going to explode; I just knew it.

I also confirmed what Bruce had told me during the processional. There was a section in the book dedicated to the "Dangers of Mixing," which read like some backward attempt to justify racism…or, in this case, speciesism.

Alters must know it is in their utmost best interest to pair bond and mate with those of their own species. Not only are personalities suited and breeding issues nullified—especially when preserving the purity of Great Families—but it minimizes the risks of going feral or beastly transformation.

This seemed to be the second most important guideline the book set, after preserving the secret of alteration from humans. Breaking either law carried the same medieval punishment—execution. The book went into insane detail of tragedies past, in which humans learned of our secret—or flamingo laid with sheep—and the alters' secret world nearly crumbled. Some of the stories read like autopsy reports rather than parables, and I couldn't read many.

The book's descriptions of what it felt like to be in animal form, however, were mystically vague to the point of being useless. I realized at some point that the person who had written this book—Cargus North—had been a carrier and not an alter themselves. They didn't know what the change was like first-hand and for whatever reason hadn't asked for testimonials from anyone who did. Or no one would tell him.

This, in addition to the lava bolts of heat that streaked through my body at all hours, convinced me that this couldn't possibly be the "gift" Cassian thought it was. It was a chronic madness. Cyclical insanity. Mrs. Margolyes assured me this was something that only happened the first time, right before terrorizing me with her own tale of alteration, in which hedgehog spines erupted from her body and shed for days while she waited for the full moon. Even more worryingly, when I asked when she had learned to control her alteration, she laughed at me.

"You can't control your inner nature, my dear," she said. "Best not to try."

Easy for her to say. At her most hedgehoggy, she might bite someone's toe off. I was hours away from being the size of a monster in a Greek odyssey. With bowie knife claws and skull crushing fangs. I'd already seen what Archer's inner nature inspired him to do.

Cassian didn't come to see me at all that week, but each morning I woke to a new flower wrapped in a silk ribbon laying on my pillow. It only made me angrier that he wasn't there with me, where he should have been.

The only true comfort were the dreams. No nightmares plagued my nights; instead, beautiful half remembrances crept into my sleep. I was within my own mind staring out through two almond-shaped viewing windows in a body that was and was not mine. One that started to feel *more* like mine with every passing day. There was no up or down. I was a little thing swirling in an ocean of color, wind sliding across my fingers as thick as water. I saw the world as a vast maze of spaces I'd never explored before under stars splattered across the night sky as thick as spilled milk. I was warm and light and whole. And all around me, a singing voice unlike any I'd ever heard before filled the air. One I couldn't locate no matter how hard I looked.

Always—*always*—the dream ended the same, with the sweep of something dark from above.

On the morning of my alteration, however, the dark sweep was accompanied by the sound of cannon fire and the growling wail of a dying man. I was out of bed like a shot, running down the main stairs to the front door before my night guards could stop me. Mrs. Margolyes stood by the open front doors, a look of the grave about her.

"Who is it? Is it Cassian?"

"Go back upstairs, child," she chastised.

I ducked around her, but the front door men caught me anyway. There was an ambulance in the driveway and a small gathering of hunters helping a young man into the back. A young man with red hair.

"Cassian!"

"I can't hold her!"

"Let *go* of me. I am not a prisoner."

"Ca' canny! She's going feral!"

The pair leapt away from me instantly, staring at the slender, unignorable *claws* that had grown out of the tips of my fingers overnight.

"Haud yer wheesht," Mrs. Margolyes growled. "Don't let the others hear you say that. Get out of here, now."

The two men *bolted* down the stairs, practically tripping over each other, as thc ambulance drove away, revealing Cassian completely intact and unscathed among the group that remained behind. My heart sank—he looked like he hadn't slept since the night I told him about Marix.

"Come back inside, girl. Don't be ridiculous now."

I hardly heard Mrs. Margolyes. Between the claws and seeing Cassian alive but unwell, I couldn't focus on anything. Cassian seemed to realize something was wrong. In seconds, he was at my side.

"Natalie, you're pale," he said. "Has she fed yet?"

"No, pet, but she's sure putting on a show."

Cassian finally noticed my hands, which I couldn't look away from. The claws were black inch-long crescents erupting from cuticles of darkest purple. I looked like a banshee, some ghoulish queen of black magic.

Cass's eyes widened as he lunged out and hid my hands in his immediately.

"What's happening to me?"

"You're all right, come on."

He pulled me inside then helped Mrs. Margolyes heave the gargantuan front doors shut behind us. He led me down the hall to the dining room, where a buffet stretched the entire length of the fifty-foot table.

"Is this for the hunting party?" I asked, my mind in a haze, as he pulled out a chair and placed me in it.

"Hardly," said Archer, who I realized sat at the far end of the table eating from a giant's platter of Scottish breakfast. "This is fuel for us, although I usually eat this much myself."

"We need to feed them, Cass," I said, trying to pull my claws out of his hands so I could stare at them again. He wouldn't let me.

"We're feeding them, don't worry."

"What's happening to me? Am I going fer—"

He darted forward suddenly to whisper into my ear. "No, my darling."

"I can hear you," grumbled Archer.

"I need you to focus on your humanity for me right now," he said. "Can you do that? Think of an entirely human moment. A happy one."

An impossible task, it suddenly seemed. Flashes of Archer's masked party rose clear as crystal. The graveyard fox. Cass nibbling my ear—

I closed my eyes tightly. I shivered, yet my body reeled from another hot flash.

I thought of my mom. Scarlett. My birthday, only a few weeks ago, before all of this had happened. The dining table my mom had lovingly sanded, the table I had painted for her. My old clunker yellow car. The smell of pizza and spilled soda and mopping liquid.

There was a sudden slice of pain across my hands.

"That's it," said Cass. "Hold onto that memory."

I opened my eyes, blinking with disbelief as he held up my own hands for me to study. The claws were gone—merely the hallucination of an exhausted mind.

No. Not a hallucination. I watched Cass kneel in front of me and carefully collect ten fallen black crescent claws from the carpet; delicate, brand-new fingernails had reformed in their places on my hands.

Without saying a word, he stood and grabbed a plate for the buffet.

"You need to eat," he said. "Any cravings?"

"Yes," said Archer. "Less of this, you'll put me off my breakfast."

Cass ignored him, waiting patiently for me to speak. But it hardly seemed like the time for food. It was already half past nine. In less than twelve hours, I'd shed my body like a suit, becoming something else entirely.

"No—"

"No black pudding, I know," he said, smiling. "Let's do you some eggs. Fruit. Berries are lovely right now."

"Berries?" groaned Archer. "I thought those were decoration. The salmon's divine; although, you will grow sick of it come September."

The plate of eggs and fruit weighed heavy in his hands as Cass set it before me. His eyes were already distracted, watching the men through the windows as they returned to the woods to hunt.

"Cass," I said, drawing his attention away. "I'm scared to be alone."

"You're not alone," said Archer. "I'm right here."

I eyed Cass until he understood that Archer's words did the opposite of reassure me. I would be trapped in that grotto all night with the man who had done this to me.

"Eat, all right?" he said. "Go up and rest. I'll come to you shortly."

"Promise," I said.

"On our life," he replied.

"Again," said Archer. "I am right here."

"It's not about you, Archie!" Cass snapped. He kissed my temple and left in the blink of an eye. After he was gone, I found Archer studying me from across the room.

"Is your hair getting darker?" he asked. "And why are you so pale? You must make an effort to go outside more."

"I'd love to," I said. "Since I'm being kept prisoner, why don't you come over here so I can break the window with your face?"

Archer's face quirked stupidly. "Rude."

I decided to eat in my room, which resulted in Mrs. Margolyes summoning Mary to gather a second portion of the already massive plate Cass had served me and carry it behind me up the stairs to my door.

"You must eat, miss," said Mary. "Process takes a lot out of you."

She had that same nervous energy I'd witnessed last month around this time, but now she had a strong, nutty smell as well. Obviously an alter.

"When did you first change?" I asked.

"Oh gosh, years ago now," she said. "Mum and dah were so proud. I was an early bloomer—first of six. But that's to be expected with squirrels."

"Do you have any advice?" I asked. "For my first time?"

"Take the pills," she said without missing a beat. "We're lucky the Mahon's get them for us. Makes it all so much more enjoyable and not everyone's so fortunate. Oh…and don't hesitate."

"Hesitate?"

"When the moon pours like silver honey, step in all at once. It's like jumping into cold water—the fear makes it so much worse. Get it over with and enjoy your new nature."

"I…I'm scared."

She was suddenly there with a sweet hug.

"Don't be, my lady, we're all rooting for you." She pulled away with a smile. "Never had a sweet-smelling bear here before."

Mrs. Margolyes had been right about the food. Both plates were gone in a few minutes. Then I went to the sink and drank glass after glass of water until I felt fit to burst… Archer was also right. My hair was the color of black coffee now. Any olive that had been in my skin was long gone. I looked…like winter. Like snow on fresh soil.

Cass appeared in the doorway behind me, still as gaunt as before.

"If it's possible, you look more beautiful every time I see you," he said.

My eyebrow arched high in derision.

"You look like a ghost," I said. "When did you last sleep?"

"I'll sleep when you're safe."

I took him by the hand and guided him into the bedroom. It was his turn to lay down and let me care for him, but the second he was down, he took hold of my hand and pulled me down right beside him, into his chest. His stubble tickled fiercely as he breathed me in.

"What do I smell like now?" I asked.

"Let's see." He sniffed again, trailing kisses as he went. "Honey…and tangerines…and alpine breezes."

"You just made that up."

"I would never." He kissed me, smiling to his dimple. "And rain. It's intoxicating."

"Do you want to know what you smell like?" I asked.

"Human deodorant. The latest trendy soap called something manly like turbo glacier vortex or something."

I leaned my chin into his, letting his stubble tickle my skin. "You smell like fire and burning wood."

"Pyro."

"Mmm. It's my favorite smell in the world."

I'd expected him to love that; instead, he pulled away, his eyes withdrawn and nervous.

"Is something wrong?"

"Natalie, you know you don't need me, right?" My brow furrowed. "You've handled yourself exceptionally well given everything that's happened to you. You know that no matter what happens, you can navigate any difficulty."

"Where is this coming from?"

"I need you to say it," he said. "I need you to tell me you can take care of yourself, no matter what happens."

Lightning-bright fear shot through my body, cauterizing as it went.

"You're not…having second thoughts about me?"

"Far from it," he said.

"You can say so if—"

"Your life is bigger than this moment. And it's only just beginning. After tonight, you'll be nearly invincible. Safe, so long as you avoid silver and the cruelty of other alters. You'll find yourself on a new path full of possibilities that may or may not include me."

"…I'd like it to include you," I said. "Is this because of the claws? Those door men called me feral. Is that why you're talking like this?"

"No, of course not. And you're not going feral. The ones who *can't* return to their human forms—so caught up in their animal natures they've entirely lost their humanity—they've gone feral. That's not you."

"Then what's happened?"

He pressed his forehead to mine, his eyes warm and full of love. "Just say the words for me, please."

"I can take care of myself," I said. "No matter what happens."

"Thank you," he said, tucking my hair behind my ear.

"But I can take care of you, too," I added.

He didn't reply. He simply reached under me and turned me away so he could wrap his body around mine, the large spoon to my little.

"I can only stay a little while before I have to leave again," he said.

"I'll see you in the morning, right? You'll be safe in the panic room?"

"Curating your animated viewing experience in the grotto," he purred. But there was a tone to his voice I didn't like.

I stayed awake as long as I could, but the faint puffs of his own sleeping breath against my ear lulled me to sleep before I knew it, and I woke hours later. Alone.

There was a small platter displaying two of Dr. Martin's pain pills as well as white Dior robe waiting for me on a hanger by the door, along with a note that told me to either go commando underneath or only wear underwear I didn't mind ripping to shreds. The thought of going commando around Archer made me queasy, but then I realized I was going to be bear naked anyway. By the time I walked downstairs in a warm haze of medicated unfeeling, the entire house seemed apocalyptically empty, save for the trail of left-on lights leading right to the dungeon door.

As I walked down the dungeon stairs, I realized the medication only worked to dull physical feeling, not raw psychological terror. I held onto the very human memory I had landed on this morning, hoping against hope that I wouldn't lose all of myself in the moonlight. Even though the others all seemed to love the change, it felt to me like leaping into the void, initially freeing then terrifying. And there was nothing and no one to catch you as you fell.

The dungeon had been cleaned in the days since my tour. Fresh straw. Fresh scratchy mats along the walls. The padlocked cellar doors were now wide open facing an animal trail leading deep into the Eastern Wood, to the grotto. A single strip of deep fuchsia dusk was visible just above the tree line. It was almost time.

But…where was Archer? As little as I wanted to spend the most vulnerable night of my life with him, it seemed worse to not know where he was. And it only got worse as the minutes ticked by and the sky's fuchsia deepened to indigo.

He didn't come when the first stars appeared.

Or when the crickets' lullaby swelled into a symphony.

I watched the last blues and pinks disappear into the black strip overhead like neon weights sinking into the sea. There was a single moment of impenetrable darkness and then all at once…light.

Everywhere.

Through the cellar doors, translucent molten silver poured heavy across the lawn and then dappled into the forest, which had bloomed with extraordinary color. Patterns crept up the stems and leaves of the tiniest plants. Tree trunks *breathed.* Leaves glowed. It was as if the illusion had fallen away, exposing the real world underneath. I could smell the aromatic magic like a fine meal placed before me—vanilla and peaches cut with the cool earthy splendor of ferns.

The molten moonlight flowed into the dungeon as well, filling in the square area where it could reach like a swimming pool of mercury. My toes were inches from the threshold of everything that laid beyond. One big step would change my life forever…and to my surprise, I wanted to take that step.

There was nothing left to do but leap.

CHAPTER 28

I took a deep breath and reached for the knotted belt along my waist. This was it. I would bound across the threshold of light and darkness and become something else on the other side. Something more.

A charge raced across my skin the closer I inched toward the moonlight. My body called to it, *longed* for it, and the moonlight responded. It was singing the song I'd heard in my dreams.

I just needed to step through—

In the brightness, something suddenly screeched, breaking the song's hold on me. I blinked, trying to process.

A dark thing rushed across the moonlight at the top of the stairs.

"Jesus!" I recoiled from the threshold of moonlight, still human, as something rushed out of the light toward me. It was a ginormous badger, almost the size of a giant anteater I'd once seen at a zoo… "Bruce?"

Magic swirled around him like a silver aura, rippling through his coat. He turned, searching the room for something, before he glanced once more at me and bolted away into the night.

A mighty roar leeched out of the forest—Archer's bear. Faintly, I heard a human man speaking as well. Cassian.

"That idiot!" I said.

He'd followed his monstrous brother into the moonlit darkness to find Marix…which was insane. Even *I* didn't know where she was…or did I?

The crypt. I felt so stupid. Why hadn't I thought about it before? We'd been talking about that crypt forever. But when the animals had led me there before, she hadn't joined me in the gully where the massive crypt rested. Almost like she couldn't.

I turned and ran for the stairs. Then I sprinted down the ground floor hallway, dodging rays of moonlight pouring in through the windows. Up the stairs again to my bedroom. I had to crawl under the moonlight splashing across my bed to the darkest corner where I could reach into the tattered headboard and retrieve the crypt key. I navigated back down to the ground floor again and headed for the library.

The green hollow outside was far denser here than it was outside the cellar doors. Moonlight dappled the ground rather than flooding it.

I opened the patio door and limpetted myself to the wall outside, eyeing the ground for dark spaces before taking my first step. Then the next, then the next.

Even the dappled light sang to me. All around me, a faint soprano. The whispers of someone trying to get my attention. And the warmth the light promised…

I couldn't give in.

I pushed on, seeking the shelter of the trees, then the darker, deeper forest. The world was colorful in here, too, but muted where the moonlight couldn't penetrate. Without the moon's warmth, the way was cold and unpleasant. I could feel eyes watching me in the dark. Thousands of them. Animals quietly observing. Judging. I could sense that I was *denying* something by being here in this form, some critical part of myself, and the darkness was punishing me for it.

The deeper I went, the louder Cassian's words became until I could almost understand them.

"*I offer…if this is…protect her…*"

Roars and chuffs responded. He was with Archer, that much I knew.

But there was someone else out there. It didn't feel like Bruce. It felt like a shadow. Through the thick foliage, I could sense the person. Then I could smell them.

Pungent violets—Marix.

They didn't know she was there. How was that possible? The stench was overpowering. So strong it was nauseating.

I picked up my pace and ran.

Marix moved, darting sideways at impossible speeds.

"Cassian!" I shouted. "She's here. She's coming!"

"Natalie?"

"She's here! Run!"

A horrible roar split the night. I rounded a tree at the edge of a moonlit clearing in time to watch Marix's oversized fox form leap out of a high tree and tear a chunk out of Archer's back upon landing, spilling thick blood across his fur. His monstrous form reared back, at least twenty feet fall, swiping at her with his sickle claws.

But she had already leapt away. Before I could blink, her mouth was on his leg, ripping with a frenzied anger that left no doubt as to her intentions. She was here for the blood she'd been denied and then some.

Her eyes met mine as she backed into the shadows, avoiding Cass's cricket bat as it crashed down inches from where she had been. Archer was injured. Badly. His leg, the missing chunk, left him immobile on the ground, and Cass was beside Archer instantly. Right where she wanted him.

"Cass, get away from him," I said.

It was too late. I heard that sickening squelch I'd heard in the graveyard as Marix retook her human form and emerged from the darkness wearing patches of her own fur across her bloodied body like a pagan bikini. Before Cass could even turn, she ripped the bat away and clamped a still-clawed hand around his throat as she slammed the bat across Archer's head with a dazzling supernatural strength entirely disguised by her petite human form. It seemed impossible to take out a *bear* like that, but she had. The bear form that had so terrorized me crashed to the ground like a limp toy. The shockwave almost knocked me off my feet.

And all of it heightened the fear I felt as I realized how tight her grip was on Cassian's neck.

"Marix, please don't!"

She smiled at me then, her mouth full of blood. "It's all right, pet. You've done well."

Cass's eyes met mine, surprised and devastated.

"I didn't bring them here," I said.

"No," she said. "But you *did* tell them I was here talkin' to you. I knew it would be too much of a temptation for them."

I felt so foolish. "You used me…"

"Aw, wee lamb. You think I wouldn't recognize their stench on you and yours on them? That's not just proximity, deary, it's love. A different chemical signature altogether. You think they care about you. I cannae dissuade you of that, but I dinna need to. You'll figure out the truth of it in time. The great families dinna care about anyone but themselves…"

"Marix," I said. "It was an impossible choice."

"Nae. It was just another careless choice. Just like it was a choice to attack you instead of welcoming you into the fold. They didna care how they hurt ye. They cared only that they retained the power they've held over this land for centuries. Great family indeed."

Her hand flexed on Cassian's neck; his yelp sliced through my heart.

"I dinna hold anything against you, lass, which is why I have no plans to kill you. I'm honestly impressed you resisted the moon's call this long. You're made of stronger stock than the likes of them. And maybe you'll lead us better than they have. I truly hope so. I'd planned to come to you after I'd had my justice to ask for the key proper. But things being what they are, I'll make a deal with ye. I'll let you keep one of 'em once you've brought me whatever's in that crypt."

I took a step forward then recoiled as the moonlight's singing invaded my brain. She smiled at me again.

"Careful now. If you turn, you won't be able to do this next bit…and I won't have any reason to stay my hand."

"What do you think happens to you after this, Marix? Like you say, they don't care what I think. You killed their father. They'll come for you anyway."

Marix's face folded with surprise. "You actually care, fancy that… All the same, we both ken there is no 'after' for me. And it would please me nothin' more than to take the Mahon's down with me, so off you go."

"Natalie, just leave me—"

As her hand tightened around Cassian's throat again, I forced myself to turn away. I picked my path through the shadows around the outskirts of the clearing to the path leading into the gully. I glanced back only once as my descending elevation stole Cass from my eyesight.

Only the faintest trickles of moonlight penetrated the thick canopies overhead, but where the light touched, the crypt glowed with color. I retrieved the key from my pocket with a shaking hand and fed it into the heart of the alder tree carving—

"Ah!"

I recoiled suddenly as a tiny beam of moonlight struck my arm, scalding me. No, it hadn't scalded. It had *sliced* the skin like a laser, revealing…soft darkness underneath.

The pain was…well, it had cut clean through whatever the pills were doing for me. Whether it was the wrong dosage or a betrayal of my own body chemistry I didn't know; and in the end it meant the same thing. Altering was going to *hurt*.

There was nothing to do about it now. I shot forward and twisted the key, pulling back against a tree as the slab began to tremble and divide, revealing stone stairs underneath. To either side of the stairwell, lights had been installed, soft and silver. They buzzed and fluctuated like they were lit by non-electrical means, illuminating enough below for me to see there was a short tunnel made with the same large gray slabs used for the garden level of the house.

I pulled the Dior robe over my head and darted down into the depths, feeling another tiny moonbeam scrape across the knuckles of one of my hands, exposing more darkness under my skin. God, the animal inside of me wanted *out*. Now.

Being down here only seemed to make the craving to jump into the lunar light *worse*. Magic was everywhere in here. It was like stepping into a pool of it; fine hairs across my body rose, electrified, pulling me toward the magic's source.

I hurried along the crypt's long, mostly bare antechamber to the room beyond, which was carved from foot to crown in animals, the way the slab had been. But I barely noticed them in comparison to the artifact at the direct center of the room.

Tendrils of magic held the object aloft in a delicate cyclone, spinning it rhythmically above a golden spire as fine as the tip of an ink pen. It wasn't a cube, exactly, although the spinning made it difficult to tell.

There was nothing else here. Nothing else to bring to Marix.

I took a deep breath and reached for it, expecting to be electrocuted or set on fire by its magic halo. Instead, the magic began to swirl around my hand and through my fingers, searching, touching. Nibbling. It wasn't altogether unpleasant. In fact, I felt a peculiar buzz of familiarity.

It…recognized me…and yielded to me.

I plucked the artifact from the air like an apple off a tree. It was a misshapen heptagonal mass; each of its seven faces was carved with an animal as if the creature was bursting outward away from the center. It weighed almost nothing at all, and the carvings were so intricate, I was gripped by the ridiculous momentary certainty that it must be plastic…until I realized what it actually was. Obsidian. Black volcanic glass. Thin as spider's silk in some places. As I turned it over and sideways in my hand, a single word blazed across the stone, marked in a strange fluorescent magic that disappeared when the stone was still. I could just make it out—*bestia*.

It vibrated in my hand as I left, clutching it to my chest. The room behind me darkened, there was a low trill in the ground beneath my feet…and then nothing. Something had happened, but I didn't know what.

I returned to the surface with the robe over my head again and leapt into the shadows once more. Creeping up the incline, I returned to the tableau I had left—Archer unconscious at Marix's feet, Cassian nearly the same in her clawed hand. But in Marix, there had been a shift. Her eyes were a vulpine copper again. Her muscles were tense and straining under her skin. Resisting the call of the moonlight all around her was taking its toll.

Her eyes snapped to me as I appeared. "Finally! What was it? Show me what you found."

Her teeth were sharp points in her blood-stained mouth; her grin stretched Cheshire wide as I held the animalmass I had found aloft for her to see.

"This was all there was," I said.

"Throw it to me."

"Release him."

She grinned again, holding the cricket bat over Archer's already-battered skull, poised to strike.

"Which one? Make your choice."

I blinked.

"Please, just let them go, Marix. Take this and leave."

"The time for negotiations is over, child. Choose now, or never."

In the same motion, she raised both the bat and Cassian off his feet.

"Okay-okay!" I said. "Cassian."

"No, Natalie!" Cass could barely speak, barely breathe. Every second his face was turning a deeper shade of purple, blue against the pink undertones of his skin.

Marix, too, seemed angered by my choice. Her smile fell as swift as a guillotine blade, as if she had expected a different choice…or for it to take me longer to decide.

"No," she said. "Choose again."

"That wasn't the deal, Marix," I said. "You said it was my choice. I choose Cassian. Let him go."

"He *killed* my child!" she screeched.

"I know! I know. There is *nothing* I can say or he can do that will *ever* make up for what you've lost. Nothing. I don't ask for his life lightly or at the expense of hers. Mael deserved better."

At the sound of her daughter's name, I saw a twinge in her eyes. Confusion, devastation, some mental *twist*.

"I'm sorry for his mistake…but that's what it was. A mistake. A childish, unfathomable mistake. In no version of the world was her life worth less than a vial of liquid. Even if it was the last cure they would ever have, the choice was clear—Mael should have lived. Cass knows that, Marix. He does. He hates himself for it. Look at him."

His self-loathing was a brutal red blush of defeat, his tears thick and slow, all exaggerated by the dribbles of blood flowing from the spots where her claws were already digging into his neck. Her scattered gaze returned to me.

"I cannae let him go," she whimpered. "This is my mercy, lass."

"And I can't let you kill him without a fight," I said.

"Child," she said, almost exasperated. "Don't be manipulated by puppy love."

"I'm not going to fight for him because I love him," I said, realizing the truth of the statement like a punch to the gut. "But because who would I be if I didn't?"

Beyond her pain, I thought I saw the slightest glimmer of respect.

"You hold the power here," I said. "All you have to do is release him like you promised. That was our agreement. This is nothing more than a bargain struck. Run. Heal. Please, Marix."

She hesitated—at least in that, I knew she wasn't truly lost…even if it didn't matter in the end.

"No," she growled.

As her grip around his throat tightened further, I walked to a nearby stone and gripped the animalmass in my hand. Her panicked copper eyes darted to it like a favored ball.

"Honor your promise or I'll destroy this."

"You don't even know what it is."

"Neither do you," I replied.

Marix unleashed a thunderous roar. I lifted the mass higher.

There was only a single second of tense silence before she tossed Cassian back against a tree like a ragdoll and leapt for me through the moonlight, altering her form in midair. I felt her piercing needle teeth latch onto my flesh, the tearing as she eviscerated my arm with four sets of sharp claws, climbing my body so I could see her vicious gaze before she lunged for my throat, and I stepped back into the flooding silver moonlight.

What felt like flames tore across my body in a blazing backdraft as the liquid lunar light surged down my throat, drowning me. Torrential pain ravaged my body. Singing shattered my brain. The ground abandoned my feet underneath me. I was floating, weightless, timeless, frozen inches in front of Marix's hungry open maw.

The eruption of my body was over in an excruciating few seconds, shedding flesh in a font of viscera, but my mind… I felt myself detach from my former human body and retreat to the space behind the almond-shaped windows I'd seen in my dreams.

All at once, time unfroze. Marix's jaws snapped shut in front of me as my new form recoiled and spiraled upward into the air out of reach.

I…

I was *flying*.

Soaring.

A flutter of shining black feathers crossed my vision as I made a hairpin turn and glided, dodging branches and leaves with acrobatic grace. I felt my talons land on a branch and grip it as I cocked my head to study the forest below. It blazed with neon color; the world *danced* with it. Through the trees, I could see the movement of other animals hunkered down and other alters awash in their own glowing coats of magic. And distantly, many dozens of golden eyes peering at me. No, not eyes—windows. The village.

Within my body—my new body—I registered the strangest sensations. Wings. Feathers. The wind's soft caress as it ran across them. The exaggerated bend in my legs. The beak I could see when I lent my vision more strongly to one eye, then the other. I was all these things and none of them.

But…what others had called a lack of control didn't feel like that. There was no *mindlessness*, just a sense of forgetting who I had been before. If anything, there was a second spirit here waiting to converse with me. It could control itself or I could, if I asked.

I wasn't just an *I* anymore. I was a *we*.

"I don't understand."

A human voice. We cocked my head to study the clearing below me and found three lives along the ground—the bear, the sleeping human—*my heart thrummed, did I know him?*—and the fox hiding its magic inside a human's body. This last one reeked of blood and violets; it sat on the ground with something small and shiny in its hands.

Shiny! My second spirit yearned for it. And so did I, although I didn't know why.

Important. Yes, it was important somehow.

We leapt off the branch as we heard a sudden *crunch.* This human-fox was *banging* the shiny on a rock. *Smashing it.*

Shiny! My second spirit cawed frantically, demanding action.

We dove for it—for her—in a frenzy of wings and claws extended. Our talons gripped the shiny as our beak plunged deep into the human-fox's eye and tore.

She screamed and shoved, tossing our body to the ground by the sleeping human.

Fire.

My second spirit seemed to hesitate, dropping the eyeball from our beak.

Warmth.

We peered up at the sleeping creature against the tree.

"He's dead! He's dead, you bitch!"

Her shadow fell across us both. My second spirit demanded flight, warning of impending death.

Mate, I replied. The word floated away from me into the darkness in my mind, where the second spirit seemed to absorb it.

There was a terrible ripple across our body, a purging of feathers, a loss of claws, a horrifying disjointing as my human jaw pushed the beak up and off like a lost tooth. Excruciating pain shot through my back as it elongated; more pain wrapped around my legs like spirals of thorns as the ankles broke and reset. The black skin pulled taut and split as skin as soft as a peach replaced it. My second spirit folded inside me, becoming a bit of origami on the shelf of my mind, biding its time.

When Marix came for me, it was a human hand I raised in defense. It was a cricket bat I swung to keep her back.

"That's…impossible," she said. She staggered back a step, eyeing me like an aberration, before her single eye narrowed. "However you please, my lady. Raven heart or human—I've eaten my fair share of both."

But she never got the chance. There was a sudden *chitter* along the ground, a flash of black and white as Bruce's badger lunged for her leg. It was all the distraction I needed.

I caught her on the chin with the bat before slamming it into her stomach so hard I heard the crunch of bone beneath her skin, the shockwave ripple into her chest and down into her pelvis. Her legs buckled beneath her, the bat collided with her head again, and she collapsed at my feet, all but dead to the world.

Inside me, I heard the flap of wings, my second spirit calling me back to the moonlight. But what did that matter if Cass died?

I dropped to my knees beside him and felt for a pulse—it was there! So strong under the skin.

"Take care, my lady. I've got him."

I shielded my eyes just in time to *not* see Bruce's naked body as he ran by, pulled a length of rope from around Archer's neck, and tied Marix down.

"Bruce, Cassian's hurt. Archer, too."

"I know. I've called for help."

"I need to return to the moonlight."

"Go. I can take care of them from here."

"I'll go to the dungeons at daybreak. Please tell me he's all right."

"Of course, my lady," Bruce said, dropping down beside Cass as I backed away.

The silver light washed over my body again and split the seams of my humanity, peeling it away to free my animal form. It hurt as badly as the first time, but this time I knew I could get through it. I braced against the blinding moments of agony then rejoiced in its passing as my wings unfolded around me. Bruce watched me go, slack jawed. Then the world enveloped me in color, I surrendered completely, and my raven carried me away.

The next thing I remember, I woke on a bed of straw in the dungeons, more rested than I had ever felt before in my life. Cassian had covered my naked form with a cashmere blanket, even tucked it around me. I could smell his smoldering wood scent on the blanket's fringe.

"It's going to be all right, I promise," I heard Cassian whisper.

For a single moment, I believed him.

"You've made unkeepable promises before, Cass," replied Bruce, also whispering.

"Does this mean the king has a second stronghold now?" asked Archer, not whispering at all. "Are we relegated back to the peasantry?"

"Keep your voice down," shushed Bruce. "And of course not. We'll figure something out."

I pushed myself to stand amidst the shed feathers and claws of my former self, wrapping the blanket around me as I stepped out to greet them. I had expected relief, joy, maybe even camaraderie after the terrible almosts of the night before. Instead, Bruce looked horrified, and the boys with their matching head bandages and brain-battered expressions looked more apprehensive than I'd ever seen them.

"What's happened now?"

"Your alteration didn't go how any of us thought it would," said Bruce after a long pause.

"What does that mean?"

"You took the wrong form," said Archer. "I marked you, it's my form you should have taken, but you didn't."

"I've never heard of anything like this happening, my lady," said Bruce. "It shouldn't be possible."

"I'm still…me," I said, with less conviction than I'd hoped. "Nothing's changed."

"Everything's changed," said Archer.

"Why?"

"A bear *must* rule the Eighth Kingdom, my lady," said Bruce.

Bruce pulled the heptagonal obsidian animalmass from his pocket. It looked lifeless in his hand. As he rolled it around, I could see Marix's destruction had been thorough; not a single animal face had escaped unscathed.

"We've already received panicked calls from the heads of three other Great Houses," he said. "Whatever this was, it wasn't meant to be broken."

"She would have killed Cass and Archer," I said. "*Killed* them, Bruce."

"I understand, and I'm grateful with my entire soul, my lady, but…William never told us about this…this *thing*." He tossed the animalmass to me with an anxious flick of his wrist. "No doubt it has something to do with your *ruined* alteration. No doubt worse will happen because of it. It's beyond me. I-I…don't know what to do."

I turned to Cass, hoping to find solace there. He had yet to utter a single word or look me in the eye. He was a stone pillar at the edge of a frightened sea, which scared me more than anything Bruce and Archer had said. Even more so when he finally looked at me. Tears glistened in his heartbroken eyes. Devastation wasn't the word for it; he looked as if some core piece of him had shattered forever.

When he finally spoke, his voice rang resolute and almost cold, shattering a piece of me as well. "There's only one thing we can do. We must surrender you to the Court of the Raven King."

THE END

Continue reading this story in

RAVENOUS

Book 2 in *The Garden of Beastly Delights*

CHAPTER ONE

I now knew that it was possible to fly away from every single problem in my life. It was as easy as running. Easier. My wings weighed almost nothing at all.

For the three days of the full moon of my First Alteration, I soared in and out of the moonlight, dove through the night's many hidden colors, deafened my broken heart's wail with the moonlight's siren's song.

I hid from the inevitable end of my first and only love.

Each morning, I woke in a nest of feathers on the dungeon floor with Cass by my side. Each day, I watched him bid me goodbye at my bedroom door without meeting my eye. Each evening, he walked me silently down to the dungeon to watch me loosen my human form and take to the air as a raven.

I wanted him to hold me. To tell me everything would be okay. To love me anyway, even though it was forbidden. Bear and raven, raven and bear. I'd heard of stranger pairings.

Worse still, it shredded my heart to know that he could so easily give me up, forget what we had shared, and turn into a silent guardian without human feelings.

Had…had it all been some strange strategy on his part? To make me love him? To keep me close when I turned away from his brother, Archer?

On the fourth morning when the full moon's light dimmed, the raven form folded away inside of me, stripping me of the only escape I had. The sun—for its power and brilliance—didn't sing like the moon. The world seemed mute in the light of day.

While I'd been away, Mary had packed my entire closet in a dozen cases, some larger than I was. And someone had taken my phone and revoked my internet privileges. Isolating me. Trapping me. The Mahon's were afraid I would try to run…and even more afraid that I would try to stay.

"You can't possibly think I'll let this go, Bruce," I said when I confronted him.

"Just a precaution," he said, not quite meeting my eye. "They'll be returned to you on the plane to Denmark."

"I'm not going to Denmark."

"There's no remaining here for the time being," Bruce had said. "Birds must flock together. I could no more teach you to roost than you could teach me to hibernate."

It meant exactly nothing at all. I was being sent to a new kingdom before my destiny in this one had been decided. And Cass was just…going along with it. When I demanded he give me his phone so I could reassure my mom I was okay, I learned they had taken his phone, too.

"Be patient," became his repeated answer to any question I asked…until I couldn't stand it anymore.

I cornered Bruce in the great salon.

"Find me a phone. Now. Or I'll break this estate into pieces and sell it for a quid an acre," I demanded. When he barely moved, barely reacted, I tacked on the obvious. "You do understand I can just fly away at the next full moon, right?"

He only responded by blithely pulling out his phone and agreeing to transcribe a text from me to my mom, letting me see it, then sending it on my behalf. Little more than *I love you, I miss you, I'm okay, will call soon*.

Holding the estate captive was the only card they'd really left me to play, but it at least afforded me the barest civility from the staff.

After all, I was the Ninth Marchioness of Ayr. My name was indelibly etched on the deeds and contracts and rental agreements of hundreds of properties Will had left me. They had paraded me around the country as the Eighth Kingdom's next great leader. If this world of shapeshifters had its own currency, no doubt my pale face would already be on it, distributed into circulation as a promise of reliability for *our people*—the alters who lived in secrecy among the humans.

Instead, the grand ruler of all Europe—the Raven King to whom I was being shipped like an artist's doodle discovered behind moldy floorboards—had sent a private jet for me.

Mrs. Margolyes, who had remained mostly neutral to this point in the chaos after my alteration, was sent to fetch me.

"I'm leaving *now*?"

"It's all arranged, my lady," she said.

"Just like that, huh?" Disappointment dripped from every syllable.

I was starting to understand my mother's words so many years ago now, when she had called herself a visitor in this world. I was just a doll to these people, dressed up and sent out to represent them, and easily cast aside if need be. They wouldn't fight for me at all, after everything they'd done. Anger festered in me like an abscess, infecting the part of me that had once been so polite and accommodating. No more of that. What had it gotten me but abuse and scorn?

I closed the door on Mrs. Margolyes and admired my rooms here one last time. My throat strained, trying to hold back the tears rampaging toward my eyes. Despite everything, I had been happy here for a little while. I'd fallen in love here. I'd survived here. I gathered the last of my effects, including the box Will had once hidden for me in the castle garden and the animalmass Marix had destroyed, and wiped my face.

"I'll take that, my—"

I stepped past Mrs. Margolyes, clutching the box, and didn't look back as I walked down the hall to the stairs and through the main foyer where the staff bowed to me in passing. I walked as quickly as I dared, not looking to either side, afraid I might burst into tears where they could see. Stoicism would be cleaner for all of us and just the way they seemed to want it.

For the last time, the house's front doors opened ahead of me, spilling sunlight across the floor. I just needed to make it another twenty steps to the car, and I'd be free to cry and carry on and leave this place behind as coldly as it was prepared to leave me.

But of course, it couldn't be that simple.

My feet halted halfway down the stairs as I looked up and saw *him* waiting by a limousine for me. Cassian, the ~~*only*~~ last person I wanted to see.

Might as well have shot me in the chest with hot, molten hate. I hated the part in his stupid gold-laced copper hair. And the tender wave right at the ends that teased of beautiful curls cut short. I hated the mesmerizing color change from the bright metal of his hair to the dark rust of his sleepless stubble. I hated how his stormy gray eyes saw right through me. I hated the curve of his chin where I had kissed him so many times. I hated the way he breathed, deeply and shallowly in a strange rhythm that suggested he was a moment from ripping his heart out and handing it to me. I hated his stench, that overpowering smell of burning cedar that brought me *nothing* but deep comfort and ease and relaxation when I wanted to smell nothing good at all. When I wanted to wallow in the despair his coldness inspired.

I hated that he opened the car door for me and said, "My lady."

"Cassian."

I hated how delicately he shut the door. How quickly he rounded the car to get in on the other side. I wanted so badly to tell him not to come, and I hated that I couldn't do it.

I steeled myself for another forty minutes of silence and breathing through my mouth when the partition rolled up between us and the stoic very un-Dave-like driver up front.

I could feel Cassian's attention scattered across my person again. Where once it had kissed my skin as individual snowflakes, now it stung like ashes.

"Natalie."

I couldn't look at him. I'd break. Damn it, it wasn't my responsibility to be the bigger person all the time!

"Please."

I closed my eyes and turned. "What?"

"Don't do that."

"I don't know what you want me to do."

"Look at me."

"I can't."

He sighed, filling me with his cruel, comforting scent.

"At least you know now why I asked you to tell me you could survive anything."

"Please stop talking."

"If that's what you want."

Anger flashed red hot inside me—he wasn't going to fight for me, either. A self-loathing chuckle escaped me like a bark.

"What I want is for you to tell me it was just some cruel scheme of yours."

"What was?"

"Whatever we had…or didn't have." My tongue clicked in disgust. "I feel *so* stupid. My heart feels like it's been torn in half, but you seem completely fine sending me away. I thought you actually liked me—"

His hands slid across my cheeks and pulled me into the soft fullness of his lips before I could breathe. My eyes opened as I pushed him away.

"What are you doing?"

"I love you to the very center of me," he said, bringing his hand to his chest in some attempt at a solemn vow.

The words didn't reach me correctly, even as they wrapped around the part of my mind that so wished to hear them. "Don't…say things like that."

"Like what?"

"Things you don't mean."

He blinked softly at me, brushing tendrils of my hair behind my ear. His fingers lingered there, caressing the helix of my ear, as the corners of his mouth rose into the saddest, loveliest smile I'd ever seen.

"I assure you I've never meant anything more." He took my hand and pressed it to his chest. The thrum of his heart was strong, raging just under the skin. "Every beat belongs to you."

"Then why have you been avoiding me?"

"I've never belonged to anyone before. I've been trying to think of what to say to you. How to tell you all the ways in which knowing you has made me realize what a fool I've been."

I blinked, feeling my eyebrow rise of its own accord. The words were at odds with the deep warmth in his voice; they made me angry and confused simultaneously, but I wanted so badly to give him the benefit of the doubt. "Do you realize how what you just said sounds?"

"I've been a fool my entire life, Natalie. Before I met you, I thought there was no greater duty, no greater honor, in this world than protecting what my family had built here. I thought I had to suffer for it, like my blood, sweat, and tears would nourish it. I thought I'd be rewarded for it. By whom, I don't know. I'd spend the rest of my life here, wasting away in the guise of some sad gothic ghost, haunting all who would wish it harm, wondering if it was enough. Wondering if I'd ruined myself enough to make up for choices I couldn't take back. And then you…" He leaned forward and brushed his lips across my cheek, my temple, my eyelid, my brow, scattering sparks through me. "You ruined me in a way I never expected."

The bastard smiled at me then. *Smiled* at me. Like ruining someone was a *good* thing. "Again, how do you want me to take that?"

"I remember sitting in that car with you on the drive here, trying to measure you in the grand scheme of all this. Trying to imagine *what* about you was so incredible my father would choose you over us. When I realized you didn't know our secret, I tried to measure you again. And then again during the interview…and when the king bowed to you. Every time, my measure failed. I found myself trying to force your hand to measure me instead. I *wanted* you to see me as I saw myself. I wanted you to despise me."

"Is that why you were so insufferable?" I asked, smiling despite myself.

I felt the soft friction of his callused fingertips as they curled around my ear again and pulled me toward him. His lips collided with mine like they never would again. I reached for him, raking my fingers through his hair, tugging him closer and keeping him there until he finally pulled back just far enough to press his forehead to mine.

"Then, I started measuring myself against you. And that didn't work either. You were—*are*—will always be immeasurable."

"You shouldn't be measuring at all." But hadn't I done exactly that myself when I saw his books on the desk in my room?

His eyes flew open, full of what looked like relieved panic. "I know that *now*...you ruined my system entirely. Shifted the entire geography of who I thought I was. Razed my self-pity. Dissuaded me of my vow of suffering. Your every glance, every judgment, every forgiveness was an offer to be happy. And I was suddenly happier than I've ever been...and more miserable than you can possibly imagine because I'd already told Archer to be for you what I wanted to be. And in the end, the best he could offer you was an approximation of love. His affection was a sketched, static flame while mine just kept growing until it burned through the masterpiece I would have painted with you. And when I had the chance to be with you, I seized it like the gift it was. *Not* to love you would be insanity."

He was so deliciously dramatic. Too sincere. Entirely marvelous. I kissed him again for good measure before teasing him: "Such a broody poet."

"Somehow you still like me."

"I do. I also love you." Just saying it sent my heart galloping around my chest. The next kiss between us was the sweetest yet. So tight, so intense, so breathless, and at the same time all the breath I'd ever need again.

"Tell me why." The joy in his voice filled every part of me. "It's the only part I don't understand."

"I don't think you'd believe me if I listed everything I love about you...but when you begged me to name my price..." Heated embarrassment coursed through me as I thought of what I needed to say next. My eyelids closed themselves, almost in defense. "I couldn't. Even then I think I knew you were priceless."

A low yearning sigh escaped him before he spoke again: "The second greatest mistake I've ever made was wasting time not being with you when I could."

My heart soared inside me. Every word was poetry. Every heated glance was like a secret revelation—

Until a terrible realization struck me, right between the ribs, about why he was telling me all of this. If I had been standing, it would have taken the legs out from under me. I was leaving. This wasn't the beginning of something spectacular; it was an ending. In this stupid secret world I didn't even know well yet, we were already over.

"Don't say goodbye to me," I begged.

"If this is the only chance I have to tell you how I feel, I'm taking it."

"Cass—"

"I am so grateful to know you, my heart," he continued. "Even if all I get to be is a chapter in your extraordinary life."

The pain crept in like a floating ember, catching and scalding my breaking heart.

"You just had to go after Marix, didn't you..." I tried to pull my hand from his chest, but he held it. "None of this would've happened—"

"You were a raven before you opened that crypt in the forest."

"No, it did something to me. Bruce said it changed my alteration."

"Bruce doesn't know what he's talking about."

"And you do?"

"Yes."

"How?"

"Because I applied the bandages to your back and neck," he said. "You healed from your injuries relatively quickly."

"Except near my neck, I know."

"*Including* your neck. I left the bandage there for so long because the claw marks along your spine changed as they reached your shoulders. They looked...like wings. There were tiny black feathers growing along the scar lines."

I reached for the spot on my neck with my free hand; I could feel the scars, but nothing more.

"I prayed to gods I don't believe in that I was wrong," he said. "But I knew."

The ember became a red-hot poker lodged in my heart. The calluses on his hands became sandpaper, abrading the delicate skin of my ear. Before I knew it, there were tears on my cheeks. He brushed those away with his thumb, utterly ruining me.

"It's not fair," I sobbed. "Because of something I can't control, it means we can't be together?"

He gulped painfully. "It is forbidden, my lady."

I grabbed the collar of his coat and pulled him in again. I wanted to taste him one more time, to feel his rhythm, his love.

It was over too quickly, even though he continued to comfort me wordlessly until we reached the private airfield. And when we parted, the cold that washed against my cheeks set my soul on edge.

"You'll find someone else in time," he promised. "Someone better."

"You're such an idiot," I said. "For choosing the peer pressure of dead people over this."

"I assure you the peer pressure is very alive and deadly."

There was a glint in his silver eyes, though, like he was fighting against himself to tell me something.

"What? What aren't you saying?"

"Letting me go is the easiest way for you to thrive on the journey ahead."

"What's the hard way?" He looked away. I cupped his face and brought him back to me. "What's the harder way?"

"Running where no one would ever find us. Leaving today and slipping into the cracks within shadows."

"Let's go. Right now."

A flash of buoyant hope surfaced in his eyes, even as he shook his head.

"New names. New places. Harsh lemon and salt baths *every day* to obscure our scent. *Fugitives on the run for the rest of our lives*. Your mother left to assume you disappeared without a trace."

"We could bring her with us—"

"They would *never* stop hunting us—or her—for the bounties on our heads. I don't want that for you. You deserve *a real life*. With me, this becomes your life. Without me, you'll be everything my father dreamed you could be." He pressed his own hand to mine over his heart and I felt it leap inside him. "But my fate was sealed the moment I met you, so it's your decision. Say the word and I will run with you forever."

RECEIVE A FREE PROLOGUE FOR THIS NOVEL

Building a relationship with my readers is one of my favorite things about writing. It feels like magic, connecting with someone through worlds created and stories shared.

I offer those on my mailing list a free bonus chapter or selection of free stories each month as well as details about new releases, special offers, giveaways, art reveals, and other bits of news about *The Garden of Beastly Delights* series.

You can join my enchanted circle of newsletter readers and receive *Feral's* **free** prologue by signing up here:
https://dl.bookfunnel.com/gegv95srvj

IF YOU ENJOYED FERAL...

Reviews are insanely powerful for a self-publishing author like me because they help me draw attention to my stories. Someday, I might be lucky enough to have the financial might of a big wig publisher on my side, but for the moment it's just me.

Committed and loyal readers are an amazing gift. Honest reviews help me find other passionate readers, which in turn makes it possible for me to keep writing stories for you all.

If you've enjoyed this book, I would be eternally grateful if you could spend just five minutes leaving a review (it can be as short as you like) on the book's Amazon page.

Thank you so much!
Xoxo Sierra

ABOUT THE AUTHOR

Sierra Prynne is a cheeky little pen name inspired by a run-in with a lovely drunk lady who told me: "You can wake up ten years from now living the life you have or the life you want."

The women in my family have a tradition of using their middle names and Sierra is mine. Prynne is a gift to a certain complex and self-possessed literary character who deserved better. I'm learning about who I want to be as I write these stories and I think she'd respect that.

As for who I am, well, I'm a hopeful romantic who believes you can find true love if you're brave enough not to settle for less than extraordinary. Also, I probably like fantasy a little too much for my own good and when I'm not writing, I can be found wandering through theme parks, national parks, and book parks…those are a thing, right?

You can check out more of what I'm up to at **www.sierraprynne.com** or email me at **sierra@sierraprynne.com**.

And, if social media's your style, please support me with a follow:

Facebook: **https://www.facebook.com/SierraPrynne**
Instagram: **https://www.instagram.com/sierraprynne/**

COPYRIGHT

A LURING PRESS book.

First published in the United States in 2024 by LURING PRESS LLC

Manuscript edited by the marvelous Rebecca Jaycox.
Cover art designed by the glorious Lisa Amowitz.

www.ingramcontent.com/pod-product-compliance
Lightning Source LLC
LaVergne TN
LVHW091115080826
845145LV00008B/1930

* 9 7 8 1 9 6 4 6 4 0 0 0 6 *